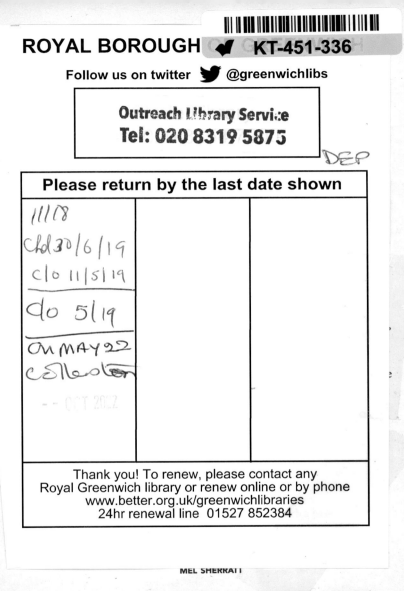

ROYAL BOROUGH

Please return by the last date shown

MEL SHERRATT

'A beautifully wrought thriller that had the kid in me cowering beneath the bed covers. One of the best thrillers of my year'

CJ CARVER

'Distu

If you like

David Jackson is the bestselling author of *Cry Baby*. His debut novel, *Pariah*, was Highly Commended in the Crime Writers' Association Debut Dagger Awards. He lives on the Wirral peninsula with his wife and two daughters. Follow David on Twitter: @Author_Dave, or via his website davidjacksonbooks.com.

Also by David Jackson

The DS Nathan Cody Series

A Tapping at My Door
Hope to Die

The Callum Doyle Series

Pariah
The Helper
Marked
Cry Baby

DON'T MAKE A SOUND

David Jackson

ZAFFRE

First published in Great Britain in 2018
This paperback edition published in 2018 by

ZAFFRE PUBLISHING
80–81 Wimpole St, London W1G 9RE
www.zaffrebooks.co.uk

A CIP catalogue record for this book is
available from the British Library.

ISBN: 978–1–78576–390–8

Also available as an ebook

3 5 7 9 10 8 6 4 2

Typeset by IDSUK (Data Connection) Ltd
Printed and bound in Great Britain by Clays Ltd, Elcograf S.p.A.

MIX
Paper from
responsible sources
FSC® C018072

Zaffre Publishing is an imprint of Bonnier Zaffre,
part of Bonnier Books UK
www.bonnierzaffre.co.uk
www.bonnierbooks.co.uk

For Lisa, Bethany and Eden

PART ONE

1

'What are you up to?'

The words startle him. But then Malcolm Benson finds the mental echo of the chuckle he failed to contain. He turns from his place at the sink, the amusement still written on his face.

Harriet is at the table, mug of tea cradled in her small hands. It's her favourite mug – the one with Snoopy on it. He made certain to give her that one on this special morning. She has her eyebrows arched in that endearing way of hers. One of the features that first attracted him to her thirty years ago.

He flicks soap foam from his Marigolds, then touches a finger to the side of his nose.

'Wouldn't you like to know?' he says.

Her suspicions confirmed, Harriet lowers her mug to the raffia coaster. 'You're planning something.'

'I'm always planning,' he says. 'You know that. Planning and plotting.'

Her eyes shine at him. 'What is it?'

'You'll have to wait.' He faces the sink again. Dips his gloved hands into the suds. He knows she will be staring at the back of his head, trying to read his mind.

'It's not my birthday for another month,' she says casually.

He remains silent.

'Is that it? Something to do with my birthday?'

He looks at her over his shoulder. In her fifties, and yet still full of such child-like innocence and wonderment.

'It *is* a present. But not for your birthday. It couldn't wait that long.'

'Malcolm, you're teasing me now. Tell me. Please!'

He had been hoping to draw things out a little longer, but it wouldn't be fair on her. Besides, he's as excited as she is to bring it into the open. He has kept it to himself for far too long.

'All right,' he says. 'Wait there.'

He peels off his gloves and removes his apron. As he heads towards the kitchen door, he sees how Harriet claps her hands in anticipation.

He smiles as he walks all the way up to the tiny box room that is his study, and all the way back down again. This is a huge moment for both of them. The culmination of an immense amount of effort and patience.

He pauses before re-entering the kitchen. 'Close your eyes. No sneaky-peekies.'

'Okay,' she answers. 'I'm not looking. Promise.'

He walks through the door, his gift held out before him. Harriet has her hands tightly clasped over her eyes. There is a discernible tremor in her fingers.

'Right,' he says. 'You can look now.'

She parts her fingers. Slides them slowly down her cheeks. Her face registers puzzlement and then disbelief at the sight of the large, leather-bound book.

'It's . . . it's the album.'

He nods. He knows she's about to blub, and already a tear is forming in his own eye.

She lifts her gaze to lock with his. 'You haven't?'

'I have.'

'You've found one?'

He smiles.

'Oh my Lord,' she says. 'Oh my Lord. Show me, show me, show me!'

She leans across to drag one of the chairs around so that it's right next to hers. Malcolm sits down and places the album on the table between them.

'Are you ready for this?' he asks.

'Malcolm, you know how much I've wanted it. Open the book.'

He locates the silk tab inserted into the centre of the album. Opens the book at that position.

The reflected glow from the page lights up Harriet's face. Her hand jumps to her mouth. Tears spring from her eyes and run down the back of her hand.

'I hope those are tears of joy,' Malcolm says.

It's all she can do to nod her head as she continues to marvel at the contents of this treasure chest. This is better than any birthday.

She reaches out and turns the page. Emits a gasp. Malcolm studies her as she gets caught up in the dream. Watches her cry and smile and laugh as she turns page after page. He wishes he could do this for her every day.

The questions start to come then. Harriet wants as much information as she can get, down to the last detail. Malcolm is sometimes stretched to answer, but he does his best.

When Harriet reaches the last page, she goes back to the first. Gently touches a finger to the photograph affixed there. Malcolm knew she would love that one best of all.

And then a cloud of doubt seems to cross her features.

'This isn't just more teasing, is it, Malcolm? I mean, this is definite?'

'Oh, yes. You can see how busy I've been. Look at the photographs. It's all set.'

'All set? When? Soon?'

Malcolm strokes his chin. 'Well, that's the difficult part. These things take time. It's a question of logistics, you see.'

Her face drops. 'Oh.'

'So I thought . . . I thought *tonight*. Would that be soon enough for you?'

Huge eyes now. Eyes brimming with ecstatic incredulity.

'Malcolm!' She throws her arms around him, pulls him into her warmth. 'Malcolm, you are an amazing man. I love you.'

She releases him finally. 'It won't be dangerous, will it? I mean, you're sure you can do it?'

He takes her hands in his. 'It won't be easy. I'm not as young as I used to be. But yes, I can do it.'

She hugs him again. Returns her gaze to the album. And then something occurs to her, and she glances up at the ceiling.

'Can we tell her? Can we tell Daisy?'

'I don't see why not, do you?'

*　*　*

Daisy hears them coming upstairs, so she puts down her pencil and sits up straight. She knows how much they like it when she sits to attention.

She has been writing a story about a mouse. She has never been good at writing stories, and doesn't know much about mice, so it has been quite a challenge. She hopes they like what she has done. Later, she will do some more fractions, and then some reading. She has a very busy day ahead.

The door eventually opens, and as the adults enter she stiffens her posture even more.

She notices how much they are smiling this morning. In fact, this is probably the happiest she has ever seen them. She wonders what that might mean.

'Hello, Daisy,' says Malcolm.

'Hello, Daddy,' she replies.

Malcolm and Harriet sit opposite her at the small worktable. They are still smiling.

'We've got some news for you,' says Malcolm. 'Something we're very excited about.'

Daisy doesn't reply. She's not sure how she is meant to answer. She sits and waits patiently.

'Don't you want to know what it is?' asks Harriet.

Daisy nods, although she's not sure she does want to know.

Harriet looks at Malcolm and nods for him to break the news. Malcolm leans forward across the table. Gets so close that Daisy can see the blackheads on his nose.

'You're going to get . . .' he breaks off, leaving a huge gap of expectation, then – 'a little sister!'

Harriet flutters in her chair. Gives a little clap of delight.

Daisy, though, is still not sure how to react. She expects they want her to be as euphoric as they are, but somehow she cannot find it within her. Seeing their eyes on her, she opens her mouth, but no words emerge.

'What do you think about that?' says Malcolm. 'Isn't it wonderful? Just think of all the things you can share together.'

'You can show her your toys,' Harriet says. 'And you can read to her, and explain how everything works. Best of all, you won't be on your own anymore. You'll never be lonely again. How fantastic is that?'

Not wanting to cause an upset, Daisy frantically searches her mind for something meaningful to utter.

'What's her name?' she blurts out.

Malcolm looks at Harriet. Harriet looks at Malcolm. 'Good question,' they say to each other.

'Her name's Poppy,' says Harriet. 'A flower name, like yours. And she's blonde like you, too. And only six years old. She's adorable, and I'm sure you're going to love her.' She turns to Malcolm again. 'Isn't she, Daddy?'

They get lost in each other's eyes again, giving Daisy a chance to formulate her next query.

'When? When is she coming?'

'Another excellent question,' says Malcolm. 'Hang on to your hat, Daisy – it's pretty fast! How does tonight sound to you?'

Something lurches inside Daisy, and she has to fight not to show it. 'Tonight?'

She realises too late that there is a tone of negativity in her voice. She sees how Malcolm's lips quiver slightly as they struggle to hold on to their smile.

'Yes, Daisy. Tonight. That's all right with you, isn't it?'

'Yes, Daddy,' she answers quickly. 'I mean . . . I was just wondering where she's going to sleep.'

Malcolm looks across at the bed. He frowns, as though the problem had not occurred to him until now.

'Well, I'm afraid you'll have to share that bed for a short while. We'll sort something out.'

'Details, details,' says Harriet. 'We don't worry about things like that in this house. It'll all be fine. It'll be more than fine. It will be the best thing ever!'

It seems to Daisy that Harriet could explode with joy. She could suddenly burst apart at the seams and splash onto the walls and ceiling.

She closes off the thought. Stares down at her story in an effort to distract herself.

'So,' says Malcolm. 'That's our amazing news. I knew you'd be pleased, Daisy.'

Daisy doesn't know the word 'sarcasm', but the tenor of Malcolm's voice tells her she is not reacting the way he wants her to.

'Don't worry,' she tells them. 'I'm a big girl. I'll look after Poppy.'

It's the most positive she can be, and the most truthful. It seems to do the trick.

'Well, we'll leave you to do your schoolwork now,' says Harriet. 'I'll pop up later to see how you're getting on.' She wags a finger. 'Don't expect me to be much help today, though. I don't know whether I'm coming or going, I really don't.'

They leave her then, almost floating out of the room on the cloud they have created. She watches them go. Waits for the door to close. For the familiar noise that always comes next. The grating sound that seems to reverberate in the centre of her chest.

The sound of the bolts being drawn.

She is alone again. She spends so much of her time alone. Because of that, a part of her really does think that it will be wonderful to have another child here.

But she wouldn't wish that fate on anyone.

She looks around her bedroom. Sometimes she wonders how long it would take a visitor to work out the true purpose of this room were it not for the external locks. They would see the bed in the alcove across from the doorway. To the left of the door they would see the shelving unit containing books, toys and a flat-screen television. Next to that, the chest of drawers, on top of which sits a doll's house and more toys. In the middle of the room, the foldaway table and stackable plastic chairs.

Nothing particularly unusual.

But then they might question the absence of bulky wardrobes. They might wonder why, instead of storage, there is a small washbasin in one corner and what looks like a shower curtain in another. And when they peered behind that curtain they would probably be surprised to find that it hides not a shower but a manky old commode.

And, in an effort to shed some natural light on the puzzling features of this gloomy room, they might wish to draw back the window curtains, only to discover the wooden boards screwed in place behind them.

At that point they might finally realise that this is not merely a bedroom, a room in which to sleep. It is a room for *everything*.

It is a prison cell.

Daisy has learnt not to complain to the adults about her situation. To the people she calls Mummy and Daddy, but who are not her real parents.

This is not the place to bring another child, she thinks.

It wasn't the place to bring *this* child.

She is not sure precisely how long she has been here, but she has a rough idea. She was forced to celebrate her tenth birthday recently. And she knows she was seven when she was snatched.

That makes it about three years that she has been trapped inside this room.

2

'Is this him?'

Detective Sergeant Nathan Cody follows Detective Constable Megan Webley's pointing finger to its target. Through the grimy windscreen he sees a figure coming towards them along the pavement, hands deep in his pockets, collar up against the cold.

'Nope. Nothing like him.'

Ed Sheeran is playing on the radio. Cody taps his fingers on the steering wheel to the beat. He looks into the shop window next to the car. It's full of skimpy lingerie. He wishes he'd parked a bit further back.

'What about this guy?' says Webley.

Cody sighs. 'No. Look, are you going to ask about every bloke who walks past?'

'If I do, it'll be your fault.'

'Why is it my fault?'

'Your idea, wasn't it? Plus, you said he'd show up at five o'clock on the dot, and it's already three minutes past.'

'He'll be here. Have patience.'

Webley indicates how much patience she has remaining with an emphatic folding of her arms.

'I'm cold and I'm tired and I'm hungry. I had no lunch today.'

'You're not the only one. Bit of a mad dash to court, wasn't it?'

'You were very good, by the way. In court.'

'You think?'

'Yeah. That barrister met his match there. I could see the sweat running down from his wig, the arrogant git.' She gestures towards him, raising her eyebrows. 'I noticed you wore a new tie for the occasion.'

Smiling, Cody sits up and straightens it. 'Yeah. Like it?'

'No.'

'Oh.'

After a short pause she says, 'Do you ever miss the old days?'

Cody feels a hot flush coming on. He suspects she's about to bring up the time when they were a couple. Back when she had a say in what ties he wore.

'Which old days?'

'When you were undercover. Do you miss that side of it?'

Phew, thinks Cody. 'Yeah, sometimes. This is good too, though.'

'Ever think of transferring back?'

'Why? Fed up of me?'

'No. Just wondering. It used to be such a big part of your life.'

He shakes his head. 'Doubt it. I still like doing the occasional small job, but I don't think I could do it full-time again.'

'Because of what happened?'

Cody thinks carefully before answering. It's a natural enough question. For most people, the experience of four men in clown masks forcibly removing parts of your body and then gruesomely murdering your partner would be enough to persuade you to seek other avenues of work.

'Yeah, but not just for the obvious reasons. To be honest, I thought the move to Major Incidents would only be temporary, but it opened my eyes. I thought I'd miss the buzz of UC work, but I don't. I like our team, and I like the work we do.'

'Wouldn't be the same if I wasn't on it, though, would it?' She smiles, and he sees her dimples appear.

Before he can reply, Webley's phone rings. She glances at the screen. 'Footlong,' she announces, then answers the call.

Cody looks in his rear-view mirror at the unmarked car parked yards behind them. He can make out the face of DC Neil 'Footlong' Ferguson, lit by the glow from his own phone. Alongside him is another DC from the squad, Jason Oxburgh.

Webley listens, then turns to Cody. 'He wants to know how long we're expected to sit here. He wants to know if your CHIS for this op is reliable.'

CHIS is cop-speak for Covert Human Intelligence Source. An informant.

'Tell him my intel is impeccable,' says Cody, 'and that he needs to have a bit more faith.'

Webley passes on the message, then listens for a few more seconds before ending the call.

'What did he say?' Cody asks.

'Nothing.'

'Go on, what did he say?'

'He asked if you're doing your best to keep me warm in here.'

Cody turns away, shaking his head in despair, but he thinks that the heat returning to his cheeks should be more than enough to keep both of them warm.

He's glad of the distraction when he notices a movement through the car window.

'Aye, aye,' he says.

'What?' says Webley. 'Is it him?'

Cody continues to observe. He sees a woman at the cash machine. She has her purse in her hand, but has left her bag wide open. A young man in a dark tracksuit has begun moving up behind her.

Cody lowers his window. 'Fitzy, get over here!'

The young man jerks to attention. Hands in pockets, he saunters over to the car.

'All right, Mr Cody. How's it going?' He bends to look across at the passenger. 'All right, love.'

Cody has to stop himself from smiling. He knows that Webley will be bristling at being called 'love'.

'What are you up to, Fitzy?'

Fitzy shrugs. 'Nothin'.'

'Didn't look like nothing. Looked to me like you took a very sudden interest in that woman at the ATM.'

'Oh, her! No, I was just keeping an eye on her, like, you know what I mean? Doing my bit as a good citizen. I don't think she realises there are certain types around here who might take advantage of a situation like that. Know what I mean?'

'Yeah, right, Fitzy. Glad to hear it. I'll put you in for the Pride of Britain Awards. Off you go, then. Chasing you through the streets is the last thing I want right now.'

Fitzy doesn't budge. 'What's happening here, anyway?'

'Nothing to concern you,' says Cody.

Fitzy grins, revealing a gap where one of his front teeth should be. 'Are you waiting for the coast to clear so you can take your missus in there?' He points behind him at the lingerie shop. 'It's okay, you know. These are modern times. No need to feel embarrassed, know what I mean?'

Webley leans towards Cody's open window. 'I'm not his missus. Now do one, before we nick you.'

Fitzy puts his hands up in surrender. 'All right, love. Just being friendly.'

It's then that the wheels seem to start turning in Fitzy's mind. He peers along the street towards the other unmarked car.

'They're with you, aren't they? What's going on? You gonna raid the frilly knickers place?'

'Something like that,' says Cody. 'Now go and bother someone else, Fitzy. And stay out of trouble.'

Fitzy shrugs, then saunters away. As he goes past Footlong's car, he gives the occupants a little wave.

Cody closes his window.

'God,' says Webley, 'I could do with a drink after this. Fancy one?'

'No.'

'Why not?'

'It's February. I don't drink in February.'

'You don't drink any frigging month. I bet you didn't even have a drink at Christmas.'

'I'm sure you quaffed enough for the two of us,' he answers. But she's right: he didn't drink at Christmas. He spent Christmas alone, in his flat. While everyone else was carving turkeys and pulling crackers and getting pissed, he was tucking into a microwaved curry and nursing an ankle sprained in the line of duty. He didn't tell Webley that, of course. He told her that he spent time with his parents and with his ex-fiancée, when in reality neither seemed overly keen to spread the festive cheer in his direction.

'Come on,' Webley urges. 'It'll be fun.'

'Nah, I'm knackered. I just want to put my feet up.'

'Christ, Cody. You sound like my nan, and even she manages to get out to t'ai chi and bingo every week. Are you sure you're not ninety-six beneath that boyish exterior?'

'Another time, Megs. Okay?'

She smiles at him.

'What?' he asks.

'Megs. You used to call me that all the time when we were going out.'

'Sorry.'

'No. It's nice.'

Hot flush time again. Cody is grateful when Webley's phone blares into life once more.

Webley answers the call. Listens. Says, 'Footlong again. Thinks we should knock this on the head. His suggestion is—'

'He's here,' says Cody.

'What?'

Cody points. 'He's going in now.'

He watches as a dark-haired man puts a key into the door of a shop front to open up, then disappears inside. Cody starts to get out of the car.

'We're on!' says Webley into her phone.

The four detectives assemble on the pavement, then head briskly in the direction of the shop.

Cody pushes open the door. Inside, the man he has been waiting for turns to stare at the new arrivals.

'What can I do for you?' the man asks.

Cody listens to the action taking place in the back room. He breathes in the odours.

His mouth waters in anticipation.

'Fish and chips four times, please. And can you make my batter extra crispy?'

*   *   *

Cody pulls rank and insists they eat in Footlong's car. The food is excellent, the company even better, but when the topic of a few beers is raised again, Cody declines. He drives back to his flat alone.

Home is the top floor of a Georgian building on Rodney Street, above a dental practice. The practice is closed now, so Cody has the building to himself. He could have invited his colleagues back here. He could have suggested they buy some alcohol on the way. Could have put on some music.

He did none of those things.

In his kitchen, he puts the kettle on, empties his pockets, and removes his jacket and tie. When he has brewed his tea, he takes a seat at the small breakfast bar.

He thinks about Webley. There have been a couple of occasions in recent weeks when she has suggested going for a drink. Sometimes he wonders if she has an agenda, but then he worries that he is being arrogant. She's probably just being friendly.

Besides, there are barriers. Too many things in the way. The job, for one. Cody and Webley have to work together, to rely on each other.

Then there are the partners. Okay, ex-partners. Cody doesn't think there is much chance of his own ex-fiancée taking him back, but he expects that Webley will hook up with her bloke again. They have been apart only since Christmas. Time yet for a reconciliation.

And then, of course, there is the other matter. The thing he can't talk about.

Webley touched upon it earlier. The event that caused him to abandon undercover work. She knows how traumatic it was for him. How it led to horrific nightmares, hallucinations and a loss of control.

What she doesn't know is that they are back in his life.

The clowns.

They have made contact. They have been sending him weird messages. They have even been here, in his flat.

They have been quiet since Christmas, but he knows they'll come again. And when they do, it won't be pretty.

That's the real reason he can't allow Webley, or anyone else for that matter, to get too close.

3

Malcolm checks his watch. Just a few minutes more. Soon it will be four o'clock, and that's when he has decided he will go in.

He thinks that four in the morning is a good time. Most people are in their deepest slumbers then. Nobody hears a thing. And if they do, they just turn over and go straight back to sleep.

Harriet will be awake, though. She will be too excited to sleep. She will be perched at the bedroom window right now, anxiously awaiting his return.

It's a quiet road, this. A leafy cul-de-sac of semi-detached houses near Otterspool Promenade. Not much chance of traffic down here at this time of the morning.

He has parked here before, at various times of the day. Watching the comings and goings. Taking countless photographs and videos. Listening to the chatter of the residents as they amble past his van, oblivious to the man sitting in the rear of it, behind the dark tinted windows.

Yes, he has done his research. Tons of it. You can't rush these things. Not if you want them to go smoothly.

He knows that there are just the three of them in this house. Poppy and her parents, Craig and Maria. At about eight o'clock, Craig will leave the house, get into the Mondeo, and drive to work. Maria and Poppy will exit a few minutes later and drive away in the other car, a red Polo. The house will be empty for most of the day, until Maria returns with Poppy at about four o'clock.

But an empty house is no good to Malcolm. He needs what's inside. He needs Poppy.

He has considered other options. He knows, for example, which primary school Poppy attends. He has sat outside that school on several occasions, looking for openings, for opportunities.

It would be too risky. Maria always arrives on time, before the school bell. And the teachers stand guard with the young ones in the playground, releasing them only when a parent is clearly visible on the other side of the gates.

He has tried following them to the shops, too. Maria never lets her daughter out of her sight. Most of the time they hold hands. It would be impossible to snatch Poppy in those circumstances.

And so this is the only way of doing it. Not without its obvious dangers, of course, but he downplays those for Harriet. She shouldn't have to worry about such things. There is no need to dull the edge of her anticipation.

It's not as if he's awash with choice. Yes, there are plenty of other children who would be much easier to take – he is constantly amazed at how cavalier and inattentive some parents are – but none of them fits the bill. Candidates like Poppy don't crop up very often. It has to be her, and it has to be now.

It's four o'clock.

He gets out of the van, taking with him the black sports bag that was on the passenger seat. He closes the van door as gently as he can, leaving it unlocked. Then he walks down to the house and onto the driveway.

He doesn't pause, doesn't dawdle. The less time spent out here, the better. Instead, he continues straight to the wooden gate that closes off the route to the rear of the property. The gate is closed and bolted, but it's a simple matter for him to scale the fencing and drop down on the other side. He might be in his fifties, but he keeps himself in pretty good shape.

Before pressing on, he slides back the bolt on the gate, to make his escape easier. Then he waits and listens, just to be sure his arrival has gone undetected.

When he is satisfied, he moves into the garden, keeping close to the walls to avoid activating any light sensors.

The house isn't a new build. Late thirties, probably. It has a conservatory, but even that must have been added at least twenty years ago. Which is welcome news for Malcolm.

Malcolm is a plumber by trade. Doesn't do so much of it now – just the occasional boiler repair, or the moving of a radiator. He's a family man now, with commitments.

He has learnt a lot in his time – not just in his own specialism, but others too. He has worked with a number of building firms and double-glazing companies who have called on his services. Along the way he has picked up a fair amount of knowledge about home security. In particular, he knows how to circumvent it.

Malcolm sets his bag on the ground and unzips it. He reaches in and brings out the first of the tools he needs: a short length of metal pipe that fits snugly over the protruding key barrel of the conservatory door.

A few seconds of effort later, he has removed the barrel. It takes just another minute to insert a screwdriver into the hole and retract the locking bars.

And then he's in.

He's inside somebody else's home. The place where they feel safest.

They have no idea.

4

Poppy comes awake.

She has no idea what time it is. Actually, she doesn't really know how to tell the time. She thinks she should learn soon, because she got a Disney watch for Christmas and she hasn't used it yet. She doesn't think it's time to get up, though. Her parents always get up first, and she can still hear them snoring in the next room.

It's very dark in here. She doesn't like the dark. She worries that night time is when monsters come out. And rats. And burglars. Even on Christmas Eve she was alarmed by the idea of a strange man rooting around in their living room, presents or no presents.

She considers putting the light on. But since she doesn't have a bedside lamp, that would involve getting out of bed, and it's too cold for that. Too scary, as well. And besides, if she did put the light on, she would probably never be able to get back to sleep again.

So she tells herself to close her eyes and think of nice things, just like her mummy told her.

She thinks about her friends at school. She thinks about how much they laughed the other day when one of the boys split his trousers.

She starts to drift . . .

And comes instantly awake again when she hears a noise.

At least she thinks she heard a noise.

She blinks furiously, but can hardly see a thing. Raising her head, she looks down the length of her bed to the outside wall. Her curtains aren't very thick, and so she can just see the outline of the window. But she can also make out a shape silhouetted against one edge of it, and now she's wondering what it could be. Try as she might, she cannot work out what is blocking the meagre light.

It's nothing, she tells herself. It's always there. If I get out of bed and put the light on, I'll see that it's only furniture or toys.

But the more she stares at the shape, the more she believes that it's moving.

Nothing significant. Just a few millimetres or so. To the left, and then the right. As though . . .

As though it's somebody standing there, trying to keep statue-still but not quite managing it.

Poppy ducks under the covers. Her hands reach down for Huggles, her teddy bear, and she pulls him into her, crushing him against her chest.

You're being silly, she tells herself. There's nobody there. It's just a shape, and it's not moving at all. And if you start calling out for Mummy or Daddy, they'll be really cross with you for waking them up.

But now she can't sleep. Not until she knows for certain. Not until she can prove to herself that there isn't a monster or a burglar in her room.

Get out of bed now, she commands herself. Go to the light switch and put it on and show yourself how silly you're being. Go on!

She throws back the duvet. Sits up. Looks again towards the window. Sees . . .

Nothing.

There is no shape there now. Which would have been a comfort the last time she looked. But not now. Because now she knows the shape has moved. It definitely was there before, and it definitely isn't now. So it's moved. And there's a smell here, too. An alien smell.

She opens her mouth, ready to yell.

The call doesn't reach the air. It is cut off when something is clamped over her mouth and nose. It feels like cloth – cold and damp. And it stinks. The strange smell, but really intense now. She tries again to cry out, but all she can manage is a muffled noise.

She flails her arms. They slap ineffectively at someone – or something – large and powerful behind her. Her legs kick out, but they get tangled up in the undersheet. And all the while, the smell seeps into her. It enters her brain, and her thoughts quickly become fuzzy. She forgets her reason for panicking, and a curious calm descends.

The blackness and the silence become total.

* * *

When she wakes up again, she knows instantly that she is in the back of a moving vehicle. She can hear the roar of the engine, feel every bump of the road. Her hands and feet are tied up, and the movement tosses her around like a plaything, making her feel sick.

And she cries.

This is beyond her understanding. She cannot reason about this. She knows only that she has been snatched from her bed, her parents, her home. Only fear is in her mind now – an overwhelming dread of the situation she is now in.

She tries to call for her mummy, but her mouth is covered with some kind of sticky tape. Over and over again she tries to yell the single word that should bring comfort and reassurance. It has always worked in the past. When she has fallen and hurt herself, or when she has been frightened, one of her parents has always responded to her bleating.

But not this time. Nobody comes to soothe away her distress.

And as each minute passes, she realises she is moving further and further away from her family. She has no idea how long she has been unconscious. She could be anywhere by now. She might never see her parents again.

And what will happen at the end of her journey? Who has taken her, and what do they want to do with her?

The unanswered questions multiply her anxiety beyond measure. She is cold and she is shaking and she feels she is turning inside out with her crying. She prays for this nightmare to end.

And then the van comes to a halt with a squeak of the wheels. She hears the ratcheting of a handbrake being applied. The engine dies. A door opens and closes. There are footsteps moving away from the vehicle.

The seconds pass. Poppy begins to wonder if she has been abandoned. Left here in this freezing cold van to die.

But then more footsteps, coming towards her now. The handle on the rear door of the van is operated. The door swings open, and the dim light of the stars and the moon and the street lamps floods into her tiny prison.

She twists her head to look out of the van. Sees that a figure is looking back at her. A woman. Not her mother. Much older than her mother. But kindly. At least, that's the impression she gets. The woman has the countenance of someone seeing her baby for the first time. A look of . . . love.

Poppy wants to beg her to help. If the tape were removed from her mouth, she would do her best pleading. She would promise the woman anything in return for being taken back home. She would pledge not to do anything bad for the rest of her life, if only she could be delivered safely into the arms of her parents.

The woman smiles. It's a warm smile, a comforting smile. She reaches out a hand and strokes Poppy's hair. The gentle caress is the first signal of reassurance Poppy has received, and she tries to hold on to that feeling.

'So pretty,' the woman whispers. 'So beautiful. I'm so happy.'

Poppy wonders why the woman is happy. Is she like the wolf in the Red Riding Hood story? Is she about to gobble up the meal she has been brought?

But the woman seems far too nice for that. She reminds Poppy of her friend's guinea pig. Small and skittish, with tiny bright eyes and bulging cheeks. Her hand slides across Poppy's hair, down her forehead, over her eyes.

'Hush now,' she says. 'You don't need to be afraid. You're safe here. We'll look after you.'

Her palm is soft and warm. It blocks out all the light now, and Poppy suddenly feels incredibly tired. She starts to believe that perhaps these people don't intend to hurt her after all. Whatever their purpose is, it is not to cause harm.

And then she feels the sharp prick of pain in her arm, and all her fears surface again for a few brief seconds before being sucked under with her drowning consciousness.

5

Maria hates the dark, cold mornings. When the alarm goes off, it always seems too early to get up. She could easily manage another hour in bed. She turns over, closes her eyes, feels the beckoning of her recent dreams.

The bed bounces as Craig clambers out of it. Without warning he turns on his bedside lamp. She moans.

Craig slaps her on the curve of her hip. 'Move it, soldier. Don't you know there's a war on?'

'With respect, Colonel,' she says, 'you can kiss my arse.'

Craig laughs heartily. He sounds far too bright and breezy. It seems unfair to her that he seems so refreshed while she could willingly curl up in a ball and go into hibernation for a month or two.

Perhaps it's a sign of age, she thinks. In a couple of days she will be thirty. *Thirty!* That's ancient. Another complete decade will have been put behind her. That's hardly something to celebrate.

She moans again, but somehow manages to summon up the energy to drag herself out of bed. There's so much to do, and in so little time. It's all right for Craig, she thinks. He only needs to jump in the shower for two minutes, throw on the clothes I've ironed for him, swallow down a bowl of cereal, and head out. I, on the other hand, have to get two females ready – myself and Poppy – and that takes a lot more time.

She pushes her feet into some fluffy slippers. Shuffles across the room and takes her dressing gown from the back of a chair. She hears the shower hiss into life.

Stifling a yawn, she drags herself out onto the chilly landing. Despite the central heating, this house never seems warm enough in the winter.

Her first surprise is a relatively mild one.

Poppy's door is wide open. She never leaves it open so much. Never fully closes it either. She likes it ajar just an inch or two.

Curious, Maria heads towards Poppy's room. It's still dark in there, the curtains drawn. Maria enters and turns on the light at the wall. She fully expects a groan of complaint, but none comes.

'Poppy, darling, it's time t—'

And then Maria sees the bed.

The empty bed. The bed with its duvet on the floor and its undersheet all rumpled. The bed with no Poppy in it.

There's a smell here, too. An unfamiliar smell. Like something you might notice in a hospital.

And there is Huggles the teddy bear, lying on the floor in the unnatural pose of an accident victim, its dark eyes turned on Maria as if condemning her for not turning up sooner.

Maria returns to the landing. 'Poppy!' she calls.

No answer. Only Craig's tuneless singing in the bathroom.

Perhaps the spare bedroom. Perhaps Poppy had a bad night and needed a change of scenery to help her sleep.

She flings open the door of the third bedroom. Its contents are undisturbed. Nobody slept here last night.

Back on the landing. Heading down the stairs now. 'Poppy! Poppy!'

The shower goes off. Craig shouts, 'Are you calling me?'

She ignores him. Picks up the pace as she reaches the bottom of the stairs with still no response from her daughter. 'POPPY!'

Into the living room. Maybe she's sleeping on the sofa. She's done that before when ill.

But then why didn't she call me? If she's sick, why wouldn't she come and get me?

Not in the living room either.

'POPPY!'

The kitchen now. But why would she be in the kitchen and not be answering my calls?

Maria sees immediately that there's nobody here. Where is she? Where could she possibly be hiding? Why isn't she answering?

Through the kitchen. Into the conservatory with its empty wicker chairs and its unoccupied two-seater sofa and . . .

Its open door.

And now Maria's heart is in her mouth. This scene is so, so wrong. That door is kept locked at night. The key is always taken out of the lock and placed on top of a high cupboard. Poppy couldn't reach that key. She couldn't have opened the door. What the fuck is going on here?

She's through the door then. Out into the murky morning. The bare trees look skeletal and menacing. Even the birds don't seem inclined to sing.

'Poppy! Poppy!'

The only answer is from a neighbour's dog. Maria turns and looks back at the house. Have I missed something? she wonders. Am I overreacting, or is this as bad as it seems? Is this the start of the nightmare it appears to be?

She sees it then. The hole in the door where the lock should be.

'Oh, God! Oh, God!'

She knows. Someone has entered the house. Someone has broken in and they have . . . they have . . .

She goes around the side of the house. Sees that the wooden gate – the gate that always has its bolt drawn at night – is yawning wide open.

'POPPY!'

Her calls are screams now – frantic, panic-stricken yells. Give me a word, she thinks. A single word, or even a cry of pain. Anything will do. Anything that will tell me you are still here with me.

If she's here, I can fix her. But if she isn't . . .

Maria passes through the front garden. Out into the street. She is crying now. She clutches at her hair, not knowing what to do. You can't prepare for this. You can't be ready to deal with a situation in which your child—

She's been taken.

She has. That's what's happened here. My beautiful Poppy has been taken.

A voice from behind her. Craig, running up the driveway. She doesn't know what he's saying. Doesn't acknowledge the stares of neighbours as they appear on their doorsteps, summoned by her desperate calls. All that is irrelevant now. Only one person matters.

And she has gone.

6

The girl called Daisy comes awake when she hears the bolts being drawn back on her bedroom door. She sits up, rubs the sleep from her eyes.

They switch the light on as they come in. Harriet first, beaming with excitement. Behind her is Malcolm. There is a child in his arms.

The child looks dead. A sleeping child would waken with all the jostling, but this one is like a rag doll. Her limbs droop and swing. Her eyes are closed but her mouth is wide open. It's hard to tell if she's breathing.

Daisy wonders if she looked like that herself when she was first brought here. Sometimes she wishes she'd never woken up from that deep unknowing.

'Hello, Daisy,' says Harriet. 'Look what we've got. We told you, didn't we? We always keep our promises.'

Malcolm stoops a little, affording Daisy a better look at the child. She seems so fragile, so lacking in substance.

'Is she asleep?' Daisy asks.

'Yes,' says Harriet. 'A very special kind of sleep. She'll wake up soon, though. We thought you might like to keep an eye on her for us. You can let us know when she wakes up. Would that be all right with you?'

Daisy feels uncertain about this. She has never looked after another child before, especially one who appears as close to death as this. But she knows better than to be negative.

'Okay,' she says.

'Let me put her on your bed,' says Malcolm.

Daisy gets off the bed, stands at the foot of it while she watches the girl being placed gently onto the mattress, her head on the pillow.

Harriet moves in front of her husband and bends to give the new arrival a gentle kiss on the forehead. 'See you soon, Poppy,' she says.

The two adults turn to face Daisy. 'We're trusting you to look after your new sister,' says Harriet. 'You will do that, won't you?'

Daisy nods. 'Yes.'

'Tell us as soon as she's awake, okay?'

Another nod.

'All right, then.' They back out of the room, their eyes very much on Poppy. Harriet gives a little wave towards the bed before she closes the door.

And then the bolts are slid into place once more, and the children are alone.

Daisy stays where she is for a full minute, just staring at the still form of the six-year-old. She looks tiny, but then Daisy probably wasn't much bigger when she was brought here.

She takes a step forward, then another. A sister, she thinks. She looks a bit like me, too. This is probably like looking at a photograph of myself from three years ago.

The thought pricks at her eyes. Three years without her parents, without family, without friends. She has not seen a single beam of sunlight in all that time.

She holds up her arm, looks at how pale her flesh is. Then she leans forward and lays it alongside Poppy's. The difference is staggering. She feels like a ghost in comparison.

There are marks on the girl's wrists: pink indentations where rope has dug into them. Daisy is pierced with another sharp memory of her own marks when she was similarly bound.

Her hand brushes against Poppy's flesh. She recoils at how cold it feels.

Daisy climbs back onto the bed. She pulls the duvet over both of them, then snuggles into Poppy.

'Please don't die,' she whispers. 'Please don't die.'

7

A long, shuddering intake of breath. Then a groan that turns into a cry of bewilderment and fear.

Daisy tries to keep Poppy close, to comfort her, but the child pulls away and sits up. She scans the unfamiliar room, then stares at her bedfellow.

'Who are you?' she demands.

'My name's Daisy,' she says. She doesn't know how else to answer. It doesn't sit right with her to say that she's her new sister. She doesn't feel they know each other well enough.

'Where's my mummy?'

'I . . . I don't know. I don't know where you came from.'

'I want my mummy.'

'I know, but . . . I'll look after you, I promise. I'll take care of you.'

She reaches out for a hug, but Poppy puts on an expression of disgust at the invitation. 'I don't want you. I don't like you. I want to go home.'

She slides off the bed. 'Mummy!' she yells. 'Mummy!'

Daisy goes after her, grabs her by the arms. 'Hush, Poppy,' she says. 'Don't shout. They don't like it when you shout.'

But Poppy doesn't heed the advice. 'Mummy! Daddy! Where are you?'

She yanks herself from Daisy's grasp. Heads straight for the door. Turns the handle to no avail.

'Let me out! I don't want to be here. I want to go home.'

Daisy feels her own tension mounting. She thought it would be easier than this. Thought that Poppy might be willing to listen to her older and wiser roommate. But it seems that Poppy is headstrong. She has an independence that could attract danger.

'Poppy, please. You need to keep quiet. There are rules here. We have to obey the rules.'

'I want to go home!'

She starts kicking the door with her bare feet. Daisy's heart jolts with each bang. She races across, encircles Poppy with her arms and drags her away. Poppy responds with more kicks, this time into Daisy's shins. She begins running around the room, a whirlwind of devastation. She knocks chairs over, pushes all of Daisy's schoolwork onto the floor, drags books from the shelves, pulls the roof from a Lego house.

'Poppy! No! Please.'

And then Daisy hears them. The footsteps coming up the stairs. She turns towards the door, and then back to Poppy, and she realises how clearly her fear is written on her face. She sees how easily Poppy reads it, how abruptly she abandons her trail of destruction.

The bolts are drawn back. The door opens. Harriet and Malcolm enter in solemn, disconcerting silence. Their collective glare alights on Daisy first, and the force of it pushes her back into the corner of the room.

'I thought you were going to let us know when she was awake,' says Malcolm. His voice is calm, quiet, but Daisy is experienced enough to detect the undercurrent of threat.

She looks across to the button on the wall that she can press to summon her keepers.

'I . . . I was going to. I'm sorry. Poppy was . . . she was really upset. I was trying to help her.'

All heads turn to look at Poppy. There is defiance in her eyes. Her chest heaves with her fury and the effort of her exertions.

'Is that right, Poppy?' asks Malcolm. 'You were upset? Why is that?'

'Go away,' says Poppy. 'I don't want you. I want my mummy and daddy. I want to go home.'

Malcolm finds a smile for her. 'Don't be like that. It's nice here. You'll like it once you get used to it.'

Poppy looks to her right, sees three dolls sitting in a row on top of a bookshelf. She sweeps them onto the floor.

'It's shitty here. Shitty, shitty, shitty.'

Daisy sees how each expletive hits Harriet with the force of a punch. Harriet can't abide swearing.

Harriet turns to her husband. 'Daddy, I hope you're not going to let our daughter talk to us like that.'

'I'm not your daughter,' says Poppy. 'And I'll say what I like. You stole me. I'm going to tell my dad, and he's going to punch you.'

Harriet keeps staring at Malcolm, urging him to exert his authority. 'Well?' she says.

Daisy senses the agitation building in both of the adults. Malcolm is bunching and unclenching his fists now. The veins have begun to bulge in his forearms and on his temples. Soon he will snap.

He takes a single step towards Poppy. She takes a step backwards, maintaining the distance between them.

'Go away,' she says.

Malcolm raises a warning finger. 'Poppy, you need to start behaving yourself. You should be grateful to us. We brought you here to look after you.'

'Fuck off!' she yells.

Harriet brings her hands to her ears, which only encourages Poppy to escalate her cursing.

'Fuck off, fuck off, fuck off. You fucking bitch. You fucking bastard.'

'Stop her, Daddy!' says Harriet. 'Stop her!'

'Yes,' says Malcolm distractedly. 'Yes.'

Backed against a wall, Poppy begins screaming as loud as she can. Malcolm glances to his right, and it seems to Daisy as though there is a glint of fear in his eyes. She knows that soundproofing has been fastened to the walls of this room, but perhaps it is not perfect. Perhaps the banshee scream of a young child could still penetrate through to the neighbours or the outside world.

'Come here, please, Poppy.'

But then Poppy takes off again. She heads for the door, but Harriet blocks the way out. She runs back to the centre of the room, attempts to duck under Malcolm's outstretched arms . . .

And is caught.

Malcolm snatches her by the wrist and whips her towards him. She begins to scream again, but Malcolm clamps his other hand over her face. She writhes in his powerful grasp, her cries muffled.

Malcolm fixes his gaze on the wall opposite, his eyes glazing over. When he speaks, his voice is flat, emotionless.

'You see, Poppy, there are rules here. We're not hard parents. We're here to help you. We want to love you. But you have to help us in return. You have to do what you're told.'

Daisy's eyes shift from Malcolm, in his almost hypnotic trance, down to Poppy. Malcolm's huge palm is covering both her mouth and nose. Her struggles now are not in defiance, but to take a breath.

To Daisy's left, Harriet silently leaves the room, closing the door softly behind her. She knows how much of a disciplinarian her husband can be. She doesn't need to witness it.

'Spare the rod and spoil the child, the saying goes. Do you know what that means, young Poppy? It means that letting children do what they want isn't good for them. And we need to do what's good for you, do you understand? It'll hurt now, in these early days, but you'll soon get used to it. You'll soon come round to our way of thinking. And one day you'll see how right we were.'

He continues with his monologue, seemingly unaware that Poppy is weakening rapidly in his arms. Her flailing has become mere aimless waving of floppy limbs. Her eyes have become unfocused and uncoordinated.

Daisy has seen Malcolm like this before. For the most part, he can act like a normal human being. In his own way he can be generous and helpful, albeit somewhat lacking in humour. But at times of stress it is as if his body is taken over by another force. He becomes a shell for some entity that is no respecter of the bounds of what is acceptable. At those times, the line between punishment and extreme violence becomes blurred.

Daisy knows exactly what Malcolm can do at times like that.

'Yes, you'll see,' says Malcolm. 'In a day or two we'll all be getting along like a house on fire. You'll be wondering what you made such a fuss about.

We're nice people, your mum and me. We want only the best for you. Only the best. You'll see.'

But Poppy can see nothing. Her eyes have rolled back in her head. Her face has turned an alarming shade of blue. Her body has become as limp as a wet dishrag.

The need to act seems to hit Daisy's legs before her brain can review it. Heedless of the danger zone she is entering, she rushes across the room to where Malcolm has the young child in a bear hug that seems to have crushed the life out of her.

Daisy touches her fingers tenderly to the back of Malcolm's hand. 'Daddy,' she says, 'let me have her now.'

Malcolm's eyelids flutter. He drops his gaze slowly to Daisy. 'What?'

'She's quiet now. Leave her with me. I'll explain the rules to her. She won't be naughty again. I promise.'

Malcolm looks at what he is holding, as if only just becoming aware of what he has done. He releases his grip, allowing Poppy to crumple to the floor. Then he raises his own arms above his head, as though trying to keep them as far away from the child as possible. An expression of pain contorts his face.

'Yes,' he says. 'Talk to her. We won't put up with that sort of behaviour in this house. You know that, don't you, Daisy? Explain it to her.'

Daisy drops to the carpet. Puts a hand to Poppy's face and begins to stroke it. She thinks it might be too late, and she wants to cry, but she holds her tears in. There has been enough emotion in this room this morning. She doesn't want to push Malcolm over the edge he has just stepped back from.

'Yes, I will, Daddy. I'll make her understand. Don't you worry.'

Still dazed, Malcolm lowers his arms and starts walking backwards towards the door. 'Call us,' he says. 'When she's better, and a bit calmer, press the button. Okay?'

'Yes,' says Daisy, but it's hard to get the word out. Her voice is cracking. Her veneer is cracking. She desperately wants to wail, to scream, to command this monster to get out of her room, out of her life.

She continues to stare at Malcolm, her chest heaving, her eyes filling up. He seems to take an age to back out of the room.

It is only when she hears the bolts being put back into place that she allows herself to weep. Silently, of course.

She leans in close to Poppy, allowing her warm tears to drop onto the girl's ice-blue flesh. She thinks of a fairy story she once read, where a single tear was enough to bring a princess back to life.

She prays for the same to happen here.

8

Cody hates children.

In his police cases, that is. Not generally. Kids per se are wonderful.

But not in his cases. Not when they become victims. There should be a line drawn there. Adults, with all their wisdom and understanding, can knock seven bells out of each other if they want. But keep children out of it. Let them enjoy life for a few years. Let them believe that the world is a peaceful, friendly place, at least for a short while.

He has a bad feeling about this one. He knows that Webley, now standing at his side, feels the same way. This isn't going to end well.

He's not going to say that to the couple currently inviting them into their home, of course. Not directly, anyway. But neither will he put on a show of unfounded optimism. He's not going to raise any hopes, knowing full well that they are likely to be dashed again.

It's a lovely home. Very tidy and clean. Parquet floors and modern furnishings. Freshly cut flowers in glass vases.

It seems inconceivable that a demon has visited this place. It feels to Cody that there ought to be signs of devastation from such a hellish visitor. A rank odour, perhaps, or claw marks on the wallpaper. A child snatcher should not be able to breeze in and out without leaving a clear signature from the underworld.

They sit down in the living room. Craig and Maria Devlin crush into each other at one end of the sofa, each needing the comfort of the other.

Through the bay window, Cody sees a uniformed officer stroll past, clipboard in hand. They are already knocking on doors, talking to neighbours.

One sighting, thinks Cody. That's all they need. One glimpse of the abductor, or a vehicle. *Something* to go on.

But he has a feeling that luck won't be on their side today.

He starts gently, taking the couple through the morning's events. Stuff the uniforms have already asked them, but which needs to be confirmed. What time did they wake up? When did they notice that Poppy was missing? Where have they looked for her? Did they hear anything in the night? Have they noticed any strangers or unusual activity on the street in recent days?

His questions are standard, but this is not a run-of-the-mill kidnapping, and he's going to have to bring that fact very much into focus.

'This is going to sound like a really odd question,' he says, 'and you may feel as though you don't want to answer it, but is there anyone you know – anyone at all – who you think might have wanted to take Poppy?'

The confusion on their faces comes as no surprise.

'What?' says Maria. 'What do you mean, someone we know?'

Cody looks down at his notebook while he thinks about how best to rephrase his question.

'I'll be honest with you, this one's pretty unusual. Most child abductions are by opportunists. They see a child left alone outside a shop, or in a park, or walking home from school by themselves, and they act on impulse. But here – it's almost as if you have been targeted.'

Confusion turns to shock. 'Targeted?' says Craig. 'I don't . . . You mean somebody wanted Poppy specifically?'

'I could be wrong, but that's how it looks on the surface. Somebody went to a lot of trouble, and took a hell of a big risk, to break into your house in the middle of the night. Snapping that lock would have created some noise. The intruder was in danger of waking someone up – you two, Poppy, a neighbour – but they still went through with it. It's almost as if not just any child would do, as if it *had* to be Poppy. That's why I'm wondering if it's someone who knows Poppy, and therefore someone *you* might know.'

Maria shakes her head vigorously. 'I've never come across anyone like that. I mean, I'd know, wouldn't I? You'd have to be demented to break into a house and steal a child. Nobody normal would do that.'

Cody looks at her husband. 'Mr Devlin?'

Craig seems almost surprised he has to answer. 'No. Of course not. It's a ridiculous question. Maria's right. Nobody's perfect – I mean, we've all done things we're ashamed of, haven't we? – but kidnapping a child . . . well, I mean, that's several levels up again, isn't it? That's psycho territory.'

He seems to realise what he has just said – that his beloved daughter might now be in the clutches of a sadistic maniac – and he grasps Maria's hand.

'Okay,' says Cody. 'Maybe not a friend, then, but what about a stranger? Somebody who might have been in or around your home recently? A workman, perhaps? An estate agent? A gardener or a window cleaner? A decorator? Anyone like that who might have spent a little time in Poppy's company?'

Craig shakes his head. He seems bewildered, and a little frightened.

Cody continues the line of questioning: 'What about people you might have antagonised? Is there anyone you can think of who might have reason to hate you? Someone you've upset in the past, even if it was unintentional?'

The pair descend into a gloomy quiet. Cody senses he is wearing them down.

'All right, look,' he says. 'I realise I'm giving you a lot to think about. You don't have to do it now. Take your time. When we're gone, cast your minds back to all the people you can think of who might have been in your house, or might have seen Poppy and found out where you live. Anyone who might want to get back at you for some reason. Make a list for us. Can you do that, please? And err on the side of caution. Unless you're one hundred per cent sure about them, put them on the list. It's better that we clear someone's name than never consider them at all. Is that okay?'

The couple look at each other, then back at Cody. 'Yes,' says Maria. 'But it's a horrible thought. I mean, that someone we allowed into our home, someone who might have sat right where you are, could have had ideas about Poppy. And then the thought that they came back and . . . and . . .'

She loses control then. Brings a tissue to her eyes while she sobs quietly. Craig rubs a hand up and down her back.

'What else can we do to help?' he asks. 'We need to find her.'

'I know,' says Cody. 'We'll do everything we can, I promise you.' He gestures through the window. 'Right now, we're talking to all your neighbours about what they might have seen or heard last night, and also about strangers they might have witnessed in the area. Do you have somewhere you can go for a few hours?'

'Why?'

'We want to bring in a forensics team to search the place. The intruder may have left clues to his identity here. I know you've been running all over the house since then, but the longer you stay here, the more chance there is that you'll contaminate vital evidence. Would you be okay with that?'

Maria sniffs and looks up at her husband. 'We can go to my mum's,' she says. She turns to Cody. 'She's only in Grassendale.'

'Great. We'll be as quick as we can, but we have to be thorough. As soon as it's done, you can come back.'

'I need to look for her,' says Craig. 'I can't just sit on my arse for the next few hours. I need to be out there, even if it's just driving around.'

'I understand how you feel,' says Cody. 'But it would be much better if you could leave the searching to us for now. One of the things we'll do is call a press conference to alert local media. We'll also bring in the dogs unit to see if we can pick up a trail from the house. We'll need something with your daughter's scent on. Her bedclothes, perhaps, or a toy she always kept close to her.'

Maria looks across to a sideboard. A teddy bear is sitting on top of it.

'Is that hers?' Cody asks.

Maria nods. She stands and walks across the room, then brings the bear back. Before handing it to Cody, she presses her face into it and breathes in its fragrance.

Cody realises then that the reason the toy is in this room is that Maria has been carrying it around with her, holding it close as if it were her daughter.

'This is Huggles,' she says. 'She always kept him with her when she was in the house. She slept with him every night. She'll be missing him.'

'I understand.'

She reaches the bear out towards Cody. He takes hold of it, but she doesn't release it immediately. She stares Cody directly in the eye.

'I want to be the one to give this back to Poppy. I want to be there when her eyes light up at the sight of him. Promise me that you will do everything in your power to make that happen.'

'I promise,' he says. But this is a promise only to do his best. It is not a promise to return Poppy. He is already dreading the moment he may have to tell these loving parents that their only daughter is never coming home again.

Maria entrusts the bear to Cody's safekeeping, then resumes her place on the sofa.

'I don't understand,' says Craig. 'Why would anyone do this? What possible reason could they have for taking our Poppy? We're not rich, so . . .' As he says this, he looks up at Cody with a glint of optimism in his eye. 'Do you think that's it? Do you think they want us to pay to get her back? Because I'll do it. I'll find the money somehow. If this is a ransom demand—'

'I don't think it's that,' Cody says. 'Like you just said, you're not rich. And, to be honest, I think they would have been in touch already if that were the case. They would have warned you not to involve the police.'

He watches the spark leave Craig, and it pains him to have been the one to extinguish it.

'Then why? Why would they come for her?'

Cody shakes his head. 'I have no idea.'

What he can't voice is his suspicion that this is the work of someone not entirely rational. Someone who is willing to go to such lengths to obtain a particular child, to put his own liberty at risk to achieve that goal, must be driven by desire more than sense. And that makes the kidnapper highly dangerous.

He doesn't want to think about what that might mean for poor Poppy.

And what he also cannot say here is that he already has some suspects in mind for this crime.

He's looking at them right now.

He doesn't want to believe it, of course. In any public forum he would be lynched for admitting such a notion. These people are victims, he would be told. Have you no sympathy, no shame?

But Cody is a police detective, and he has been trained well. The ABC of investigative work has been drilled into him: Accept nothing; Believe nobody; Challenge everything.

And so, as much as a very human part of him is determined to deny it, there is another part that has these two in his sights. He doesn't know how much of their story to believe, how much of their distress is genuine. He has been fooled by such displays of emotion before, and will be again, no doubt. He looks at the Devlins now, crying and fretting, and he hates himself for distrusting them. But there it is: that's what he has become. What salves his conscience is that it might just be the only thing that can save Poppy.

'I have another question,' says Maria. 'But I'm not sure I want the answer.'

Cody has a feeling he knows what's coming, but he waits it out.

'What are the chances?' she says. 'When a child is taken like this, what are the odds of getting them back?'

Cody's reply isn't instantaneous, even though he realises that the couple will fill his silence with negativity. But there is no easy answer. When it comes, he could win a prize for dodging the issue.

'The point is,' he says, 'I've never seen a situation like this. And because of that, I don't know what we're dealing with. I don't understand the motive. We have to hope that such an extraordinary set of circumstances means that all the usual stats about child abduction go out the window.'

'Meaning that the usual stats don't offer much hope,' says Maria.

You got me, thinks Cody. You saw through me.

He says nothing, and sees again how his silence cuts them.

9

Treble twenty.

Malcolm's first dart beds into the red fibres with a satisfying thud. He moves a few inches to his right on the oche, takes aim, lets fly with his second arrow. It narrowly squeaks into the same small arc, clicking against the metal frame as it penetrates. He adjusts his stance once more, lines up his dart . . .

He knows it's going low even as he releases it. A perfect throw can be felt. He doesn't need anyone to tell him that it's going into the black by several millimetres.

He's not as good as he used to be. No chance of extending the line of trophies gleaming at him from the top of his bookcase. Doesn't matter, though. He does it more for the hand-eye coordination now. Plus the mental arithmetic involved in working out how best to achieve his target score. All good for the brain. Even the doctors said so.

On his way to retrieve his darts, Malcolm makes a slight diversion and looks at himself in the mirror. Facing straight ahead, chin up, nobody would ever know.

But then he drops his head a little, and it becomes obvious.

If he had more hair it wouldn't be so bad, but on a bald pate like his the deformity screams for attention.

The surgeon did a great job, but from the start he was honest about the outcome. A great big metal plate screwed onto your skull is never going to be quite as streamlined as the original bone.

He has almost forgotten what life was like before the accident. It changed him in so many ways.

Often he wishes he hadn't been so ambitious. If only he had stayed a simple local plumber, picking and choosing his jobs, taking his time, not being pressurised . . .

But it's easy to think like that now. When you've got a mortgage and bills to consider, and someone comes along and offers more money and regular work – well, you take it, don't you?

He was only a year into the job with the new firm when they almost killed him.

His supervisor should never have sent him up that ladder. A proper scaffolding platform should have been erected.

The legs of the ladder were on the flat roof of an extension. It looked a sound enough support. Turned out it wasn't. While he was at the top of the ladder, the roof gave way, and Malcolm plummeted onto the paved patio.

The hospital didn't hold out much hope for survival. In fact, he died once on the operating table. And even when they started to believe they could keep him alive, they remained doubtful about his chances of leading a normal life ever again.

The problem was his head. They explained it to him later. Told him how his brain had been catapulted against the inside of his skull when his head impacted the stone paving. Bruised and battered, his brain began to swell up like a balloon, expanding to fill the confined space. The only way to give it more room to grow was to cut away a section of his skull.

He still remembers how he looked back then. A huge depression on one side of his head, as though some vicious animal had taken a bite out of it.

They fashioned the metal plate eventually. Screwed it into place during yet another operation. The medical experts seemed rather proud of what they managed to achieve.

Malcolm, on the other hand, felt like a freak. Some kind of cyborg. He noticed how people's eyes tended to drift upwards when they were speaking to him.

What the doctors couldn't tell him was how much damage had been done to his brain, and whether his personality might be affected.

He soon found out.

Before the accident he had always been a happy-go-lucky man. Nothing bothered him. But the bang on his head seemed to shake out his darker feelings.

He became morose, quick-tempered. He would suffer blackouts.

On a train from Carlisle one day, he became convinced that a gang of youths were talking about him. Analysing it afterwards, he wasn't sure it was even true, but at the time he felt he had become the butt of their cruel jibes. He thought they were sneaking glances at the discoloured lump on top of his head, that they were making jokes about it. His anger growing, he could no longer concentrate on his newspaper or the picturesque scenery through the window. He wanted only to put a stop to the perceived mockery.

When the lads stood up to leave the train, he followed them with vengeful eyes. He should have felt relief that they were exiting his life, probably never to be seen again, but he couldn't let them depart so easily. A few seconds after the last youth stepped onto the platform, so did Malcolm.

He doesn't remember much of what happened next. He has vague memories of following three of them into a quiet side street, and then a blur of fists and shouts and blood. He came home with cuts and bruises, but also visions of the youths laid out on the ground, moaning and beaten.

For days afterwards he expected a call from the police, but none came. Presumably the lads were too embarrassed to admit to their thrashing. But still, it came as a shock to Malcolm to realise he was capable of such precipitous and violent action. He vowed then to avoid confrontation and stress as much as possible, for fear of what he might do.

But sometimes he is pushed too far. Sometimes the more rational part of his mind fails in its duty to intervene and calm him down.

Like this morning, for example.

He hopes he hasn't damaged Poppy beyond repair. That would be terrible. Harriet would be so upset.

He didn't plan it that way. He just needed the child to quieten down. But then it all went misty. Everything disappeared from view.

He moves back to the oche. Throws his next dart. Another treble twenty. That's more like it.

It's another reason he plays darts. It takes him away from his worries. Allows him to relax when his stress levels start to build.

He spends a lot of time up here in the back bedroom. It has become his study, his den, his fortress of solitude. Harriet doesn't mind. She sees what a difference it makes to him.

Darts isn't the only pastime that keeps him here. He has his computer, too. He often wishes he had been clever enough to study computing, but even without a formal qualification he is more expert than most. It's another way of exercising his brain.

Plus, it has proven a fantastic tool for helping him plan his missions.

There were only so many times he could patrol the areas frequented by Poppy and her family without attracting attention. Using online maps, he was able to walk up and down her street as many times as he wished. He paid virtual visits to her school, her local park, her friends' houses. In minute detail he plotted out all the places he could employ as observation posts or as possible bases for ambush.

Using search engines, he was able to find out what time the school opened and closed, what the term dates were, when outings were taking place. He found out when the bin collections were scheduled for Poppy's road. He discovered the opening times of the hairdresser's where Poppy's mum works. He even managed to unearth an old listing from an estate agent, which contained a detailed floorplan and interior photographs of Poppy's house.

He drew all of this information together into a comprehensive bank of data, each item cross-referenced with many others. He wanted to leave nothing to chance.

In the end, he decided that his best option was to go into the house itself. But it was a decision based on extensive background research that would have been impossible without his good friend the computer.

Treble one. Not one of his best efforts.

He thinks, What if she's dead? Not just injured, but dead? Harriet will never forgive me. I will never forgive myself. We're supposed to be providing a loving home for these kids.

I should've asked Harriet to give the girl another injection. Knock her out again.

Yes, but she has to learn some time, doesn't she? We can't keep her in a permanent coma. She needs to fit in. If she's to live with us, she has to learn to abide by the rules.

He thinks he should go back to the girls' bedroom and check, but a part of him doesn't want to face up to what he might have done. He doesn't want to deal with the consequences.

A five. A single five. Concentrate, man. You can do better than that.

He remembers when he first unveiled his grand scheme to Harriet. He wasn't sure how she'd take it. He thought she might be mortified. Thought she might never want to speak to him again.

The accident led to a claim for injury, which in turn led to enough money for him to reduce his plumbing work to the minimum and think about how to spend the rest of his life.

Like starting a family, for instance.

They were unable to have children by natural means, and that had always been a source of great distress to Harriet. His injury and subsequent psychiatric problems also rendered him unsuitable for adopting.

But this . . .

This could work. This would solve a number of problems at a single stroke. Yes, there were risks involved, but another of the side effects of the brain injury was that he was less concerned about danger in all its forms. He was not frightened by anyone or anything. He wanted only to keep his wife happy.

He needn't have worried. Harriet took one look at the photographs and instantly fell in love with Daisy. The idea of having her here as her own daughter wasn't so much of a hard sell after that, especially when Malcolm described the research he had done.

It worked perfectly. Everything went precisely according to plan. Malcolm never believed that things would line up so seamlessly ever again.

But that was three whole years ago. He never gave up searching. Harriet, bless her, deserves the opportunity to extend her mothering skills.

He hopes he hasn't given with one hand and taken back with the other. That would be a disaster. Especially after all that hard work.

Treble twenty again. Nice.

10

Daisy remembers too well the fear, the confusion, the ache of separation. She sees it now all wrapped up in Poppy's tiny body.

'Are you all right?' she asks.

Sitting on the bed, Poppy nods and sniffs.

Daisy hands her another tissue. 'They don't like it when we don't do what we're told. Malcolm can get very angry.'

'He hurt me.'

'I know. That's why you can't break things or make loud noises. If you're good, they won't hurt you again. Do you understand?'

Poppy nods again. 'Yes, but . . . I don't want to be here. I want to go home.' She gestures towards the door. 'Your mum and dad are horrible.'

'They're not my mum and dad.'

Poppy's eyes widen. 'What do you mean?'

'They brought me here, just like they brought you.'

'Why? Why did they take us?'

'I think . . . I think they just want a family of their own.'

'Well, they can't just take children who aren't theirs, and then be horrible to them.'

'They can be nice. All you have to do is be nice back to them.'

Poppy raises her head and looks around the room, taking it all in. 'Do you live here?'

Daisy nods. 'Yes. Do you like it?'

'No. When can I go?'

'I don't know. Would you like to play with my dolls? I've got a nice rabbit here.'

'I've got my own toys. I've got a teddy bear called Huggles.'

'That's nice. Do you have a doll's house like mine?'

'Mine's better,' says Poppy. 'Is it daytime or night-time?'

'It's daytime. It's the morning.'

Poppy looks towards the window. 'Then we should open the curtains. It's too dark in here.'

'No,' says Daisy. 'There's really no—'

Before she can finish, Poppy jumps off the bed and runs around it to the window. She yanks the curtains aside.

Daisy's heart sinks. She hates the sight of the tongue-and-groove panelling nailed over the window space.

Poppy runs her hand across the wood.

'How do you open it?'

'You can't. It's . . . They prefer it like this.'

'What do you mean? How do you look at things outside?'

The question stabs at Daisy, making her want to cry. She hasn't seen the outside for three years. She hasn't seen the sun or a tree or a bird or even a blade of grass for almost a third of her lifetime.

She can't tell Poppy this. She can't make her aware of the extent of her imprisonment. Not before she has settled in a little.

'I don't need to see outside,' she lies. 'I have everything I want in here.'

'But what about when you want to go out to play?'

'I . . . I don't play outside.'

She can see how stunned Poppy is. Not spending a part of each day in the fresh air is an alien concept to her. Just as it once was for Daisy.

Poppy and Daisy. Two flowers. They need sunshine and rain and the touch of soft earth so that they can grow and bloom. Otherwise they will wither.

'What?' says Poppy. 'Never?'

'No. It's . . . It's safer in here.'

A lie, but it seems such a necessary one. Best to make Poppy afraid of the outdoors, to quell her desire to escape.

She sees a look of worry on Poppy's face, and immediately hates herself for scaring her.

'Are there bad things out there?' Poppy asks in a much quieter voice. 'Is that why you have no windows – so that you don't have to look at them?'

Daisy doesn't want to utter another untruth. She wants to say instead that there is nothing to be frightened of out there. The monsters are here, in this house, and she would like nothing more than to run as far away from them as possible.

But instead she simply nods and says, 'You're better off in here.'

Poppy scans the room again. 'What if I want to use the bathroom? How do I tell them?'

'You don't. Look . . .'

Daisy walks across to the small curtained area in the corner of the room. The metal rings scrape along the track as she draws back the curtain to reveal the commode.

'Here's the toilet,' she says.

Poppy shakes her head. 'That's not a toilet. It's just a chair.'

'No, it's a special kind of toilet. See – it has a container below the seat to catch everything.'

'But where's the handle? How do you flush it?'

'You don't. Malcolm comes and empties it twice a day.'

Poppy looks disgusted. 'I'm not using that. I want a proper bathroom. How do I have a bath or a shower?'

Daisy points to the tiny basin. 'We get washed there. I've got a big sponge and a—'

'No, I am not doing that. They'll have to let me use the bathroom. When are they going to unlock the door?'

It hits Daisy that Poppy still doesn't get it, still doesn't realise that these four walls are her impassable boundaries from now on.

But clearly she is starting to suspect. She looks to the door, then to the boarded-up window, then back to Daisy. Immense sadness tugs at the corners of her mouth.

'Am I in prison?' she asks. 'Have I done something really, really bad?'

Daisy goes to her. Takes her by the shoulders, guides her to the bed and sits her down.

'No,' she says. 'It's not a prison, and you haven't done anything wrong. Malcolm and Harriet just want to look after you for a while.'

'How long?'

For ever, is the correct answer, but Daisy can't say that. It took her a while to accept it for herself. Poppy needs to be allowed a sliver of hope if she is not to bring trouble to their door.

'Maybe not very long at all. I think probably the best thing to do is to just go along with what they want. You don't have to like them. Just obey their rules, keep them happy. Then maybe they'll let you go back home again. How does that sound? Do you think you could be good for a while?'

'Have *you* been good?'

'Most of the time.'

'How long have you been here?'

'Not long. Tell you what, let's both be extra good together. What do you think?'

Poppy looks down at her bare feet, swinging above the carpet. 'I'll try. As long as they don't hurt me again.'

'They won't. Promise.'

Poppy takes hold of her pyjamas and twists the material between her fingers. 'I can't stay too long, though. My mummy and daddy will miss me.'

Daisy spreads her arms wide. 'Would you like a hug?'

Poppy nods, and Daisy folds her arms around her. Looking over the young child's shoulder, she wonders about her own parents. Wonders how worried they must have been.

Wonders, too, if they have now given up searching for her.

11

'Right then. The subject of our search: Poppy Eliza Devlin.'

DCI Stella Blunt stands at the front of the Major Incident Room, clicking on a remote control to display photographs of Poppy on the monitor next to her. Blunt is unarguably a physically large woman, but her presence would be imposing even without that. Each member of the team, Cody included, hangs on her every word as she takes them through the picture gallery.

'She is six years old,' says Blunt. 'Blonde hair and blue eyes. Imprint this face firmly in your minds, ladies and gents. I want you looking for her everywhere you go, even when you don't have a file of photographs to consult.'

She moves on to another picture. Poppy standing on her bed, with Huggles the teddy bear clutched tightly in her arms. She is wearing pink pyjama bottoms and a white top with pink butterflies on it.

'These are the very pyjamas that Poppy was wearing when she was put to bed last night. That doesn't mean, of course, that she still has them on, but keep an eye out for them anyway.'

Blunt keeps clicking. Two new figures appear on the monitor.

'Poppy's parents. Craig and Maria Devlin. Craig is thirty-four and works as a buyer for Boothroyd's department store. Maria is thirty-two and works part-time as a hairdresser on Aigburth Road.'

Blunt turns to the faces in front of her. 'One thing we need to make very sure of from the beginning is that we are not being made fools of. I do not want to see this team chasing ghosts. So, first question: Does this story hold water?' She points to the faces on the monitor. 'Do we believe them?'

'If I had to call it,' says Cody. 'I'd say yes. Webley and I spent some time with them this morning, and they seemed genuine enough to me.'

Webley adds, 'I'd second that. They were absolutely distraught. Why would they fake this?'

'Why indeed,' says Blunt. 'But we all know that it wouldn't be the first time. Perhaps the parents have murdered her and are trying to cover it up. Perhaps they just like being in the media spotlight. Who knows? I accept we've only just started this investigation, but so far nobody has offered any support for the claims being made by the Devlins. Nobody saw or heard anything during the night, and we've had no reports of any suspicious behaviour in their neighbourhood in recent weeks. Until someone comes up with proof positive that the Devlins are clean, we have to keep them in our sights.'

'Meaning what, exactly?' asks Cody.

Blunt answers with a question of her own: 'Where are the parents now?'

'At Maria's mother's place while CSI do their stuff.'

'Right. Intensify the search. I want that house scoured from top to bottom. Look at every scrap of paper they own. Examine their bank records, their phone records and their medical records. Take their computers and check every file they contain. Find out who they talk to, how they spend their time, how they vote, who they might have pissed off, who they owe money to, and why they haven't had any more kids. I want to know if they've had so much as a parking fine or a demand letter for unpaid bills.'

One of the assembled detectives raises a point that is probably on everyone's mind. 'That's going to take a long time, ma'am. The house search itself—'

Blunt rounds on him. 'Yes, I'm fully aware of that, thank you. And I hope *you* are aware that there's a young child's life at stake here.'

There is a level of emotion in her voice that Cody has rarely heard before. Like everyone else in the room, he remains silent while Blunt composes herself again, then turns her eyes on another detective.

'Jason, you're the FLO, right?'

Jason Oxburgh, known to many of his colleagues as Oxo, nods his flame-haired head. As the Family Liaison Officer, it will be his job to keep the parents up to speed with developments in the case.

'Yes, ma'am,' he says.

'Explain the situation to them. Collect some overnight things for them and move them into a hotel for the night. If they've got nothing to hide, they shouldn't kick up too much of a fuss.'

'I'll do my best, ma'am.'

'I want better than your best on this case, Jason.' She scans the room. 'That goes for the lot of you. No shortcuts, no laziness. Grace, is there anything in your technological bag of tricks you can pull out for us?'

Cody swivels in his chair to get a better look at Grace Meade, the Intelligence Analyst seated at the very back of the room. For the most part, Grace tends not to call attention to herself, but Cody can testify what an asset she is to the team. He has seen for himself how much of a whiz she can be when it comes to computers.

Grace stands up. She always seems to feel the need to get to her feet when called upon to contribute. She looks nervously at all the expectant faces, then clears her throat.

'Well, I'll collate all the intelligence as it comes in, of course, and I'll look for correspondences and mismatches. That's standard. I'll make sure we get a dump of phone records and I'll analyse them. I'll also liaise with HCU to make sure we search any computers owned by the family, especially if Poppy had access. I know she's only six, but it's amazing how young some people are when they start using computers nowadays, and parents don't always supervise their activities. It's a long shot, but I've got a lot of clever software I can use to help me search. I might just get lucky.'

Cody interjects with a thought that has been burning in his mind. 'And if they're clean?'

Blunt shifts her gaze to him. 'Cody?'

'The Devlins. What if we do all this checking and we satisfy ourselves that they really have played no part in this?'

Blunt nods solemnly. 'Then we've got one of the strangest and most ominous abduction cases on our hands that I've ever encountered. This wasn't a simple burglary of an empty house. Whoever did this went in knowing that there were people inside. Think about the risks involved. Either of the parents could have been woken up. The child could have screamed the house down. What sort of person does this? And why?'

Neil 'Footlong' Ferguson chips in. 'What if it was a mistake? What if it started out as a straightforward burglary, but the intruder was discovered by the girl? Maybe he didn't even know there was anyone in the house.'

Blunt thinks for a second. 'You mean he had to silence her before she yelled? Okay, but then why take her with him? Why not just leave the body there and scram?'

'Because maybe he didn't kill her. Maybe he's not that kind of guy. He couldn't leave her there because she'd seen his face, and now he doesn't know what to do with her. Or, if he *has* killed her, maybe he doesn't want to be done for murder, so he's hidden the body somewhere.'

Blunt mulls it over some more. 'I don't know, Neil. All the indications are that the intruder went straight up to Poppy's bedroom. Nothing downstairs was touched. Why would a run-of-the-mill burglar act like that?' She pauses. 'All right. I don't want to rule anything out at this stage. Start ferreting out some of the lags we know about. Find out what they've been up to lately. Touch base with informants, too; see what they can tell us. Anyone got any other theories about why Poppy Devlin suddenly became prize of the century?'

Cody hesitates, but knows he has to give voice to something else that is on everyone's minds.

'Hate to say it, but we need to start talking to registered sex offenders in the area.'

Blunt's head lowers as if the weight of Cody's suggestion has dragged it down. It's clear to Cody that his boss is finding this case as emotionally difficult as he is – perhaps more so.

'You're right, of course,' she says. 'In the absence of a ransom demand, we have to consider motives other than financial gain. Start drawing up a list and knocking on doors. Anything else?'

'Yes. We can't be certain that Poppy was his first. He may have taken other children in the past, or at least made attempts.'

'Good point. Okay, do some digging. Look at past cases, both solved and unsolved. I don't know of anything as audacious as this one, but maybe he's been working his way up to it. Maybe the danger is part of the thrill for him. I'm sure Grace can help you look for patterns.'

Cody looks back at Grace again. Sees a flash of a smile before she buries her head behind her monitor.

'There's a lot of work to do,' Blunt announces to the throng. 'A lot of people to interview. Get on it. If anyone can find Poppy Devlin, you can.'

12

He finds Harriet in the kitchen, furiously stirring some cake mix. He can't see her face, but he suspects that more than a few tears have dropped into that bowl.

He comes up behind her, slips his arms around her waist. 'What are you making?'

'Chocolate cake,' she says in a squeaky voice.

'Lovely,' he says. Then: 'Are you okay?'

She stops stirring. Puts the bowl down. 'Oh, Malcolm, have we done the right thing? This new girl, she seems so . . . defiant. You know I can't cope with badly behaved children. I get so upset.'

'Hush, dear. It'll be fine. Have you taken a tablet?'

'Yes, but I don't think it's helped.'

Harriet self-medicates. She has boxes full of drugs, all dating back to the time she worked in the hospital. She stole them in the period leading up to her breakdown.

What a pair we make, he thinks. Me with my bashed-in skull. Her with her nerves. It's a wonder we manage to cope.

'What you have to remember,' he says, 'is that Daisy was rebellious as well when we first got her. And now look at her! She's a little angel.'

Harriet twists in his arms to face him. 'I know, but I don't think she was ever this bad. She was never this destructive, and I certainly never heard her swear. That language from Poppy was disgusting. You know I hate those words.'

'I know, dear, I know. Give her time. I'm sure she'll settle in. You can already hear how quiet she is.'

Harriet glances up at the ceiling. 'Did you . . . Did you have to hurt her much?'

He doesn't know the answer to this. He still hasn't been into the bedroom to check. It worries him that it has been deathly silent up there since his intervention.

'I didn't really *hurt* her,' he says defensively. 'I just restrained her until she calmed down.' He wants to believe this. Wants to be convinced that he used minimal force. But he's not sure.

'Good,' says Harriet. 'Well, maybe she has learnt her lesson. I hope so. I want us to be a proper family, Malcolm. I want Poppy to feel she can be happy here with us. I mean, we've done a good job with Daisy, haven't we?'

He beams a smile at her. 'We've done an excellent job. And it's all thanks to you, dearest. You're everything a good mother should be.'

He kisses her on the forehead then, and she embraces him. They stand like that for a while, lost in each other's warmth.

And then the buzzer sounds.

They both look out towards the hallway. It's not a visitor at the front door, but a signal from Daisy's bedroom. It's what she uses to tell them they're needed.

Harriet's agitation returns. 'If she's causing trouble again, I don't want to know. You go, Malcolm.'

Malcolm swallows hard. He'd rather not go up there. Despite what Harriet has said about mischievous children, she will be devastated if Poppy is . . .

He doesn't want to think about that.

'Okay, my love,' he says. 'I'll go.'

He pulls away from Harriet, leaving her to resume her baking while he trudges into the hallway and then up the carpeted stairs. On the landing he pauses and listens, but can hear nothing. He slides back the bolts, then opens the door.

He does not enter, but stands in the doorway, absorbing the scene in front of him. Taking a breath, he calls over his shoulder. 'Harriet! Harriet, you'd better come and see.'

He hears his wife come up the stairs after him. She halts at the top step, still wiping her hands on a tea towel.

'What is it?' she whispers. 'Is it bad news? I don't want to know if it's bad news.'

He beckons her with a flick of his head. 'Look.'

She comes up behind him. Peers around his shoulder.

Daisy and Poppy are sitting quietly at the table. The room is tidy once more: the furniture upright, the toys in their rightful places, the bed made.

'We drew a picture,' says Daisy.

She holds it up for them to see. Most of it has been done in blue crayon by Daisy. It shows Malcolm and Harriet holding hands with Daisy. At the end of the chain of people, Poppy has added her own crude rendition of herself in green.

'We thought you might like it,' says Daisy. She looks at Poppy. 'Didn't we, Poppy?'

Poppy doesn't speak or smile. She simply nods. But that's enough.

Malcolm steps forward. He takes hold of the picture and examines it more closely. 'That's beautiful,' he says, a lump rising in his throat.

He takes the drawing over to Harriet and shows it to her. 'Look at this, Mummy,' he says. 'Isn't it wonderful?'

Harriet is already crying. She can find no words.

He puts an arm around her shoulders. 'You see? I told you it would all be fine. We're a family now. A proper family.'

13

DC Jason Oxburgh loves this side of his work. It's why he volunteered for the Family Liaison Officer training. He likes the human touch, the closeness to the people who, as a policeman, he has elected to help.

Some of his colleagues think of FLO work as a bit too touchy-feely. They prefer detachment, objectivity. They don't like emotions getting in the way of what they believe should be a logical process. They're quite happy making phone calls, interviewing suspects, and taking down criminals. FLOs are, in their view, a bit 'soft'.

Oxo would be the first to admit that he's a little on the sensitive side. But he doesn't believe that makes him a bad copper. In fact, he is stronger for it. At least, that's what he tells himself.

There are times, though, when he thinks he should have taken up a different career. A counsellor, perhaps, or a psychologist. He likes to know what's going on in people's heads. It's why he moved from uniform to CID as soon as he could: it seemed to him that detectives have far more opportunities to explore the motivations of criminals, and the effects their crimes have on victims. But the downside of such an empathetic nature is that sometimes the contents of other people's heads stay with him for far too long.

He cried just last week. A murder-suicide, it was. MIT were brought in because at first it looked like a double homicide. Turned out the man had shot his wife in their bedroom, and then, at the top of the stairs, turned the gun on himself. The blast had sent him tumbling down the steps, leaving the gun on the landing.

To many cops, establishing the facts of the case would have been enough. Man kills wife; man tops himself; case closed. Nobody left to arrest, no leads left to follow.

Oxo, though, needed to know the whys and the wherefores. He needed to *understand*.

And what he discovered was that the woman had been told just before Christmas that she had terminal cancer. Her husband didn't want to watch her rapid decline, and he didn't want to live on without her. So he brought things to an end. In the note that was eventually found on his computer, he said that he was simply 'deleting one more episode of pain and misery from a world that can do without it'.

Oxo read out that line to his wife, and they cried together.

He wonders if any of his colleagues ever cry over a case.

This one could do it, he thinks. If anything can turn on the water-works, it's the victim being a young child. Such cases almost invariably end in tragedy.

He's not going to say that to the couple now sitting in front of him, of course. Craig and Maria Devlin. Perched on the edges of their seats with expectation written on their faces.

It's a difficult balancing act, being an FLO. His role here is as an intermediary. He will bring the family updates on the progress of the investigation, while at the same time not revealing confidential intelligence. Conversely, he will do his utmost not to demolish the trust of the family when conveying useful snippets of information from them back to the detectives. He must also strive not to raise false hopes or cause undue distress.

Not everyone could do this job, he tells himself.

They are in the living room of Maria's parents' house, a new-build detached property in Grassendale. Taking a hint, her parents have gone out for a walk, leaving the three of them alone.

Oxo begins by explaining to the couple, in the simplest and clearest terms, exactly who he is and what he will be doing for them.

'We'll be seeing a lot of you, then?' says Maria.

'You can see as much or as little of me as you like,' he says. 'Some people like to have constant updates, while others prefer to have as little to do with the police as they possibly can. I'm not going to judge you. If you want me to stay away, I will. Or if you find you don't get on with me, and would prefer someone else as your FLO, that can be arranged too.'

When Maria looks to Craig for his view, Oxo quickly adds, 'You don't have to decide right now.'

Maria nods. 'I think at the moment we're so focused on Poppy . . .'

'I understand. So let me tell you what we're doing in the investigation.'

He spends some time outlining each of the actions being taken by the team, stopping at frequent intervals to make sure they understand, and to give them an opportunity to pose questions.

Then he takes a deep breath. So far, so good, but there are a couple of other things he needs to bring into the conversation that could prove more controversial.

'As I mentioned, we've alerted the media, and we've got them on board. Anyone who picks up a paper or turns on the news will hear about what's happened to Poppy. Her face will be everywhere. This is the kind of story that attracts attention, and so there are going to be huge numbers of people looking out for any sign of your daughter. What we need to do is to make sure that the case registers fully with as many people as possible. That's where you come in.'

'Us?' says Maria. 'What do you mean?'

'We've arranged a press conference, for tomorrow morning. We'd like you to put out an appeal for the safe return of your daughter.'

The couple exchange glances again.

Maria says, 'So we'll be on camera? We'll be in front of reporters, asking us questions?'

'Yes, but it's nothing to be frightened of. You've done nothing wrong. You're not accused of anything. All you have to do is answer truthfully. Don't try to hide your emotions, either. Let people see how devastated you are by what's happened. They're more likely to be sympathetic then. The more people we have on our side, the greater the chance of finding Poppy quickly.'

'All right,' says Maria. 'If you think it's a good idea.'

'Absolutely. But the most important thing of all is what you say to your daughter's abductor.'

The mention of this phantom figure causes alarm to leap into Maria's eyes.

'Her . . . her abductor?'

'Yes. Whoever did this is also likely to be watching news reports. They'll want some idea of how successful they've been. They'll want to know whether they're getting away with it, or if the police are hot on their trail. They may even get a kick just from hearing people talking about them.'

'They?'

Oxo waves the question away. 'At this stage, I'm trying to avoid getting fixated on a preconceived idea of who the perpetrator is. It could be a man, a woman, or several people acting together. The point is—'

'A woman? You think a woman could do this?'

'Why not? Burglars are almost exclusively male, but this isn't your standard burglary. Somebody, it seems, desperately wanted your child.'

He sees how Maria lowers her gaze while she tosses his suggestion around in her mind. It's as if it has opened a whole new realm of possibilities for her.

'As I was saying,' he continues, 'the point is that Poppy's abductor is probably going to hear whatever message you send out. This is your prime opportunity to make a connection. You need to think carefully about how best to do that. You don't want to frighten them off, but at the same time you need to convince them that they've made a huge mistake, and that it's not too late for them to put it right.'

Craig shifts forward in his seat. 'It's . . . it's a huge responsibility. What if we get it wrong? What if we say something that triggers the kidnappers to . . . to . . .'

'We'll help you,' says Oxo. 'We've got experts in this kind of thing. Write down some thoughts as to what you might say, and we'll knock it into shape for you before tomorrow morning.'

Craig nods, but still looks a little unsure and bewildered. Oxo isn't relishing what comes next.

'There's one other thing,' he says. 'As you know, we're conducting a search of your house . . .'

'Okay,' Craig urges.

'Obviously, we're primarily on the lookout for forensic evidence that may have been left by your daughter's abductor, but we also need to make sure that the two of you cannot possibly have fingers pointed at you for being involved.'

'I don't understand. What does that mean?'

'It means we need to extend the search. We need to examine the whole property. That includes your personal possessions and documents.'

Craig stares at him for several seconds. 'No. I still don't get it. You mean you'll be going through our things? The private stuff in our rooms?'

'Yes. We'll also need to take a look at what's on your computer.'

'My computer? Why?'

'We have to see if there's anything that could help us to identify possible suspects.'

'But . . . but Poppy has never been allowed on the computer by herself. She's too young. It's not as if anybody could have groomed her online or anything.'

'Even so, we need to check.'

'Why? What's the point of that? How can that possibly—?'

'Oh, my God.'

This from Maria, who has just brought a hand to her mouth.

She says, 'You think it was us, don't you?'

'What?' says Craig.

Oxo raises a placating hand. 'No, not at all. We just need to—'

'You do. You think we're responsible. You think we've harmed Poppy, our own daughter. Oh, my God.'

'No. Listen to me. I'm not suggesting anything of the kind, but there are people who will. There have been cases like that. You must have heard about them. People who have invented stories about their missing children. And—'

Craig finally seems to grasp what his wife is saying, and his anger surfaces. 'Invented? Why the fuck would we invent this? Are you seriously accusing us of—'

'I'm not accusing you of anything. What I am saying is that there are members of the public, possibly fuelled by the press if we don't handle things properly, who will try to blame you for this. We have to nip that in the bud. We have to prove to them as soon as we can that you are completely innocent victims of a terrible crime.'

'And to yourselves,' says Maria.

'I'm sorry?'

She wrings her hands as she gathers her thoughts, then looks him in the eye. 'One of the first things you said to us today was that you wouldn't lie to us. You might have to keep things back, but you wouldn't lie. Isn't that what you told us?'

'Yes. Yes, it is.'

'Then don't lie to us now. Let's start as we mean to go on. Do you or do you not suspect us for the disappearance of our daughter?'

Good question, thinks Oxo.

'We haven't ruled out that possibility,' he says.

Craig's fury snaps him into a standing position. 'I don't believe this.'

Maria continues to hold Oxo's gaze. 'Thank you,' she says.

Craig looks down at his wife in disbelief. 'What are you thanking him for? Did you hear what he just said? He thinks we did it. He thinks we did something bad to our Poppy. How can you just sit there and—'

'I'm thanking him for being honest. Look at it from their point of view. They've—'

'I don't want to see it from their point of view. I want them to see *ours*. We're the victims here. I want them to be working *for* us, not against us.'

'And we are,' says Oxo. 'Believe me, we fully intend to find your daughter and whoever took her. But to do that—'

Maria cuts him off. 'To do that,' she says to Craig, 'they need to have faith in us, so that we can work together. Think about it. Think about what they can see from the outside. They see a couple they know nothing about, whose child has been reported missing. They have to investigate everyone who knows the child.'

'But we're her parents.'

She reaches up and takes Craig's hand in hers. 'Which is all the more reason to look at us under a microscope. Suppose little Sophie Landis across the road had gone missing. Or Katrina Everly. Wouldn't you think it weird if the police didn't investigate the backgrounds of their parents?'

She has sapped Craig's energy. He collapses on to the seat next to her, tears filling his eyes.

'I just want her back,' he says. 'The police should be out on the streets, finding her kidnapper. Not invading our privacy. It's wasting precious time and manpower. They need to find her. They *need* to find her.'

Maria pulls her husband in close, rests his head on her shoulder.

And suddenly it feels to Oxo as though this raw intimacy drives him out of existence. As though this couple who may never see their daughter again have lost the ability to see him too.

14

'It's nice round here,' says Webley. She's looking out of the side window of the car. Cody is driving. They are on their way to interview a man called Gavin Quigley, who is of interest to them for two reasons. The first is that his registered address is near to that of Poppy Devlin. The second is that he was once accused of attempting to abduct a young girl. Cody has already spoken to Quigley's mother, who directed him out into the sticks of the Wirral.

'Nice big houses,' Webley continues. 'Wish I could afford to live here.'

Cody grunts. He's not sure where this is going.

'Doesn't Devon live round here somewhere?'

And now he knows. Devon is his ex-fiancée.

'Yeah. Hoylake.'

Webley turns and looks at him. He doesn't look back, but he can feel her eyes trying to see into his skull.

'Big house, is it?'

'Pretty big.'

'Garden?'

'Yup.'

'On the prom?'

'Not on the front, but pretty close.'

She nods thoughtfully. 'Nice.'

Cody risks a glance towards her. 'That's the third time you've used the word "nice" in the past few seconds.'

She raises her eyebrows. 'All right, Mr Roget. We're not all frigging walking thesauruses, you know.'

They lapse into silence. But only for a few seconds. Cody knows that Webley hates an unfilled gap in a conversation.

She says, 'Do you fancy dropping in while we're here?'

'Dropping in where?'

'Devon's place. Just for a quick cuppa. You could introduce me.'

'Why would I want to do that?'

'Well . . . why not? Don't you think the two most important women in your life should meet?'

'What makes you think that—'

He stops himself. Just in time.

'Go on,' she urges.

'Doesn't matter.'

'No, go on. You were about to suggest that one of us – either me or Devon – isn't all that important to you.'

'That's not what I was going to say at all.'

'Yes, you were. So which of us was it?'

'You misunderstood. What I was about to say was . . .'

'Yes?'

'I was about to ask what makes you think that either you or Devon is more important than Cath.'

He can almost hear Webley's jaw landing on her lap. 'Cath? Who the frigging hell is Cath?'

'The new woman in my life. She's a barista.'

'A barrister? You're going out with someone who wears a wig all day?'

Cody laughs. 'No. A barista. She works at Starbucks in town. Don't know if she wears a wig, though.'

And now Webley's stare has become positively searing.

'How did you meet her?'

'How do you think? I went in there for a coffee.'

'Hold on. You're telling me that you went to a coffee shop, and you chatted up the waitress?'

'Barista. There's a lot more to it than just serving. She even puts those little pictures on my coffee foam.'

'I don't think I want to know what tricks she does with your foam, Cody. And you haven't answered my question.'

'Yes, I chatted her up.'

'No. You didn't.'

'I did.'

'You didn't. Did you?'

Cody clams up. Makes a show of looking out for his next turn-off.

'You're lying,' says Webley.

'Here we are,' says Cody. He puts on his indicator, then makes a right turn. It takes them off the main road and onto a street leading down to the promenade.

They are on the north coast of the Wirral peninsula – the finger of land that is separated from Liverpool on the east by the River Mersey, and from Wales on the west by the River Dee. Straight ahead is the Irish Sea.

'So what's her surname then?'

'Whose?'

'Cath's, you idiot.'

'You won't know her.'

'I know a lot of people. Try me.'

'She's a postgraduate student from France. Do you know any French students?'

Webley's voice goes up a notch in both volume and tone. 'Just tell me her sodding name, will you?'

'Okay. It's Tierre. So do you know her?'

'No.'

Cody starts his countdown. Doesn't get very far before—

'You bastard!' She smacks him hard on the arm. 'A coffee maker called Cath Tierre! Very fucking funny, Cody.'

He can't stop laughing then. Continues laughing for the next few minutes while Webley sits next to him in grumpy silence, her arms tightly folded.

It's evening now, at the tail end of rush hour. Being February, it's already dark. It gets even blacker as Cody takes the car away from the residential streets and onto narrow country lanes. When he reaches a lay-by, he pulls the car in and switches off the engine and lights.

'I'll bet we're not the first couple to have parked up here in the dark,' he says.

'Hmm,' says Webley. 'Perhaps you could bring Cath here some time. Hot and dark, is she? Good at perking you up in the morning?'

Cody smiles at her, then opens his door and climbs out of the car. His feet crunch on the gravel.

Webley gets out too. 'Why the hell are we parked here? There aren't even any houses. Are you planning to bump me off or something?'

'He lives in a field,' Cody answers.

'Who, Quigley? What do you mean, he lives in a field? Have you brought me all this way to interview a frigging scarecrow?'

'Follow me,' he says.

He walks over to a fence and starts to climb it. Notices that Webley is still standing next to the car.

'Coming?'

She moves towards him. 'I swear, Cody, if this is another little joke, I will not be amused.'

Cody starts plodding up the field, not even breaking stride when Webley calls after him.

'Wait for me,' she says. 'I'm not exactly dressed for farming. This skirt was expensive.'

When she catches up with him, Cody audibly draws in a chestful of air. 'Smell that,' he says. 'There's nothing like a bit of sea air.'

'I'm more worried about the smell of whatever I might step in. There aren't any animals in this field, are there?'

'What, like lions, you mean?'

'No, Mr Funny Man. I mean horses or cows or other farmyard residents. Animals that have no second thoughts about where they choose to leave their deposits.'

Cody laughs. 'Come on. Nearly there.'

As they approach the far end of the field, the breeze grows stronger, bringing with it spots of rain and the pounding beat of the waves. The sky is only a shade above black now, but it's enough to reveal to Cody the rectangular silhouette for which he has been searching.

He lowers his voice. 'This is it.'

Webley squints. 'This is what? I can't— Oh, wait! A caravan? He lives in a caravan?'

'Yup. Just like being on holiday again, don't you think?'

'No, I do not. Give me a villa on Skiathos any time. This place gives me the creeps. I wouldn't spend a night here if you paid me.'

They walk up to the caravan's door. Cody cannot hear anything from inside, but he can see chinks of light through the closed curtains.

Webley whispers, 'What do we do now?'

'We go back to the car. I just wanted to show you what a caravan looks like in the dark. What do you *think* we do now?'

Ignoring Webley's look of annoyance, he raps on the door.

Nothing.

He knocks again. Same result. He tries the handle, finds it locked.

'Nice to see you came prepared for every eventuality,' says Webley. And when Cody frowns, she adds, 'See, you're not the only one who can do sarcasm.'

'Check the windows,' he says.

He goes one way, Webley the other. When he meets up with her at the rear and she shrugs her shoulders, he realises he's in for a lot of stick on the drive back to Liverpool.

And then everything changes.

The crash is the sound of the door being flung open and hitting the side of the caravan. Cody races around to the front, Webley hot on his heels.

He sees the figure of a man – presumably Quigley – racing through the field towards the sea wall, and he gives chase.

'Police!' he calls. 'Stop!'

But Quigley keeps on running. Sprinting as hard and as fast as he can, as though his life depends on it.

Cody picks up the pace. He's fit, but his quarry is no slouch either.

He sees Quigley fling himself over the boundary fence. A few seconds later, Cody tries the same manoeuvre, but the jacket of his suit catches on a jagged piece of wood, and he winces as he hears the cloth rip apart.

By the time he has untangled himself, Quigley has already scrambled across the dunes and disappeared over the wall. Cody gets to the same spot as quickly as he can, bounding over the wall without even thinking about how deep the drop might be on the other side. The last time he made such a foolish decision he sprained his ankle. This time, he is relieved to find that the drop is only a couple of feet.

He is on a concrete pathway, often used by walkers, joggers and cyclists, but fairly deserted now. Ahead, the concrete slopes down into the lapping sea, its cold blackness punctuated in the distance by the winking red lights of wind turbines and, beyond those, the fierce burning of gas platforms.

But Cody has no time to lament the passing of the more natural vista that once existed here. He is running again, accelerating along the path towards Leasowe lighthouse. He thinks, but isn't sure, that Webley isn't that far behind.

The gap closes. He can hear Quigley now. Panting, yes, but is that the sound of sobbing too?

They are separated by a distance of just a few yards. Cody digs into his energy reserves. Reduces the gap to mere feet. Then almost touching distance . . .

And then Quigley suddenly changes course. Leaves the path to head down the slope. Towards the sea that threatens to swallow him whole.

'No!' Cody shouts.

But Quigley continues, and Cody has no choice but to follow. He needs to stop the man before this ends so, so badly.

He considers attempting a leap, a rugby tackle – anything that will bring this to an end. But the risk is too great: the pair of them would end up barrelling into the sea's icy clutches.

And then the decision is taken from him.

Just above the waterline, a large stretch of slimy algae robs his shoes of their friction. Cody loses his footing. Suddenly he is no longer running but falling.

He hits the concrete hard, but his momentum keeps him sliding across the algae. He knows what's coming, and he tries to flatten himself out to brake, but still he plunges down to the sea edge.

He braces himself, takes a deep gulp of air in readiness for going under.

His feet break through the waves. He closes his eyes as he prepares himself for the punch of cold and the terrifying embrace that will deny him sight, sound and breath.

And then his feet hit solidity and he comes to a stop. He realises that the water is less than two feet deep here, just up to his knees.

If he had time to feel both relieved and foolish, he would, but behind him there is a lot of noise, and he turns to see that Quigley is slipping and sliding in the algae himself, while above him Webley is shouting all kinds of things he cannot quite make out.

It takes Cody several seconds to pull his feet free from the sucking grip of the wet, oily sand. By then, his prey has managed to scramble back towards the path.

But not before Webley can head him off.

She leaps at Quigley like a woman possessed, knocking him to the ground and firing a salvo of expletives at him.

Exhausted, Cody inches himself through the algae on hands and knees, daring to stand only when the ground feels dryer and more secure. He looks down at his sodden legs, but cannot see very much. Not, that is, until he is suddenly bathed in a pool of light.

He lifts his gaze to see a man who has been walking his dog along the path, but who has now stopped to sweep his torch alternately between the two spectacles in front of him: a suited figure who has just emerged from the sea like the creature from the Black Lagoon; and a woman who is sitting astride another man while she curses at him and applies a painful arm lock.

'Evening,' says Cody, raising a hand in greeting. 'Looks like rain again.'

15

They huddle around an old Calor gas heater on the floor of the caravan. Cody thinks it looks dangerous – like it could suddenly burst into flames or even blow up. But at least it kicks out some heat.

Gavin Quigley is twenty-four years old. Physically, that is. His mental age lags some way behind.

His dark hair is short at the sides, long on top, and looks as though it hasn't been washed for at least a week. He keeps flicking his head to shake the fringe out of his eyes. He is wearing a grubby woollen polo-neck sweater and jeans that are shiny with grease. His leather boots have been tied with one white lace and one blue.

It suddenly hits Cody that he's not in a good place for throwing stones right now: his own appearance is hardly straight out of a menswear catalogue. His jacket was almost ripped in two by the fence he climbed, and looks as though it could part company with him any time soon. The rest of his attire is covered in a slimy green stain, as though crawled over by a gigantic slug. To top it all, his shoes squelch when he walks, and the gas heater is turning his drenched trousers and socks into generators of considerable steam.

Webley isn't helping matters either. She keeps eyeing him up and smirking.

'First thing's first, Gavin,' says Cody. 'What's with the impromptu jog along the prom?'

Quigley has trouble maintaining eye contact. His head bobs and twists as he tries to find something else on which to focus.

While Cody does his best to follow the nomadic gaze, he takes in how much of a tip this place is. It's littered with cardboard takeout boxes from fast-food chains. The sink is piled high with encrusted dishes. There are food stains everywhere, and the air is rank with the perfume of rotting leftovers and sweaty feet.

The only things adding a touch of cheer are Quigley's drawings. Every surface is strewn with his childish pictures in crayon and felt-tip. They lie on the floor, the seats and the worktops. They are taped to the walls and the cupboards. Cody finds it hard to say for sure, but it seems that the local geography has been a huge inspiration for most of them. They contain what appears to be beach and sea, plus the occasional seagull or passing ship. A number of the pictures – presumably Quigley's favourites – have been given titles. Beneath one that seems to be Leasowe Lighthouse are the words *Litehouse by Gavin Quigley*. Cody's eyes linger on another now, yellowed and curled by the sunlight. He guesses it's of the Leasowe Castle Hotel near to the lighthouse, which does have tessellated walls, but which Quigley has made look far too much like a real castle. Below this one is written *Castell by Gavin Quigley*.

'You like to draw,' says Webley.

No longer in the best of moods, Cody aims a sharp glance at her to let her know he is still waiting for an answer to his question.

But Webley doesn't seem to notice. She has morphed radically from the foul-mouthed she-devil on the footpath. In this more controlled setting she has affixed her best calming smile – the one she uses when dealing with distressed and vulnerable people. The sort of smile Cody cannot hope to match given his current state of mind.

It seems to work. Quigley's eyes settle on Webley for the briefest of moments, as if he's trying to decide if she is being genuine.

'Yes,' he says. 'I like to draw.'

'They're lovely pictures,' she says. 'Happy.' She points to one on the floor. 'I like that one with the big sun smiling.'

Quigley allows his gaze to swoop low, before raising it again. 'That's a bird. It's not a smile.'

Webley glances across, presumably to check that Cody isn't laughing at her. He keeps his face straight, so she continues.

'Oh, yes. So it is. I'm too far away, aren't I? Which is your favourite, Gavin?'

He looks around, his expression perceptibly brighter. When he points, it's the emphatic straight-arm gesture of a kid singling out a particular type of confectionary on a high shelf.

'That one. I like the whale.'

'A whale? You saw a whale here?'

He shakes his head, and his lank fringe curtains his eyes again. 'No. I drew that one in Wales. That's why I put a whale on it, because it was Wales. I didn't really see the whale. I did see some dogs, though. And jellyfish. And dead crabs.'

'When did you go to Wales? Recently?'

'Last summer. When it was hot. I like to go to beaches. I go to lots of beaches, all over the place.'

'All over? How do you get around?'

'Trains and buses. You can get to lots of beaches on trains and buses.'

'So that's why you're living here? Because you like the beach so much?'

'Yeah. It's peaceful here. Quiet.'

'Yes, I can see that. Don't you ever get lonely?'

'I like being alone. People are always nasty.'

'Do you ever go back over to Liverpool? To see your mum?'

'Sometimes. But I don't think she wants me there. She's got a new boyfriend, and he hates me.'

'What makes you think that?'

'He calls me bad names. Swearing names, like you did before.'

Webley blinks. 'Yes, I'm sorry about that, Gavin. I got a bit . . .' She lets the sentence trail off. 'Doesn't your mum stick up for you?'

'She doesn't know about it. He calls me names when she's not there. She thinks he's a nice man, but he's not. I'm in the way there, so I come and live here instead.'

'Whose caravan is this, Gavin?'

'My mum's friend. She lives near here. She said I can live in it as long as I want.'

'Does she know you're not looking after it? It's a bit of a mess in here.'

Quigley lets his eyes rove around the space, as though this report of its untidiness is a revelation to him. Accepting the news, he merely shrugs.

'She doesn't care. She was going to get it towed away. She said it's falling apart.'

Cody decides it's time to resurrect his question. 'Why'd you run, Gavin?'

As Quigley ventures a momentary look at Cody, his expression becomes more sombre. Cody wonders whether it might have been best to allow Webley to continue with her own line of interrogation.

Quigley frowns. 'I didn't know who you were. You frightened me. I thought you came to hurt me.'

'You always run a mile when someone knocks on your door?'

'Nobody knocks. Nobody comes here. That's why I like it.'

'Uh-huh. When was the last time you were over in Liverpool?'

'I don't know. Weeks ago.'

'Weeks? Not yesterday or today?'

'No.'

'You sure?'

'Yes, I'm sure.'

'Do you know why we're here, Gavin?'

'No.'

'Care to make a guess?'

'I'm not good at guessing.'

'Have you got a radio here?'

'Yes.'

'Do you listen to the news?'

'It comes on sometimes. I don't really listen. I prefer music.'

'Have you heard any news today? Read any papers?'

'No.'

'Then you don't know about the little girl? The one that's gone missing?'

And this is it. The start of the real questioning. He suspects from the look on Webley's face that she would have taken more time to get here, that she thinks he's being a bit clumsy in wanting to get straight to the point. But he's growing impatient.

It's as if Cody's query has landed on Quigley and clamped his jaws shut. His head begins to swivel again, as though he is searching for an emergency exit.

Cody continues to press. 'Well, Gavin? Do you know anything about this? Everyone's talking about it. They're saying she's been taken away by someone. She's only six years old. Just like—'

'NO!'

The word is fired at them like a cannonball. Quigley's face has contorted in a display of inner torture. His fingers dance in the air, as if plucking at some invisible musical instrument.

'No,' he says again. 'I didn't . . . It wasn't . . . They said it . . . They wanted to hurt me . . .'

Webley takes it upon herself to cut through the rambling. 'Gavin, you know we have to talk to you about this, don't you? You know why?'

Tiny sobs escape Quigley's lips as his eyes scan the drawings on the walls. It seems to Cody that he is trying to find some inner peace from them.

'I . . . I know why,' says Quigley. 'But it wasn't me. I just want to be left alone. That's why I live here, so everyone will leave me alone. You just want to hurt me.'

'No,' says Webley. 'We don't want to hurt you. We want the truth, that's all. Tell us the truth, and then we'll go away and leave you in peace. All right?'

Quigley doesn't answer, but his tics subside a little.

'The truth.'

'Yes.'

'Okay. But . . . but I don't know anything.'

'Then that's fine. A few more questions and we'll be done.'

Quigley's head bobs. Could be a nod, or simply a twitch.

'The girl who has just gone missing,' says Cody. 'Her name is Poppy Devlin. Have you ever heard that name before?'

Quigley's head movement is clearer this time. A definite no.

'Her home is in Otterspool. In fact, it's just a couple of roads away from where you live with your mother.'

'I . . . I don't live there no more. I live here.'

'But you know the area, right? You know Larkwood Close?'

'Yes. I know it.'

'Ever go down there?'

'Long time ago.'

'Why?'

'I like to walk. I like fresh air.'

'I see. Did you ever speak to anyone on that road? A child, perhaps?'

'No.'

Cody reaches into his pocket and brings out an envelope. He's surprised to find it in one piece, given what he went through during the chase. He opens it up and takes out a photograph of Poppy. He shows it to Quigley.

'Does this girl look familiar to you?'

Quigley drags his eyes to the picture.

'No,' he says, with some effort. 'Never seen her.'

'Are you sure? Take a good look.'

'Don't know her.'

Cody suppresses a sigh as he puts the photograph back in his pocket. He doesn't relish what has to come next, and guesses that Webley will be happy to let him continue to play the role of bad cop.

'Do you ever talk to any other young children, Gavin?'

He detects the agitation building again. Quigley is looking like a newly caged animal.

'I don't talk to no one. I live by myself now. Nobody likes me.'

'What about when you're outside, when you're on the beaches? You must see people then. You must see kids playing.'

'I see them. But I don't talk to them. Not allowed.'

'Not allowed? Why isn't it allowed, Gavin?'

'You know. You know why. You'll hurt me again. That's why you're here.'

'Why do you think that, Gavin? Have you done something that needs to be punished?'

'No. But that's what you think. You won't believe what I say. You didn't believe me last time.'

Cody nods thoughtfully. 'Let's talk about last time, Gavin.'

'Don't want to.'

'It was about two and a half years ago, wasn't it? Down by the light-house. In the car park there.'

Quigley remains silent.

'Her name was Courtney. You remember her, don't you? You remember what you did?'

And now Quigley is making small whimpering noises. His fingers are plucking the air again.

'You took her, didn't you, Gavin? Why did you do that? Why did you take that little girl?'

Quigley jumps to his feet. Cody tenses, expecting him to do a runner again.

'Sit down, Gavin,' he orders.

'I didn't do nothing. I'm not a bad person. I was just trying to . . . to . . .'

'To what? What did you intend to do with that child?'

'I . . . nothing. I wanted to protect her.'

'Her parents were close by, Gavin. She didn't need your protection.'

Quigley is still on his feet. He twists and turns on the spot, scratches at his greasy hair.

'I . . . I didn't know that. I thought she was in danger. I thought some-one might hurt her. I was going to take her somewhere safe. They . . . they attacked me. They called me names and hit me. They said I was a bad person. I'm not a bad person. I just want to be left alone. I won't ever try to help anyone ever again.'

'Are you sure you weren't going to do something bad to Courtney?'

'No. Please. I wasn't.'

'And what about the girl in the photo? Poppy Devlin. Someone took her, Gavin, and we're going to find out who did it. She lives near to your house. Are you still saying that you've never seen her, that you know nothing about her?'

'No. I mean yes. I don't know her. I don't hurt children. I don't hurt anybody. Everybody hurts *me*.'

Cody exchanges glances with Webley. Sees that she's in agreement.

He lowers his voice. 'All right, Gavin. Take it easy. We're going now.'

Quigley looks at each of the detectives in disbelief. 'No more questions?'

'No more questions.'

Cody stands up, squelches across to the door. Webley follows.

'If we find out you've lied to us, though,' Cody adds, 'we'll be back. Do you understand that, Gavin?'

Quigley nods. He folds his arms, as though embracing himself to calm down.

And then Cody and Webley leave. Back out into the cold February wind.

* * *

Only when the police have gone does Quigley allow himself to sit down again.

He sniffs heavily. Uses the sleeve of his sweater to wipe the tears from his cheeks.

He thought he was safe here. Thought he'd never be bothered again. He just wants to be left in peace. To walk by the sea and create his drawings. That's not asking too much, is it?

He hopes they don't come back. They frighten him. Most people frighten him. Even when they just look at him it's like they think he's weird.

The girl in the photo was pretty, with a pretty name. Poppy. Like the flower. He likes flowers. Lots of girls are named after flowers. There's Rose and Lily and Iris and Pansy and Violet . . .

And Daisy.

He's glad they didn't ask him about Daisy.

He knows a lot about her.

16

She's terrified of him.

It's understandable, he tells himself. He appeared in her bedroom in the middle of the night. He drugged her and took her away from her home. And then he smothered her until she almost died. She has every right to be afraid.

When he took up their evening meals, he noticed how Poppy shrank away from him. She didn't yell or cause a fuss, but it was obvious how much she didn't like him being so close to her.

He decides it's time to do something about it. To start building some bridges.

When he has washed the dishes and made a cup of tea for Harriet, he gives the children a few more minutes to relax before he heads back upstairs. He goes to his study first, then to the girls' room. Unusually, he knocks gently on the door before unlocking it and entering.

Daisy and Poppy are sitting on the bed, staring at him. Daisy has an arm around Poppy's shoulders, comforting her. Poppy is wiping her face, as if trying to hide the fact that she has been crying again. He guesses it's because she fears it may lead to punishment, and he feels a pang of guilt.

All he wants is for everyone to be happy.

'Hi, girls,' he says. 'Everything okay?'

Poppy says nothing. She just stares back at him defiantly.

Daisy breaks the silence. 'Yes, thank you. We're fine.'

'Good, good. I, er, I thought we might play a game together. What do you think?'

Poppy turns her face away. Presses it into Daisy's shoulder.

Malcolm's mouth twitches with annoyance. Look, he thinks, I'm trying here. I'm making an effort. The least she can do—

'Great!' says Daisy. 'That would be fun. What could we play?'

Malcolm raises a finger. 'Wait. Just one second.'

He goes out onto the landing. Returns with the items he brought from his study.

'Look what I've got.'

'Darts!' exclaims Daisy. 'Look, Poppy. A dartboard.'

Poppy twists her head slightly, just enough to get a glimpse of the board in Malcolm's hands.

She's interested, thinks Malcolm. I know she is. This is going to do it. A game of darts always breaks the ice.

He hangs the board on the nail in the wall, then moves back to the bed and opens up the plastic case he brought. The darts it contains are cheap, with gaudy plastic flights, but good enough for the kids to use.

'Pick a colour.'

'Green, please,' says Daisy.

'And what about you, Poppy? What colour darts would you like? . . . Poppy? . . . *Poppy?*'

'She'll have red,' says Daisy. 'To go with her name.'

'Red it is,' says Malcolm. 'Come on, then. Let's play. I'll go first.'

He takes three yellow darts from the case, then moves to a position as far from the board as the room allows. Taking aim, he says, 'Highest score wins, okay?'

He throws his darts, deliberately hitting one, then seven, then four.

'Well, that's a rubbish start, isn't it? I think you've already beaten me. Come on, Daisy, show us what you can do.'

Daisy takes up her own position, somewhat closer to the board than Malcolm. Her first dart misses the board completely, bouncing off the wall and landing on the carpet.

'Nice try. Don't bring your arm back so much before you let go of the dart.'

Daisy throws again. Her second dart hits the board, but lands outside of the scoring area. By some miracle, though, her third missile beds itself solidly in a treble seventeen.

'Nice throw! What are three seventeens, Daisy?'

She thinks for a few seconds. 'Fifty-one?'

'Spot on. A tough score to beat.' He turns to look at Poppy, who is now lying face down on the bed. 'Your turn, Poppy.'

She doesn't stir.

'Come on, Poppy. I said it's your turn now.'

Still no response. He can feel the heat rising in his cheeks. He doesn't like this kind of insubordination, especially in front of Daisy. Daisy is such a lovely child. He doesn't want her to get ideas. Doesn't want her thinking this kind of behaviour will be condoned.

'Poppy, did you hear what I said? I'm doing my best to cheer everyone up here. We're all supposed to be having fun. Don't you want to have fun? Don't you want to be happy here?'

But she just lies there, ignoring him. He would find this easier to deal with if she would get angry, or at least explain what she's feeling. But this idea of pretending he doesn't even exist – well, that's just plain rude. That's unacceptable.

He takes a step towards the bed. His cheeks are burning now. A mist is forming in front of his eyes. He doesn't want to be like this, but it's her fault. She's provoking him. She's ruining the moment.

'Poppy! Look at me, girl! God help me, if I have to—'

And then Daisy is in front of him. Standing between him and Poppy. There's a smile on her face. Good little Daisy.

'I'll throw for her,' she says.

'What?'

'I'll take her turn. She doesn't understand the game. I don't think she's ever played before. And she's tired. It's been a long day for her.'

Malcolm stares down at the child. So delightful. So charming.

And she's right, of course. What was he thinking? It's Poppy's very first day. He's pushing too hard, expecting too much.

'Right,' he says. 'Yes. You throw her darts. She can play next time. You can explain it to her so she doesn't feel embarrassed.'

'Yes, I'll do that. Come on, let's carry on with the game. I think I can win this one.'

His eyes follow Daisy as she moves back to stand in front of the dartboard. He sees the intense concentration on her face, and then hears the squeal of delight as her dart hits the twenty.

His mind begins to clear. There are things he needs to tell Harriet. Things that can't wait much longer.

But the time has to be right. The new girl has to be more settled. Harriet has to be happy with the family they have.

When that happens, he'll reveal his plans to her.

17

It shouldn't be like this.

This is a school day, thinks Maria. I should be making Poppy's lunch. I should be brushing her hair and putting it into a ponytail. I should be making sure she finishes her breakfast and brushes her teeth. I should be telling her how smart she looks in her school uniform. I should be letting her know about all the wonderful things that life has in store for her.

Not this. Not sitting in the back of a car, on my way to a police station. Not agonising over what I can say to bring back my precious child. Not wondering if Poppy is even still alive.

Maria didn't sleep a wink last night. Of course not. It wasn't even worth trying. She and Craig spent the entire night downstairs in her parents' house. When they weren't crying, they were trying to make sense of it all, but every suggestion they made defied logic.

There is no sense to this. This is nothing less than pure evil. Nobody puts a child through something like this unless they are a monster.

And that's what gives Maria the most pain. Monsters don't care. Monsters don't listen to reason.

So what do I say? she wonders. What words can I use that will make any kind of impact on this creature?

She looks across to Craig. He seems not to notice her eyes on him, willing him to offer comfort. He stares straight ahead. His own eyes are red-raw.

When she reaches for his hand, she feels him jolt at her touch. He turns his grief-torn face to her. They speak to each other without words. They exchange their loneliness.

Because that's how this feels. So lonely. They are victims, but it seems as though everyone is against them. Where there are no outright accusations, there are certainly insinuations. And where there are no insinuations, there are looks of disbelief and suspicion.

Take Maria's own mother, for Christ's sake. Her questions last night. *Is it possible you said something to Poppy that would make her want to leave? Was there ever a time when you left her alone with a stranger?*

I mean, fucking hell, Mother. What kind of questions are those? What kind of parents do you think we are? What happened to your own maternal instincts all of a sudden?

Maria turns to look at the back of Jason Oxburgh's head. Even he isn't on their side, she thinks. Not really. Yes, he makes all the right noises, but what he shows them is the tip of the iceberg. There's a vast unseen mass beneath the waves. Things he knows but can't reveal. Things he believes but cannot voice. Suspicions he harbours. He's a policeman, after all, and being cynical is his job. He'd lock them up in a heartbeat if he had grounds.

But he can't have grounds, she thinks, because we are innocent.

And so we sit here in silence and try to hold back the pain.

* * *

It's a circus.

She doesn't think she has ever sat in front of more than one camera simultaneously. Now there seem to be dozens of them. The continual flashes are blinding. Journalists shout out Maria's and Craig's names, trying to get them to stare directly into their lenses.

The hubbub dies down when the policeman at their table begins speaking. He's a senior officer of some kind – a superintendent, Maria seems to recall being told. She reckons he is trotted out for a lot of events like this. Someone who won't embarrass the force in front of the media, but who probably has very little to do with the case directly.

Most of what he says doesn't penetrate Maria's consciousness. She's heard it all before, and the awareness that her turn is coming is too terrifying to allow her to concentrate.

The superintendent keeps it brief, then hands control to Maria and Craig. Cameras click and flash again. Maria clears her throat.

When the words tumble out, it's as though they aren't under her control. She feels like a ventriloquist's doll, opening and closing her mouth mechanically as somebody else provides her voice. All her careful preparation goes to pot as her emotions take over and purge her of what she really wants to say. It could be nonsense – she has no idea. She knows only that she has to tell the world how much she loves Poppy and how much she wants her back unharmed.

When she can go on no longer – when she breaks down and has to cover her eyes with the tissues somebody has passed to her – the bombardment of questions begins, and she is glad that Craig takes over to handle them.

She wants only to get out of here now. Baring your soul to millions of viewers is too difficult. Relief floods in when the superintendent says a few closing words to plead for anyone who has any information, however insignificant it may seem, to get in touch. She lowers the tissues. Becomes aware of Craig grasping her other hand tightly in his.

And then something else. Something that will stay in her mind for a long time.

The detectives. Jason and the others dealing with their case. She sees them in the audience – a small knot at one edge of the room. They are staring at her. Their collective gaze is intense, tightly focused. Their expressions are impassive.

She knows then that they are appraising her.

Like a pack of hyenas, they are waiting for her defences to fall, her weaknesses to be revealed.

18

The return journey seems a continuation of the one that brought them there. Stony silence. Empty stares through the windows.

Eventually she can stand it no longer.

'Did we pass?'

In the driver's seat, Oxo turns his head slightly.

'What's that?'

'Did we pass? Did we pass the test?'

'I'm sorry, I'm not sure what you—'

'I saw you. You and the other detectives. The way you were watching us. You were waiting for us to make a mistake. You still don't believe us.'

Beside her, Craig suddenly becomes aware of what she is saying. He takes her hand again.

Oxo shakes his head. 'No, that's not true, Maria. What you have to realise is that we have a lot invested in you when you're on a public stage like that. What you say up there can make or break a case. Your voice is our voice, and so obviously we want what you say to have maximum impact.'

'Hmm,' she says.

Craig speaks up then. 'So what did you think? Will it help? Will crying our eyes out in front of millions of viewers make any difference?'

'Absolutely. I'll check when I drop you off, but right now the police switchboard will be on fire. I guarantee it. I won't lie, a lot of it will be a waste of time, but all we need is one crucial piece of information. Just one. So yes, it was worth it. I thought you did a brilliant job back there.'

Maria bites her lip. This whole thing seems so theatrical, such a charade. The facts seem to be secondary. All that matters is the show they put on, the masks they wear, the characters they play. The audience insists on actual tears, on physical and mental breakdown. Nothing less will do if this crowd is to honour the actors with its begrudging support.

That's how it feels to Maria. And she's had enough.

'I want to go home,' she announces.

'Don't worry,' says Oxo. 'No more interviews for now.'

'No, I don't mean my parents' house. I mean *home*. Our home.'

'I, er, I don't think that's a good idea. The press will be camped outside, and—'

'I don't care. That's my house. It's where Poppy lives. It's where she'll head back to if she can. I want to be there, with all of Poppy's things around me.'

Oxo hesitates before replying. 'Let me make some calls, okay? We'll go to your parents first, I'll make the calls, and if they say it's okay—'

She blows up then. 'What is this? Am I under arrest or something? I just want to go home! Is that such a strange fucking request?'

Craig leans into her. Puts a hand on her thigh. 'Maria,' he says, 'stay calm. Remember what you said to me yesterday. They're just doing their job.'

'I don't care what I said yesterday. I've had enough of this shit. I've had enough of being made to feel like a criminal. I'm going home whether you and the police like it or not, and you can't stop me.'

'I'll make the calls,' repeats Oxo. 'We'll see what we can do.'

* * *

It takes an age.

Maria sits in front of an untouched mug of tea while her mother fires more questions at her. Through the window she can see DC Oxburgh meandering up and down the garden, his mobile phone clamped to his ear and his free hand gesticulating as he tries to cut through whatever red tape is in his way.

When he finally comes back in, he tells her that her request should be authorised, but that it'll be another couple of hours before the search teams complete their work and get out of there.

So she waits. A fresh cup of tea appears, and she watches this one go cold too. Craig hovers, paces, consults his watch, checks the television news. She wishes he would just sit next to her and offer some reassurance. At the same time, he probably senses that she would bite his head off if he were to utter so much as a single misjudged word. He has never felt comfortable with his in-laws. Right now, she can't blame him. It's as if they have completely failed to find the right perspective on things.

She wonders if they, too, have their suspicions about her and Craig.

Could that be possible? Her own mother and father? Could they entertain the notion that she has committed an unspeakable act against their granddaughter?

She's not going to confront them. She doesn't want to hear any lack of conviction in their replies. She'd rather not have another agony to pile onto her existing woes.

It's lunchtime before Oxo gets the all-clear.

The relief galvanises Maria into action. She rushes upstairs, throws her things into her travel bag. Yells at Craig to get his arse into gear.

She doesn't care that her goodbyes to her parents are hurried. They fling question after question at her as she hastens to the car: *You'll let us know if there's any news, won't you? You'll ring us if you want us to come over?* She says yes to every one of them. She's not really sure if she means it.

It turns out that Oxo was right about the press. At the first sight of the approaching cars, they put down their sandwiches and flasks, and spring into action brandishing microphones and cameras.

Oxo reminds her and Craig to say nothing, then ushers them through the chaotic scrum. Maria finds it easiest to duck her head and keep her eyes on the ground. She wishes she could block out the sounds too: more than one question is couched in terms that suggest she might know more than she's telling. She wants to punch those tabloid journalists in the face.

They eventually bob under the police tape at the gate to their house. Beyond this, there are no vultures shrieking for titbits of news.

There's a uniformed copper at the front door. He nods at Oxo, but doesn't even acknowledge the presence of the real homeowners.

And then they are inside, and the door gets closed behind them. The journalists fall silent.

She didn't expect to feel overjoyed, but she did at least expect some kind of warmth, some sense of being bathed in familiarity. Some connection with what has been lost.

Not this, though.

She sees the wrongness as soon as she enters. It's not wanton vandalism, but it's certainly disrespect. Things out of place, pictures askew, black marks on the walls.

Oxo sees her studying the dark smudges. 'Fingerprint powder,' he explains. 'Sorry. I'll get it cleaned off.'

She says nothing. She walks from room to room, noting the disruption. She suspects that Oxo won't see all of it, that even Craig will hardly notice. But every little alteration shrieks at her. They tell a story of infiltration, of probing at her most personal possessions.

She turns and heads upstairs. Craig touches her arm as she passes him in the hall, but she shrugs him away.

She knows to expect change in Poppy's room, but the scale of it stuns her. The dark stains are everywhere here, as though some hellish creature has left its imprint on everything. Furniture has been shifted out of place. Drawers have been left half-open, their previously neat contents now jumbled and spilling out. Poppy's bed has been completely stripped, leaving only a bare mattress.

This is devastation. This is worse than it was after the intruder entered. It's as if he has been back to finish the job, to make his impact on this torn family even more keenly felt.

Poppy seems further from them than ever before.

Leaning against the wall, Maria stares at the cold, empty bed until the tears cloud her vision and the screams erupt from her mouth.

PART TWO

19

'A week!' yells Blunt. 'A whole bloody week. And what have we got to show for it? Fuck all – that's what!'

The detectives assembled in the incident room keep their counsel. It's never wise to interrupt their boss when she's in full flow, and especially when she's as incandescent as this.

Even Cody, usually Blunt's most favoured soul, decides not to raise his head above the parapet on this occasion.

She's right, of course. A week has gone by since the abduction of Poppy Devlin, and the team has made zero progress in finding her. They don't know why she was taken. They don't even know if she is alive or dead, although the latter is a pretty good bet after all this time.

'Cody!' says Blunt. 'Prove me wrong. Status report.'

Shit, he thinks. So much for trying to stay below her radar.

He sits up, clears his throat. 'Right. Okay. Well, we've extended the house-to-house in the area. Talking to everyone we can who lives there, works there, or has visited there.'

'Fine. And?'

'Er, not much to go on so far. We've been interviewing a large number of people known to us for various offences, specifically crimes involving children, but also others who may have operated in the Otterspool area. Whoever got into the Devlins' house knew something about breaking and entering.'

'What about those on the Devlins' list? Anyone promising there?'

After repeated pressure by Oxo on the Devlins to come up with the ranked list of people who might want to do them harm, the couple had eventually relented. Cody understands the reticence: it can be difficult to look at everyone around you – friends, colleagues and even family – and question whether it's possible, just *possible*, that they might consider acting in a way that might hurt you. If the answer is yes, for whatever reason, then they should appear somewhere on the list.

'I'm afraid not. We've interviewed every one of them, some more than once. At the moment we've got no reason to suspect any of involvement.'

'Sightings?'

'Lots of reports of little girls supposedly matching Poppy's description, but so far we've discounted every one. We even had one woman who called us in to take a look at her neighbour's daughter, despite the girl having lived there since she was born. The woman thought her neighbour might have made a swap.'

Blunt sighs heavily. 'Okay. What about forensics?'

Cody shakes his head, half-expecting Blunt to blast it from his shoulders.

'Christ on a bike! Is there anyone in this room who can improve my day by sharing some *positive* progress about this case? Grace, what about you?'

As Grace gets to her feet, Cody feels a pang of sympathy for the Intelligence Analyst. She's not the most confident of people at the best of times. Being roared at by Stella Blunt is likely to reduce her to jelly.

'As DS Cody says, we've been inundated with reports since day one. I've been cross-correlating all the intelligence data as best I can, searching for matches, patterns, contradictions. I've also been examining CCTV footage from the area, although without knowing what it is we're looking for—'

'Yes, yes, Grace. Get to the point. Has all this intelligence generated any substantial lines of inquiry?'

'Nothing of substance, no.'

Blunt looks away for a moment, drumming her fingers on the desk next to her. To Cody she looks like a ticking time bomb, ready to explode.

Unsure as to whether the spotlight is still on her, Grace begins to lower herself tentatively to her seat. She springs up again when Blunt fires another salvo at her.

'And the Devlins? Where are we with them?'

'Well . . . We've examined their phone records, their computer, their bank accounts, their insurance, their emails, their—'

'Don't tell me. Nothing, right?'

'They seem clean as a whistle.'

Blunt locks eyes with Oxo. 'Jason? That your conclusion too?'

'Yes. I've spent a lot of time with them now. They seem genuine enough to me. I can't point to a single piece of behaviour that's out of line with what you'd expect from parents who've had their only child snatched from under their noses.'

'In that case, we're letting them down. Badly. They need closure. Much as I hate to admit it, we're likely to have to deliver some devastating news to them. But I want that news to consist of the truth. Not supposition, not guesswork. I want facts, and right now we don't have any. It's not good enough.'

She turns and marches away. As she leaves, what lingers most in Cody's mind is not so much that Blunt has just given every team member a bollocking, but that she herself is taking much of the blame for not finding Poppy Devlin.

Her final sentence – about not being good enough – was not directed at them.

20

He decides it's time.

Poppy is a lot more settled now. She doesn't smile much – not when he's been in the room anyway. But there have been occasions when he has put his ear to the door and heard the tinkle of her laughter as she plays with Daisy. She's eating more, too, and she doesn't mention her old parents nearly as often as she did.

But the main thing is Harriet. She seems content now. She appears happy that the new family situation is working. She will be a lot more receptive to his new idea.

He comes down from his study. Finds Harriet on the sofa in the living room, knitting while she watches *Coronation Street*.

He sits down next to her. Waits for the programme to finish. Harriet doesn't like to be distracted when her soaps are on. She gets so involved in the lives of those characters.

'Was it a good one tonight?' he asks.

'Not bad. Someone's about to get their comeuppance, I think. The next episode should be interesting.'

Malcolm nods, hesitates as he listens to the hypnotic click-clack of her knitting needles.

'There's something I've been meaning to ask you,' he says.

Harriet pauses in mid-stitch. She looks at him – slightly fearfully, he thinks.

'What?' she says. 'Is it bad?'

'No, no. Not at all. I just . . . want to put something to you.'

She lowers her knitting. The ball of wool rolls from her lap and halts precariously on the edge of the seat cushion.

'Well, go on. Don't keep me in suspenders.'

He smiles at the wordplay. It's a little joke they've been using so long it has lost its currency. Harriet isn't even aware she's doing it. Bless her.

'It's about Poppy. Kind of.'

'What do you mean? She's not ill, is she? I've got lots of medicines, you know. I can fix most things. Remember when Daisy had that fever? And when she fell and cut her arm? I make a good nurse. I can—'

'Hush, dearest. She's not ill. She's fine. And you like her, don't you? I mean, you are glad she's here, aren't you?'

Harriet releases her needles and brings her hands up to cradle Malcolm's face. 'Of course I am. She was a handful at first, but then so was Daisy, wasn't she? Remember when she ripped the wallpaper that time? And when she smashed that expensive lamp? And look at her now. She's the perfect daughter. Poppy's getting there too. I don't know how you do it, Malcolm. You have a gift. You make a wonderful father, and the girls look up to you.'

He's not sure how to answer that. It's nice that Harriet believes it, but he can't tell her the truth. He can't tell her about how he almost killed Poppy a week ago. He can't tell her that Daisy's cut wasn't the result of a fall.

Sometimes he wonders just how far he could go.

But now, as he looks into the eyes of his darling wife and sees what happiness his actions bring to her, he realises he would go to the ends of the earth to maintain that sparkle.

'What's the matter?' Harriet asks.

'Nothing. Just thinking. I want to be a good father, and I want to give you every opportunity to be a fantastic mother.'

'So, then . . . what's the problem?'

He takes a moment to gather his thoughts.

'As you know, I spent a lot of time and effort finding both Daisy and Poppy. They had to be . . . right, you understand.'

'Yes, I know. It couldn't be just any old child. We discussed this. We had our criteria, and we stuck to them.'

'Yes. So that's why it took so long. That's why three years went by before I could suggest Poppy to you.'

'Malcolm, you don't have to explain. I realise how difficult the process is. I don't fully understand all the stuff you have to do to get there, but I know it's not easy. And I really appreciate it, more than you can imagine. No other man would do this for his wife. No other man would be capable of it. A family is the most precious gift in the world, and you have given it to me. I was happy enough with one child, but I'm a thousand times happier with two. The wait was worth it.'

'Good,' he says. 'I'm glad you see it like that. You see . . . the thing about Poppy . . .'

'Yes? What?'

'I . . . I had to make a choice . . .'

'What do you mean, a choice? Malcolm, you're getting me all worried again.'

He takes her hand. 'No, don't worry. I just need to explain it to you. There's so much work involved. And there's risk, of course. I don't care about that, but, well . . . there's only so much I can do. I can't fit everything in. And I needed to see how well you got on with Poppy. I didn't know what I'd do if you hated her.'

Harriet gives him a reassuring smile. 'Well, I don't hate her. She's wonderful. You made the right choice. You could have kept quiet about her. You didn't have to say anything at all, but you chose to bring her to me. I'll always be grateful for that.'

'No. That's not what I mean. That wasn't the choice.'

'I don't understand.'

He takes a deep breath. 'There were two.'

Harriet's eyes flicker as she searches for his meaning. 'Two what?'

'Children. I had a choice of two. Poppy and another little girl. I chose Poppy.'

'Two? I . . . There were two possible candidates?'

He forces out a laugh. 'Yes. Like buses, eh? You wait three years and two come along at once.'

Harriet doesn't join him in his laughter. 'You . . . you didn't tell me about the other one.'

'No. I didn't want to confuse the issue. In the end I chose the one who looks most like Daisy, and also because she has a flower name and the other one doesn't. I thought if they were going to be sisters . . . But . . .'

'Go on.'

'But I also chose her because it seemed less of a risk, and now I feel such a coward about it.'

'Malcolm—'

'I should have told you about both of the girls. I should have let you decide. I should have talked it over with you at least. I'm sorry, Harriet.'

'Malcolm,' she says, 'don't be daft. I'm sure I would have picked Poppy too. It doesn't matter now. You've given me a wonderful second daughter. And she does look like Daisy. You couldn't have done any better. Stop beating yourself up about it, and go and put the kettle on.'

He nods as she strokes his arm, but he doesn't budge from the sofa.

'Malcolm,' she says. 'Is there something else you want to tell me?'

He struggles to find his words. 'What if . . . What if you could have them both?'

'What do you mean?'

'Poppy and this other girl. What if we brought both of them into the family?'

'Both of them? Malcolm, what are you saying?'

He becomes more animated then, more excited as he starts to paint a new future.

'You waited three years for another daughter. That's how often these opportunities come along. We might never have another chance of growing the family. Like I said, it was a hard choice for me to go for Poppy. I wasn't even sure we could cope with another child. But you've just told me, haven't you? You've just said how well it's worked out. So what I've been thinking is . . . well, what if we grasp the nettle right now? We have one more child while we can.'

'Another child? *Three* daughters?'

'Why not? The alternative is to leave this other kid where she is, and I don't know how long it'll be before her situation changes. She might move house or something. If we don't act now, we might lose this chance for ever.'

Harriet drops into silence. Then: 'Three children?'

'Yes. We can cope, can't we? We're still young enough. And that's another thing: a few years more and I could be too old to do any of this again. It's now or never, dearest.'

Harriet pulls her hand from his. She sets her knitting aside, gets up from the sofa. She walks softly to the other side of the room and pulls aside the curtain. She stands there for a full minute, just staring into the darkness outside.

Finally, she turns. 'Show me,' she says.

Malcolm leaves his seat and races upstairs. Minutes later he's back again, the album in his hands.

'You've already prepared it,' says Harriet.

He flashes her a cheeky smile. 'I had a feeling.'

They resume their places on the sofa. Malcolm flips open the album to the place he has bookmarked. He watches Harriet's face.

'She has dark hair,' says Harriet.

'Yes. Nothing like the other two, really. She's the same age as Poppy, though. Just six.'

'She's cute as a button.'

Harriet turns the pages, her eyes growing brighter as they soak up each new image.

She says, 'And the criteria? She satisfies them?'

'Yes. I wouldn't lie to you about that.'

Harriet reaches the final photograph. She touches a finger to the child's beaming face.

'When?' she asks. 'When would you get her?'

21

No time like the present.

That's what he told Harriet. There was no point giving her all that spiel about this being a tiny window of opportunity, and then leaving it until the window was firmly bricked up. It had to be tonight.

So yet again he's parked up in his van in the middle of the night, waiting for his four o'clock call to action.

He hopes he's doing the right thing. It's much, much trickier, this one. Opting for Poppy was a no-brainer when he'd had a choice.

He'd hate to get caught: he's got a family to support.

But he was right to mention it to Harriet. It would have preyed on his mind for the rest of his life if he hadn't. She deserves it. Ellie deserves it, too.

That's the new girl's name: Ellie. Ellie McVitie. Like Poppy, she's an only child.

Don't worry, Ellie. You'll have a bigger family soon, with two new sisters to play with. Won't that be great?

The difficulty with this one is access to the property. He's done his homework, and there's no way he'll get in through any of the doors and windows on the ground floor – not without making a racket and attracting attention.

So that leaves the first floor.

There's only one way in. The bathroom. The McVities always leave the transom window open a couple of inches in that room. It probably doesn't seem much of a risk to them. After all, nobody could fit through it; and even if they could, how would they get up there?

Malcolm intends to give them an answer to that.

And now's the time to do it. Four o'clock, on the dot.

He leaves the van, taking his bag of tricks with him. The house is detached, and from the street there doesn't appear to be any route to the rear.

But Malcolm knows better.

He strolls up the side path of the neighbour's house, which isn't as secure. His presence causes a security light to come on, but he ignores it. Unless someone is at their window, they are unlikely to see it.

When he gets to the back of the brick-built garage, he waits for the lamp to go off again, then squeezes into the narrow gap between the garage and the boundary fence. The fence is low – just a couple of feet. Easy enough to step over into the McVities' garden.

He is behind a wooden shed here. Well hidden. Which helps for the next phase of his mission.

The McVities keep a ladder hanging from metal hooks screwed to the concrete fence posts. A padlock and chain prevent it from being removed.

Unless you have the right tools.

Malcolm opens his bag, pulls out the bolt cutters. They snip through the chain like scissors through card.

He takes his time slipping the ladder off its supports. It's not heavy, but it's long and made of aluminium. One slip could make a hell of a noise.

When the ladder is free and lying on the grass, he pauses to take a much-needed breather. So far, so good, but there's a long way to go yet.

He picks up the ladder, carries it to the rear wall of the house. No security lights here, thank goodness.

He raises the ladder into a vertical position. Gently angles it towards the wall. It makes contact with barely a sound.

Retrieving his bag from behind the shed, he sets it down next to the feet of the ladder. He takes out another couple of tools, then stares up at his target.

He is standing directly below the open transom of the bathroom.

As soon as he puts a foot on the bottom rung, a deluge of memories hits him. He was up a ladder when that roof gave way all those years ago. When he came hurtling to the ground, smashing his skull like it was an egg.

Not going to happen this time, he tells himself. Think about why you're doing this. Think about Harriet's joy when you come home with her new baby. Ellie is up there right now, just waiting to begin her new life. Go to her.

Slowly, step after careful step, he ascends the ladder. When he is within a couple of feet of the top, it suddenly strikes him how brazen, how daring this is. Harriet was right: nobody else but him would be capable of a feat like this. This is special. This is bravery at its finest.

Emboldened, he creeps up the final few rungs. He pulls the transom open as wide as it will go, then puts his arm through. He can't reach the handle of the adjoining section of the window, but he guessed that would be the case. It's probably another reason why the McVities believe themselves to be safe.

The tool he uses is something he fashioned at home. Just a twisted piece of metal on the end of a stick, really. One piece of the metal juts out like a thumb; below that it becomes a hook.

Malcolm slides the tool through the gap, careful not to tap it against anything. He spends some time manoeuvring it until the hook is around the window handle and the metal thumb is positioned over the release button. All he has to do then is apply pressure to push down the button, and then make a twisting motion to turn the handle.

And *voila*, the window is open.

He swings the window wide, then reaches in and moves aside some toiletries on the sill before squeezing himself through. He's a big man, and this is not a large window, so it takes both time and effort.

He lowers himself to the bathroom floor, then reattaches his makeshift tool to his belt. From the belt he slips out a torch; he has taped a piece of material over the end to dim and diffuse the light, leaving him just enough to spot obstacles. He switches it on, allows himself a minute for his eyes to adjust.

The bathroom door is ajar, so getting out of this room is not a problem. When he's on the landing he spends a moment getting his bearings, working out which room is which. When he figures out where Ellie is sleeping, he has to resist the temptation to go right in and grab her. There is more preparatory work to be done first.

Coming through that bathroom window was a struggle. There is no way he can go back through it and down a ladder with an unconscious child thrown over his shoulder. He needs another, simpler exit.

Malcolm heads downstairs, then through the hall to the front of the house. The door there is bolted on the inside and has a chain in place, but when he tries turning the catch of the Yale, he discovers that it hasn't been locked.

He shakes his head. Belt and braces, folks. Don't you know there are criminals everywhere?

He slides back the bolts, takes off the chain. His escape route is ready.

And now for Ellie.

As he moves back up the stairs, he feels a curious urge to start whistling a tune. This seems so like a job – a mundane, everyday task. It's too easy, too straightforward. Too—

It's just as he reaches the landing that a light comes on and he whirls to see Ellie's father staring at him.

22

They stand frozen in time: Malcolm acting as if becoming a statue will suddenly endow him with the power of invisibility, and McVitie glued to the floor by the shock of finding a stranger in his house.

And then it becomes chaotic. Both men reacting without thinking, driven by the sudden surges of adrenalin. McVitie heading towards Malcolm, yelling stuff at him, ordering him to get the fuck out of this house, and what are you doing here, you fucking bastard, what the fuck do you think you're doing, call the police, Eva, call them now.

And Malcolm, wanting to run, but knowing he can't. Knowing his face has been seen, that if he shows his fear he will be set upon, that if he wastes a second the police will be alerted.

Which is why he does the opposite of what McVitie probably expects. Instead of turning tail, he moves towards him, swatting him out of his way as he goes into the bedroom, where he sees Eva – McVitie's wife – sitting up in bed, lamp on, phone in hand, but screaming, not knowing what to do, physically unable to jab the buttons that will summon help.

And Malcolm feels it. He feels the darkness descending, the mist closing in. His senses begin to distort reality. The sight of McVitie advancing on him again, teeth bared and spittle flying, holds no fear for him. He sees only a ludicrous little man in his pyjamas, and with a single hand he pushes him away with an unexpected force that sends him flying across the room. And when McVitie comes back again, this time with fists bunched, this time filled with wrath and the super-human energy that comes with the urgency of defending family and home, Malcolm is ready.

He doesn't know that he is ready. His consciousness has abandoned him and handed the fight to the rest of his brain. He doesn't know that his readiness comes in the form of a craft knife that he has slipped from his pocket. He doesn't know that his thumb has fully extended the razor-sharp blade.

McVitie knows none of this either. He would run otherwise. He would look at that blade and accept that he cannot win this fight, that he must surrender to such overwhelming odds.

But he sees nothing. His rage, his incredulity are total. He is immersed in the act of removing this unwelcome stain on his home. He is not aware that Malcolm holds his life in his hand.

He realises only when it is too late. He realises only when he sees the intense red warning signals. And when he staggers back, away from Malcolm, it is because he senses that the redness is his, and it should not be visible. It should be inside him, coursing through his vessels, keeping him alive. But there it is, yes, there it is, everywhere, on the walls, the floor and even the ceiling, slashes of crimson that he continues to paint, because it still sprays and gushes from his body.

And as he looks down at himself and tries to fathom what is happening, he finds that a curious detachment begins to settle in him. He finds that he cannot respond adequately to the vision of this attacker who has now turned his attention to Eva, his wife, his beloved wife, who is still in bed, still holding the phone while she shakes and screams and pleads. He cannot help her now, cannot save her, even though he would give everything he has to do so.

He can only watch, while his breathing becomes ragged and his pulse flutters and his heart struggles to find something substantial with which to work. He can only watch as Eva is dispatched to join him on the other side, and he prays that such is the case, prays that anything bad he has done in this life will not prevent him from being reunited with her in the next.

I'm sorry, Eva. Forgive me.

* * *

Malcolm doesn't cry. Doesn't yell. Doesn't run.

When his faculties eventually come back to him, he reacts only with puzzlement. His confused brain takes some time to make the connection between the carnage before him and the knife still tightly clutched in his blood-slicked fingers.

It's all their fault. He hadn't wanted this. They shouldn't have interfered. They shouldn't have got in his way.

That's a lot of blood.

He doesn't remember spilling it. He doesn't recall the intense violence that must have gone into creating this scene. Which is probably a good thing. It will make it easier to live with what he must have done here.

He reaches up and fingers the deformed area of his skull. Marvels at the effect such an injury can have on one's whole personality and behaviour. He tries to think back to what kind of man he was before the accident. Would he have been capable of something like this?

It's time to go.

He doesn't know how long he has been here, but it's time to leave.

It's only as he turns that he remembers what he came here for.

And that's because she's standing in the doorway.

She's tiny, and she's silent. Her eyes appear hugely magnified against the chalky whiteness of her face. Her whole body is trembling, and she is standing in a pool of her own urine.

Malcolm smiles down at her.

'Hi, honeybunch,' he says. 'Let's go home.'

23

After he has backed the van onto their secluded driveway, Malcolm remains behind the wheel.

Harriet is quick to appear. Watching her in his mirror, Malcolm reads the excitement in her bustling form. He cracks the vehicle's window open an inch as she approaches.

'How did it go?' she asks.

'Fine,' he says. 'She's in the back. Do you want to take her in?'

Harriet looks doubtful.

'By myself?'

'It's okay,' says Malcolm. He spots the syringe in her hand. 'You won't need that. Just take her inside. Put her in the kitchen, see if she'll have a glass of milk or something.'

Harriet hesitates. 'What about you? Aren't you coming in?'

'Yes. In a minute. Take the girl in first.'

She nods. Slips the hypodermic into her pocket. Goes around to the rear of the van.

When she opens the doors, Malcolm knows instantly that any concerns she has immediately dissipate. He hears how she coos, how she melts.

'Hello, gorgeous one,' she says. 'Come to Mummy. That's it. Come on, darling. Let's get you inside in the warm. Would you like a biscuit?'

He doesn't hear a peep from the girl. Hasn't heard a sound from her since he first encountered her in the house. He didn't even need to knock her out. Just picked her up, light as a feather, and carried her out to the van.

She goes quietly with her new mother now, good as gold. Harriet leads her along the driveway and takes her inside. Malcolm gives them a couple of minutes to get settled, then climbs out of the van and heads indoors.

Walking into the living room, he catches sight of himself in the mirror. He gets the curious sense of knowing his image should shock him, and yet not finding it alarming at all. It's just . . . weird. Like being one of the walking dead.

But now he doesn't know what to do. He can't sit down for fear of marking the furniture. He worries that he is already leaving marks on the carpet.

He can hear Harriet's chatter. The encouragement to eat, drink and . . . well, maybe not be merry just yet. Give her time.

And then Harriet's questions directed at him, growing in volume as she emerges from the kitchen.

'Malcolm, what are those marks on Ellie's—?'

She cuts off her sentence with a hand clamped to her mouth as she sees him in the light. He lifts his arms slightly, lets them fall again. As if to say, *I'm home. What do you think?*

'Malcolm!' She rushes towards him, eyes scanning him urgently for injury. 'Oh my God! What's happened? Are you hurt? What happened?'

'I'm okay. I'm fine. It's not my . . . it's not mine.'

'Not yours? You're not hurt?'

'No. Honestly. I'm not hurt at all. There was . . . there was a fight.'

She brings her hand to her mouth again, lowers it. Tears are in her eyes.

'A fight with who? The parents?' She drops her voice to a whisper, fearful that Ellie may hear. 'Ellie's mum and dad?'

'Yes. They tried to stop me. I had to . . . I had to get forceful with them.'

'Forceful? Was it bad? I mean, are they badly hurt? Won't they tell the police about you? Oh, Malcolm! Are we in trouble?'

Malcolm reaches out towards her. He wants to touch Harriet, to reassure her, but he's afraid of staining her.

'Shush now. We're not in trouble. They . . . they won't be going to the police.'

Harriet opens her mouth, closes it again. Malcolm can almost hear her mind working as she analyses his words, looking for any implication other than the obvious one.

She could come right out and ask. She could say, 'Are they dead?' But she won't do that. She understands his meaning all right, but she will prefer to leave it unsaid. That's how Harriet gets through life: stepping around things she'd rather not know for certain.

She says, 'So . . . So we're safe?'

'We're safe.'

'Because Ellie is a beautiful child.'

'She is.'

'She needs us. She needs to be looked after.'

'Yes. Yes, she does. And we can do that now.'

Harriet nods. She waves a hand, indicating the bloodstains splashed across her husband.

'You should get out of those clothes, Daddy. You need to look respectable for your new daughter.'

24

For a few moments, Cody thinks he's having another of the panic attacks that used to plague him. He's finding it difficult to get enough oxygen into his lungs, and his legs are beginning to tremble, as though they're preparing to get him out of here as fast as they can.

He takes a few deep breaths, then pinches himself hard through his Tyvek suit to keep himself grounded in this room of horrors.

When he is calm enough to take in his surroundings in a more objective way, he sees that Webley is staring at him, concern filling her eyes. He gives her a brief smile to tell her he's okay.

It's difficult for anyone to be okay at a scene like this. It seems worse, somehow, that this isn't a dump of a house. There are no drug needles littering the floor, no empty bottles of booze, no overflowing ashtrays, no dirt and decay. A dead body or two might not seem out of place in a setting like that.

But this is a beautiful, clean, modern house. This house shines.

Except in here. This room doesn't belong. This is the odd one out. This is where all the depravity and rot in the world has been gathered and left to fester. The smell of death here is so strong it leaves an aftertaste.

Cody always feels a little ineffectual at a scene like this. He knows it's important to see it, to get a proper idea of what he's investigating. But he also knows that the real work here is being done by the CSIs and the pathologist and the photographers and the sketch artists. He's just a bystander, waiting to have it all explained to him.

Not that there's much explanation needed. There's a ladder against the outside wall, an open window, and two sliced-up bodies in the bedroom.

He's an experienced enough detective to put the story together from that evidence.

He has also worked out a motive. And that's what's really worrying him.

A six-year-old child lives here. And now she's missing.

It has all the hallmarks of the abduction of Poppy Devlin, only now with deadly force thrown in for good measure. That's not good. That's not good at all.

There's only one positive fragment of information to come from all this mayhem, which is that the detectives are now fairly certain that the attacker was male. If the strength and sheer violence needed to overcome two people determined to protect themselves and their child from harm were not enough of a clue, then the size-twelve bloody footprints are more of a giveaway.

When he feels he's lingered long enough, Cody makes his escape. After he has stripped off and bagged up his protective clothing, Webley joins him outside.

'Cody, what the hell is this guy playing at? What kind of maniac are we dealing with here?'

Cody looks back into the house. 'I haven't the foggiest. Hard-faced bastard, isn't he? Did you see how he got into the house? Put a ladder up against the fucking wall and climbed it, for Christ's sake. While the whole family were sleeping inside! Who does that?'

Webley shakes her head. 'To be honest, this case is really starting to freak me out. I know I haven't got kids, but . . . Jesus, this is fucked up. Snatching them in the middle of the night like that.' She shakes her head and then looks at Cody hard. 'You know she probably saw it, don't you?'

'What?'

'The child. Ellie McVitie. They're saying the signs are she saw her own parents being slaughtered. She left a puddle of urine in their bedroom.'

'Shit.' Cody looks to the heavens. 'Could it get any worse?'

A female uniformed officer approaches them along the path. 'Sarge, there's someone you should speak to. A woman says she saw something last night.'

Cody races out to the street, Webley close behind. A witness! Could be the first real break they've had. A tad late, mind, but he'll take anything right now.

The woman is probably in her late fifties. Her hair is dyed a curious purple colour. She shifts her weight from foot to foot, and keeps peering along the street as though she's expecting someone.

Cody introduces himself, invites the woman to reciprocate.

'Helen Morley. My husband is Trevor Morley. He's an accountant.'

Cody isn't sure why she's telling him this. He wonders if he's supposed to have heard of Trevor Morley, but his list of famous accountants doesn't stretch very far.

She says, 'Is it right, what they're saying? About what went on in there?' She tilts her head to the left, indicating the McVities' house, but keeps her eyes focused on a point at the end of the road. Cody follows her gaze, but sees nothing.

'I'm afraid I can't give out any details at the moment,' he says. 'I hear you've got some information that could help us, though.'

'Well, that seems a little unfair. I mean, if I tell you stuff but you don't give me anything back, doesn't that seem a little unfair to you?'

Cody glances at the uniformed officer, who looks apologetic but offers no help.

'I'm sorry, Mrs Morley, but it doesn't work like that. All I can tell you is that a very serious crime has been committed, and we'd appreciate any information you can give us to catch whoever did it.'

'When you say serious, you mean murder, don't you?'

'I'm afraid I can't confirm or deny that.'

'Other people, they're saying murder. Mrs Robertson at number nine, she's always spot on about such things, and she's got an artificial hip.'

'Well . . .' says Cody.

'It's murder. I know it is. Who got killed?'

'Again, I'm afraid I'm not at liberty to—'

'It was her, wasn't it? Eva. Her husband killed her, and then he drove away. That's it. I knew it.'

Cody takes a back seat while Mrs Morley makes up her own version of events. He doesn't care if she says later she got it straight from the detective's mouth, as long as she gives up her own nugget of information first.

And then something hits him.

'Hold on. What do you mean, he drove away? Why do you say that?'

Mrs Morley squints purposefully down the road, as if to distract Cody from his line of questioning. He senses she is feeling the discomfort of having just lodged her foot in her overly busy mouth.

Cody presses her again: 'Mrs Morley, this is important. Did you see someone drive away from the house during the night?'

'It woke me up. We sleep at the front of the house. We moved out of the back bedroom because of the gas.'

'The gas?'

'The boiler. It's at the back of the house, and it makes a racket. The man from the gas company says they can't make it any quieter, but what does he know? He has a terrible stutter.'

Cody tries not to be thrown by the latest non sequitur.

'So you sleep at the front of the house. And a noise woke you?'

'Yes. Which is unusual for me, because I normally sleep like a log unless I eat chocolate liqueurs after seven-thirty.'

'What kind of noise was it?'

'Well, I don't know. I was asleep, wasn't I? But it was something. So I went to the window and looked outside.'

'What time was this, do you know?'

'About four-thirty in the morning, I think.'

'And what did you see?'

'A van. Driving away from here.' She gestures to the kerb in front of the McVities' house.

'Definitely a van? Not a car?'

She frowns at Cody. 'If it was a car, I'd have said so, wouldn't I?'

'Do you know what kind of van it was?'

'A white one.'

'White? Okay, you're doing great. Do you know the make? A Ford, maybe, or a Vauxhall? A Peugeot?'

She shrugs. 'Could have been.'

'Big or small?'

'What do you call big?'

'I mean, was it just a little bigger than a normal car, or was it something you could fit a wardrobe into?'

'I'm not sure about a wardrobe. You'd probably manage some garden furniture. Or a few illegal immigrants. You can get quite a lot of them into a small space, can't you?'

Cody dodges the question. He has already formed an opinion about what sort of newspapers this woman reads.

'That's brilliant, Mrs Morley. I don't suppose you got the vehicle registration number?'

'You're lucky I could see it was a van. I didn't have my glasses on. I should have them on now, really, but I thought I might get on the telly. Are they here yet?'

'Who?'

'The TV people.'

'I'm sure they're on their way. Now if you can just cast your mind back to last night. Did you see any people outside? Anyone in the van, or going to or from the house?'

'No. Just the van. Which was a bit strange, really.'

'Strange? In what way?'

'Well, Eva's husband doesn't usually drive a van. I've never seen it here before.'

Something clicks in her mind, and for the first time she forgets whatever it is that has been occupying her at the end of the road, and locks her gaze on Cody.

'It wasn't Eva's husband, was it? It was somebody else.' She looks up at the McVities' front-bedroom window. It is clear that lights are burning behind the closed curtains. 'Oh, my Lord,' she says.

Cody thanks her for her assistance. Lets her know that another detective will take a full witness statement from her.

He moves away, thinking about how cases can sometimes rest on a knife-edge of probability like this. If only Mrs Morley had thought to put her glasses on. If only she had managed to see the registration number. If only she had got out of bed a few seconds earlier and witnessed the killer heading towards his van with the little girl.

If only. Two words that could change everything but are worth nothing.

'This changes everything.'

The words are from Blunt, coming towards them from the house. Cody can almost see the dark cloud hovering above her head. Her face carries the discomfort of its presence.

'Ma'am?' says Cody.

She turns to him. Her eyes are dark, as though tinged with the evil she has encountered here.

'Have either of you seen *Chitty Chitty Bang Bang*?'

The question sounds a bit like one of Mrs Morley's: seemingly random and inappropriate.

'Er . . .' says Webley.

'The Childcatcher. I had nightmares for years after I saw that film. I kept thinking someone was coming to get me while I was asleep. And now it's come true. This is real. One kid was bad enough; how many others is he going to snatch? Did you see what he did in there? Did you see how determined he was to get that child? He will stop at nothing.'

Cody finds himself lost for words. His boss is almost always a shining example when it comes to staying in control of her emotions and her team. But right now she seems on the verge of losing it.

She gives him a look. He suspects it's one that few others ever receive, and he wonders what must be going through Webley's mind as she observes it. It's a look of understanding, of sharing, of empathy. It's a look that speaks to Cody of the truth of human misery.

'Find him,' she says. 'Find those girls.'

25

There is something about today.

Daisy doesn't know what it is, but something isn't quite right. When Harriet came into the room earlier, she seemed suspiciously happy. She carried a warped smile that hinted at surprises to come.

And then Harriet did a curious thing. She started opening drawers and pulling out clothes until she was able to put a complete outfit together. It was from the stuff that had been bought for Poppy, but Harriet took the clothes away with her without even suggesting to Poppy that she might wear them.

That was half an hour ago. And now Daisy can hear them coming back upstairs.

She looks at Poppy, who is busy flicking through a comic. The cartoons are doing little to lighten her spirits. She seems so sad all the time, so serious, so in need of her real parents.

The bolts scrape back again. The door opens. Harriet pokes her head around, but doesn't fully enter. She is wearing that stupid grin again.

'Hello, girls. I've got a surprise for you, but first you must shut your eyes. Go on, then, close them.'

Daisy sees Poppy place her palms over her face. Then she clamps her own eyes shut. She wants to make a wish. Wants to wish for something happy. But she doesn't, because she knows it won't come true.

'Okay,' says Harriet. 'You can open them again.'

Daisy does as she is told, and the sight in front of her makes her want the world to end. It is another girl, or rather, the pale imitation of one. She is tiny and fragile and trembling. Her long dark hair emphasises the whiteness of the face it frames. The girl's lips are thin and purple. Even the modern clothes she's wearing do not stop her from looking like one of the starving Victorian street urchins in Daisy's books.

But above all, there is something about her eyes. Even Daisy can tell that these are eyes that have seen things no child should see.

'This is Ellie,' says Harriet, her hands on the girl's shoulders.

Daisy and Poppy continue to stare, neither making a sound.

Harriet glances behind her at her husband now filling the doorway, then back to the children.

'Well? Aren't you going to say hello to your new sister?'

So that confirms it. Daisy guessed, of course, but now she is certain that this girl is here to stay. The Bensons have another prisoner. How many more will they take?

Daisy slides off the bed, walks across to Ellie. She attempts a smile.

'Hello, Ellie,' she says. 'Would you like to come and play with us?'

She knows what the answer is. She knows that, even if the girl hears the question, the answer will be negative. Ellie doesn't want to play. She doesn't want to be here at all.

But Daisy doesn't even get a 'no'. Ellie doesn't shrink away or shake her head or look down at the floor. She just stares straight ahead, right through Daisy. As if she sees things that nobody else can.

Harriet says, 'We'll leave you three to get acquainted. Ellie's had nothing to eat this morning, so I'll bring along a snack later when she feels a bit more relaxed. Make her feel at home, won't you, Daisy?'

Daisy nods, but she suspects she's got a job on her hands. Ellie doesn't seem all there. It's like she's sleepwalking.

Harriet and Malcolm back out of the room, all smiles and cutesy little waves. Daisy waits for the locks to be put back in place, then turns her attention to the new arrival.

'My name's Daisy, and this is Poppy. We're going to look after you.'

Poppy moves closer, her eyes fixed on Ellie's unmoving form.

'What's wrong with her?'

'I don't know,' says Daisy. 'Maybe she's just frightened.' She looks again at Ellie. 'Is that it, Ellie? Are you a bit frightened?'

But Ellie says nothing. She breathes and she blinks and she shivers, but these are the only signs she is alive.

Daisy reaches for Ellie's hand. It's like ice.

She leads her over to the play table. It's like helping someone who's really old or sick.

'We're looking at comics. Would you like to read one? Or draw a picture? You can sit down in my chair if you like.'

Again Ellie doesn't budge, and Daisy has to apply gentle pressure to her shoulders to lower her to the seat. Daisy slides a piece of paper in front of her, but when she gives her a crayon she has to fold her fingers around it.

'There you go. You can draw now if you like. How about some flowers? Or you could draw me?'

But there is still no response. Ellie is like a doll, capable of being pushed and pulled into position, but unable to do anything for herself.

Poppy comes up behind Daisy. Takes her hand.

'What's wrong with her?' she asks again.

Daisy has no answer to give. She understood Poppy's behaviour. Shouting and screaming and swearing and breaking things made perfect sense in a situation like this.

But Ellie is beyond her comprehension, beyond her experience.

The closest she can get to describing what she sees comes from something she read in a book once. Something about a character looking as though they had seen a ghost.

Yes, that would account for it, all right.

It's as though Ellie has looked into the face of death.

26

Oxo gets to the Devlins' house as fast as he can. They need to hear this from him, before the media get their greedy mitts on it and turn it into whichever contorted version of the truth will make them the most sales.

It's much quieter outside the house now. With little progress on the case, the paparazzi have moved on to more salacious revelations elsewhere. They'll be back imminently, though – as soon as the news breaks.

The Devlins greet him with expressions that reflect hopefulness held in check by the need to avoid crushing disappointment. He can see the struggle on their faces. One word from him could send their emotions soaring or plummeting. Such is the responsibility he carries.

It's funny. His wife told him she had a feeling in her water (perhaps the baby telling her) that there would be a break in the case today.

This isn't the kind of break he thought she meant.

He can see that the Devlins want to ask questions, but are afraid to. They are wondering whether this is just another regular update of no substance, or a matter of crucial importance. He tries not to give anything away until he feels they are ready to deal with what he has to deliver.

'There's been a development,' he tells them.

A *development*. A solidly neutral word. Nothing to be misinterpreted there. At the same time, he is sure the Devlins are aware that he wouldn't have shrouded the news they really want to hear in such camouflage.

'What kind of development?' Craig asks.

He takes a deep breath. 'In the early hours of this morning, a young girl was abducted from her parents' house in Crosby.'

He gives them a moment to absorb the information. He sees how their faces and their body language change as they filter the news, analyse it, formulate questions. Their sympathy for the victims will understandably be washed away by their need to comprehend what this means for their own case. Above all, is this good news or bad?

'How young?' says Maria.

'She's six.'

'Like Poppy.'

'Yes.'

'Who . . . Who are they? Do we know them?'

'At the moment, we have no reason to believe that you know the family concerned. I should also tell you that I can't give out all the details right now, and that includes their names. A police statement will be made shortly, but there are checks we have to do first. We have to make sure we don't get things wrong, or say anything that might jeopardise the investigation. The reason I'm telling you what I can now is so that you don't hear it from a journalist first. I wanted you to be prepared.'

'I . . . I don't understand. Do you mean . . . Are you saying this is the same abductor? That he's taken another child?'

'It's much too early to jump to that conclusion without a lot more evidence. But clearly there are similarities.'

Maria suddenly becomes ravenous for detail. Questions fly from her mouth.

'What happened? Was he seen doing it? Do you have some promising leads? Has he made contact with the parents?'

Oxo raises his hands. 'Please. I know this is difficult. Believe me, this is difficult for me, too, but—'

'I don't care how bloody difficult it is for you,' she cries. 'It's not your child out there, is it? Come back in a few months' time when your wife has had the baby and it gets snatched from its pram, and then you can tell me how difficult this is.'

A silence descends. A silence filled with embarrassment and regret and hurt.

'I'm sorry,' she says. 'I didn't mean that. I don't want you to suffer like we're suffering. I just want . . . I want to know what this means. I just want my Poppy back. Please.'

Her final plea splinters Oxo's heart. He wishes he could give them what they want. Wishes, too, that he didn't have to make this so much harder for them.

'Bastards!'

This from Craig, suddenly springing to his feet. He marches to the window, pulls aside the curtain, puts up two fingers to whatever press people are out there. He seems not to care that the image could be on the front pages tomorrow.

'Craig!' says Maria. 'What the hell are you doing?'

He moves back into the centre of the room. 'Them! The bastards. They'll know now, won't they? They'll know it wasn't us. All those nasty, spiteful little twats who said we must have had something to do with it. All the people who've been staring and pointing at us. Even so-called friends who smile to our faces, then stab us when our backs are turned.'

He rounds on Oxo. 'And you lot! You know now as well, don't you? You know this is the same fucking guy, even though you're not saying it. How about finally crossing us off your suspect list, eh? Maybe even a word of apology? All that work you did looking into us when you should have been chasing after the real criminal. Shame on you!'

Oxo holds himself in check. It won't do to become defensive now. What Craig has said is perfectly true. Although Oxo has gradually come to trust the Devlins since Poppy's abduction, he has always tried to keep some cynicism in reserve. Just in case.

'Craig!' Maria says again. 'Sit down. This isn't a time to celebrate. It's not about who's right and who's wrong. Another child has been taken. She could be with Poppy right now. We have to focus on what this means for finding them and setting them free.'

She turns to face Oxo. 'Please, is there anything else you can tell us? Anything that this latest development might mean for us and for Poppy?'

There's that word again: *development*. It hides so much.

'This crime has some definite similarities to your own. We think it was carried out some time before four-thirty this morning. The house was broken into. A child, the same age as Poppy, was taken. There is a report of a white van being seen driven away from the house. Later, when you've got time, I'd like you to take another look at the list you gave us, and work out whether anyone on it might have access to a white van.'

'Okay,' says Maria. But she continues to stare at Oxo. She knows there is more. 'What else?'

Oxo locks eyes with her. 'Whoever took this girl was more determined than ever to get her. So determined, in fact, that he didn't run when her parents discovered him in their house.'

'Hang on. They saw him? They know what he looks like?'

'Like I say, the intruder didn't run away. There was a fight. Unfortunately, both of the parents were killed.'

It's like the Devlins have both been punched in the stomach. Their mouths drop open, and they seem unable to breathe.

'Oh, God,' says Maria.

'Shit,' says Craig. 'Jesus fucking Christ.'

Maria brings a hand to her mouth. 'I think I'm going to be sick.'

Craig stands up again. Pushes his hand through his hair. Blows out some air.

'He killed them? Both of them?'

'It looks that way.'

'That could have been us,' says Maria. 'Oh, my God, that could have been us.'

And then the bigger thought hits her. 'Oh, no. No, no, no. Poppy. Our Poppy. Please don't let him hurt Poppy. Please, God. Please . . .'

Her words become drowned in sobs, and as these turn into heart-piercing wails, Jason Oxburgh thinks back to what she said about his own imminent parenthood and what he would do if his baby were to be taken from him.

27

Daisy doesn't know what to do about Ellie. The girl seems lost in another world. What is left here is a mere shell. A dried-out husk that could be carried away by the slightest breeze.

She scares Poppy. Poppy won't go anywhere near her.

She scares Daisy, too, but for different reasons. What Daisy sees when she looks at this tiny waif is severe disturbance. She guesses that Ellie hasn't always been like this. She was probably a little bundle of fun and energy before she came here. She probably danced and played mischievous pranks with her parents, and laughed as she ran around the school playground with her friends.

So that means something happened to her. Something terrible. It makes Daisy fear that Malcolm is capable of behaviour far more terrifying than anything he has exhibited thus far.

Which means he could do it again. He could be getting worse, more unpredictable.

They have to keep him happy. They mustn't do anything to push him over the edge again. The next time could be fatal for all of them.

Daisy realises that it's down to her to ensure their collective safety. The others are too young to realise the danger they are in. Daisy must lead the way.

Which is easier said than done with this pair.

Poppy isn't too bad now, but she is still prone to fits of bad temper. Only yesterday she threw a chocolate eclair on the floor and ground it into the carpet under her heel. Daisy spent ages cleaning up the mess while Poppy wailed on the bed.

But now there is Ellie, whose problems are altogether different. Her lack of communication is the least of Daisy's worries. A far bigger one is that she refuses to eat and drink. She has gone all day without anything passing her lips.

There's a meal in front of her now. Fish fingers, mashed potato and beans. Poppy wolfed hers down and went back to sit on the bed. Ellie's is untouched.

'Go on, Ellie,' says Daisy. 'Have a few beans. Everyone likes beans.'

But Ellie just sits and stares at the plate and its rapidly cooling contents.

Daisy takes another mouthful of her own food. She would normally polish off a meal like this without giving it much thought, but Ellie's attitude is infectious. It makes Daisy wonder about the worth of staving off hunger. Why even bother to survive in a prison like this? Why not just starve to death and be done with it?

'Please, Ellie. For me. It will make you feel much better.'

She doesn't really believe that. Food isn't going to cure whatever it is that ails Ellie.

Daisy hears Malcolm and Harriet coming up the stairs. She looks at the door, then at Ellie's plate, then back to the door. She feels the need to do something to save the situation, but she doesn't know what.

Harriet comes in first, holding the door wide while Malcolm bundles in with a new mattress.

'Can't have you all sleeping in one bed, can we?' says Malcolm. 'That would be a bit squished.'

He props the mattress up against the chimney breast. 'When you've finished eating, we can put the table and chairs away, and that will leave room to put the mattress next to the bed. In the mornings, we can slide it away in the space between the bed and the window.' He turns to Harriet. 'Will you sort out the sheets and pillows, Mummy?'

Harriet beams. 'I certainly will.' She looks down at Ellie. 'You'll be as snug as a bug when I've finished. Don't worry. This is just for now. We'll get you a proper bed soon.'

And then Harriet's smile droops.

'You've not touched your food, Ellie. Is it all right for you? You're not ill, are you?'

Ellie doesn't even look up. It's as though Harriet's words have passed straight through her.

Daisy watches the adults exchange concerned glances. Sees how Malcolm's mood begins to darken.

'She's been playing,' says Daisy. 'She's been far too busy to eat.'

Her eyes dart to Poppy, warning her not to contradict.

'Playing?' says Harriet. 'Really?'

I've gone too far, thinks Daisy. I shouldn't have said she was playing. She doesn't look anything like a kid who has just been playing. She looks exactly the same as she did when she first got here. She looks like a dead person.

'I mean . . . not playing, exactly. But trying to play. When you brought the food, it was quite hot, so I said we should leave it for a few minutes, and while we were waiting we played pretend. We said Ellie should be the baby, and Poppy and me would put her to bed. So we put her in the bed and sang nursery rhymes to her. But then she fell asleep. So me and Poppy had our meal.'

Daisy doesn't think she has ever spouted such utter rubbish in all her life. She has told small white lies before – what kid hasn't? – but nothing like this.

They know, she thinks. They're looking at me like I'm mad. They know I'm making it up.

But then Harriet finds a hesitant smile again, reflected instantly by Malcolm.

'I was like that when I was your age,' says Harriet. 'Never could sit still long enough to eat. Always wanting to play outside on the swing while—'

She seems suddenly to realise what she is saying: that she is taunting them with childhood experiences they will forever be denied.

'Anyway,' says Harriet, backing out of the room, 'I'll sort out those sheets.' She wags a finger at Ellie. 'You eat up now.'

Malcolm follows her out, but before he leaves, Daisy catches a look on his face that says, *Don't make me have to punish anyone.*

As soon as the door is locked, Poppy bounces across to the bottom of the bed.

'You lied,' she says. 'Why did you tell all those lies? We didn't play with *her*.' She emphasises the final word, as though the very idea of taking part in any activity with Ellie is unthinkable.

'I had to. If they think Ellie is just being naughty, they'll get mad, and then they'll punish us.'

'They'll punish *her*.'

'No, Poppy, it doesn't work like that. Malcolm doesn't always think like we do. He'll say we're not trying hard enough, or we've done something to upset Ellie, and then we'll all be in trouble.'

She turns to Ellie again. 'Please, Ellie. Eat something before they come back. Just a couple of mouthfuls.'

'I know,' says Poppy. 'Throw it down the toilet.'

'It's not a proper toilet, Poppy. They'll see it. I can't put it down the sink either, because it will clog it up.'

And then she hears footsteps again. They're coming. They will walk in and see the disobedience, and Harriet will demand that Malcolm deal with it, and then Malcolm will unleash a whirlwind of devastation that will snap the children like brittle twigs.

Daisy has no choice. She grabs Ellie's fork, scoops up some mash and beans, stuffs it into her own mouth. Although her stomach is already full, she forces herself to swallow the unchewed mass. She chops up a fish finger, piles on some more beans, throws it down her gullet.

Footsteps on the landing now, just outside the door.

Another attack on the food. Daisy retching as she takes another couple of gulps, even though there seems no room for it and it is just sitting solidly in her throat, queuing for space.

The bolts being drawn back.

Daisy frantically pushing the food around the plate, spreading it out to give the impression that inroads have been made. Then one final touch as the door swings open: Daisy dipping two fingers into the bean sauce and wiping it across Ellie's mouth.

'How are we doing?' says Harriet, beaming while her husband stands behind her, awaiting her command like an attack dog. She has sheets and blankets draped over one arm. Malcolm clutches a pillow far too tightly, reminding Daisy of the way he held on to Poppy when she was naughty.

Daisy tries to summon a smile of her own, but finds it difficult to manipulate facial muscles that are focused on holding back a volcano. She nods emphatically, hoping that will make up for it.

Harriet cranes to look past Daisy at the food on the table. Daisy's own eyes slide sideways, to where Ellie is sitting. Doubts rush into her brain. She worries that her attempt at deceit is plain to see. It's too rushed, too obvious.

A ball of food threatens to spring back up Daisy's oesophagus. Her hand automatically jumps towards her mouth to prevent an eruption, but at the last moment she manages to divert it to her cheek, which she casually scratches.

Harriet's eyes switch back to Daisy. They appear laden with suspicion.

But then Harriet smiles once more. 'You managed to get her to eat something.'

Daisy nods again, fighting against the internal pressure.

'Fantastic,' says Harriet. 'Nothing like a good meal to make people feel better.' She points to the plates. 'All finished?'

More nods from Daisy. She looks to Poppy for support, but gets no response.

'Good girl,' says Harriet, patting Ellie on the head. Ellie doesn't seem to notice. 'Now, let's sort this bed out.'

Harriet collects the plates and passes them across to Malcolm, who carries them out of the room. Daisy and Ellie move over to the bed while Harriet wipes down the table, then folds it away and stacks the chairs. When Malcolm returns, they busy themselves preparing the mattress.

Daisy feels relieved as the attention shifts away from her. She uses the opportunity to take a few hard swallows, desperately trying to compact food into her overstretched stomach, which grumbles in complaint. She glances at Poppy, who appears to be filled with a mixture of delight at the con trick being perpetrated, and trepidation that it will all be uncovered. Poppy fidgets as her wide eyes flit between Daisy and the Bensons, waiting to see who will win this battle.

'There,' says Harriet. 'All done. Doesn't that look cosy?'

It doesn't look cosy at all to Daisy. She would hate to be that close to the floor, where unseen things might crawl across you at night.

'Great,' she croaks, the first word she has managed to let loose since the adults walked in.

When the Bensons have left, Poppy bounces on the bed with excitement. 'We did it! We fooled them.'

Daisy clutches her stomach and groans. 'Move over, Poppy. I need to lie down.'

She gets on the bed. Spends several minutes massaging her abdomen in an effort to coax the food through her system. Stops when she feels an urgent tapping on her shin.

She sits up. Follows Poppy's gaze.

Ellie is moving soundlessly across the carpet. She doesn't look at the other two girls, doesn't seem aware of their existence. Daisy watches her, wondering whether to intervene.

When Ellie arrives at the far side of the room, she turns one hundred and eighty degrees, then slides her back down the wall until she is sitting on the floor. Finally, she draws up her legs, crosses her arms over them, and buries her face. There is no further movement.

Poppy twists her head to look at Daisy, but Daisy has no answers. She has no idea what is going through Ellie's head. She knows only that her behaviour could mean the end for all of them.

28

It's bedtime.

Daisy left Ellie where she was for at least an hour. She doesn't know whether the child slept or simply cut herself off from the world, but she couldn't leave her like that any longer.

By the time Harriet returned to announce that they needed to get ready for 'sleepy-byes', Daisy had Ellie sitting on the bed, a book in her hand. She wasn't reading it, of course. Wasn't even seeing it, probably. But it at least gave the impression she had some interest in being alive.

Now Daisy takes the book from Ellie and eases her off the bed. She undresses her, leads her to the sink and washes her down. Then she helps her into a pair of warm pyjamas. Throughout the whole process Ellie doesn't murmur once.

Daisy turns to Poppy. 'Poppy, I don't think Ellie should sleep alone tonight.'

Poppy looks horrified. 'I don't want her in our bed. She's creepy. Anyway, there's no room.'

'I thought . . . I thought maybe you could sleep on the mattress, and Poppy could get in with me.'

'On the floor? I'm not sleeping there. There might be spiders down there or . . . or mice or something.'

'You'll be fine. There's nothing down there. Please, Poppy. Look at her. She needs hugs, like the ones I gave you, remember?'

'No. It's horrible down there.'

'It's not horrible. It's . . . Look, if you sleep there tonight, I'll give you my dessert tomorrow. How does that sound?'

Poppy stares at the bed while she mulls it over. 'What about your biscuits?'

'All right, yes. You can have my biscuits too. Do we have a deal?'

'Okay. But if anything crawls on me in the night, I'm going to scream the house down.'

Daisy gets herself washed and changed, then helps Ellie into bed. She climbs in next to her and pulls the covers over them. Ellie stays flat on her back, staring up at the ceiling.

'Put the light out,' she tells Poppy.

'Why can't you put it out? If I do it, I'll have to find my bed in the dark.'

'It's easier for you, Poppy. If I do it, I'll have to climb over Ellie or stand on you.'

Poppy huffs and puffs as she gets up from the mattress and stamps over to the light switch. When they are in blackness, Daisy hears Poppy quickly retracing the steps back to her bed.

Daisy remains still for a minute, listening. She thinks she can just about hear Ellie breathing, but it's ever so faint. She stretches her hand out beneath the covers. When her fingers touch Ellie's flesh, it still feels like ice.

Daisy slides herself across until she is pressing against Ellie. She wraps her arm across the child's body.

'It's okay,' she breathes. 'I'll look after you. I promise.'

'Stop whispering,' says Poppy from below. 'It's creepy.'

* * *

Daisy has no idea what time it is, or why she has woken up. She reaches out a hand.

Ellie isn't there.

Daisy dives off the bed. She heads for the light switch, stumbling as she tries to get across Poppy's mattress. Poppy comes awake with a yelp.

'What's the matter? What's the matter?'

Daisy finds the switch. Turns it on. And then she sees.

Ellie is standing in the middle of the room, screaming.

Or rather, she looks like she's screaming. No sounds leave her mouth. She keeps bending at the waist and opening her mouth as wide as she can, letting out what ought to be an almighty roar. All the emotion contained in that tiny frame spewing out of her in eerie silence, again and again, while tears stream down her face.

'What's she doing?' Poppy yells. 'Make her stop. Make her—'

Daisy drops to the mattress and clamps a hand over Poppy's mouth. The adults mustn't hear this. They mustn't come in and see what Ellie is doing. They won't like what they see, and they will hurt her.

'Hush,' says Daisy. 'Hush.'

She doesn't know what she's watching. Doesn't understand what is happening to Ellie – what *has* happened to Ellie. She knows only that Ellie must be allowed to do this. She needs to get it out.

Whatever it is, it shouldn't be inside this poor little girl.

29

'The Pied Piper! The Pied bloody Piper!'

Blunt slams the newspaper down on the desk at the front of the incident room. It's a depressing start to another day. The tabloid sensationalists have had plenty of time in which to concoct slogans and catchphrases that will stick in Joe Public's memory. And they've gone to town.

'It's sick, and I hate it,' says Blunt. 'And before you give me any accusing looks, DS Cody, yes, I know I said yesterday that this is starting to resemble the work of the Childcatcher, but that was for internal consumption only. We're allowed to think such things. What I don't want is for the people of this city to start believing that some mysterious maniac is rounding up their children and leading them away, never to be seen again.'

'No, ma'am,' says Cody. 'But we shouldn't be surprised they're borrowing from fantasy. I mean, this is pretty damn weird.'

'Weird doesn't begin to cover it. This is unprecedented. But what that tells us is that there has to be a rational explanation. These attacks weren't random or impromptu. They were carefully planned. In each case, the perpetrator needed to take a specific child. No other child would do. And once he'd decided to take them, nothing was going to get in his way. Including the parents. So, ladies and gents, my question is why? Why did he abduct these particular girls, and why was he willing to go to such lengths to get them?'

'Maybe he has a type,' Cody ventures.

Blunt gestures to the back of the incident room. 'Grace, put some pictures up for us, will you?'

She doesn't have to wait long before photographs of the two girls appear side by side on the central monitor.

'All right, Cody. Let's explore that. Similarities?'

Cody stares at the images. The girls look nothing like each other. If the abductor covets a certain type, it goes beyond mere appearance.

'All right. Both are female. Both are six years old. Neither of them has any siblings. All the parents are employed – I mean, the McVities *were* employed . . .' He continues to wrack his brain, but manages to shake out nothing of significance.

'What else?' Blunt pushes. 'Grace, anything on the intelligence front that might link the two?'

Grace stands up. 'Nothing yet. It'll be a while before I can get full data on the McVities, but so far I've found nothing. I'm analysing phone dumps right now. If the Devlins ever called the McVities or vice versa, or if either of them had a conversation with the same intermediary, I'll know about it. But nothing has been flagged yet. Same goes for their computers. HCU are cross-checking the sites they visited, the emails they sent, and so on, but it could take a while.'

'There has to be a link of some kind,' says Blunt. 'Maybe Devlin and McVitie both did some work for the same guy at some point. Maybe they once drank in the same pub. Maybe the children were in the same Brownies pack.'

'Rainbows,' says Webley.

'What?'

'Brownies comes later. At six you'd be in Rainbows.'

'Whatever. Our perp targeted these kids because he knew something that connects them. If we can work out what it is, we've cracked this case.' She pauses. 'Forensics given us anything?'

'The killer stepped in blood,' says Cody, 'so we've got shoe prints. Apparently they were size twelve CATs. We've also got several fibre samples. The problem is finding something to match against. We're working our way through potential suspects again, looking for items of footwear or clothing that might have been used.'

'What about the methods of entry? This guy knew what he was doing.'

'He did. At the McVities' house it looks as though he used some kind of tool to open the window from the inside. That suggests he knew exactly where to go to get hold of such a thing, or he was skilled enough to construct it himself.'

Blunt nods. 'That's useful information. Okay, what about this white van that was seen?'

'We brought Mrs Morley in, showed her some pictures. She's very vague about it. She thinks it was about the size of the smallest Ford Transit, but she couldn't say anything about make or model. Anyway, we went back to the neighbours of the Devlins, and asked them specifically about a white van. Lo and behold, a couple of them now think they remember seeing a white van parked on the street on a couple of occasions. Could be just coincidence, but on the other hand . . .'

Blunt's eyebrows shoot up. 'You're not suggesting one of the Devlins could have been driving it, are you?'

'There's no indication of that. More likely that someone was using it for surveillance on the Devlin property. That's assuming it wasn't just a builder working at one of the houses nearby. We're still checking that.'

'But I don't suppose anyone got a registration number there either?'

'Afraid not.'

'Grace, anything to add?'

Grace gets to her feet again. 'Only that I'm scouring CCTV for recordings of white vans on nearby roads at that time of the morning. I'm also analysing local ANPR data for plates belonging to white vans. It's a long shot, but worth a try.'

Blunt nods slowly. 'We're missing something,' she mutters. 'Nobody does this kind of thing without a reason. What's his reason?'

She starts to pace the room.

'Why?' she says. 'Why?'

The explosion is as shocking as it is sudden. Blunt lets out a shout of frustration, then sweeps her arm across a desk, sending papers, pens and trays sailing across the room.

She whirls round to stare at her stunned team then stabs a finger at them. 'This man is a stone cold killer. He has two children in his clutches. They are not dead. I refuse to believe they are dead. We *have* to find them.'

And then she turns and marches away.

*   *   *

'Ma'am?'

Cody keeps his voice quiet, hoping its calmness will carry to his superior.

He's not sure he should be here at all, but he knows that nobody else will take the risk. Perhaps they know better than he does. Perhaps he should leave well alone.

But then again, maybe she needs someone right now. Blunt always seems such a rock, an island. But she's also a human being.

'Ma'am?' he says again.

Blunt turns from her office window to face him. 'Nathan,' she says. 'What brings you here? A major break in the case since I left you five minutes ago?'

'No, ma'am. I just wanted to . . . I just thought I should check if you were . . . if you are . . .'

'That's what I like about you, Nathan. Your directness.'

She smiles. Relieved, he smiles back.

'Shit,' she says. 'Made a bit of an arse of myself out there, didn't I?'

'Well, I wouldn't say that. It's just that I've never seen you act that way. You took me by surprise.'

'Well, I don't like to be too predictable.' She pauses. 'Scratch that. I do like to be predictable. I want you and the rest of the team to believe that I will always be someone who can be relied upon to stay in control and to get the job done. I don't think I did that out there today. That's why I'm seriously considering handing this case over to someone else.'

The shock of the statement is like a punch to Cody's gut. 'Ma'am, that's . . . I mean, you can't possibly . . .'

'Maybe I'm getting soft in my old age, I don't know. This case is getting under my skin. I'm not being objective, and that means I'm not doing my job effectively. The team deserves someone who is. Those two young girls deserve it.'

Cody takes a deep breath. 'If I can speak frankly, ma'am, what those two girls need is someone who *cares*. What's obvious to me – what's obvious to the rest of the team – is that you care about this case more than anything. What you also need to know is that your determination is infectious. Every person in that incident room sees how you act, and it makes them want to be just as dedicated, just as involved. It reminds us how important these two young lives are. If you want the best out of your team, you need to stay.'

Blunt drops her gaze while she thinks about this, then she smiles at Cody. 'Well, this is a right turnaround, isn't it? I never thought I'd see the day when I'd be getting behavioural therapy from you. I'd always thought you'd be the one ending up in the psychiatrist's chair.'

Could still happen, thinks Cody.

'All right,' says Blunt. 'You've convinced me. But if that lot complain they're getting a rough time from me, you can tell them they've got you to blame.'

Cody smiles, but doesn't move.

'Something else?' she asks.

'I just thought . . . well, maybe you'd like to hug it out?'

Her eyes widen. 'Fuck off, DS Cody. What kind of place do you think I'm running here, a fucking hippy commune? Now get back to work before I throw you through that door.'

When Cody turns and leaves, it is with a huge grin on his face.

30

'Morning, girls!'

Harriet flutters in like a mother bird returning to the nest. She is carrying a tray of breakfast cereal and juice. As always, Malcolm stands guard at the door while she fusses over her pretend family.

'Rice Krispies today. Plus some toast. And I've got some new DVDs for you to watch. I'll bring one up later. How does that sound?'

A movie is always presented as a special treat. The television isn't connected to an aerial. Daisy knows it's to prevent her from finding out what's going on in the outside world.

'Great,' says Daisy. 'It'll be nice to have something new to watch.'

She wonders if she sounds a little overenthusiastic. For a moment, Harriet looks at her suspiciously.

'Right,' says Harriet. 'Well, eat up! Breakfast is the most important meal of the day.'

She bustles out. Malcolm stares at them for a few seconds before he too departs.

Daisy herds the other girls to the table. There is a lump in her throat, because she knows this isn't going to be as straightforward as it ought to be. Having breakfast shouldn't be an ordeal. You sit down, you eat and it's done. Only it won't be like that, will it? It will be exasperating and stressful. Everything is stressful now.

She picks up the jug of milk, pours it onto each bowl of cereal.

'Look at that,' she says. 'Doesn't that look good?'

Poppy gives her a puzzled look. 'It's only Rice Krispies.'

Daisy glares at her, then turns back to Ellie. 'Can you hear them, Ellie? The snap, crackle and pop? Would you like some juice to go with it? It's nice and sweet.'

She pushes the glass closer to Ellie. Then she picks up a spoon and puts it in Ellie's hand.

'There you go. Dig in now. You must be starving.'

Poppy is already tucking in. She brings spoonful after huge spoonful of cereal up to her mouth.

'Please,' Daisy says to Ellie. 'You've got to eat. You'll waste away. You'll get ill. You've—'

She realises she is crying. This is too difficult. It's too much responsibility. Life shouldn't be this much of a hardship when you're ten years old.

Poppy stops eating. She stares open-mouthed at Daisy, masticated food visible on her tongue.

'What's the matter?' she asks.

Daisy jumps out of her chair. She marches across to the wall and, raising her arms, leans her face against them, like she used to when she played hide and seek all those years ago. When she had friends. Real friends. Not these two strangers, these cellmates, these children who are dependent on her to keep them alive.

She wants to play hide and seek now. She wants to close her eyes and count to ten, and when she turns around the other children will be gone. The adults will be gone. This house will be gone. There will be just her, out in the open, and she will run and run and run, because there will be no walls to stop her, no people to hold her back.

'What's the matter, Daisy?'

Poppy, at her side now, tugging on her cardigan.

Daisy whirls around, sees how it causes Poppy to flinch.

'I can't do this anymore. I can't help you. We're all going to die in here.'

Poppy blinks in sudden fearfulness. 'Don't say that.'

'It's true. You won't help me. You keep getting angry. She won't eat. What am I supposed to do? How am I supposed to help you if you won't help me back? It's not fair.'

She buries her face in her arms again. Her body begins to shake as she sobs silently.

It's a while before she notices Poppy pulling at her cardigan again.

'Daisy! Daisy!'

She pushes away from the wall. Sniffs as she looks down through blurred eyes. 'What?'

Poppy turns. Points. 'Look.'

Daisy follows her gaze. She wipes her eyes to get a better look.

It's Ellie. She is eating.

It's slow at first. The spoon moves at a glacial speed from bowl to mouth. But gradually, as she becomes reaccustomed to it, she speeds up.

A bark of hysterical laughter escapes Daisy's lips. Slowly she walks across to Ellie and sits opposite her. Ellie doesn't even seem to notice. She just stares at the table as she fills her mouth with food.

It's for me, thinks Daisy. She's doing this for me.

'Thank you,' she says. 'Thank you, Ellie.'

31

The call takes Webley by surprise.

She's at her desk, but it's not her police extension that rings; it's her mobile. She reaches into her pocket and takes out the phone. Sees that the call is from Parker.

Shit.

She debates rejecting the call. Or at least letting it go to voicemail. But people are looking at her.

She thumbs the answer button. 'Hello.' She keeps her voice flat, emotionless.

'Hi. It's me. Long time no see.'

It's me. Well, that's a dumb opening. And 'long time no see' is stating the bleeding obvious.

I'm angry, she thinks. *But then I've every right to be.*

'I'm on duty, Parker. What is it?'

'I . . . I was hoping we could talk.'

'What about?'

'Well . . . us. We've hardly spoken since before Christmas.'

'No, we haven't. And whose fault is that?'

'I . . . You were pissed off with me. I thought I should let you cool down a little.'

Let me cool down? As if I'm the one at fault here?

'I can't talk now, Parker. Believe it or not, I've got some really serious matters to deal with.'

'No, I understand that. I've called at a bad time. But . . . I'm really missing you, Megan. It's not the same without you.'

Now why'd you have to go and say that, Parker? Why'd you have to go and tug at my heartstrings?

'I don't know what you want me to say.' She looks around her. None of her colleagues is staring at her directly, but she knows that ears are wagging.

'Say that you'll meet up with me, so that we can talk about this properly.'

'I'm not sure that's a good idea.'

'Why not? What harm would it do to talk? Was what I did really so bad?'

A good question. Was it so bad? He didn't sleep with another woman. He didn't steal money from her account. He didn't beat her up.

So was it so bad? Or was she just eager to grab at the first excuse that came along to end a relationship in which she wasn't entirely happy?

Yes, he overstepped a mark, but wasn't that simply because of his jealousy? Is that something she can't forgive?

'I'll think about it,' she says.

'You will? Seriously?'

'I said so, didn't I? Look, I need to get back to work. I'll text you.'

'Okay. Great. When?'

'Soon, all right? Don't pressurise me.'

'No. You're right. Okay. Just let me know.'

'Bye, Parker.'

'I love—'

She hangs up before the rest of his sentence can reach her.

* * *

'Cody!'

He thinks that almost everyone in the building must have heard his name being yelled. Blunt wouldn't need a megaphone to do crowd control.

He gets up from his desk.

'You should take a notebook,' says Webley.

'Why?'

'To put down the back of your pants before you get your spanking.'

He gives her his best 'We are not amused' look, but still he wonders why he is being so emphatically summoned.

When he gets to Blunt's office, he sees that Grace Meade is there. She gives him a coy smile.

Blunt wastes no time with such niceties. 'Tell him,' she says to Grace.

'Well,' says Grace, 'I've been looking into past cases of missing children, trying to find any similarities with the current ones. Until now, I haven't had much luck.'

'Until now? You've found another one?' The thought horrifies Cody. Two is bad enough.

'I'm not sure, but it's a possibility. It doesn't follow the same pattern. It wasn't in the local area, it didn't involve a break-in, and it wasn't at night.'

Cody senses he's missing something. 'So . . .'

'The white van. An anonymous caller said that they saw the girl being forced into the back of a white van.'

'Which case are you talking about, Grace?'

'Daisy Agnew.'

The name rings a bell with Cody. 'Daisy Agnew! That was over two years ago, wasn't it?'

'Three.'

'And it was in North Wales, right? I thought the father was the main suspect.'

'He was. The parents had split up, but he wanted Daisy to live with him. When she disappeared, he was the natural suspect. The Welsh CID looked into it, but couldn't pin anything on him. The girl still hasn't been found, but everyone in the community believed he did it. He had to move away in the end.'

'And he drove a white van?'

'Yes. He was a plasterer.'

Cody weighs up the information, and finds it lacking in substance. 'I don't know. Seems a tenuous link to me. For one thing, it's a completely different MO. And then there's the huge separation in both distance and time. Why wait three years and then switch your focus from Wales to Liverpool? There's also the anonymous phone call. Why wouldn't a witness to something like that come forward? Unless, of course, they didn't want to get caught lying about the father's part in it.' He looks at Grace. 'You're not suggesting that Daisy's Agnew's father might be responsible for the latest abductions too, are you?'

'No. He started a new life in Spain in the end, and I'm sure it wouldn't be hard to confirm he's still there. But what if he really didn't have anything to do with his daughter's disappearance? What if it was another white van driver – the same one who took Poppy and Ellie? Daisy was seven at the time she went missing – not so different from the other two.'

Cody is still sceptical, but Blunt heads off his objections.

'I want it looking into,' she says. 'Send someone over there. Talk to the investigating officers and re-interview any witnesses. In particular, get the mother's story. But whatever you do, don't get her hopes up. Any case involving a child missing for three years is unlikely to have a happy ending.'

Cody looks at Grace again. 'Remind me of the details.'

'Daisy was having a picnic on the beach with her mum and her mum's new partner. She went up to play in the sand dunes with another kid. A few minutes later, the adults realised that the second kid had rejoined her family, but Daisy wasn't with her. That's when they started to worry. They searched the dunes for ages, but there was no sign of her. I remember something similar happening to me when I was little: climbing up on some sand dunes and then losing my bearings. I cried my eyes out when I couldn't see my parents. It didn't seem such a big deal to them, but to me—'

Cody interrupts: 'Where exactly was this?'

'I think we were somewhere in Cornwall. We—'

'Not you. Daisy Agnew.'

'Harlech. It's got a beautiful long beach. There's—'

Cody turns to Blunt. 'I need to go, ma'am.'

Blunt eyes him up. 'I've seen that look before, Cody. What is it this time?'

'I'm not sure. There's just something I need to check out.'

'In Harlech?'

'No, ma'am. Much closer to home.'

32

'That nice Italian restaurant on Dale Street?' says Webley.

'Nope,' Cody answers.

'The Indian on Water Street?'

'Stop thinking about your stomach.'

'You said you were taking me to one of my favourite places. I happen to like those restaurants.'

They're in the car, Cody driving.

'Guess again.'

'All right,' she says. 'John Lewis?'

'Nope.'

'Hotel Chocolat? No, wait, that's my stomach again. Boodles?'

'Nope.'

'A clothes shop? A flower shop? A bar?'

'No, no and no.'

'I give up. Tell me.'

'What, and ruin the surprise?'

She doesn't have to wait long. It comes to her as soon as Cody turns off towards the entrance of the Mersey Tunnel.

'Oh, pissing hell, Cody. Please don't tell me we're going to see Quigley again.'

He turns, smiles.

She slaps him on the arm. 'Why didn't you say? At the very least I'd have changed my shoes.'

'Hey, I'm the one who ended up looking a right state last time. You hardly even smudged your lipstick.'

'Yeah, well that just shows what a superhero I am, doesn't it, seeing as I'm the one who caught him.'

He lets her fume for a minute, while he drives into the tunnel that will take them through to the Wirral.

'So why do we need to talk to Quigley again?' says Webley.

'I just need to check something out.'

'Good. Well, that's clarified that one. You need to start holding things back, Cody. I'm drowning in all this information you're giving me. Loose lips sink ships.'

Another pause. And then it seems as though Webley has decided to launch a counter-offensive.

'I've been meaning to ask you for ages,' she says. 'What is it with you and Blunt?'

He gives her a puzzled look. 'How do you mean?'

'Don't act daft. There's something between you. A *special* relationship.'

'What, you think I'm getting it on with our boss?'

'No. But there's something. She doesn't talk to the rest of us in the same way she talks to you. And before you say it, it's nothing to do with rank. It's like when we were at the McVitie murder scene. She looked at you like you both knew a secret – like you were in the Masons or something. And when she threw that wobbler in the incident room, none of us would have dared go near her. You did, though. You knew she'd open up to you.'

'That's because I have charm, tact and diplomacy.'

'And modesty. Don't forget modesty. Seriously, though, what's going on between you two?'

Cody shakes his head. 'To be honest, I've no idea.'

'Come off it.'

'No, really. I'm not trying to dodge the question. She's been that way with me ever since I joined. At first I thought it was just because of what I went through when I was undercover, but I think there's more to it than that.'

'Why don't you ask her?'

'Are you kidding? I may get on all right with her, but I'm not stupid. Anyway, speaking of relationships . . .'

He feels the full force of Webley's glare. 'What's that supposed to mean?'

'You and Parker Penn. What's the latest?'

'His surname isn't Penn, and it isn't Carr either. And I still don't know what you're talking about.'

'Yes you do. That was him earlier, wasn't it? On the phone.'

'Might have been. None of your business.' She pauses. 'Okay, it was him.'

'Is it back on, then?'

'Not at the moment, no. He wants to meet up. To talk things over.'

'Are you going to?'

'Haven't decided. Do you think I should? Actually, don't answer that. It's none of your business.'

'Well, since you asked – yes, I think you should. He's a nice bloke, despite the ridiculous name. A bit possessive maybe, but then who wouldn't be jealous of a guy like myself?'

She stiffens in her seat. 'You know what, Cody?'

'What?'

'Never mind. Drive. And I hope you end up in the sea again.'

33

Cody raps on the caravan door. Gets no response.

'Gavin, it's us again. The same two police officers you spoke to before.'

'Go away.'

'So much for your charm,' Webley mutters to Cody.

Cody tries again. 'Can you open up, please, Gavin? We just need to ask you a few more questions.'

'I don't know nothing.'

'Well, then, it won't take very long, will it? Come on, Gavin. We're not going away till you speak to us, so you might as well get it over with.'

The caravan shakes a little as Quigley thuds across it. When the door is unlocked, Cody tenses in the expectation that he will have to go running along the Wirral coastline again.

But Quigley just throws open the door and steps back inside, leaving Cody and Webley to follow.

Nothing has changed in here. It's still a tip. Cody's lip curls as he breathes in a whiff of burger grease. He remains standing as Quigley settles back into his seat and begins sucking on the plastic straw protruding from a carton of blackcurrant cordial.

Cody points to a piece of paper on the cushion next to Quigley. It has just a few squiggly lines on it at the moment – nothing recognisable.

'New drawing?'

Quigley nods. Continues sucking up his juice.

'What's it going to be?'

It's a few seconds before Quigley releases his grip on the straw. When he does, he seems out of breath.

'The marina,' he says. 'West Kirby.'

'When did you go there?'

'This morning. On the train.'

'That's right. You like to travel around the coast, don't you?'

Quigley returns to his juice box, his lips tightly pursed on the straw.

Cody steps across to the cupboards, points to one of the drawings taped there.

'This is Leasowe Lighthouse, isn't it? I think it's a pretty good likeness, myself. What do you think, DC Webley?'

Webley nods vigorously. 'Definitely. You're quite the artist, aren't you, Gavin?'

'Now this one . . .' says Cody, moving along the row, 'this one had me puzzled. When I first saw it I assumed it must be the Leasowe Castle Hotel. You've even written *Castell* below it, haven't you? But it's not Leasowe Castle, is it, Gavin?'

Quigley's eyes cross a little as he tries to focus on the carton just inches in front of his face. As though he's trying to shut the rest of the world out of his field of vision.

Cody says, 'Didn't you tell us you travel quite a distance to visit some of these beaches? I think you even mentioned you get as far as Wales. I'm right about that, aren't I, Gavin?'

Quigley takes a long, hard suck on his straw, draining the carton noisily and causing its sides to collapse.

Cody points again at the legend below the drawing. 'Where'd you get that spelling, Gavin? Off a road sign when you were there? That's the Welsh word for castle. And the castle itself – I think that's Harlech Castle.' He pauses. 'It *is* Harlech, isn't it?'

Quigley keeps sucking air from his empty box. Webley moves across and gently prises it out of his grasp.

She says, 'It's okay, Gavin. You can talk to us. We're not here to hurt you.'

'When did you go to Harlech, Gavin?' says Cody.

Quigley shrugs his shoulders.

'Well, was it in the past couple of weeks? A few months ago?'

'Ages. I don't remember.'

'Ages? Do you mean years? Like, maybe three years ago?'

Quigley's eyes flicker up to Cody, then back down again.

'Gavin,' says Cody, 'have you ever heard the name Daisy Agnew?'

A tremor passes through Quigley's body.

'Daisy Agnew was a little girl who went missing three years ago,' Cody continues. 'It happened on the beach in Harlech. You were there, weren't you, Gavin? You were there when it happened.'

Quigley presents a pleading face to Webley. 'It wasn't me. I had nothing to do with it.'

'Did you take Daisy Agnew, Gavin?' asks Cody. 'Did you lead her away from the beach, just as you tried to do with Courtney a few months later?'

Quigley keeps his eyes on Webley. 'He's making things up. I didn't take any girls. I don't do that. I don't hurt people. People hurt *me*. They always hurt me.'

Tears are streaming down his cheeks. Webley looks up at Cody, then back to Quigley.

She says, 'You can see how it looks, can't you, Gavin? You can see why we have to ask these questions? Three years ago a girl went missing, and you happened to be in the same place at the same time. Six months later, you were caught leading another little girl away from a car park in Leasowe. And now yet another little girl called Poppy has been taken from her house in Otterspool, just a few streets away from your family home. It's all starting to look a little suspicious, don't you think?'

Cody notices how Webley doesn't mention Ellie McVitie, for whom there is currently no evidence of a connection to Quigley. And he accepts that this isn't the only hole. So far, there has been nothing to suggest that Quigley was anywhere near his mother's house when Poppy was snatched. And then there are the break-ins themselves: does this wreck of a man sitting here really possess the requisite skill and audacity? And what about the white van? Can Quigley even drive? He certainly doesn't have a licence.

But Webley is simply following Cody's lead. They have to keep piling on the pressure. It's beyond belief that all of this could be sheer coincidence.

Quigley is trembling. He looks like a trapped animal.

'I didn't take her,' he says. 'I was trying to help her. I thought she was lost.'

'Who?' says Cody. 'Daisy?'

'No. The other girl. Courtney. I thought she couldn't find her mum and dad. I didn't want the man to come and snatch her.'

Cody exchanges glances with Webley. 'Which man, Gavin?'

'The man. The one who took Daisy.'

'What man? Are you making this up, Gavin? Wasn't it you who took Daisy?'

'No. I swear. I saw him. I told you. She didn't want to go, but he made her. He put her in his van.'

And that's the word. *Van*. They haven't mentioned it to Quigley, and it hasn't been on the news. How does he know about a van?

Cody finds a seat next to Webley. 'Are you saying you saw that happen? You saw a man putting Daisy Agnew into his van?'

'Yes. I told you. I said all this before.'

'What do you mean, you—' And then realisation hits him. 'You phoned us! You're the anonymous caller, aren't you?'

Quigley nods. 'I thought you needed to know. I thought it was the right thing to do.'

Excitement surges through Cody's system. If what Quigley is telling them is true, then he's not a suspect at all. On the contrary, he's a witness. He could be the best lead they've got to catch the real offender.

He takes out his notebook and pen. 'Tell me about that day, Gavin. What happened exactly?'

'I went to Harlech beach. It took me a long time to get there.'

'How long?'

'About five and a half hours. I had to change trains at Wolverhampton.'

Cody scribbles down a reminder to check out the train schedules.

'You went there and back in a day?'

'No. I slept on the beach, up in the dunes.' He points to a scruffy back-
pack in the corner of the caravan. 'My tent's in there.'

'Okay. So when did you see Daisy and the man?'

'The next day, when I was coming home. I went to the toilet in the car
park. When I came out, they were there.'

'All right, Gavin. You're doing well. What happened then?'

'The man was holding the little girl's hand. She was pointing behind
her, back towards the beach. I think he was telling her to hurry up.'

'He wasn't carrying her?'

'No. She was walking with him, but then I think she changed her mind.
She started crying. When the man opened the back of the van, she started
shouting for her mummy.'

'You could hear her saying that?'

'Yes. She was very upset.'

'What did the man do?'

'He picked her up and pushed her into the van. She was screaming. But
then he leaned into the van. After that she went quiet.'

'Could you see what he did to her?'

'No. I don't think it was very nice.'

'And then what?'

'He closed the back of the van. Then he got in and drove away.'

'And what did you do?'

'I went home.'

'You went home? Is that it?'

Quigley blinks at Cody as though he's just been told off. 'I didn't want
to miss my train.'

'You didn't tell anyone what you'd just seen?'

'I . . . I didn't know what I saw. I thought it was just a girl being naughty
with her dad. I didn't know what was happening. Not till much later.'

'How much later?'

'A couple of days. I heard it on the news. They said her name was
Daisy Agnew, and they described what she was wearing. I knew it was
the same girl.'

'And that's when you decided to call?'

'Yes.'

'Did you call on your mobile?'

'No. I don't have a mobile. I used a payphone.'

'Where was this?'

'Blackpool. I went to Blackpool beach, but I didn't like it. It was too busy, too noisy. And I saw all the newspapers about the missing girl, so I called the police and told them what I saw.'

'But you didn't give your name or tell them how they could find you?'

Quigley hangs his head. 'No.'

'Why not?'

'I was scared. Police ask lots of questions. I didn't want to be asked lots of questions.'

'So what did you tell them?'

'I told them I saw Daisy being put in a white van by a man.'

'And that's all?'

Quigley thinks about this for a second. 'I told them what the man was wearing.'

'Which was?'

'Jeans and a blue hoody. That's all I could remember.'

'You didn't see his face?'

'No.'

Cody leans back, sighs in exasperation. Their only witness is not telling them anything more than they already know.

Webley takes over. 'Tell me about what happened six months after that. When you saw the little girl in Leasowe.'

Quigley shrugs. 'I saw her. She was alone, and she looked upset. I thought she was lost. And then I thought about the bad man in that van, and I didn't want the same thing to happen to this girl. I was worried about her.'

'So you went up to her, is that right?'

'Yes. I said I would help her find her parents, and she took hold of my hand, and then . . . and then . . .'

'You were seen, and you were attacked.'

Quigley's mouth droops. He seems to be on the verge of tears.

'And that's the only reason you approached the girl, to help her find her family again?'

'Yes. I told them that, but they didn't believe me. Nobody believed me, not even the police.'

'So when the police questioned you, didn't you tell them why you were so worried for Courtney? Didn't you tell them about what you'd seen in Harlech?'

'I couldn't. How could I? They would have thought that was me, too. They would have blamed me for everything. I haven't told anyone about that. Only you, now. Does that mean I'm in trouble? Are you going to take me away and lock me up?'

Webley looks to Cody, who says, 'No, Gavin, we're not going to lock you up. You've told us about it now. You've done the right thing.'

Cody gets up from his seat. Puts his notebook away. 'We're going to leave you alone now, Gavin. Thank you for talking to us.'

He steps across to the door, Webley close behind him.

'Do you want to see my picture?' says Quigley.

Cody glances at Webley. It seems they've made a friend, but there's work to be done elsewhere.

'Maybe another time, eh, Gavin?'

He turns towards the door again. Reaches for the handle.

'It's got the van on it. And the girl.'

Cody freezes. Slowly turns back to Gavin.

'What?'

'I did a picture of them. It was a long time ago. I just thought . . . I thought you might like to see it.'

Cody opens his mouth, but it's Webley who speaks first. 'Yes. We'd love to see it. Do you have it here?'

Cody joins her in scanning the rows of drawings on the walls, but sees nothing relevant.

Quigley gets up. Goes to his bedroom. Comes back with a thick plastic wallet under his arm. He sets it down on the table, unbuttons it, then starts dragging out piles of drawings.

'It's here somewhere,' he mutters. 'That's not it. Not that one, either. Here! This is it!'

Cody takes the piece of paper from him. Holds it up so that he and Webley can get a good look at it. It shows the rear end of a van. At the back window is a young girl's face, cartoon tears dotting her cheeks. Beyond the van, a hill is surmounted by Harlech castle.

'You saw this?' says Cody. 'You saw the girl crying at the window when it drove away?'

Quigley squirms in his seat. 'Well, no. I couldn't see her then, but I thought it was okay to draw her in. Artists are allowed to do that.'

Cody is already framing his next question. He puts his finger on the relevant spot of the drawing, shows it to Quigley.

'The number plate,' he says. 'You've written "DOGGY" on it.'

'Yes.'

'Is that what it said? "DOGGY"?'

Quigley squirms some more. 'No. Not exactly. I drew this picture about a week after the man took Daisy. I couldn't remember what it said. I just know it was something about dogs.'

'Think carefully, Gavin. What do you mean when you say it was something about dogs? You mean a breed of dog, or maybe a famous dog? Is that what you mean?'

Quigley presses his hands to the side of his head. 'I don't know. I don't remember.'

Cody sighs again. A solid clue to the killer seems tantalisingly just out of reach.

But perhaps this is enough.

He has to hope so.

34

'Did he come into your bedroom?'

Daisy puts down the comic she has been reading to Poppy. They are lying together on the bed. Ellie is sitting at the table, staring at her own comic. Daisy isn't sure if she has bothered to turn the pages.

'Who?'

'Malcolm,' says Poppy. 'When he took you, did he come into your bedroom?'

'No. Why? Did he come into yours?'

'Yes. I thought there was a monster in my room. He sneaked into our house and put something over my face that made me sleep. Then he brought me here.'

This is the first time Daisy has heard this tale. She has always assumed that Poppy's story would be similar to her own, but thought it best not to ask.

'No, he didn't do that with me. We were on a beach.'

'A beach? Where?'

'I don't remember. I think it was Wales, but I'm not sure.'

'Were you with your mum and dad? Didn't they try to stop him?'

'My dad wasn't living with us then, but my mum was there. She was with her new boyfriend. They were being all lovey-dovey with each other, so I started playing with another girl. Her name was Olivia.'

'I know an Olivia too.'

'Yes. It's a nice name. I still remember what she looked like. We went up into the sand dunes and played there for ages. But then Olivia left me. She just went, and I was all alone.'

'Were you frightened?'

'Not at first. But then I tried to find my way back to my mum, and I couldn't see her anywhere. There were lots and lots of people on the beach, but no sign of my mum. Then I started to cry.'

That memory is still vivid in Daisy's mind. Despite the horrors she has endured since then, she still has flashbacks to that time on the dunes, running and wailing and believing herself to be lost forever. Sometimes, during her especially low moments, she finds herself blaming her mother and her boyfriend for what came next.

'What happened then?'

'Malcolm found me. He was smiling, and he made me feel better. I thought he looked like a big, friendly teddy bear. He said to me, "You must be Daisy." And I said yes. And then he said, "I work in the car park. Your mum and dad are there, they've been looking everywhere for you. Shall we go and find them?" And then he put out his hand, and I held it, and I went with him.'

'You're not supposed to go with strangers,' says Poppy.

'I know,' she answers. 'I know.'

She wishes now, of course, that she had heeded that advice, drummed into her constantly by her mother and her teachers. But she had been so frightened, so upset. And then along came this huge, cuddly teddy bear with his daft smile and his massive outstretched paw of friendship. He knew her name, too. What was the worst that could happen?

This. This is what could happen.

'You told me fibs, didn't you?' says Poppy.

'What? When?'

'When I first came here. You told me you'd only been here for a short while. It's not true, is it? You've been here a long time.'

Daisy looks at her friend. She cannot lie now. 'Yes, I've been here a long time.'

She sees the tears welling up in Poppy's eyes, and she puts an arm around her shoulder and pulls her in close.

'But not for much longer,' she tells her. 'We'll all be out of here soon. Promise.'

* * *

The DVD that Harriet has chosen for them is *Toy Story*. Daisy blew a sigh of relief when she saw what it was. She had worried that it might be *Mary Poppins* or *Bambi* or any number of films dealing with family relationships. She's not sure how the other two girls would cope with something like that right now. *Toy Story* is more about friends, and that's okay. It's about trying to survive against impossible odds, just as the girls in this room are doing. And although there isn't much laughter going on at the moment, at least the film is keeping everyone entertained. For a short while, they can forget their problems.

On her chair in front of the television, Daisy thinks back to her conversation with Poppy. It was a gamble telling her about how long she's been trapped here, but she's glad she did. The honesty was a release. And she believed her own note of optimism when she voiced it. Together, the three of them are surviving. Perhaps they will do so long enough for someone out there to discover their whereabouts and rescue them. They will beat the odds, just as Woody and Buzz and their pals are doing.

Daisy turns to her right. Sees that Poppy is engrossed in the film, her eyes wide. There is no smile on her lips, but neither does she appear troubled.

Ellie silently joined them earlier, sitting some distance behind, but still wanting to take part. It showed Daisy that Ellie was becoming more aware of her surroundings. She's reluctant to swivel round and check on her now, for fear of breaking the spell. So she waits for the closing credits, the final sing-song. And then she turns.

To find that Ellie isn't there.

Ellie isn't in her chair because she is over at the chimney breast. She has a red crayon in her hand. She has drawn a massive picture across the wallpaper.

'Oh no!' says Daisy. 'No, no, no.'

She leaps out of her own chair. Races across to where Ellie is standing. 'No, Ellie!'

Ellie draws back, crayon still tightly clutched. Daisy stares at the girl's handiwork, expressed in a sea of red. She does not attempt to understand what she sees. Right now the message is less important than the medium. This is vandalism. This is devastation. All this redness is a beacon of alarm, of peril, of danger.

Just when things seemed to be going so well.

Daisy snatches the crayon from Ellie's hand and flings it across the room. She grabs Ellie tightly by her arms.

'Why, Ellie? Why did you do this? Why?'

It's a pointless question. She knows there will be no answer. Knows, too, that she has to find a way to fix this.

She pushes Ellie away, then dashes over to the sink. She doesn't know how much time she's got. The movie has finished, and Harriet and Malcolm could return at any minute.

She turns on the tap, soaks a flannel, runs back to the wall. She starts rubbing, and while she rubs she prays. Prays that this will work. Prays that someone up there will be on her side for once.

Some of the crayon comes off, but not all of it. Not enough. Daisy feels the panic setting in. Tears sting her eyes.

She goes back to the sink. Sees the water turn pink as she squeezes out the flannel.

She soaks it again and returns to the wall. More frantic rubbing, but now the wallpaper is beginning to come away. The top layer turns to mush and forms clumps beneath the facecloth.

'No!' she sobs. 'No.'

She continues rubbing, not knowing what else she can do. She rubs until her arm aches and she can no longer see through her tear-blurred eyes.

She steps away, sobbing.

She squeezes her eyes tightly shut, forcing out the tears. Please, she thinks, please let the wall look okay now. Please make it into something nobody would notice.

But then she opens her eyes and sees the mess. It couldn't be any more obvious. Her prayers have gone unanswered.

The other girls are staring at her now, waiting to see what she will do next, how she will fix this. They will be thinking that she always has a solution, that she will know exactly what to do.

But she doesn't. She has no next move.

And here come the footsteps.

Up the stairs . . .

Onto the landing . . .

Outside the door . . .

35

The bolts are drawn back. Poppy and Ellie continue to stare, as if willing Daisy to get a move on and sort out this mess before it's too late.

Daisy doesn't move. She watches the door swing open. Unaccompanied, Malcolm steps into the room, dartboard in hand. Initially he wears a smile, apparently excited to announce a new game.

His eyes are drawn immediately to the wall's angry red stain. His smile wilts and his shoulders sag. He puts down the darts and board, closes the door, then moves across the room. He seems oblivious to the children as he wanders past them and up to the chimney breast.

Daisy stares at the back of the man's misshapen head, wondering what thoughts are going through it, and how he will react. She cannot see his eyes at the moment, cannot tell if they have already misted over to signal a violent outburst.

'Who did this?' he demands.

Nobody answers. Nobody dares speak.

Malcolm turns his head to his left, drops his chin to focus his gaze on Ellie. It is clear he has his suspicions.

'Who did this?' he asks Ellie.

To her credit, or perhaps simply because she has lost the ability to care about her fate, Ellie locks eyes with him. She seems curiously unafraid.

Malcolm bunches his fists. He squares up to Ellie. He is Goliath to her David, but she has no catapult, no weapon of any kind. He could crush her tiny frame in an instant.

His voice booms. 'I want you to tell me who did this.'

Ellie stands her ground. It is almost as though she has already resigned herself to her fate.

Malcolm stretches out his arms. Rests his powerful hands on her shoulders. His fingers are so close to her slim white neck.

He takes a deep breath. 'I said—'

'Me! It was me.'

The words tumble out of Daisy's mouth. She sees how Poppy looks at her and opens her mouth to object, but Daisy shakes her head violently to cut her off.

Malcolm freezes, his damaged brain slow to deal with this unexpected input. Gradually he straightens up and takes his hands from Ellie. Then he turns to face Daisy.

'You, Daisy?' He points to the chimney breast behind him. 'You did this?'

'Yes.'

'Why? Why would you do such a thing?'

'I . . . I got upset. We finished watching the film, and then I wanted to draw. But Poppy and Ellie took all the paper, so I didn't have anything. I got in a temper.'

Her eyes flicker towards Ellie. She's not sure, but she thinks she detects a slight movement in her, as though she wants to intervene. Daisy wills her not to.

'You know what this means, don't you, Daisy?' says Malcolm. 'You know I have to punish you?'

Daisy nods. She expected nothing less.

Malcolm turns his gaze on each of the other girls in turn. 'You two. Get behind the curtain. Close it tight.'

Poppy starts across the room, but then halts between Daisy and Malcolm.

'You can't punish Daisy. She didn't do anything wrong. She—'

Daisy sees how Poppy's words are hitting Malcolm and stoking a dreadful fire within him. She leaps forward and wraps her arms around her.

'It's okay,' she whispers in Poppy's ear. 'It's better this way. I'll be all right, I promise.'

Poppy looks at her with wet eyes, but Daisy pushes her in the small of her back, urging her to do as she has been told.

Poppy moves towards the commode. She collects Ellie on her way, then draws the curtain on its rail, cutting off their view of what is to come.

Daisy awaits her fate. She watches Malcolm approach with his belt in his hand, and doesn't try to run away. He will do what he must, and any attempt to prevent it will only make things worse for all of them. Better to take her medicine and be done with it.

As he lashes her with his belt, he tells her things. He tells her he does this because she is loved so much, and that real love sometimes necessitates deep pain. He tells her that he hopes she understands. He tells her that it will bring the family closer. He tells her that it is for the best.

And while he says all these things, Daisy thinks about the picture that Ellie drew on the wall. A confusing blaze of red, like something burning fiercely inside Ellie's head. As with the silent screams, it had to be let out before she exploded.

And what gets Daisy through her ordeal is knowing that the pain she is feeling now is nothing compared to that which Ellie must be experiencing.

* * *

They come to her later.

When Malcolm has long gone, and the room is filled only with the sound of Daisy's soft cries, the youngsters hesitantly draw back the curtain and creep up behind Daisy.

She feels Poppy's touch first. A gentle stroking of the back of her hand. She blinks away her tears and forces out a smile of reassurance.

'What did he do?' Poppy asks.

'It's better not to know,' says Daisy.

'He hurt you. A lot.'

'Yes.'

Poppy whirls on Ellie standing behind her. 'This is *your* fault. *You* did this. Daisy keeps trying to help you, and you just keep making things worse. I hate you. You're a . . . You're a bitch!'

'Poppy, no,' says Daisy. 'She doesn't understand. She's been through so much.'

She stands with difficulty, wincing with the pain. She puts her arms out. 'Come here, you two. Give me a hug.'

They come to her, and she wraps an arm around each of them. They have changed things so much, these two. The way Malcolm and Harriet described Poppy's promised arrival almost made it sound exciting. At times she believed the presence of sisters would make life here much more bearable.

Now she believes the opposite. This isn't working. It was better when she was the only child. Poppy and Ellie's presence here has introduced only pain and turmoil.

More than ever, Daisy wants to go home.

She pulls the girls in tighter and starts to sing softly to them.

The song from *Toy Story*.

You've Got a Friend in Me.

36

Sometimes he finds it difficult to tear himself away from the job.

Like now, for instance. He could have gone home hours ago. Back to his little house and his pregnant, not-so-little wife.

But at this moment the Devlins need him more than she does. They need someone to talk to, to pour out their feelings to.

He can do that. He's a good listener.

The Devlins have had a lot to drink. Maria downed most of a bottle of red wine. She seemed to lose the equivalent amount of fluid through her tear ducts. When she could endure it no longer, she took herself off to bed, bouncing off the walls like a pinball as she went.

Craig has stuck to beer. Some cheap Spanish brain-pounder, straight from the bottle. He keeps repeating himself, including his offers of alcohol. Oxo is thinking of writing a note to say he doesn't want beer, and taping it to his forehead.

They are facing each other across the kitchen table. Over Craig's shoulder, Oxo can see the kitchen clock ticking away his life.

'I've never really liked coppers,' says Craig.

Oxo thinks about responding that he doesn't like insult-throwing drunkards, but restrains himself. What is it that makes some people think it's okay to slag off a police officer to their face?

'But,' Craig continues, 'you've changed my mind. All coppers should be like you.' He takes another gulp of beer. 'We can talk to you,' he says. 'Maria and I can talk to you. And that's important. It's important to talk.'

'Yes,' says Oxo. 'Yes, it is.'

'Do you think she's dead?'

It comes out of the blue. Direct and to the point.

Which leaves Oxo in a quandary. Because such an unambiguous question deserves an equally unambiguous reply.

It also demands honesty, and this is the problem. Because yes, on the balance of probabilities, Poppy Devlin is almost certainly dead. That's the truth of it.

But Oxo cannot deliver that message. Cannot give weight to what the man in front of him already knows. It is enough that he is already dissolving in his own tears.

He becomes suddenly agnostic. 'I don't know,' he says. 'I hope not. I like to think there's still hope.'

Craig raises his beer in the air. 'Bottle half full kind of guy, eh?' He takes a long swig, wipes his mouth with the back of his hand. Then he gets up from the table, looks out into the hallway, and closes the kitchen door.

He flops back into his chair. 'Man to man,' he says. 'Okay?'

'Okay,' says Oxo, unsure as to where this is leading.

'A man takes a kid, right? He breaks into her house and he takes her out of her own fucking bed. Right?'

Oxo says nothing.

'There's a reason for that. Has to be. And I've been wracking my brain for it. I have considered every possible reason. And I can only think of one.'

And now Oxo realises where this is going, and he wishes it would stop.

Craig says, 'Men do things like that, don't they? They do horrible, disgusting things. Sometimes I'm embarrassed to be a man. Do you know what I'm saying? Sometimes I'm ashamed of what we're capable of doing. To women. To kids.'

'Craig, we don't know—'

'But you do! You know. More than most. You know what men do to the young girls they snatch. And you know what? It's tearing me apart. God help me for saying this, but . . . I can tell you this, can't I? I can say this without you judging me?'

'You can say it.'

'It's just that sometimes . . . sometimes I wonder if it might be better if Poppy is dead.'

The words are out, because Craig needs them to be out. The relief opens the floodgate to a further cascade of tears down his cheeks.

'I mean, if the alternative is that she has to suffer, that she goes through pain, that she wishes she were dead, then . . . Do you understand? Do you get what I'm saying to you?'

Craig takes hold of Oxo's forearm and grips it hard.

'I can't say this to Maria. I can't say that it might be better if our only daughter never comes back to us. How can I say that? But it's what I feel.' He puts the bottle down, and then he starts banging his fists against his temples. His voice becomes shrill. 'I can't get the images out of my head. I can't stop seeing what this guy is doing to my daughter. And it's killing me. It's killing me.'

And then Oxo is out of his chair. He comes around the table. He puts his arms around this man and he holds him tightly while he sobs his heart out.

37

'It's all your fault.'

This from Webley, sitting next to Cody in an unmarked car on the way to Childwall.

'What is?'

'This! Van-checking duty. White van man isn't my favourite species in the first place, and for the last two days we've done nothing but look at vans and talk to their owners. I'm sick of it.'

'So how's that my fault?'

'Have you forgotten your little joke with Blunt? "We've got a lead," you said. "A dog lead."'

A smile breaks out on Cody's face. 'Oh, yeah. I did say that, didn't I?'

'Yes, you did. And I don't think Blunt saw the funny side. And now we're stuck with this rotten job.'

'Could be worse. If it hadn't been for my idea to talk to Quigley, we could be checking every white van out there.'

Webley lapses into silence. It's true that the scale of the task has been reduced, but Cody can't take all the credit. Grace Meade, for one, deserves some recognition. From the vehicle registration database she extracted entries for all medium-sized white vans registered in the Merseyside area. Next, she wrote some code to pick out all those cars with registrations that might have some connection with the word *DOGGY*, which naturally involved a lot of guesswork and creativity. The search terms she used included *DOGGY* itself, of course, but also *DOG*, *DGY* and anything else she could think of, such as *WOOF*, *BARK*, *WAG*, *K9* and even *GRR*.

'It's still a bloody long list of vans we've got to check,' says Webley, 'and that's just in Merseyside. What if the guy doesn't live in this neck of the woods? He could live in Harlech, or somewhere between Harlech and here, or anywhere else in the frigging country for that matter. We don't even know for definite that the guy who took Daisy is the same guy who took Poppy and Ellie.'

'So,' says Cody, 'by following this dog lead, you're saying we could be chasing our tails?'

Webley gives him a look that lets him know she's not impressed by his crap joke.

'Or, to put it another way,' Cody continues unabashed, 'we could really be barking up the wrong tree here.'

Webley shakes her head slowly in dismay. 'Have you finished?'

Cody takes a second to consider this. 'I haven't said anything about dogging yet. I wasn't quite sure how to work that in.'

'Well, don't even try. If you can be serious for one minute, have you given any thought to how many possible ways a car number plate could have some connection with dogs?'

'Actually, no, it's not something that keeps me occupied at nights.'

'And that's assuming Quigley's brain works like ours. Hell, the guy can't even spell. For all we know, the number plate he saw might have contained K-A-T. And then there are all the idiots who use black screw covers on their number plates to make one letter look like another. We've no hope of finding it if it's one of those.'

Cody glances across at her. 'You okay? Only you sound a bit . . .'

'A bit what?' she snaps.

'A bit out of sorts.'

'That's because I am.'

'Want to talk about it?'

'No.'

'Okay.'

'Yes,' she says.

'Yes, what?'

'Yes, I do want to talk about it. I've done something, and now I'm not sure I should have done it.'

'What have you done?'

'I've agreed to something.'

'Right. Care to elaborate?'

Webley hesitates. 'It's Parker. He phoned me again. He still wants to talk things over in person. So I've agreed.'

'Well . . . good. That's a great start.'

'Is it?'

'Yes. You know it is. Otherwise you wouldn't have agreed.'

'I'm not so sure. Sometimes I go along with things I shouldn't, just to keep others happy. It's my biggest failing.'

'Well, I wouldn't say it was your *biggest* failing . . .'

'Shut up, Cody. You're not helping.'

'Sorry. Okay, serious face on now. What's your plan?'

'Plan? What do you mean?'

'I mean what's your negotiating stance? What are your desired outcomes?'

She stares at him. 'Negotiating stance? Outcomes? Cody, what are you going on about? I'm having a friendly discussion with my ex-fiancé, not attending a G8 summit meeting.'

'All right, I'll put it another way. Do you want him back?'

Webley looks out of her side window for a few seconds. 'I don't know.'

'You don't know? Why don't you know?'

'I . . . I don't know why I don't know. Maybe I'm not missing him as much as I thought I would. Maybe I'm enjoying my independence. Maybe I think I could get a better offer.'

'Is that likely?' Cody asks.

Webley gives him her frostiest glare. It irritates her that, again, he's not taking her seriously. It further irritates her that she ever entertained the notion that a 'better offer' could come from Cody himself, because she certainly wouldn't want that to happen. Definitely not.

Cody seems to sense that he is dicing with death here – so much so that he doesn't even risk a pun about being in the dog house.

He says, 'Don't you think you need to make a decision about all that before you meet up with him?'

'I've made a hundred decisions since his last call, each one different from the last. The problem is I don't know what I want. I think I want to hear what he's got to say first. If he's an arsehole, I'm walking away.'

'And if he's not?'

Good question, she thinks. What if he's charming? What if he's delightful? What if he's all the things that made me want to become his fiancée in the first place?

'We'll just have to wait and see,' she says.

'What if – and I'm merely trying to get you to consider all the possibilities here – but what if he proposes again?'

'He won't.'

'But what if he does? What if he gets down on one knee and gives it the full Monty – ring and all?'

'He wouldn't do that. He wouldn't put me on the spot like that. Not after all we've been through. He wouldn't want to risk the embarrassment of me turning him down.'

'If you say so.'

'I do.'

Cody goes quiet again. But only for a short while. 'Where's the meeting?'

'I'm not telling you. You'll show up, just to enjoy the show. You'll probably even heckle.'

'All right, then. When is it?'

She decides that's not sensitive information. 'Friday.'

'Friday? I see. Who chose that?'

'Parker did. Why do you ask?'

She studies Cody's face, sees how difficult he's finding it to suppress an emerging smirk.

'What? What's got into you?'

'Friday. You know what day that is, don't you?'

'Yes, it's the day before Saturday. Cody, what are you—?'

'Valentine's Day. Friday is Valentine's Day. A special day for all love-struck couples.'

Webley's mouth drops. She stares at Cody for a full minute while he enjoys himself.

'Oh, fuck,' she says.

38

Malcolm hates it when people come to his door. They feel like unwelcome intruders. They never bring good news. Usually, they are just trying to sell something, or ask for charity. He doesn't give to charity; he has a fear that word will spread of his generous nature, and hordes of insistent do-gooders will come from far and wide to pester him.

He opens the door, just a few inches. Anything wider would appear too welcoming.

There's a man and a woman on his step. Young, and smartly dressed. Official-looking.

'Malcolm Benson?' says the man.

Malcolm doesn't like it when people know his name. It implies they have other information about him, and Malcolm likes to keep his life private. He also doesn't like the way the woman can't keep her eyes off his head injury, the cheeky bitch.

'Yes?' he says.

The young man holds up a small dark wallet. It contains a badge of some kind, plus an ID card with his photo.

'Police,' says the man. 'I'm Detective Sergeant Cody, and this is Detective Constable Webley. We've just got a few questions. Mind if we come in?'

Malcolm's mouth twitches. He has never had police at his door, and it worries him that they are here now. Did he make a mistake? Did he leave a clue at one of the houses?

And yet these two don't seem overly concerned about him. If they really suspected him of abduction and murder, wouldn't they be more heavy-handed? Wouldn't they have him in cuffs by now?

'What's it about?' he asks.

'Just routine. We're talking to a lot of people about a case we're investigating. Your name cropped up on a list, that's all.'

Malcolm relaxes a little. Routine, is what he said. Routine is nothing to get worked up about. It's just a coincidence.

But he really doesn't want them in his house, snooping around. He doesn't think he's left anything on show that would give him away, but he can't be certain. Did he put away the photograph album? Are any of the kids' clothes lying around? Harriet was doing some ironing earlier. Are those family DVDs still on the bookcase?

Harriet appears at his side. 'What is it, Malcolm? Who are these people?'

Go away, he thinks. I love you dearly, Harriet, but sometimes you can say or do the wrong thing.

'It's all right,' he says. 'Let me handle this.'

He turns to the officers again. Lowers his voice to a conspiratorial whisper. 'My wife suffers with her nerves. Can we do this another time? Perhaps when she's gone shopping?'

'It really will only take a few minutes,' Cody says. 'I promise we won't upset anyone.'

Malcolm realises they're not to be fobbed off, and that if he refuses to cooperate, he's only going to make them suspicious. But how to make sure it's safe to allow them in?

'Look, I don't mean to be funny or anything, but I hear a lot of stories about con men turning up and robbing people. And if you don't mind my saying, you look a bit young to be a detective sergeant. Mind if I take another look at your ID?'

Cody reaches into his pocket again for the wallet, opens it up and hands it across.

Malcolm squints at the identification. 'I need my glasses. Hang on.'

As he turns, he gives Harriet a look warning her not to question his actions or do anything silly. Then he goes into the house, still clutching the wallet.

His eyes scan the hallway. Nothing untoward here.

He does the same in the living room. Nothing here belonging to the children, or to indicate that they are in the house.

Just one more thing to do . . .

He moves over to the television. Leans across its top edge to look behind it. He hasn't had to use this for a long time.

It's a switch, screwed to the wooden shelf supporting the television.

He reaches behind the television. Flicks the switch . . .

* * *

The bedroom is plunged into blackness.

Or almost-blackness. A tiny red light on the wall flashes every few seconds.

'What happened?' Poppy shrieks.

'Hush!' says Daisy. 'Come over here, to the bed.'

'I can't see you. I can't see where I'm going.'

'Follow the sound of my voice. I'm just here. Walk slowly so you don't bump into anything. Keep walking.'

'Daisy. I can't . . .'

'We're just here. Reach your arms out.'

Daisy puts out her own arms. Makes contact with Poppy.

'That's it. Come here. Sit on the bed. Cuddle in with me.'

She puts her arms around the frightened young girls on either side of her.

'What happened?' Poppy asks again. 'Why did it go all dark?'

'See that little red light? That means it's Quiet Time,' says Daisy.

'Quiet Time? What's that?'

'It means we have to be very, very quiet. It's gone dark so we don't move about. It's very important that we don't make a sound. If we do, we'll be punished. We'll be punished really badly.'

'Like you were before?'

'Yes.'

'Why? Why do we have to be quiet?'

'We just do. It won't be for long. Stop talking now, and just sit here next to me.'

She doesn't give them a full explanation. She doesn't want them to be tempted to call attention to their presence.

She knows, though, that strangers have arrived at the house.

39

'You've got it nice in here,' says Cody.

He doesn't really think that. Yes, the living room is very tidy and clean, but the décor and furnishings are a bit dated for his liking. Stuff his mum and dad would have. Still, does no harm to be friendly.

He continues with the chit-chat: 'Just the two of you living here?'

'Yes,' says Malcolm. 'Just me and Harriet.'

'Kids flown the nest, then?'

'No. We never had kids. Never wanted them.'

Cody nods. 'Right. Well, we don't want to keep you any longer than necessary. As I said, we're just making some routine inquiries.'

He reaches into his pocket and takes out his notebook.

'According to our records, you're the owner of a Ford van, registration number . . .' He flips open his pad, finds the information he needs and reads out the number.

'Yes,' says Malcolm. 'Yes, that's right. Sorry, have I broken the law? Did I run a red light or something? Because I haven't had any letters about it.'

Cody smiles. 'Nothing like that. Actually, DC Webley and I are from the Major Incident Team. We're investigating some very serious crimes, possibly involving the use of a van like yours. All we're doing at the moment is going through our list, ruling out people where we can. I'm sure you've got nothing to worry about.'

Malcolm nods. Taking her cue from her husband, Harriet nods too.

They both seem nervous, but Cody understands their unease. They seem like a couple who like their peace and quiet. The very fact that they haven't wanted kids is indicative of that. They probably prefer to sit alone in front of their television, wearing their slippers and cradling their mugs of cocoa, and not being bothered by the outside world. The last thing they want is two coppers from a Major Crimes squad bringing the realities of death, destruction and mayhem into their oh-so-tidy home.

Webley says, 'Can you tell us why you own a van?'

Malcolm looks perplexed by the question.

'What I mean,' says Webley, 'is why a van rather than a normal car? Is it because of your business?'

'Oh,' says Malcolm. 'Yes. I'm a plumber. I don't do so much of it now, but I've still got the van.'

'You've retired?'

'Kind of.' He points to his battered skull. 'I had an accident.'

'I see. Do you drive the van much?'

'Not much. We've got a little Renault Clio too. We tend to use that more these days.'

'So when's the last time you used the van?'

Malcolm rubs his chin. 'Ooh, must have been just after Christmas. I took the Christmas tree away to be recycled, plus some other rubbish.'

'But not since then?'

'Don't think so. I've got a central heating job in Toxteth next week, though.'

Cody makes some notes. This one doesn't seem promising. If Benson is their man, it seems unlikely that he would tell such a barefaced lie. All it would take is one sighting from a neighbour of him driving his van off the premises, and his story would be in tatters.

'Ever been to Harlech, Mr Benson?' Webley asks.

Malcolm blinks. 'Harlech? You mean Harlech in Wales?'

'Yes.'

'Well, yes. I've been there. But not for a long time.'

'How long?'

'Years.' He looks at his wife. 'I don't think we've ever been there together, have we, love?'

Harriet shakes her head.

'So,' says Malcolm, 'it must have been at least thirty years ago when I was there.'

'But not since? Definitely not in the last five years?'

'No. I'm sure of that. We tend to stay in England for our holidays now. We like Cornwall and Devon.'

Cody snaps his notepad shut. 'Okay. I think that'll do us for the moment.' He sees the relief on the couple's faces, and then he adds, 'We'll just need to take a quick look at the van, if that's all right.'

'The van?' says Malcolm. 'You want to see it?'

'Yes. Is that a problem?'

'No. It's in the garage. I just . . . I just need to find my keys.'

He shambles off, heads upstairs.

Cody rocks on his feet, exchanges glances with Webley, smiles at Mrs Benson.

'Do you work, Mrs Benson?' he asks.

'Me? No. Not now. I used to be a nurse, but I had to give it up. Health problems.'

'I see,' says Cody. He wonders if she met her husband in the hospital when he was having his head seen to, but doesn't ask.

Malcolm reappears, jangling the keys in his hand.

'Found them. Haven't needed them for a while. Shall we go outside?'

He leads the way out to the front driveway, then to the garage. He reaches down, grabs the lever and pulls up the garage door.

There's a van in there, all right. It has the right number plate, too, the registration ending with the three letters 'PUP'.

There's only one problem.

It's black.

Cody moves into the garage, then circles the van. On its sides it has a gold sign for 'M Benson, Plumbing and Heating', followed by a phone number.

Cody takes a closer look at the paintwork. It is showing clear signs of aging, including numerous scratches and nicks. It certainly wasn't done recently as a cover-up job.

He says, 'I'm sorry, Mr Benson, but our records say that the van with this registration number is white.'

'Ah,' says Malcolm. 'Yeah. It used to be white. I had it resprayed. Thought it looked classier like this.'

'When was this?'

'Ooh, about four years ago. I think I've still got the invoice in the house if you want me to dig it out.'

'No, that's okay,' says Cody. 'You do know that you're supposed to inform the DVLA when you change the colour of your vehicle, don't you?'

'Am I? Sorry, I wasn't aware of that. Nobody's ever told me.'

Cody exits the garage. Takes one last look at the van. Sighs.

Another wasted journey, he thinks. If a van really was used for the abductions, it definitely wasn't this one.

40

The Bensons spend a good couple of minutes at their front door, reassuring themselves that normality has resumed. But when they retreat once more into their living room, Malcolm can tell that Harriet is still fretful.

'Oh, Malcolm!' she says. 'The police.'

'Stay calm,' he tells her. 'There's nothing to worry about. They've gone now, haven't they?'

'Yes, but . . . but why did they come here in the first place? Do they know about us? About the girls?'

Malcolm takes her in his arms. 'Hush now. They don't know anything. You heard them. It's the van. They're looking at vans. They're probably working their way through hundreds of them. Maybe even thousands.'

'Yes, but why? Doesn't that mean you were seen?'

Malcolm shakes his head. 'If they knew anything, they would have searched the house, wouldn't they? They're just poking about in the dark at the moment. Honestly, dear, it's just coincidence. They won't be back.'

'If you're sure.'

'I am.'

But he isn't really. He suspects that the police know a lot more than they were saying, and that worries him.

'The children were good,' says Harriet.

'Yes. Yes, they were. Maybe we should let them watch another DVD as a reward. Why don't you dig one out for them, eh?'

'Yes. All right. And then I'll put the kettle on. Can you end Quiet Time now?'

He nods. And while Harriet totters off, he goes over to the television and locates the switch hidden behind it.

He realises then that he hasn't explained Quiet Time to Poppy and Ellie. It's been a long time since anyone else has been allowed into the house, and so the necessity of informing them simply didn't enter his head. Daisy must have told the others what was going on, because there wasn't a peep out of them.

He doesn't want to think about the consequences if they had broken this particular rule.

* * *

The lights come back on. The red warning light no longer winks at them.

Daisy breathes a long sigh of relief. She had been so worried that one of the other girls would make a noise. She had put her arms around them not only to comfort them, but also to keep them in check.

'Can we talk again now?' Poppy whispers.

Daisy smiles. In a normal tone of voice she says, 'Yes, of course. It's all over.'

She lets her arms drop from the children's shoulders. Poppy slips from the bed and turns to face Daisy.

'I could hear voices,' she says. 'Downstairs. There were voices.'

Daisy knows there is no point in denying it. 'Yes. They had visitors.'

'What visitors? Who were they?'

'I don't know. It could have been anyone.'

'But why did we have to stay so quiet? What if we make a noise when there are visitors? Would they come upstairs? Would they find us? Would they take us back home?'

Daisy has wondered this herself. There has been only a handful of occasions during the past three years in which she has experienced Quiet Time, and on each occasion she has agonised over the choices available to her.

She has heard the voices. She has stared into the blackness and tried to picture their owners. She has put her ear to the floor in an attempt to catch their words, to determine if they are people who might be brave enough to intervene.

She has tried imagining what would happen if she were to stamp her feet on the floor or bang on the door and cry for help. She has imagined the visitors defying the Bensons and rushing to her aid, breaking down the door and taking her in their arms. She has imagined the tears of joy and relief, and the subsequent ecstasy of being reunited with her parents.

But the dark thoughts always intrude, swamping her optimism and depriving it of oxygen. They tell her of a different outcome: of the visitors being fobbed off with a simple lie, and walking away from this house none the wiser. And then they tell her of what would surely come next: of the bolts being drawn back, and the appearance of Malcolm, more angry and unhinged than ever before.

And when those images appear in her head, Daisy always resigns herself to erring on the side of caution. She remains still and quiet, waiting for the awful finality of the goodbyes and the closing of the front door on what may have been her only hope of freedom. And for days afterwards she will wonder what might have happened if she had acted differently, and it will continue to twist a knife in her belly.

So now she looks into the shiny-bright eyes of her questioner, and knows that she can't allow Poppy to suffer the pain of these decisions. It would be unfair to give her that power.

'No,' she says. 'They wouldn't take you back home. Malcolm and Harriet wouldn't let that happen. And if you ever break the rules at Quiet Time, they will be so angry they will cut off your legs so that you can never run away.'

She watches the fire die down in Poppy's eyes, to be replaced by the leaden greyness of despair and subjugation.

And Daisy hates herself for what she has just done.

41

Cody is beginning to think Webley might be right about this being a wild goose chase. The idea of checking out vans in the area doesn't seem to be getting them anywhere, and might even be distracting them from more fruitful lines of inquiry. Not that he can imagine what those other lines might be. They have so little to go on.

It's been a long day, and he's tired. Perhaps tomorrow will be better. Perhaps the break they need is just around the corner.

He enters his building on Rodney Street. Trudges up the steps to the first floor. Unlocks the door to his flat. Sets his alarm again before going up another set of stairs.

He goes into the kitchen first. Snaps on the light. His unwashed breakfast dishes are still on the draining board where he left them. He also sees the unwrapped loaf of bread that he forgot to put away, so that will be nice and dried-out now.

He sighs. Goes to the fridge. There are a couple of pork escalopes in here. He checks the best-before date, finds that it was two days ago. I'll risk it, he thinks. Two days isn't going to kill me.

Cup of tea first.

He closes the fridge door. Fills the kettle and switches it on. While it hisses and pops because it needs descaling, he starts to unburden himself of the objects in his pockets. He tosses his keys, wallet, notepad, pens, coins, phone, Polo mints and tissues onto the counter, then he takes off his jacket and tie and hangs them on the back of a chair. He returns to the counter, drops a teabag into a mug, pours boiling water onto it.

And then it hits him.

He moves along the counter. Scans his belongings.

Where's my ID?

He goes over to his jacket. Checks all the pockets. Nothing there.

Back to the counter. He moves the items about, looks under his wallet. Definitely not there.

So where is it?

He looks through the doorway into the hall. Could he have dropped it? Perhaps when he took his keys out at the front door? Surely he would have heard it fall? And besides, he keeps his keys and ID in different pockets.

Shit, he thinks. I'm in trouble if I've lost that.

Think, man! When did you last use it?

And then he remembers.

The last house they went to. What were they called? Oh, yes, the Bensons.

Mr Benson took his ID from him before disappearing into the house to examine it. Did he give it back, though?

Cody replays the episode through his mind. The more he does so, the more certain he is that Benson never handed it back. It wasn't even in plain sight in the living room.

That must be it, he thinks. I left it at the Bensons' house.

So I'll go round and pick it up in the morning.

Except . . .

I've got an early briefing in the morning. What if the Bensons aren't early risers? Or what if they leave the house even earlier than I do? I'll be in deep shit then.

Crap. I'll have to go now, otherwise I'll never relax. Besides, it's only a fifteen-minute drive away.

Cody grabs his keys, leaving the other items where they are. I'll only be gone for a short while, he thinks.

He leaves his jacket on the back of the chair too, but takes a fleece from its peg as he goes back into the hall.

As he heads downstairs, he allows his thoughts to drift back to the current case.

Where was I? he thinks.

Oh, yeah: I was hoping that the break we need is just around the corner.

42

He pulls up in his car. The house looks dark, unoccupied. He hopes they haven't gone away for a few days. All he wants is his warrant card. Then he can go back home and eat his pork escalopes and relax with a good book. Not too much to ask, surely?

He walks along the driveway. Knocks on the door. Waits.

He knocks again. Inside, a light goes on. Good, he thinks. They're still here.

The door opens. He hears Harriet's voice saying, 'Did you forget your—?'

Then she sees him. Her eyes widen. She looks startled.

'Oh,' she says. 'I thought . . . I wasn't expecting . . .'

'Sorry to bother you again, Mrs Benson,' says Cody. 'This won't take long. I think I may have left my warrant card here.'

'Your . . . your what?'

'My badge and warrant card. My identification. Do you remember? I was here earlier, and your husband took it into the house. I don't think he gave it back to me before I left.'

Harriet's lips quiver, but she seems to struggle to voice whatever it is she wants to say. Cody wonders why she appears so anxious.

'I . . . I think you must be mistaken. I haven't seen it anywhere.'

'Are you sure? It's in a small black wallet. It's got "Property of Merseyside Police" written on it.'

'No. I don't remember anything like that.'

'Then maybe your husband could tell us where he put it? Do you mind asking him for me?'

'He's out. He went to the shop. We're out of ketchup. He likes ketchup with his sausage and chips.'

She doesn't budge from the doorway, but she keeps turning her head to look back into the house, as though listening out for something.

Cody's radar pings. Something isn't quite right here.

He says, 'Do you mind if I wait for him then? We could have a quick look for it while we're waiting.'

She seems uncertain, but Cody knows she can hardly turn him down without appearing even more suspicious.

'I . . . I suppose that would be all right.'

She opens the door, allows him in. He sneaks a glance at her as he enters, notices that her eyes are turned up towards the ceiling.

What is she worried about?

He starts to move towards the living room, but Harriet overtakes him. She seems in one hell of a hurry. Cody picks up his own pace, and as he reaches the doorway he sees her straightening up by the television, a sheepish look on her face.

'Had a thought?' he asks her.

'Sorry?'

'About my ID. It looked as though something just occurred to you.'

'What? Oh. No. I was just turning the television off.'

Cody is convinced he hadn't heard the television when he came in. And even if it was on, why the sudden urgency to switch it off? Harriet doesn't seem the type to be watching porn movies.

'Oh, right,' he says with a smile. But he's even more intrigued now. The woman's behaviour is beyond strange.

'Shall we have a quick search?' he asks.

'Er, yes. Okay.'

He nods, smiles again. He starts moving around the room. He picks up cushions on the sofa, moves magazines on the coffee table, peeks behind the ornaments on the mantelpiece. Harriet's actions are similar, but her attention doesn't seem to be devoted to the task. Every time Cody glances across at her, he finds her eyes on him. It's almost as though there's something she doesn't want him to find.

He straightens up. Harriet does the same. They face each other across the room. Cody decides it's time he asked her some serious questions.

And then he hears it.

The thud.

From upstairs.

43

'What was that?' says Daisy in a harsh whisper.

'My book,' says Poppy. 'I dropped it. I'm sorry, Daisy. I didn't mean to.'

Daisy hears the sniffles starting. Poppy knows how serious this could be.

'It's okay,' she tells her. 'Maybe they didn't hear.'

'I'm sorry. It was an accident. I'm sorry.'

'Shush. Don't make it worse now. It'll be okay if we stay quiet.'

But she doesn't think it will be okay. She thinks they are in trouble.

* * *

'What was that?' says Cody, looking up.

Harriet follows his gaze. Her mouth works furiously again as she tries to find an explanation.

When their eyes meet once more, she says, 'The cat. He likes to sit on the windowsill. Makes a heck of a noise when he jumps down again. Sometimes he knocks things over, too.'

Cody nods slowly. He's not convinced, and he's finding it increasingly difficult to hide that fact.

'Mrs Benson—'

'Tea!' she says. 'Shall I make some tea, while we're waiting for Malcolm?'

She doesn't wait for his answer. She goes bustling out of the room, her cheeks red and blotchy.

Cody isn't quite sure whether he is meant to follow her out. He takes one last look around the room, then starts towards the door. Stops again when another thought strikes him.

He walks across to the television. It's a large flat screen device on a pine stand in the alcove. He looks over the top of the set to find the vents on the rear. He puts his hand to the vents. There's no residual heat.

And then he sees the switch. It's behind the television, fixed to the wooden stand. His eyes follow a cable leading from it to the wall. The wire travels up the corner of the wall, then disappears into the ceiling.

Was that what Harriet was doing? Flicking the switch?

He looks at it again. It's a simple toggle – on or off. What could possibly be its function?

It occurs to him to try it out, but then he decides better of it. Perhaps Harriet or Malcolm can enlighten him.

He takes a step back, still puzzling over the set-up here, and Harriet's bizarre behaviour.

Then something else catches his eye. There's a slight gap between the edge of the pine stand and the chimney breast. Where the gap joins the floor, something is protruding.

Cody bends down, pulls out the object.

It's the wallet containing his badge and warrant card.

Cody stands there for a few seconds, wallet in hand. The very fact it's here suggests that this was the first place Malcolm came to when he disappeared into the house. And now Harriet has just done the same.

So what is it about that switch? The switch that controls something above the ceiling.

From where the noise came.

Cody decides he's not going to reveal the fact that he has found his warrant card. Not just yet. Not until he's got answers to a few questions.

He slips the wallet into the pocket of his fleece, then heads out to the kitchen.

Harriet is only just filling the kettle. Cody wonders what she has been doing out here since she left him alone. Fretting, perhaps? Panicking?

'You okay, Mrs Benson?'

She jumps at the sound of his voice behind her, causing water to slosh over the sides of the overfilled kettle. Realising what she has done, she pours some of the water out before flicking the lid shut.

'Yes, yes. I . . . I forgot what I came out here for. It's my nerves. My brain doesn't work so well now.'

'Mrs Benson, where did you say your husband was?'

She switches on the kettle. 'The local supermarket. Ketchup. He went for ketchup.'

Not upstairs then? Why would she lie about that?

'So he'll be back in a minute?'

'Yes. Any minute now.'

She opens a cupboard. Takes down a box of Typhoo. 'How do you like your tea?'

'Milk, no sugar, thank you. Is there anything I can do to help?'

'No. That's all right.'

He notices her hand trembling as she takes out the tea bags and drops them into a teapot. She taps her fingers on the counter as she waits for the kettle to boil. She seems to be avoiding making eye contact with him.

Cody looks around the kitchen. It's neat and tidy. Unlike his own place, there are no unwashed dishes on show. Not even any washed ones. Everything has been put away. There are no empty shopping bags. No newspapers or mail. No . . .

No what?

What's missing?

His eyes dart as he tries to work out the thing that should be here but isn't. Why is he so sure that's the case? It's just a kitchen, isn't it, with everything a kitchen should have. Everything two human beings need.

Yes, human beings.

But not an animal. Not a cat.

Where are the cat's food and water bowls? Its litter tray? Its scratching post? Its toys? How can you own a cat and possess none of those things? There isn't even a cat flap in the back door.

'Excuse me, Mrs Benson,' he says, 'but do you mind if I use your loo?'

She almost drops the cup that's in her hand. 'My what?'

Cody points a finger upwards. 'Your toilet. Do you mind? I won't be a sec.'

He doesn't wait for her to think about it, to come up with an excuse. He just leaves the kitchen and heads for the staircase.

He hears her follow him into the hall. He turns and gives her another smile. 'Top of the stairs, is it?'

'Er, er, yes. On the left. The one with the light switch outside.'

'Thank you. Won't be long. How's that tea doing?'

He waits for her to slink reluctantly back into the kitchen, and then he starts up the stairs.

When he gets to the landing, he sees there are two doors to his left. Only one of them has a light switch outside. The other . . .

Well, the other is bolted.

Why would that be? Why on earth would anyone put bolts on a bedroom door? And on the outside?

The only reason that Cody can think of is to lock something in. Or someone.

Building a quick mental map, Cody realises that the bathroom is over the kitchen, and the locked room is directly above the living room. The noise he heard must have come from inside this bedroom.

Cody opens the bathroom door, then snaps on the light as he steps inside. He pulls the door shut with a slight slam. Stamps heavily across the tiled floor, whistling as he goes.

And then he sneaks back to the door. Opens it quietly.

He steps back onto the landing. Goes up to the other door – the one holding all the secrets. He puts his ear to it, but hears nothing.

He reaches up, carefully slides back the upper bolt. Then he does the same with the lower one. He grasps the doorknob. Twists it slowly.

He pushes the door open carefully, not sure what to expect.

It's black inside. If there *is* someone in here, why would they be sitting in the dark?

He reaches a hand to the wall. Slides it around until he locates a light switch. He flicks it on.

Nothing. Still pitch-black. He wishes now that he had put a landing light on. Only a faint gloom reaches him from downstairs.

He swings the door wider, blinks as he tries to adjust to the darkness. He takes a cautious step forward, then another.

The thing that immediately catches his attention is a tiny blinking red light. He can't make out what it's connected to. Presumably it belongs to a computer or other technical appliance, but it seems awfully high up.

He is more puzzled than fearful. There doesn't seem to be anybody here, but he can't quite work out what the purpose of this room is.

Maybe the Bensons are just weird. Maybe they really do have a cat, but they keep it confined to this room, along with its food and things.

Yeah, but that doesn't explain the locks, does it? Not unless this particular cat knows how to turn doorknobs. And why the red light? And what gives with the switch behind the TV? Is it the switch that causes the red light to come on? Is it a security system of some kind?

So many questions.

His eyes are beginning to make out vague shapes now, but they are just shades of grey against the black. Nothing he can define.

He decides it's time to go, before Harriet becomes suspicious.

And then he hears a rustle.

At least, he thinks he does. Was it? Did something move in here?

'Hello?' he whispers. And then slightly louder: 'Hello?'

But he gets nothing in return. Maybe it is a cat.

He shakes his head. You're spooking yourself, he thinks. Making up ghosts where they don't exist. Let's get out of here.

He decides he's going to ask Harriet about this room. Casually, of course. He'll say something like, 'I noticed you've got a room up there with locks on the outside.' And she'll laugh and give a perfectly reasonable explanation, the likes of which he can't imagine right now.

And then suddenly it all comes together. The explanation jumps into his head, almost blinding him with its clarity.

Why did I come here? he thinks. For my ID, of course. Yes, but before that. What was the original reason? It was to look for abducted children, wasn't it? And if you've got children who don't want to be with you, you need to lock them up. You need to put them in a room with locks *on the outside*. And if you don't want visitors to the house to suspect anything, you need a way of telling those children not to make any noise. You need a signalling system of some kind. Something that can be operated from downstairs. A *switch*.

Oh my God.

'You're here,' he breathes. 'You're here, aren't you? Poppy? Ellie?'

He waits. Gets nothing.

And then . . .

'Yes.'

A single word. Barely audible, yet shattering the silence. A word that changes everything, that brings with it a fundamental change of perspective. A word that charges Cody with alarm, with adrenaline, and with a renewed sense of danger.

He whirls too late, sees the silhouette in the doorway too late. Something comes at him in an arc, too fast to evade. It strikes him on the side of his head, and his world explodes in a fury of colour and pain. He feels himself falling, landing heavily on the carpeted floor. It's all he can do to raise his arms in protection, but it's futile. He hears an immense intake of breath – the kind that precedes an act requiring supreme effort.

And he hears one other thing.

It manages to penetrate just before the second blow lands, just before it seems to smash his skull into a million pieces, obliterating all his thoughts and hopes and memories and fears.

It's the sound of a child's cry.

PART THREE

44

Should've worn a hat, thinks Malcolm.

Not because of the cold. He has never in his life worn a hat because of the cold.

It's the stares.

People looking at his head as though they've never seen anyone with any kind of injury before. They wouldn't stare at a guy in a wheel-chair like that. They wouldn't think a woman on crutches was an object of entertainment and ridicule. But give them someone with a bulge in his cranium, and suddenly they've got something better than television.

He almost wishes now that he hadn't bothered going for the ketchup. The sad fuckers always seem to congregate at that mini-market in the evenings, buying their cans of ale and their packets of fags, their meals for one. And there's always a queue, mainly because the dozy staff don't seem to give a shit.

But he had to go. Bangers and chips aren't the same without a huge dollop of ketchup on the side.

He imagines that Harriet will have them cooking now. She said she would, and she always does what she says she's going to do. As soon as he walks through that door, the aroma of sizzling Cumberlands will assail his nostrils. She's that reliable. Always has been.

Chicken nuggets for the kids tonight. They like a bit of ketchup too, so that's another reason for the journey.

He sometimes wonders how things would have turned out if it hadn't been for the girls. He and Harriet experienced some tough times before that. Losing their jobs, medical treatments, their inability to conceive, depression – sometimes it seemed the whole world was against them. Their love for each other was severely tested.

Malcolm isn't quite sure whether he believes in God, but the children are certainly a miracle. He found them – or they were revealed to him – at just the right time.

They say the first child is the most difficult. You have no prior experience or knowledge. You have to learn as you go along. Of course, they are talking about natural childbirth, but the same applies here, doesn't it? In fact it's worse: there were no books or experts he and Harriet could consult before doing things their way. They could hardly go to a counsellor and say, 'We're thinking of having a child. Only it's someone else's child, and they won't be very keen on the idea. What do you recommend?'

He remembers that first abduction vividly. At the time he felt he knew what he was doing, but looking back he can see all the mistakes, all the unnecessary risks.

What did surprise him, though, was how compliant Daisy was – how readily she took his hand to be led away from the sand dunes. Yes, she fought a little at the end when she realised her mother wasn't in the car park, but for the most part she was so good. It was almost as if she *wanted* to be with them.

And the difference it has made to Harriet! She is so happy now, so content with life. Poppy is settling in nicely. And Ellie has got a few problems, but she'll come around. Give her time.

She saw a lot, that girl. Things she wasn't meant to see. That shouldn't have happened.

So, he thinks, what was it you were saying about the mistakes with Daisy? Wasn't this latest adventure the biggest mistake of all? Is it any wonder the police are on your tail?

He turns up the car radio to drown out these dark thoughts.

The police aren't on my tail. They were just doing their job. Everything is fine. Besides, there aren't going to be any more abductions now. Three children is enough. We've done our bit. Let somebody else share a bit of love if they care enough.

You can all go away and leave us alone now. Let us live our lives in peace.

He feels relieved when he turns onto his road. Sometimes his mind can get into arguments with itself. Now he just wants home and Harriet and the kids and sausages. Normal family life.

His anger resurfaces when he notices a dark car parked directly in front of his house.

He hates it when people park there. Not that he needs the space – he always puts his car on the drive or in the garage – but he still thinks it's a cheek. It's not even as if the whole road is full of cars: there's plenty of room to park elsewhere.

He wonders which neighbour it is, but he's not going to kick up a fuss. He could do without the extra tension in his life right now. If it becomes a habit, though, the car's owner might find an extra scratch or two on it.

He turns onto his driveway. Sets the handbrake and turns off the engine. Gets out of the car, ketchup in hand.

At the door, he uses his own key. No point summoning Harriet when she's busy cooking.

But then he opens the door, and wonders why he can't smell food.

'It's me,' he announces.

No answer. Something is wrong.

He hears a noise from the kitchen, so he goes straight there. Harriet is at the table, crying.

'Honey?' he says. 'What's the matter?'

He pulls up a chair next to her, puts the ketchup down on the table.

'What's up?' he asks again.

'Oh, Malcolm. I don't know what to do. I've messed things up. Promise me you won't be angry.'

'What do you mean, messed things up? What have you done?'

'Don't be angry with me. Please.'

'I won't be angry,' he says, but already he can feel the stress building inside. 'Now tell me all about it. Is it the girls? Have they been naughty?'

She shakes her head. 'No. It's not their fault. I tried my best, but I'm not very good by myself. I need you here, Malcolm. You deal with these things better than I do.'

Her sobbing increases. Malcolm wants to soothe her, but he also needs to get to the bottom of this. He wishes she would just spit it out.

'Harriet, what are you talking about? What things?'

'The . . . the policeman.'

It's not the word he was expecting, and so it passes through his defences and hits him between the eyes.

'Policeman? What policeman?'

'The one who was here earlier, asking about the van. Cody.'

'Well, what about him?'

'He came back. While you were out. Malcolm, I tried to stop him. I tried to tell him he needed to speak to you.'

'Why did he come back? What did he want?'

'He said he'd left something here. His identification – something like that. I don't know if it was true. I think he might have been lying.'

Malcolm thinks back. Tries to remember if the detective took his ID away with him. But it's all a blur, lost in the mists of his stress at the time.

'So what happened? What did he ask you?'

'Nothing, really. I don't . . . Oh, Malcolm.'

She sobs again. Malcolm grabs her wrist.

'Harriet, I don't understand. Why are you so upset? What did Cody do?'

'He *knows*. He . . . he went upstairs. I couldn't stop him. He found them. He found the girls.'

It feels to Malcolm as though his heart stops. What is she saying to him? What has happened to the girls? Why aren't police swarming all over the house right now?

'Harriet? What do you mean? Where is Cody now?'

She lifts her gaze. 'He's up there.'

Malcolm looks upwards too. His throat and mouth are suddenly parched. 'He's upstairs?' he croaks. 'With the girls?'

'Yes,' Harriet says, beginning to cry again. 'And I think he's dead.'

45

'What do you mean, he's dead? I only went out for a bloody bottle of ketchup. What the hell's been going on?'

'Don't shout at me, Malcolm. I didn't know what to do. He found the girls. I had to stop him.'

'Stop him how? What did you do to him?'

'I hit him. With the rolling pin.'

'And now he's dead? Are you sure?'

'Yes. I don't know. There was a lot of blood.'

'For God's sake, Harriet. You were a nurse. You of all people should be able to tell a dead person from a live one.'

'You're shouting again, Malcolm. Please stop being angry with me.'

He realises this isn't helping, so he takes a deep breath and counts to five.

'All right, Harriet. Here's what we'll do. We'll go upstairs, and you can check him over.'

'But if he's dead—'

'We'll worry about that when we get to it. One step at a time, okay?'

It occurs to Malcolm that it could be more of a problem if the detective is still alive, but he doesn't mention it.

'If you say so, Malcolm. Are you still annoyed at me? I didn't know what to do. I never know what to do when you're not here.'

'It's all right,' he says. 'You did the right thing. Now come on. Don't worry; I'll be with you all the way.'

He takes her hand, leads her out to the stairs. Starts to ascend. Behind him, Harriet makes small whimpering noises.

When he gets to the landing and sees the locked door, Malcolm wonders if he should have brought a weapon with him. But then if the policeman's as injured as Harriet says, he's not going to put up much of a fight.

Malcolm unlocks the door. As he opens it, he hears snivelling from the girls, which provokes more crying from his wife.

The door stops suddenly. Malcolm sees that it has caught against the feet of the prone figure. He steps further into the room to get a better look, pulling Harriet in behind him.

It looks as though the detective hasn't budged since Harriet assaulted him. The reason Malcolm knows this is the large halo of blood around the man's head. It has soaked into the carpet. Going to be a hell of a job to get that clean.

He looks at the girls. Daisy and Poppy are hugging each other on the bed, and risking the occasional glance down at the body. Malcolm sighs inwardly. He would have preferred them not to have witnessed this, but what's done is done.

Ellie, meanwhile, is behaving differently. She is standing over Cody, staring at his bloodied head.

'Move away, Ellie,' he tells her. 'Go on. Move!'

She shuffles backwards, her eyes still locked on the figure.

'Harriet, take a look at him.'

He realises he hasn't called her 'Mummy', as he usually does in front of the children, but it doesn't seem the time for niceties.

'Go on,' he says. 'He won't bite.'

Harriet creeps forward at a snail's pace. When she reaches the body, Malcolm balls his fists, just in case the bastard is playing dead.

Harriet sinks to her knees, puts two fingers to the side of the man's neck. Seconds later she looks up.

'He's alive. He's still alive, Malcolm. What do we do?'

All eyes turn on Malcolm. He feels the pressure of their expectation. He thinks, Why is it always me who has to come up with all the answers? Why can't somebody else make a decision for once?

Because they'd make a cock-up of it, that's why. Bad decisions are what got us into this mess in the first place.

Malcolm rubs a hand across the top of his head. Feels the bumps and indentations.

And then the man on the floor groans.

He emits a sound like a creaking door, followed by a cough. He tries to raise himself up. Daisy and Poppy crawl back to the far edge of the bed.

Not now, thinks Malcolm. I need more time. We can't rush into this.

'Harriet, get one of your syringes. We need to knock him out again.'

'But Malcolm—'

'Just do it!' Realising he is shouting again, he says, 'Please. Go and get the *medicine*.'

He puts emphasis on the last word, purely for the benefit of the children. Not that they are likely to believe their parents intend to help this guy – not after one of them just caved his head in.

As Harriet dashes away, Malcolm moves closer to Cody. He looks down on the man as the groans increase in volume.

I could crush him now, thinks Malcolm. I could place my foot on his neck and press until he can no longer breathe. It could even be classed as a mercy killing. The guy looks half dead as it is.

But then he notices the children watching him, waiting to see what he will do next. He thinks about what the murders of Ellie's parents did to her. And he has already talked about medicine, about helping. He can't now squash the man like an insect. What kind of lesson would that teach them?

'Be quiet,' he tells Cody.

The policeman groans again.

The girls on the bed shrink even further away. Ellie, on the other hand, takes a step closer again, her eyes greedy for the spectacle.

He could be dead soon anyway, thinks Malcolm. I wouldn't be surprised if he has a fractured skull. Maybe even brain damage. His brain could be swelling up inside his head right now. Just like mine did. Only this lad isn't going to get the operation he needs.

Malcolm feathers his fingers across his knobbly scalp again. Thinks what would have happened without his operation. His brain getting bigger and bigger inside that confined space, its tissues becoming more and more compressed until . . .

'Here,' says Harriet, breathless behind him. 'I've got it. I've got it.'

She brandishes a hypodermic as if it contains the secret of eternal youth.

'Give it to him, then.'

She looks down at the figure, again trying to push himself up from the floor. She seems reluctant to go anywhere near him.

'Malcolm, I . . .'

Malcolm sinks to his knees, starts to pull up Cody's sleeve. When Cody brings across his other arm to resist, Malcolm slaps it away.

'Come on now, Harriet. You can do this. Quickly!'

The command gives Harriet the impetus she needs. She dashes across to join Malcolm, then sinks the needle into Cody's arm and depresses the plunger.

'That's it,' says Malcolm. 'See? Wasn't hard, was it?'

Cody emits a moan, but his voice is fainter now. His eyelids begin to flutter.

And then he's gone again.

46

Daisy is terrified. For herself and Poppy, but less so for Ellie. Ellie is dealing with this differently: she seems morbidly fascinated by the whole affair.

Daisy knew something was wrong as soon as she heard the bolts being drawn back during Quiet Time. Prior to that, she had detected footsteps on the staircase, and then the bathroom door being closed. She expected that to be followed by the sounds of the toilet flushing, the taps running, the door, and then a journey back down the stairs.

So when she heard the bolts sliding out of their recesses ever so quietly, she feared the worst.

She assumed it was because of Poppy dropping the book. She expected it to be Malcolm or Harriet at the door, sneaking in to warn them not to make any more noise or else the repercussions would be fierce.

But then her mind started playing tricks on her. Nobody had ever come into their bedroom like this before. In the blackness, the slow grinding of the metal bolts scraped along her nerves.

She shuffled off the bed. Poppy's mattress was occupying the gap between the bed and the wall, so she slid it forward and dragged the other girls down into the space she had created. They remained hidden there, staring fearfully in the direction of the door.

Daisy heard the knob turning. Then the door swung open.

The faint silhouette of the man in the doorway was unfamiliar to Daisy. As she stared at the dark shape she tightened her embrace on the girls. She tried to control her breathing, to keep it inaudible, while praying that the other two would have the sense to do the same.

When he eventually spoke, she tried to use his voice to build a picture of him, but her fears insisted on endowing him with a malicious grin and eyes thirsty for blood.

She kept quiet, knowing that even if this interloper did not wish them harm, Malcolm would.

But then he asked his question. Queried their presence. He sounded concerned, compassionate. She was tempted to answer, to plead for his help, but she knew it would be a dangerous mistake.

And then Poppy took it out of her hands. Snatched away their safety in one breathy word.

Daisy clamped her hand over Poppy's mouth. Stared wide-eyed as the shadow veered towards them like a monster suddenly aware of its prey.

And then the other, more recognisable shape appeared in the doorway. Silent and deadly, it struck like a viper. The blow was like a whip-crack in the stillness, and the vague figure collapsed to merge with the inky blackness beneath it.

When Harriet raised her arm again, Daisy and Poppy cried out as one, but still the weapon was brought down without mercy.

Harriet disappeared then, like an assassin in the night. She locked the door, leaving her children with the remains of the thing she had destroyed. Daisy and her young charges cowered, trembled and cried, not understanding what had happened, and not knowing what to do if the creature were to come back to life and claim its revenge.

When the light came back on, it blinded Daisy at first, before stinging her with the viciousness of what it revealed. She saw that the intruder was just a man, blood puddling around his head, and she believed that he was dead.

What was worse was the notion that he had come to save them. Why else would he be attacked so violently? And if that were the case, what if she had acted differently? What if she had shouted out a warning when Harriet turned up?

Regrets again. They are destroying her.

But that was then and this is now. And now she knows that at least the man has survived. She has not witnessed someone being slaughtered.

It does little to dispel her distress. Though not dead, he seems on the edge of it. And despite what Malcolm said about 'medicine', it seems to Daisy that the man's welfare is the last thing on the minds of the couple. They are afraid, she can tell. And they are acting out of self-preservation. Even Daisy can sense the primitive instincts in play, as though they are cave dwellers who have managed to trap a ferocious wild animal.

It makes her wonder how long they will allow the poor beast to live.

47

'Check his head,' Malcolm says.

'What?' says Harriet, still a-flutter.

'The wound. On Cody's head. Where you cracked him one. Take a look at it.'

Harriet shifts her body, then leans forward and parts Cody's hair with her fingers as she examines him.

'It's not bleeding as much, but it's an open wound. It'll need stitching.'

'Has he got a fractured skull?'

'It doesn't look like it, but I can't be certain. Not without a proper scan.'

'Well, that's not going to happen, is it? Not unless a brain scanner is something I can knock together in the garage.'

Harriet looks at him, her lower lip quivering, and he realises his sarcasm isn't helping.

He says, 'Move over, Harriet. Let me check his pockets.'

He digs a hand into Cody's fleece. He pulls out the ID wallet and opens it up, then frowns at his wife.

'I thought you said he came back here because he'd lost his ID?'

Harriet looks back at him as though she's been caught out. 'He did. That's what he told me. Do you . . . Do you think he was lying?'

'Looks that way, doesn't it?'

Malcolm pushes the warrant card deep into his own pocket, then examines the other side of Cody's fleece. Finding a car key, he stands up and moves towards the door.

Harriet watches him in alarm. 'Where are you going?'

'Cody's car. I need to move it.'

'But . . . we'll be alone.' She gestures towards Cody. 'With him.'

Malcolm holds up an open palm. 'You'll be fine. Just keep an eye on him. I'll be back in a few minutes. While I'm gone, put some stitches in that head of his.'

'But Malcolm . . . Malcolm . . .'

He is already out on the landing, but Harriet chases after him.

'Malcolm,' she pleads again.

He halts at the top of the stairs. Waits while Harriet closes the bedroom door.

She lowers her voice to a whisper. 'Are we . . . I mean, do we have to keep him here?'

'What do you mean?'

'Can't we . . . get rid of him?'

Malcolm stares at her. 'This isn't like Ellie's parents. They attacked me. I had no choice.'

She sidles up to him. 'I know, but . . . do we have a choice now? He could ruin everything.'

Malcolm takes hold of her arms. 'He won't ruin a thing, I promise you. I won't let that happen. If I have to get rid of him, I will, but right now I need time to think. I need to work out what's going on here. Do you follow?'

'Yes. I know you'll do what's best, dearest. You always do. I just don't like the thought of him in the house.'

'I know, and I understand. Just trust me, all right, my angel?'

She nods. 'All right.'

'Good girl. Now go and stitch him up, and make sure you don't say anything to the girls about who he works for.'

With that, he leaves her.

* * *

Outside, Malcolm pauses for a moment, takes deep lungfuls of the cool February air. He pictures it filling his whole body, swirling around his head and clearing his thoughts. It seems so muddy up there at the moment. There are too many questions clogging it up.

He doesn't like the way his world has been so abruptly turned upside down. Things had been going smoothly. He had watched all the news reports, and there was nothing in there to suggest the police might be on to them.

But now this. It's a catastrophe. Their quiet family life, shattered.

What does it all mean?

He knows he nearly lost it back there. He became aware of that spongy sensation that precedes his detachment from reality. He knows he was on the verge of adding to the violence that had already taken place. If he had not pulled back from that precipice, Cody's lifeless body might have ended up in the boot of his own car.

Which could still be the eventual outcome, of course.

For now, though, Malcolm needs to take stock. He has a good brain – hasn't he already proved that with his research on the children? – but its cogs turn slowly. He has to analyse things with patience and care, to consider all the possibilities and their ramifications.

He walks up his driveway and out onto the street. It's not late, but it's already dark. The detective's car sits there like a tethered dog waiting patiently for its owner to return. Malcolm knows it can't have been there long, and that it's unlikely anyone will have noticed it.

He unlocks the door and climbs in. Takes a minute to study the unfamiliar controls before starting up the engine. He doesn't worry about leaving fingerprints or other trace evidence. This car won't be seen again.

He drives off carefully, sticking to the speed limit and small side roads. He knows that major highways have special cameras that can scan car number plates, and he has to hope that Cody's vehicle wasn't spotted on its way to the house.

It's only a short drive, but it gives his mind time to return to its many questions.

Two visits in one day, from the same copper.

Why?

The first time could have been coincidence. Perhaps the neighbours of one of the girls really had noticed a white van, and that's why the police were checking on similar vans in the area.

But then again . . .

There must be thousands of vans in Merseyside. They weren't intending to check them all, surely? They must have other information.

But what could that information be?

And then the second visit. Unannounced, and when Malcolm was out of the house. It's almost as if the timing was deliberate. Did the copper realise he was more likely to be successful with him out of the way?

Why come back at all? Did he spot something the first time round? Was something said that aroused suspicion?

Cody claimed he'd left his ID card, but that was clearly a bald-faced lie. The thing was in his pocket. Why did he need to be so underhand about his reasons for this latest visit?

Malcolm realises he needs to ask Harriet more questions. What exactly was said? What provoked Cody to go upstairs and search for the children?

And if he had suspicions about them even before he came to the house, why did he come alone? Why didn't a full army of coppers come banging on their door?

What worries Malcolm most is the idea that this could still happen. Police officers don't work in isolation; they operate as a team. They talk to each other; they share intelligence; they distribute tasks. Cody can't be a maverick enforcer. There must be others who are aware of his actions.

So when will they smell a rat? When will they come looking for their colleague?

Malcolm needs answers to all these questions.

After that, Cody becomes dispensable.

* * *

He arrives at the lock-up garage within minutes. It will mean a long walk back, but that's okay. More time to clear his head.

It's a large garage, with room for two vehicles. Malcolm started renting it years ago, back when the decision was made to have children. It was all part of the plan.

Leaving the engine of Cody's car running, Malcolm gets out, unlocks the garage door and raises it.

He gets back into the car, then drives it neatly into the free slot. Nobody will find it here.

After he has locked up the car, he takes a quick look at the vehicle parked next to it.

The white van.

Malcolm's father gave it to him, years ago when the old man became too infirm to work. It's still registered in the name of his dad, who lives down in Shrewsbury. Malcolm never told him he'd bought another van.

This is the van he used for the children.

There is bound to be all kinds of incriminating evidence in it, which is why he has used it only for his missions. Keeps the risk down. The two coppers certainly didn't seem to be aware of this vehicle specifically.

And it should be almost impossible to trace back to him. Even if it has been seen at the scenes of the crimes, the extra precaution that Malcolm has taken should keep him safe.

The fake registration plates.

Looking at the van, he realises he forgot to detach them after the stressful episode with Ellie and her parents.

He does so now. Unlocking the back of the van, he tosses them inside.

He chose the characters on the plates completely at random. Nothing that seemed to be an obvious word.

The last three letters are ODY. It never occurred to Malcolm that a simpler mind might read them as 'Odie'.

The name of the dog in the Garfield cartoons.

48

Daisy forces herself to watch.

She doesn't know why, but she feels she needs to know that the man is being properly patched up. She doesn't trust Harriet to do the right thing, despite the strict instructions handed to her by Malcolm.

The other girls have their own coping mechanisms. Poppy turns away completely and covers her ears, obviously fearful of hearing any signs of pain. Ellie, on the other hand, stands as close to the body as she can get, her eyes wide.

Daisy grimaces as Harriet pulls the edges of the wound apart and squirts a syringe of fluid into it. She wonders if that's bone she can see beneath the skin.

She grimaces even more when Harriet begins stitching. For some reason, she expected it to be totally different from stitching material – perhaps involving some clever device. But no, it is still with a needle and thread.

It's done in seconds. It doesn't look pretty, but at least the wound is closed.

An image flashes into Daisy's mind. She once owned a teddy bear that had a line of dark brown stitches on its head, just like these.

But that was three years ago. When stitches in the head meant something to cuddle.

When she has finished, Harriet closes up her medical kit, then gets up from the floor and plonks herself down on one of the kids' plastic chairs. She wipes her brow with a shaky hand. She looks ready to burst into tears.

Daisy knows what she has to do.

She slides off the bed. The other girls turn to watch her, puzzled by her actions.

Daisy pulls up a chair next to Harriet. She watches her for a second, then reaches out and grasps Harriet's hand in hers.

The simple act prompts Harriet to find a small smile, but also causes a tear to slide down her cheek.

'Are you all right, Mummy?' says Daisy.

She hates using the terms 'Mummy' and 'Daddy', but she knows how much it pleases them, and now is the time to get in their good books.

'I'm all right, Daisy. I didn't mean to . . . I didn't want you girls to . . . Never mind.'

Daisy leans her head into Harriet's arm. Leaves it resting there for a minute. She can see the other girls glaring at her, challenging her treachery.

She raises her head again. 'I'm sorry, Mummy,' she says. 'It was an accident. I dropped my book.'

She hears an intake of breath from Poppy, the real guilty party. Then Harriet looks down at her.

'It's all right, Daisy. I don't think it matters. I think he would have found you anyway.'

'Who is he?'

'I . . . I can't say. Just a bad man.'

'What's going to happen to him?'

Harriet stares at the body on her carpet, as though trying to divine the answer for herself.

'I don't know. Your father will decide.'

Daisy waits another few seconds. Then: 'Mummy . . . You won't tell Daddy, will you? You won't tell him about the noise I made? He'll be very cross, and he'll punish me again.'

Harriet shifts her gaze to Daisy. Looks at her long and hard. 'Like I said, I think the man would have found you anyway. Daddy doesn't need to know about the noise.'

For the first time since she was brought to this house, Daisy flings her arms around Harriet.

'Thank you, Mummy,' she says. 'I love you.'

The words make her want to vomit. She doesn't love this woman. Doesn't love anything about being here. What seems strange to her is how much the arrival of the two other girls has caused her to realise this. She had settled into a path of minimal disruption: obeying orders in a robotic way simply to lead a quiet life. The girls have heightened her perception of the danger present here. She needs to up her game to survive. She needs to lie, to cheat, to manipulate.

And so, as she hugs this woman, what makes it bearable is imagining she could squeeze the life out of her. She could crush her so hard she wouldn't be able to breathe. And then Daisy would be free.

She hears a noise from downstairs.

Malcolm has returned.

Daisy releases Harriet. She looks into her eyes fearfully and wonders whether she sees a little of that fear reflected back.

She gets up from her chair and returns to the other girls. It is as if the arrival of Malcolm tips a balance again. Redraws the line in the sand between friend and enemy.

Harriet seems to recognise this. She too gets out of her chair. She pushes and prods at her greying hair. Tries to appear presentable and collected.

Malcolm doesn't come straight up. Daisy can hear cupboard doors being opened and closed downstairs, heavy items being moved around. She wonders what he's up to.

And then the heavy thud of his boots on the staircase.

When he appears in the doorway, Daisy sees that he is carrying a large toolbox.

In the other hand, he carries an implement that Daisy remembers her real father using.

It's an electric saw.

49

When Malcolm looks at the body of the stranger, it seems to Daisy that he regards him as a mere blot on his carpet. He exhibits no sympathy for the man he referred to as Cody, no concern for his well-being.

He nods at Harriet. 'Everything okay?'

'Yes. I did what you asked. I mended his head.' She gestures meekly towards the items Malcolm is carrying. 'What are you going to do with those?'

Malcolm ignores the question. 'Has he given you any trouble?'

'No, no. He hasn't moved an inch since I injected him.'

'Good. Good.'

Malcolm puts the tools down on the floor, then leaves the room. Daisy looks at each of the other girls. Ellie sits cross-legged on the bed in Buddha-like silence. Poppy is shivering with fear, so Daisy takes her hand.

When Malcolm returns, he brings with him a chair and a power drill. The chair is wooden, with arms and a green padded fabric seat.

'That's one of our kitchen chairs,' says Harriet. 'Why have you brought that up?'

'He needs to sit somewhere,' Malcolm says.

The terse reply only confuses Harriet. Daisy can see it on her face.

Malcolm puts down the chair then moves to the toilet area. He draws back the curtain on its overhead rail, picks up the commode and lugs it across the room.

Poppy leans towards Daisy and whispers in her ear. 'That's our toilet. What's he doing with our toilet?'

Malcolm grabs the chair, then shifts it to where the commode was. He opens up the toolbox and rifles through it noisily, tossing out various screws and bits of metal.

He retrieves the drill next, and plugs it into a wall socket. Placing an L-shaped bracket against one leg of the chair, he fires a screw into it.

'Malcolm!' cries Harriet. 'That was a perfectly good chair.'

'I'll get you another one. I need to do this.'

He drives another screw through the bracket, but this time vertically, into the wooden floorboards beneath the carpet. Daisy can see Harriet cringing at the damage being done to her home.

When he has finished securing one leg, Malcolm moves on to the others, anchoring each firmly to the floor. He takes hold of the chair and tries to shake it from side to side. When it doesn't budge, he grunts in satisfaction.

Next, he picks up the electric saw. Plugs that in, too. He positions the serrated blade over the padded seat.

'Malcolm!' Harriet says again, but this time he just glances at her before continuing with his labours. The saw whirrs into life, cutting a circular hole in the seat without effort.

'I don't understand,' Harriet says as Malcolm collects his tools together. 'Why did you do that?'

'In case he has to go,' says Malcolm.

'Go where?'

'*Go*. In case he has to *go*. I'm going to put a bucket beneath the seat.'

Enlightenment dawns on Harriet's face.

Daisy watches as Malcolm goes to the body. He bends forward and pulls Cody into a sitting position, then puts his hands under his armpits and drags him across to the chair. Once there, Malcolm gasps and groans as he hefts the unconscious form onto it. The man's head and limbs loll around like he's Pinocchio.

Malcolm removes Cody's shoes. He pauses, a puzzled expression on his face. He rolls down Cody's sock, slides it off his foot.

'Ohmygosh,' says Poppy.

Daisy sees it too. The pink scarred flesh where the two smallest toes should be.

Malcolm removes the other sock. Two missing toes here as well.

Daisy sees how Malcolm looks to his wife for an explanation and receives only a shake of the head. How does such a thing happen? How does anyone lose the same two toes on each foot?

Malcolm replaces the socks, then looks again in his toolbox. He brings out a collection of nylon ties, then spends the next few minutes binding Cody's ankles to the chair legs and his wrists to the wooden arms.

He looks across at Harriet. 'Have you got some cotton wool in that first aid kit?'

Harriet doesn't question him this time. She opens up the box, finds some, and passes it across.

Malcolm rips away some of the cotton wool, forms it into balls and begins stuffing it into his prisoner's mouth. Daisy feels sick at the idea of all that moisture-sucking material filling her own mouth. She is certain it would make her throw up.

Harriet seems to have the same thought. 'Malcolm, he might choke.'

'He'll be all right,' says Malcolm, but he halts anyway. He takes a roll of wide silver duct tape, snips off a section, and fastens it across Cody's mouth.

Finally, Malcolm steps back and admires his handiwork.

'There. He's not going anywhere.'

Daisy doesn't like the sound of this. It implies he could be staying here for some time. She exchanges glances with Poppy, whose expression suggests she is contemplating the same thing.

Malcolm starts packing up his tools. When he is done, he takes a last look at Cody's slumped form before pulling the curtain around him.

He stands in front of the three girls, his face grim and hard. 'I'm only going to tell you this once. You stay away from that man. He is a very, very bad man. He is evil. You saw his feet, right? They are a sign. When you make a deal with the Devil, he takes some of your body parts in payment. Somehow this man found out about you, and he wants you for himself, but he won't look after you like we do. He wants to keep you in his prison. He wants to hurt you and make you do horrible things. He might even kill you if he gets a chance. So you mustn't go near him. You mustn't try to speak to him. Do you understand me?'

Daisy and Poppy nod in unison. Ellie just stares.

As Malcolm moves towards the door, the heads of all three girls turn towards the curtained section of the room. Daisy knows they are all thinking about what lies behind that thin veil of material.

Harriet picks up her things and trails after Malcolm. Before she disappears, she takes a long look at the girls. Daisy thinks she sees pity in her eyes.

But then she leaves too, locking her daughters in with the Devil's companion, as though offering them up in sacrifice.

50

Once he has put his tools away, Malcolm finds Harriet waiting for him at the kitchen table. He thinks she looks smaller than usual. Small and uncertain and fragile. He goes to her.

'What's the matter?' he asks.

She takes a while to find her words. 'I don't like this, Malcolm. I don't like the thought of that policeman in our house. What if there are others? They could be on their way now. What if they find him, and see what we've done? How will we protect the girls then?'

He takes her hand. 'Hush now. It'll be all right. We need to talk to this Cody bloke, don't we? We need to find out exactly why he came here. That's why we can't . . . you know . . . get rid of him. Not just yet. Let's find out what he knows first.'

'But how long will that take? Are you really going to keep him shut in there with the girls?'

'What choice do we have? He can't go in our bedroom, and there's no space in the study. Besides, all my research is in there, and I can't risk him seeing that. The girls' bedroom is the only room that's secure and sound-proofed. If he gets out of that chair, there's nowhere for him to go, he can't attract attention and he's got a 24-hour guard. The girls will soon let us know if he tries anything.'

'They'll be frightened. You told them he's evil.'

'I had to. They need to be frightened of him. They need to stay away from him. He'll poison their minds. He'll make them hate us. You don't want that, do you?'

Harriet looks horrified. 'No. No, I don't want that. But it's so cramped in there now. It used to be just Daisy, but now there are four people. I know it's a big room, but it's getting ridiculous.'

'It's temporary. Cody will only be there for a short while. And in the longer term I'll convert the study so that one of the girls can move in there. Stop worrying.'

He allows her time to calm down a little, and then he says, 'Can I ask you a question now?'

She sniffs, nods.

'What exactly did Cody say to you when he arrived?'

'I told you. He said he'd lost his – what do you call it? – his warrant card. He said he must have left it here.'

'And you hadn't seen anything like that lying about?'

'No. I would have remembered.'

'But he wouldn't take no for an answer?'

'No. He was adamant. He said you must have put it somewhere when you brought it into the house.'

Malcolm frowns as he tries to cast his mind back to that first visit. He remembers having it in his hand when he rushed into the living room, but that's about it. He has no recollection of handing it back, and yet he must have done. Either that or he left it in plain view for Cody to pick up again.

He digs into his pocket, pulls out the ID wallet.

'This was in his fleece. That means he was lying to us. Why would he lie? Why would he need to make something up to come back to the house?'

'I don't know.'

'He didn't give you any clue? Didn't ask any questions that sounded a bit suspicious to you?'

'No. All he talked about was the warrant card. He said that he'd wait for you to get back so he could ask you about it.'

'That was *his* idea? You didn't suggest it?'

'No. I wanted you back. I was desperate for you to come home and get rid of him, but I didn't ask him to wait.'

Malcolm tries to make all this fit together in his head. What was Cody up to? Why weren't Harriet's answers good enough for him?

'All right, so what happened next?'

'I . . . I went to make some tea.'

'You left him alone?'

'Only for a few seconds. Then he followed me into the kitchen.'

A surge of annoyance hits Malcolm, but he doesn't give voice to it. Leaving Cody in the living room was a big mistake.

But what could Cody have found there anyway? If he really was there for only a couple of seconds, as Harriet claims, what harm could that have possibly done?

'And then what?'

'He said he wanted to use the toilet.'

'What, just like that? Totally out of the blue?'

'Yes. One minute he was standing there talking to me while I made tea, and the next minute he was desperate for the loo.'

'And you let him go up there?'

'What else could I do? How could I say no? Wouldn't that have looked really odd?' She casts her gaze down. 'I thought he would just use the loo, and that would be that. I heard him go in there. I heard his feet on the bathroom floor.' She lifts her eyes to Malcolm again. 'But I knew I still had to take precautions, Malcolm. I picked up the rolling pin, and I went and stood at the bottom of the stairs, listening. I heard him quietly open the door and sneak out. And then I heard him go into the girls' bedroom, so I went up there. I did the right thing, didn't I, Malcolm? I did what you would have done?'

She is desperate for his support, so he gives it. 'Yes, Harriet. You did a good job.'

He thinks again about the events as Harriet has described them. There has to be something missing. Why the implausibly sudden excuse of a full bladder? Had Cody always intended to use this as a way of getting upstairs, or did the urge to do so come to him when he was already here in the house?

He says, 'I'm going to ask you something now, Harriet, and I want the truth.'

Her eyelids flutter. 'Of course, Malcolm.'

'You did flick the switch for Quiet Time, didn't you?'

'Yes. It's the first thing I did. I went straight into the living room and did it, even before the policeman came in.'

'Okay, good. And the girls? They stayed absolutely quiet?'

'Yes.'

'Are you sure about that? They didn't make even a slight noise?'

Another flicker of her eyelids as she hesitates. 'No. Not a peep out of them. I'm certain.'

Malcolm studies her face, waits for the cracks to show.

And then he thinks, What does it matter? What's done is done. Catching Harriet in a lie, punishing the kids – what good will that do?

'All right, Harriet,' he says calmly. 'Let's leave it there. I'll talk to Cody in the morning. We'll clear up this mess. Don't you worry about it.'

Harriet gives him a smile, but it is weak and unconvincing, as though she is still troubled.

'Malcolm?'

'Yes, my darling?'

'What if . . . what if he's not there in the morning? I mean, what if he dies? What if I've hurt him really badly, or he chokes on his own vomit? What then?'

'Well, then, he'll have brought it on himself. We didn't invite him here, did we? He came poking his nose in where it wasn't wanted, and so he'll have to suffer the consequences.'

'And you won't blame me?'

He rubs the back of her hand. 'We're family, Harriet. Family comes first. Anyone who tries to break us up will get exactly what's coming to them.'

51

Daisy and the other girls don't move for a long time. They sit together on the bed, all facing in the same direction, staring at the birds and flowers on the curtain, the bright pattern belying what it screens from them.

'I'm scared,' says Poppy.

Daisy looks at her, sees her shining, wet cheeks and the way she is wringing her hands.

'He can't hurt us. They put him to sleep.'

'But what about when he wakes up?'

'You saw. They tied him up. He can't get out of that chair.'

'But what if he does? They said he came to take us away so that he can put us in a prison and do horrible things to us.'

'He can't do that. If he tries to escape we'll hear him, and we can buzz for Malcolm to come back up and sort him out.'

'But what if he gets out while we're asleep? He might kill us or eat us.'

Daisy forces out a laugh intended to reassure. 'He's not going to do that. Stop worrying, Poppy.' She looks across to Ellie at the foot of the bed. 'You're not scared, are you, Ellie?'

Ellie gives no indication that she has heard. She continues to stare at the curtain in silence.

Daisy can't figure her out. Ellie is eating properly now, but still she won't speak, won't let anyone know what is running around in her head.

'What if I need the toilet?' Poppy asks.

'It's still here. It's just in a different place.'

'But . . . people will see what I'm doing. I can't go if people are watching.'

'The man can't see you through the curtain. And Ellie and me can turn the other way.'

'I still don't like it. I want a proper toilet. I want one like the one in my house.'

Daisy feels a stab of irritation. 'Yes, we'd all like that, wouldn't we? Sometimes we can't have what we want.' She immediately regrets the sharpness of her tongue. 'I'm sorry, Poppy. I didn't mean to snap at you. Come on, let's get ready for bed.'

'I won't be able to sleep. Not with him there.'

'We have to. Just . . . just pretend he's not there.'

Poppy's voice rises in frustration. 'I can't. Who is he, anyway? How did he find us?'

Good questions. Questions to which Daisy has no answers.

Cody. The man's name is Cody. That's all she knows about him.

Oh, and one other thing.

His voice. It sounded . . . kindly. It sounded like the type of voice she has wanted to hear for a long time. A voice suffused with concern and compassion. The voice of a prince come to rescue the princesses trapped in the castle with the wicked old trolls.

But then her memories of kindly voices have faded over time. They have been gradually eroded by the artificial benevolence put on display by Malcolm and Harriet, who have repeatedly drummed into her warnings about the terrible dangers, the predators that lie outside the shield they so generously provide.

And if she has learnt anything about monsters in that time, it is this: the clever ones are great deceivers. It's like in *Little Red Riding Hood*. They sit there, patiently and quietly, pretending to be what they're not.

And when the time is right, they unsheathe their razor-like claws, they bare their needle-sharp fangs and they gobble you all up.

* * *

She eventually coaxes the younger girls to follow her lead in preparing for bed, but their eyes hardly ever stray from that curtain. When they undress, they do so in a contorted manner, with their bodies turned away but their heads facing it. When they brush their teeth, they stand with their backs to the basin, watching and listening for the slightest movement.

Malcolm and Harriet put in their customary bedtime appearance. While Harriet tucks them in and kisses them on their foreheads and tells them how filled with love she is, Malcolm checks on the subject of her violence. Daisy finds herself craning her neck as the curtain is parted, but she sees only Cody's left side. His head remains obscured.

When Malcolm reappears, he nods at Harriet with satisfaction and says, 'He looks fine. Sleeping like a baby.'

He comes to stand at the side of the bed, his figure casting a shadow over Poppy occupying the mattress on the floor.

'Remember what I said,' he tells them. 'No going anywhere near that man. He's dangerous. He's worse than any wild animal you can think of. Worse than a shark or a tiger.'

'But,' Harriet adds hastily, 'he can't hurt you if you stay away from him, so there's no need to be too frightened.'

Malcolm grunts. 'If you need us, you know what to do. Just press the buzzer and I'll come. I'll always protect you. You know that, don't you?'

Daisy thinks about Malcolm's protection. Thinks of the agony and the fear it has caused her. She still bears the welts of his care.

'Yes,' she says. 'Thank you.'

'Good girl,' says Malcolm. 'Lights off in fifteen minutes, okay?'

The couple say their goodnights, and then they disappear. The bolts are put into place.

The girls sit up in their beds, books open on their laps. But nobody reads. Nobody so much as glances at the pages. Only one sight demands their attention. They remain that way for the full fifteen minutes.

Daisy takes away the books. Tidies them away on the bookcase. As she does so, she catches sight of the commode and realises none of them has used it tonight. They are all holding themselves in, put off by the lack of privacy and the vulnerability.

She switches off the light. Dives back to the bed before she can think too much about what the darkness holds.

She pulls the covers tight under her chin. She finds herself lifting her head from the pillow every few seconds to look in the direction of the room's only adult occupant. She can see nothing, but her mind insists on filling in the blanks. It shows the curtain moving. A slight flutter at first, and then a slow, soundless drawing back on its rail. The man called Cody is free! He moves towards the bed, seeing where the girls cannot, blood dripping from his head, which is now uncannily misshapen like Malcolm's. He comes closer and closer, gliding rather than walking, like a phantom. He reaches out. Torn, bloodied fingers stretch towards Daisy . . .

She jumps, yelps. The touch was real! It's real!

'It's me,' says Poppy. 'Can I get into bed with you? I don't like being down there by myself. It's scary.'

Daisy can hardly refuse, even though it's going to be a tight squeeze. She is just as scared herself. It will help to have the warmth of another human being next to her. Someone other than Ellie, who is still barely present.

'Get in,' she says.

Poppy climbs aboard and snuggles in. Her breath is sweet and comforting.

A minute later, she whispers in Daisy's ear. 'Why did you tell Harriet you love her?'

'You dropped a book. You made a noise when it was Quiet Time. We were in trouble, but now Harriet isn't going to tell Malcolm about it.'

'You said *you* dropped the book.'

'Yes.'

'You lied to her.'

'Yes.'

'And you were lying when you said you loved her.'

'Yes.'

'Because you don't really love her, do you?'

'No.'

'Is it all right to lie?'

'Not always, but sometimes.'

'Malcolm was lying when he said he would look after us, wasn't he?'

'Yes, I think he was.'

'But you lied because you want to help us.'

'Yes.'

'You will look after us, won't you? Malcolm and Harriet won't, but you will.'

'Yes, Poppy. I'll take care of both of you.'

'You're like our big sister, aren't you?'

'Yes.'

And then Poppy moves forwards and kisses Daisy on the cheek, and Daisy feels as though she could drown in her own tears.

52

He moves from one kind of nothingness to another.

The first nothingness was a sweet oblivion. A total absence of sensation; of thought, of emotion, of pain. Even the usual horrific nightmares and memories from the darker recesses of his mind seemed loathe to intrude into that stillness.

The second nothingness is altogether more terrifying. He is aware of this nothingness; it has his consciousness in its icy fist. It has stolen his senses and his rational thought, and refuses to give them back. He believes he is awake, but craves a return to that blissful sleep.

He thinks he is blind.

He can see nothing. Nothing at all. Even in the darkest of rooms there is usually a chink of light somewhere, seeping from behind a curtain or under a door.

He blinks furiously, becoming more and more afraid that his sight has been robbed. As he does so, a fist of pain hammers at his skull. Lights dance before him, confusing him because he does not know if they are real or imagined.

Memories begin to lap at the shore of his mind. A house. A locked room. A whispered voice.

He was attacked.

He remembers now. In the bedroom. The figure leaping at him from the doorway.

They have him. He was inadequately prepared, and now he is paying the price. He is theirs.

They have taken my eyes, he thinks. Destroyed them to make me easier to handle. Oh, Christ, please tell me I'm not blind.

No.

Don't let fear win.

It's dark, that's all. The bedroom was dark, remember? It was pitch-black in there.

So am I still in that room?

Focus. Use what other powers you still possess.

He tries to move. His legs and arms refuse to obey orders, and he can't work out why. His brain is curiously fogged, and the flashes of pain continue to stab through it, slicing apart any attempts to reason.

He listens. Nothing.

Am I dead?

He tries to speak.

Yes! Hear that? You heard that, didn't you? A real sound.

But not words. Not even a proper voice. Just a muffled inhuman cry, as though from an animal in the far distance.

Why can't I speak? Why can't I form words?

He attempts to open his mouth, but feels resistance. A tugging around his lips and face.

He tries exploring with his tongue. It pushes into a soft dryness that fills his mouth and seems to want to force its way down his throat.

He starts to gag. Bile rises from his stomach and he feels his body heaving.

NO!

He throws his head back, breathes heavily through his nostrils. He can hear his breathing now as it rasps across whatever is covering his mouth.

Don't be sick, he tells himself. If you do, you will die. It's as simple as that.

He wills himself to resist, for his nausea to subside. His temples throb with the effort. He can feel the sweat pouring out of his body. His mind wants to put him on a tiny boat in the middle of a swelling ocean, and he has to anchor himself mentally to solid ground. Has to fight the driving impulse to swallow the mass that seems greedy to infiltrate his body and expand into its spaces.

It takes him countless minutes, but he gets there. And as he gradually regains control, new sensations creep into his limbs. He feels the biting into his wrists and ankles that indicates he has been tied up. The bindings are tight and without give. He suspects that, even if his strength returns, he will not be able to break them.

So here I am, he thinks. Gagged and trussed and possibly drugged.

Why? What are they planning to do with me? And where *is* here? Am I alone?

A voice comes to him. Not in the here and now, but from earlier. A tiny whisper of a voice.

Yes.

That is what it said.

Didn't it?

I asked a question, and it answered. It said yes. It said they were here. The girls.

Are they here now?

'Hello?'

In his head, it's a meaningful utterance. In his ears it's just noise. To anyone in hearing distance it will be just noise.

But noise can attract attention. Noise can bring help.

'Hello? Hello? Please! Help me!'

He continues like this for several minutes. Calling and calling and calling.

But it seems to him that he might as well be doing it with a cushion over his face.

Nobody can hear him.

Nobody is coming to help him.

* * *

She hears it.

Eyes wide, Daisy stares into the darkness and listens to the calls.

The man called Cody is alive. The man called Cody is awake.

He wants something.

Someone to help him? Someone to free him? Or someone foolish enough to fall into his trap?

Poppy and Ellie are fast asleep, their breathing gentle and untroubled. She thinks it good that they are unaware of what is happening.

Her emotions shift in waves. Mostly she feels afraid of the stirring beast. She has no desire to leave her bed, to go to him.

But just occasionally she feels pity. She thinks of him as a lion with a thorn in his paw. If she pulls it out and takes away the pain, he will be forever in her debt. Despite his apparent ferocity, he will repay her.

But that's just a story, she thinks. Real life isn't like that. Real life is cruel.

He needs to shut up now.

He needs to be made to go away.

53

He realises that, at some point, he must have lost consciousness again. Asleep or unconscious – it's all the same. He doesn't know whether it was because of exhaustion, drugs or damage to his brain. It feels like he has been out for hours, but perhaps it has been only minutes. He has no way of knowing.

His mind seems a little clearer now. His head still pounds, but he feels more alive, more aware.

It is still black here. Still silent. Perhaps he is not in the house at all. Perhaps he has been dumped somewhere and left to die.

He tests his bindings again. Strains as hard as he can. It simply makes his wrists hurt. He tries rocking backwards and forwards. The chair he is on squeaks, and its structure flexes a little, but it doesn't give way.

The movement makes him realise his shoes have been taken from him. He can detect the softness and bounce of a carpet or rug beneath his feet.

He tries raising his right foot. The ties prevent him from lifting it higher than a few millimetres, and when he brings it down again it sinks silently into the pile. No way he can attract the attention of anyone who might be below him, then.

He is well and truly trapped.

He tries yelling again. Tries to force his voice through the cotton wool and the tape, beyond this crypt in which he has been entombed, and out into the world.

But he knows it is fruitless. Accepting the madness of his endeavour, he drops his chin to his chest.

And then he hears the sounds.

A soft sobbing in the darkness. Whispers. Rustling.

He calls out again. He is answered by an anguished cry, and harsher whispering. He thinks he hears a name.

Poppy.

Poppy Devlin. Has to be!

He yells her name, though it doesn't sound anything like her name. It is two syllables, with the emphasis on the first. Maybe she'll get it. Maybe she'll realise he is calling for her.

'Stop it!'

The shrill cry is crystal clear. An end to the mumbling and the whispering. It is intended for his ears, and it is intended to shut him up. He can hear how desperately this girl wants him to stop torturing her.

He stops calling. The girls don't want him. They are afraid of him. They will not help.

And then there is light.

It floods the space, stinging his eyes not only with its brightness, but also with the instant relief it brings him that he is capable of sight. He blinks furiously, adjusting to his new surroundings.

He is in the corner of the room, cut off from the rest by a curtain on an arc of metal rail. Looking down, he can see how his ankles and forearms are bound with nylon ties to the wooden chair.

He sees blood, too. On his trousers and the arms of his fleece. He suspects it's his own.

There is crying coming from one of the girls – Poppy, probably. Another girl is trying to comfort her with soft shushing sounds.

Another noise intrudes, and the girls suddenly quieten. Cody realises it's the sound of the bolts being drawn on the bedroom door he opened last night.

'You all right, girls?' says a gruff voice. Cody recognises it as belonging to Malcolm Benson.

'He's making funny noises,' says Poppy.

'Is he now?'

Footsteps approach. A shadow on the curtain sharpens into focus. An arm reaches up, and then the curtain is drawn briskly back on its rail.

It's Malcolm, all right. But Cody is more interested in what lies behind him. He gets only a glimpse before Malcolm steps in and closes the curtain again, but it's enough.

Three girls, sitting on the bed and staring his way.

Not two – not just Poppy Devlin and Ellie McVitie – but three.

The other is Daisy Agnew. She is three years older than the photographs he has seen, but he would recognise her anywhere.

They're alive. All three of them are still alive.

He guesses that his own time here will be much shorter than theirs.

Malcolm seems larger than when Cody last saw him. He looks stronger. Or perhaps it's just that Cody feels that much weaker now.

Malcolm steps up to him. He tilts his head to the side as he appraises his captive. Then he reaches out a meaty hand and cups Cody's chin, turning his head from side to side.

'Hmm. Could be worse,' he says.

He leans forward, rests his hands on Cody's arms.

'We'll have a proper chat later,' he says, his rancid breath making Cody want to retch again. 'A nice long talk. Until then, you need to stop frightening my girls. I've told them all about you. I've told them what'll happen if you take them away from us. And I've told them I won't let you. I'm going to protect them.'

Cody realises now why Malcolm is talking so loudly. This is for the benefit of the girls. This is to make an enemy out of Cody, to make the girls distrustful and afraid of him. That way, they won't be tempted to come to his aid.

Malcolm straightens up again.

'Now be a good lad and keep quiet. I'll be back in a while.'

There is a strange glint in the man's eye. A look that tells Cody this man is capable of anything.

54

When Webley gets into work, she is surprised to see that Cody isn't already at his desk. Poor sleeper that he is, he tends to arrive before most.

She shrugs off her coat, takes a seat, logs on to her computer, checks her emails, answers her emails.

Still no Cody.

Probably sick of looking at vans, she thinks. I know I am.

The others start to drift in. There is some good-natured banter. Footlong Ferguson asks her why she hasn't made the coffee yet. She tells him to fuck off. Five minutes later he brings over a steaming mug and places it in front of her with a wry smile.

Blunt enters. Strides through the incident room and into her office. She clutches a sheaf of papers under her arm. Webley guesses she has already had at least one meeting over breakfast. Probably been roasted about the lack of progress in the case.

Webley starts typing up a report that was due yesterday. She hates report writing. If she'd wanted to spend all day typing she'd have become a secretary.

And still no Cody.

She halts mid-sentence. Takes a look around her. A full complement of staff. Bar one.

'Anyone seen Cody?' she asks, to nobody in particular.

She gets a couple of headshakes. None of the others seems particularly concerned. It's bothering her, though.

She looks directly at Ferguson. 'Mate, have you seen anything of Cody?'

Another shake of the head. 'Not since you clocked off together yesterday. What did you two get up to last night?'

A further wry smile. She tells him to fuck off again.

She picks up her mobile phone, leans back in her chair. In her contacts she finds Cody's number and calls it.

It rings and rings, then goes through to voicemail.

She hangs up. Decides to give him a few more minutes.

He'll have a valid excuse, she thinks. Why am I getting worried anyway? It's got nothing to do with me. I'm not his mother. Or his girlfriend.

She straightens her spine. Resumes typing, more furiously now. There's work to be done. Sod Cody. If he wants to get into deep shit for being late, that's his problem.

Five minutes later she's picking up the phone again.

It goes to voicemail.

'Cody,' she says. 'It's me. Megan. Where are you? Not that we can't manage without you, but we're short of someone to make fun of. Catch you later.'

There. Just the right tone. Jocular, but showing him he's missed. He'll appreciate that.

Another half-hour passes.

He's on an assignment, thinks Webley. He got in really early, picked up a lead and has gone out to investigate it.

Without telling anyone.

Which is what seems so wrong about this. Nobody seems to have the faintest idea where he is.

Blunt comes out of her office, her face grim. It seems to have been fixed in that expression ever since Poppy was taken.

Blunt, if anyone, must know where Cody is.

'Where the hell is DS Cody?' she roars.

That's a no, then. His whereabouts remain a mystery.

'Well?' says Blunt. 'Anyone care to enlighten me?'

When she gets no answer she looks ready to blow a gasket. 'Right. Well, unless he shows in the next few minutes with the killer in cuffs, you can tell him from me he's not in my gang anymore. Got it?'

She doesn't wait for a response, but storms back into her office and slams the door.

* * *

Work doesn't wait. The world doesn't stop spinning just because Nathan Cody has decided not to turn into the office today.

For Webley, that means more vans to check out, joy of joys. She hits the streets again. One of the drivers she talks to is in his nineties and can't hear a word she says, which is fun. Another lost an arm in a cycling accident, and hasn't been able to drive for the last six months.

She ticks them off her list and moves on to the next. But her mind isn't really on the job. The seat beside her in the unmarked car shouldn't be empty like this. It should be filled with the bundle of annoyance and irrational behaviour that is Cody.

She tries calling his mobile again, only to hear the same grating invitation to leave a message.

'Cody, where the hell are you? Don't think I'm worried about you, because I'm not. But we've got a case to work, and you are really not helping. Besides, Blunt is going ape-shit. Call me.'

As an afterthought, she tries his landline. That, too, is answered by a machine.

'Fucking robots,' she says, before hanging up.

This shit is getting weird, she thinks. Too weird even for Cody.

She puts the car into gear and drives on to her next rendezvous.

55

When Malcolm eventually returns to the bedroom, he is carrying a plastic carrier bag, crammed with items.

Daisy eyes the bag with suspicion. This will have something to do with Cody. She knows it will.

'Guess who's been shopping?' says Malcolm. 'And guess who's bought you all presents?'

He plonks himself down on the edge of their bed, almost causing Poppy to bounce off the other side. Then he dips a hand into the bag and starts pulling out cardboard boxes. Daisy can see what they hold from the pictures on them. She's not impressed.

Malcolm opens up one of the boxes. Brings out its contents.

'Look at those beauties,' he says. 'Here, Poppy. Try them on.'

Poppy reaches out with uncertainty and takes the pair of headphones from him. Gingerly, she slides them over her head.

'They need adjusting,' says Malcolm. 'Lean forward.'

Poppy does as she is told while Malcolm fixes them into position covering her ears.

'Your turn, Ellie.' He hands her another pair. She studies Poppy's headgear while she ratchets her own into place.

'Good girl. And finally some for Daisy. I thought you'd prefer the jazzy pink ones.'

Daisy feels like shedding tears as she collects the offering, but not because she is overwhelmed by the apparent act of generosity. In her young heart she knows she is being bought. This gift is not out of love; it is out of hate. It is a cynical manipulation of young minds. Despite what they have been through, Ellie and Poppy retain much of the innocence of Snow White: they do not suspect the poison hidden in their juicy red apples.

'And this,' says Malcolm as he opens another, smaller box, 'is called a splitter. It lets you all listen to the same thing at the same time. Come on, girls, let's test it out.'

He moves across the room. Switches on the television and the DVD player. Squatting, he plugs the splitter into an audio socket.

'Right, come and sit here.'

He lines up three of the small plastic chairs in front of the TV, then beckons the girls to sit down. Poppy and Ellie go straight to their seats, but Daisy drags her feet.

'Chop, chop, Daisy. This'll be fun.'

Daisy sits down on the middle chair. Malcolm collects together the leads of the three headphones, then plugs them all in. He goes back to the bed, returns with yet another item from his bag of goodies.

'Right, then. Who wants to watch *Frozen*?'

He holds up the DVD as he says this, as if awaiting a massive cheer from his audience. What he gets is three solemn faces, not a smile among them.

His face drops. 'Well, that's what you're getting. You can thank me later.'

He opens up the case and extracts the DVD, but hesitates before inserting it into the player.

'Listen to me, girls. This is very important. While you're watching this film, I'm going to be over there, talking to Mr Cody. You are NOT to turn around while I'm doing that, okay? OKAY?'

They all nod. So this is it, thinks Daisy. This is the real reason for the presents. Just like I thought.

'I'll have the curtain open,' Malcolm continues, 'so I'll be able to see you. Anyone who turns around or takes off their headphones will be punished. Do I make myself clear?'

More nodding. We're his prisoners, thinks Daisy. We do as he says. So much for this being a time for fun.

Malcolm finds a smile again, and it makes Daisy want to be sick.

He loads the DVD. Waits for the movie to begin. He steps to one side, his eyes on the three girls, checking that their attention is on the screen and nothing else.

And then he disappears behind them.

Daisy finds it a struggle not to turn immediately. She wants to see Cody, wants to get a proper look into his eyes. Wants to know what Malcolm is about to do to him.

But she doesn't. She sits rock-still and stares at the bright colours emanating from the TV, the joyful songs ringing loudly in her ears, and she tries to take herself to a happy place.

56

Cody sees the shadow looming again on the other side of the curtain. He has been dreading this moment. He has no clue what plans have been made for him, but he has heard all that Malcolm has said to the children. They are not to see or hear what is about to take place, and that cannot bode well.

The curtain is whipped back. Drawn all the way round the rail. Cody gets his first proper view of the bedroom. He notices the wooden boards screwed into place over the window. He sees the three girls, all facing dutifully away from him. The cartoon images on the television seem strangely incongruous.

He wonders what is going through the heads of the children. Are they happy here? Have they been looked after or badly abused?

At least they are alive.

Malcolm looks over his shoulder. 'You can turn round now, girls,' he says.

Nobody moves, and Malcolm faces Cody again, satisfied that the headphones are serving their purpose of cutting the girls out of what is to come.

Malcolm collects a carrier bag from the bed, then sweeps up a child's chair and drops it in front of Cody. When he settles his bulk onto the miniature furniture he looks almost comical.

Almost.

'I said we'd have a talk,' Malcolm begins. 'This is it. This is our talk. In a moment, I'm going to take that tape off your mouth. First, I need to tell you the rule. The rule is that you don't try to call out to the girls. You talk in a normal, quiet voice. Is that understood?'

Cody nods.

'All right, then.'

Malcolm stretches forward. Grabs the edge of the duct tape. Rips it from Cody's face in one swift, savage motion.

Cody yells, his cry soaked up by the cotton wool in his mouth.

'Spit it out,' Malcolm orders. 'Go on.'

Cody bends his head forward and does his best to expel the stuffing. It takes several attempts to get it out, and even then there are remnants adhering to the inside of his mouth. He moves his tongue, trying to dislodge them, and it rasps as though his saliva glands have been drained. He can smell his own breath, and it is like the odour of a cesspit on a hot summer's day.

'There,' says Malcolm. 'Better? Don't worry, I've got plenty more where that came from.' He empties the plastic bag onto the carpet. Cody sees duct tape, cotton wool and a small pair of scissors. Malcolm picks up the scissors and begins toying with them – opening and closing them like a vicious snapping turtle.

'Water,' Cody croaks. 'I need a drink.'

'Well, we'll have to see about that, won't we?' says Malcolm. 'This will be a two-way street, you see, Mr Cody. You scratch my back and I'll scratch yours.'

'I . . . I don't know what you want from me.'

Malcolm smiles. 'That's easy. Nothing to worry about. All I want is some information. The answers to some questions.'

'What about?'

'About you. About the police. About what brought you to our door. What's going on, Sergeant Cody? Explain it to me, please.'

'There isn't much to explain. I already told you everything when we arrived yesterday afternoon.'

'Tell me again.'

Cody hesitates. He's not sure why, but something whispers to him that he shouldn't be too forthcoming. Shouldn't be too hasty in satisfying Malcolm's demands.

He says, 'We were . . . We were following up on a lead. The sighting of a van near the crime scenes. We produced a list of people who own vans matching the description. You were just one of many on that list.'

Malcolm continues opening and closing his scissors. Snap, snap, snap.

'You expect me to believe that?' he says finally.

'Yes. It's the truth.'

Malcolm shakes his head. 'Do I look like a fool to you? Do I look like some kind of idiot?'

No, thinks Cody. You look deranged. You look unhinged. You look dangerous. But not a fool.

Malcolm says, 'There must be thousands upon thousands of vans in Liverpool alone. You couldn't have been checking out every single one of them. You must have had more to go on than that.'

Cody still doesn't understand what happened over the van. It was Quigley's information that led them to Malcolm, and yet his van didn't fit the sighting.

'We hit lucky,' he says, because now he's starting to think that's what it was. Or unlucky.

'No,' says Malcolm. 'You knew, didn't you? You knew about my other van.'

Cody has to fight to hide his surprise.

'DIDN'T YOU?' yells Malcolm.

Cody jerks back in his chair. The wood creaks with his movement. He looks across to the girls and sees that they are still blissfully unaware of what is going on.

Malcolm follows his gaze. 'Didn't you?' he says again, quietly this time. 'You knew about my other van?'

'Yes,' Cody says. 'We knew about that.'

He has to think about the reasons for his sudden impulse to lie, and realises it's not just because it's the answer Malcolm is expecting. Something is telling him he needs to get across the notion that the cops know a lot more than Malcolm thinks.

Yes, that's it, Cody. That's what you need to do. Make him believe he's not out of the woods. Make him fear that there is still a good chance of his being caught, and that killing a cop is not in his best interests right now.

Whatever you do, don't give him the true story. Don't allow him to realise that nobody knows you're here, that he could kill you right now and nobody would be any the wiser. Because that's the harsh reality, isn't it? You're alone.

Malcolm rubs his hand across his pate. Spends a while circling that deformity in his skull. He looks uncomfortable with what Cody has just told him.

'How?' he asks. 'How did you find out about my other van?'

'I don't know.'

Anger crosses Malcolm's features. 'What do you mean, you don't know? You came to my house looking for a white van. That means you know about the van. How?'

'It doesn't work like that. What you have to realise is that what you've done is a big deal. It's major news. You must have seen it on TV. There is a massive team working on this case, and I'm just a foot soldier. I do what I'm told. So when my boss tells me to go to a certain house and ask about a van, that's what I do.'

'You're a sergeant.'

'A sergeant is nothing. Above me are inspectors, chief inspectors, superintendents, chief superintendents . . . Then there are the intelligence people – the ones who really know what's going on.'

Malcolm thinks for a second. 'It still doesn't make any sense. If you were sent on a mission to find the other van, why didn't you just come out and ask me about it?'

'There was no sign of it on your property. We weren't sure you still had it, but if you did, we didn't want to spook you into getting rid of it somehow, just in case it contained vital evidence linking you to the crimes.'

Cody is having to think fast. He's not sure how much probing his deceit will take before it crumbles into dust.

Malcolm looks around, working the scissors as he tries to come to terms with this new information. Cody thinks his lie is just about standing up, but he can't be certain. He's also more than a little worried about the signs of agitation building in his captor. If he gets caught out now, he'll be in serious trouble.

'So who else knows? Who else knows about the second van?'

'Probably lots of people. It's right there on our computers.'

'But they don't know what I used it for?'

'No. Don't you think we would have arrested you at the time if we'd known?'

'Your friend. The woman who was with you. Does she know what you know?'

Cody decides he needs to deflect attention away from Webley. He's not sure what this psychopath is capable of.

'Yes, but she's just one of many. Like I said, we're all part of one big team.'

Malcolm takes another time-out to consider this. It's clear he hates the idea that police officers could still come to his door. Cody realises this might be the only thing to keep him alive.

'Will they come?' Malcolm asks. 'Will they come looking for you?'

'When they realise I'm missing, yes. They will.'

Malcolm nods. His eyelids flutter, and his eyes seem suddenly to lose focus. It looks to Cody as though the man is entering a trance state.

And then a yell from Malcolm. A release of pent-up frustration that drives him out of his chair, has him springing towards Cody and plunging a blade of his scissors deep into Cody's thigh.

Cody screams with both the shock and the pain of the attack. He stares with wild eyes at the scissors, which are now embedded in his leg. Malcolm leans over, brings his face within inches of Cody's.

'I think you're lying. I think nobody knows you're here, and they're not coming for you. I think you're making it up to save your scrawny neck.'

'No,' Cody says through teeth clenched in pain. 'It's the truth. They'll be here. Eventually they'll come looking for me. You need to accept that, and you need to do the right thing.'

Malcolm's spittle rains down on Cody's face. 'I don't need to do anything you say. I know what the right thing is. The right thing is to look after these girls. We give them everything they need. Everything! We would die for these girls, and when it's necessary, we will kill for them.'

Cody can see in Malcolm's eyes that there is little point in arguing further. The man has moved beyond the reach of plain reason. The slightest push is all it might take for Malcolm to grab those scissors again and open up Cody's belly.

And so he says nothing. He just waits for the fire to die down.

When it does, it is as though Malcolm suddenly becomes aware of where he is and what he's done. He looks at Cody with apparent puzzlement at first, and then down at the scissors protruding from Cody's leg.

'We'll have to see, won't we?' he says. 'We'll have to see if your police friends show up, like you say they will. If they don't, I'll know you were lying. And then it won't matter.'

He reaches for the scissors then. Cody grimaces as they are yanked out. There is a spurt of blood, followed by a dark circle widening across the leg of his trousers.

Malcolm reaches for the cotton wool and starts to rip pieces from it. 'Open wide,' he says.

Cody does as he is told. He is too frightened to do otherwise. He lets his eyes drift to the three girls as his mouth is filled with the cotton wool, as though he is a soft toy being stuffed. The girls are oblivious to his torture.

He is grateful for that small mercy.

57

He'll be there, thinks Webley.

When I walk back into that incident room, Cody will be there at his desk, working away as if nothing has happened. And when I ask him about it he'll say, 'Sorry, I didn't know you cared,' or something equally stupid. And I'll hate him for it, but I'll love it that he's back with us, safe and sound, and I'll shout at him for making me worry unnecessarily. Because that's what Cody is so good at, the bastard: making me care about him, even when I shouldn't.

But then she walks into the incident room, and he's not there. His chair is empty, and none of the papers on his desk have been disturbed. And the worst thing is that nobody else seems to have noticed.

She stops at Ferguson's desk on the way to her own.

'Still no sign of Cody?'

Ferguson looks across at Cody's desk as if only just becoming aware of its lack of an occupant.

'No. Do you think maybe he's gone back undercover? A top secret mission that we're not allowed to know about?'

Webley doesn't feel the humour. 'I'm serious, Neil. This isn't like Cody. He doesn't just fail to show up like this.'

Ferguson seems to sense her unease. 'Relax. He's probably sick or something. He'll have phoned it in, and somebody will have forgotten to pass on the message.'

Webley nods, but she's not convinced. Not at all.

She takes a seat at her desk. Tries phoning Cody again. Voicemail.

Shit.

He can't be too sick to answer the bloody phone. He can't be too sick to have listened to her earlier voicemails and to have responded, even if only with a brief text.

Except that he *is* sick, isn't he?

He's got issues. Mental health issues. He was in a really dark place a few months ago. Hallucinations, nightmares, violent outbursts, insomnia. Yes, he has seemed much better recently, but perhaps he's had a relapse. What if he has totally lost it this time? What if he's done himself some serious damage?

Webley leaves her seat again, goes to knock on Blunt's door. Blunt beckons her in.

'Don't tell me,' says Blunt. 'You've had no luck with the vans. I can see it written all over your face. When in God's name is someone going to bring me good news for a change?'

'Actually, ma'am, it's about Cody.'

Blunt's expression changes. A different hue of dark.

'What about Cody? Have you heard from him?'

'No. And that's the problem. Nobody has. He seems to have disappeared.'

Blunt shakes her head. 'He hasn't disappeared. He'll be up to something. If there's one person you can count on to do his own thing around here, even when I expressly forbid it, it's Cody. He's shown me that enough times in the past. Just watch. He'll come swanning in, I'll give him a bollocking, and then he'll tell me he's solved the case, and I'll have to forgive him.'

Webley hears the words, but isn't convinced. This is Blunt trying to reassure herself that nothing untoward has happened to her favourite copper.

'Ma'am, I've been calling him all day. I've left several voicemails. Something is wrong. Finding whoever abducted these girls means as much to him as it does to you. He wouldn't go off on a tangent at such a crucial point in the investigation. You know he wouldn't.'

Blunt falls silent.

'All right, Megan. What do you suggest?'

'I'd like permission to go round to his flat. He lives above a dentist's, who is also his landlord. Maybe he can tell me something.'

Blunt sighs. 'I could really do with you here, Megan. We've got kids to find.'

'I know. I know. I'll be as quick as I can, and I'll make up the time. If I leave it till later, the dentist will have gone home.'

Blunt taps her pen on her desk. 'All right. Go.' She aims the pen at Webley. 'But if you find Cody, you can tell him from me that his days are numbered.'

58

Rodney Street. Webley loves it here. Wishes she could afford to live in a flat in one of these Georgian buildings. She knows that Cody can afford it only because the dentist is a mate of his and has done him a good deal. Lucky bastard.

Before she approaches the door, she spends a couple of minutes walking up and down the street, checking out the cars. She can find no sign of Cody's.

She goes into the building, where an effervescent receptionist greets her. Webley introduces herself with her warrant card, and asks to speak to whoever's in charge.

Simon Teller is the best possible advertisement for his business: a perfect smile on legs. A handsome beast, he oozes charm. As he shakes Webley's hand, she can imagine the number of women who have gone weak at the knees during that simple contact.

Not me, though, she thinks. Not my type.

He shows her into his surgery, and they sit on leather chairs opposite each other. He seems very relaxed, with his rolled-up sleeves and his open collar. On one of his tanned wrists he wears a very expensive-looking watch. Webley guesses he's stinking rich. There are no signs of a wedding ring.

Not that it matters, she thinks. He's still not my type.

'Business or business?' he asks.

'Sorry?'

'Well, I assume you aren't here for pleasure, so is it *my* business, in that you want me to do something about your teeth, or is it police business?'

'What's wrong with my teeth?' she asks, slightly panicky now.

'I didn't say there was anything wrong.' He leans forward in his chair. 'Give me a smile and we'll see.'

'What?'

'Go on. I won't even charge for it.'

Her impulse is to say no, but Teller has this way of making her think it would be downright rude to refuse him.

She flashes him the briefest of smiles.

'There,' says Teller. 'Didn't hurt, did it? Beautiful smile, too. Top left incisor a little crooked, but otherwise immaculate.'

She thinks, *Crooked?* What the hell does he mean, crooked?

She runs her tongue over her top teeth. They're not frigging crooked.

'Thank you for the appraisal, Mr Teller, but if you don't mind—'

'Simon,' he smarms. 'Call me Simon.'

'Right. Simon. The reason I've come to see you today is Cody.'

'Cody? You work with him?'

'Yes. We're on the Major Incident Team together.'

'Really? I can't believe he's never mentioned you.'

She thinks, Cody hasn't mentioned me. Great. Why has he never mentioned me?

'The point is, I was . . . we were wondering if you'd seen him lately.'

'Oh, not for days. To be honest, our paths rarely cross. He tends to be out before I get here, and back home after I've finished up. Why do you ask?'

'It's just that he hasn't been in work today, and we can't get hold of him.'

Teller raises an eyebrow. 'That doesn't sound like Cody.'

'No. That's what I – we thought. In fact, we're starting to get more than a little concerned about him. So we were wondering . . .'

'If you could take a look in his flat?'

'Is that okay?'

Teller shows his pearly whites again. 'I don't see why not. You've got a trustworthy face. Come on.'

He leads her back out to reception.

'Helen, can you dig out a key to Cody's flat upstairs, please?'

The key gets handed to Teller, who in turn passes it to Webley. 'All yours,' he says.

'You can come along too, if you like. It's your property.'

He shakes his head. 'I've got patients to see. You know where it is, don't you?'

'Yes. Yes, I do.'

He winks. 'Thought as much.'

As Teller heads back to his surgery, Webley wonders what he's thinking about her and Cody. She opens her mouth to say something, but changes her mind.

Let him believe what he likes.

She starts up the wide staircase. It feels weird coming up here in the daytime, when the place is bustling. On the few prior occasions she has visited Cody here, they have been the only two in the building.

She can hear chatter, the whine of a drill, the clatter of metal instruments on trays. The air is thick with the odour of sterility.

On the first floor she pauses at the door to Cody's flat. To the left is a gloomy passage leading to the dental practice's kitchen. She can smell coffee and hear the rattling of mugs and a kettle on the boil.

She tries knocking but gets no response. She tests the door. It's locked, and there is no sign of forced entry. She inserts the key, unlocks the door.

When she opens it, she sees that there is a small alarm box screwed to its other side. She doesn't recall seeing it there before. No bells or sirens go off, so for some reason Cody must have left it disabled.

The only thing in front of her is another staircase. She ascends it slowly, cautiously, wondering what she will find here. Hoping that it is not what she fears most.

At the top of the stairs is a large hall, dotted with doors. Cody gave her a short guided tour once, so she has a vague memory of the layout.

She does a quick search to begin with, just to reassure herself that the flat isn't occupied, by the living or the dead. She works her way through the living room, the bedrooms, the bathroom. On each occasion she holds her breath as she flings open the door.

But the rooms are all empty.

Only the kitchen left now.

She opens the door. Finds this room empty, too.

Except . . .

There are signs here. Signs of his last visit.

On the counter, a full mug of tea, the spoon and teabag still in it. Further along, Cody's belongings: tissues, pens, notebook, cash, wallet, and other miscellaneous items. Even his mobile phone. No keys, though, to either the flat or Cody's car.

And then, slung over the back of a chair, Cody's suit jacket and tie.

So . . . Cody comes home, empties his pockets, starts to get out of his work clothes, makes a brew, and then . . .

What?

He leaves? Why?

What was so urgent that he couldn't even drink his tea?

And why did he only take his keys?

Clearly he wasn't expecting to be out for very long. He took neither his wallet nor his mobile phone.

The phone. He must have received a call. That's it. An emergency of some kind – perhaps in the family, or affecting his ex-fiancée.

But wouldn't you take your phone with you if that were the case?

Of course: he was too flustered, too upset. He wasn't thinking straight.

Webley grabs the phone, checks the log of incoming calls. Works her way past all the calls she made herself to this number.

She finds nothing. No calls were made to Cody's phone any time between Cody leaving work and Webley calling him today.

She goes back into the hall. Picks up the house phone and checks its own history. Even fewer calls have been made to his landline.

This is insane, she thinks. It doesn't make any sense.

She goes back through all the rooms, checking more carefully this time. There is no sign of a disturbance, no evidence of a crime or a struggle. It appears that Cody simply went out on an errand that was supposed to last minutes . . .

. . . and never came back.

59

'Well?' says Blunt.

Webley tells her all she knows, which isn't much, but which isn't easily explained either.

Blunt can't dismiss this, she thinks. She'll have to do something now.

'All right, Megan,' says Blunt. 'Thank you. That'll be all.'

Webley can't believe her ears. She stays rooted to the spot in front of Blunt's desk.

'Ma'am? I'm not sure you've understood what I've just told you. I—'

'I heard every word, Megan. Cody has gone AWOL. What are you suggesting I've missed in your report?'

'That . . . that we need to do something. He hasn't just gone on holiday. He's disappeared.'

'And what are you suggesting we do about it?'

'Well, we contact the people who know him – his family and his ex-fiancée. We put in a request for information on recent fatalities of unidentified males. We ring the hospitals. We check for ANPR pings of Cody's car registration. We—'

'Megan, Megan. Who are we?'

'What?'

'Us. This unit. Who are we?'

'We're MIT.'

'Which stands for?'

'Major Incident Team.'

'Exactly. Regrettable though Cody's disappearance is, it is not yet a major incident. When it is, we'll investigate it. Until that time arises, we hand it over to Missing Persons, whose job it is to deal with such matters.'

'But ma'am—'

'DC Webley! You're not listening to me. We've got two abducted children on our books – three if you count Daisy Agnew – plus a double homicide. We are stretched enough as it is. We have neither the time nor the resources to go chasing after a member of staff who has been absent for less than a day. Bring home those missing children, lock up the man who killed two of their parents, and I'll reconsider your duties. Until then, sort your priorities out.'

'And if the two are connected?'

'What do you mean?'

'The children and Cody. What if Cody has been taken by the same man who abducted the girls?'

Blunt stares for a few seconds. 'I'll make you a deal, Megan. Give me one piece of evidence, however slender, that connects the abductions with the disappearance of Cody, and I will reclassify Cody's case. In fact, to hell with solid evidence. Give me any piece of logical reasoning that suggests they're linked. Anything at all.'

Webley says nothing. Intuition doesn't count as logical reasoning, and she's not even sure she's got that.

'I thought not,' says Blunt. 'Now get back to what you should be doing.'

Webley remains tight-lipped. She wants to call Blunt a heartless bitch, but that won't help matters.

Instead, she turns on her heel and leaves.

* * *

When Webley has gone, DCI Stella Blunt takes several deep breaths.

Poor girl, she thinks. I was tough on her, but sometimes these things are necessary. Hopefully she will realise that when she's calmer. She's a good copper. A lot to learn still, but a good copper.

Like Cody. One of the best detectives she has ever had on her squad.

Life goes on, though. She can't have favourites. There's a job to be done, cases to be solved. It's her responsibility to make sure that the team functions properly and efficiently, even when individual members go astray. To do otherwise wouldn't be fair. It wouldn't be fair on the missing girls, and it wouldn't be fair on their families. They have to be put first.

So, she thinks, where was I? What was next on my list?

She remembers. Reaches for the drawer containing the file she wanted. She opens it, starts to rifle through the tightly packed contents, checking the handwritten tags on top of each folder.

But she's not seeing them. Her mind is too preoccupied with a name, a face, a voice. She slams the drawer shut.

Damn you, Nathan Cody, she thinks. Why the hell do you keep doing this to me?

60

The hours pass.

Cody listens to the girls whispering to each other. Occasionally he hears his name mentioned. They are scared, but the simple knowledge that they are still alive keeps him from losing all hope.

But each time the bolts are withdrawn and one of the Bensons comes into the bedroom, his heart sinks. He expects the worst. He expects the end.

So far, they have always come for the girls. They bring them food. They talk to them. They read to them. They play games with them. They try to make them laugh, without success.

It is almost as if the Bensons have forgotten about the man secreted behind the curtain. Out of sight, out of mind.

But he knows it won't last.

And it doesn't.

He realises his time has come when he hears Malcolm Benson entering the room and instructing the girls to put their headphones back on.

Cody wonders if he'll still be alive when the closing credits of *Frozen* roll by.

When the curtain is pulled back, he sees that Malcolm looks a new man – as though he's taken a normality pill. He seems almost like someone who could be reasoned with, someone who might entertain an alternative point of view.

Cody realises he will have to capitalise on this brief opportunity before the rot sets in again.

As before, Malcolm brings fresh cotton wool, duct tape and scissors. He places the items on a shelf to his right. Then, with a smile and a flourish, he reaches forward and rips Cody's gag from his face.

Tears in his eyes, Cody spits out the cotton wool. Again he tastes the foulness in his mouth.

'How are we feeling now, Detective Cody? Ready for another little discussion? One without lies this time?'

'Water,' says Cody, his voice hoarse. 'Drink.'

This time, Malcolm doesn't reject the request out of hand. Instead, he walks across to a small basin, fills up a plastic beaker with water, and brings it back. He puts it to Cody's lips and allows him a few small sips.

'Better?' says Malcolm. 'Are we good to go now?'

'Toilet,' says Cody. 'I need the toilet.'

This is his plan. The only course of action he has managed to concoct during his long hours behind the curtain. Not much of a plan, admittedly, but it's all he's got.

Malcolm scowls. It's clear he is already losing his relatively cheery demeanour.

Come on, thinks Cody. Undo the ties. Surely even you wouldn't let me sit here wallowing in my own piss.

But then Cody discovers that Malcolm is a step ahead of him. As his belt is unbuckled, and his trousers and underwear are pulled halfway down his thighs, Cody wants to cry with his indignity and the disappointment of seeing his plan in tatters.

While Cody relieves himself through the hole in his chair, Malcolm partly closes the curtain again. It seems paradoxical to Cody that Malcolm feels the need to spare the girls' blushes at the sight of a man with his trousers down, when he seemed to have no problem subjecting one of them to a ringside view of her parents being slaughtered.

When he is done, and Malcolm has refastened his clothes, Cody feels defeated before his interrogation has even begun.

'So where are they?' says Malcolm, spreading his arms.

'Where's what?'

'Your cop friends. The ones who know you're here.'

'It doesn't work that quickly,' Cody says, although he's not quite sure how many hours he has been here. 'They probably think I'm just out of the station while I follow some other leads.'

He knows that won't be the case. They will be fully aware of his absence by now, and they'll be trying to trace him. Hopefully, at least one of them will be worried enough to instigate an active search.

That's the good news. The bad news is that they probably don't have a cat in hell's chance of finding him.

'Well, we'll see,' says Malcolm. 'There's time yet.'

Cody would like to know what that means. Does Malcolm have a deadline in mind?

Malcolm places his small blue chair in front of Cody again. Lowers his bulk onto it.

'Why did you come back to our house?' he asks.

'To get my warrant card. I left it here.'

Malcolm shakes his head. 'See, you're lying already. Digging yourself a deeper hole.'

'It's the truth.'

'No. It's not. I searched you when you were unconscious. Your card was in your pocket the whole time. It's a lie now, and it was a lie then. Why? Why did you make it all up?'

Cody passes his tongue over dry, cracked lips. The few sips of water have done little to replace the moisture he has lost. Again, something tells him not to let Malcolm know he found the warrant card here. Let him believe that the police are using clandestine methods of investigation. Allow him to assume their intelligence data is more substantial than it is.

'I had a feeling about you,' he says.

'A feeling? What kind of feeling?'

'Intuition, based on experience. When you spend enough time in this job, you develop a radar for these things. Something about you didn't seem right.'

'No,' says Malcolm. 'Not good enough. You wouldn't sneak back here based on a feeling. You wouldn't wait till I'd gone out so you could harass my wife while she was alone.'

'I didn't harass her.'

'Harriet is not a well woman. She has problems dealing with people. You upset her. You frightened her.'

'She didn't seem that frightened when she sneaked up behind me and cracked my skull open.'

'You're lucky I didn't finish the job when I got home. I love the bones of that woman. Anyone who hurts Harriet has me to deal with.'

Cody can see Malcolm's chest rising and falling. This is clearly a touchy subject for him.

'I had some questions I needed to ask, that's all. I had no intention of causing your wife any distress.'

'You didn't ask any questions. Not proper ones. You got into the house under false pretences so that you could sniff around. You already knew what you were looking for.'

'No. No, I didn't.'

'Then why did you come upstairs?'

Cody has to resist the reflex to glance at the girls. Malcolm mustn't be given an excuse to take his anger out on them.

'I needed the toilet.'

'I don't believe you. I asked Harriet about it.'

Oh, shit, thinks Cody. She told him. She told him about the noise the girls made.

'What did she say?'

'She said you were fine one minute, and then about to piss yourself the next. That doesn't add up to me. You came here knowing you needed to find a way to get upstairs. That was your aim all along, wasn't it?'

Cody wants to sigh with relief. Harriet has kept it from her husband. She has put the safety of the girls first.

Well, at least that's something. One of them still has some humanity left.

'You're right,' Cody says. 'I lied. I didn't need the toilet.'

Malcolm's anger subsides a little, to be replaced by sheer surprise at Cody's confession.

'Then why did you come up here?'

'I was told to.'

Surprise turns to alarm now. 'What do you mean? Who told you to?'

'It's like I said earlier. At my level of the police, we do what we're told, and we don't question it. It was suggested to me that I should check out your house again.'

'Why?'

'I don't know. New intelligence, I guess.'

Cody accepts he is taking a huge gamble here. Anyone who knows anything about how the police operate will realise he is talking complete bollocks. His hope is that he can deliver his story with enough authority to sound convincing.

Malcolm stands up. Takes two paces one way and two the other, all the while rubbing his head. To Cody's right, the girls remain rooted to their chairs in front of the television.

Cody would so like to have a conversation with those children.

'No,' says Malcolm. 'That can't be right. Why would they ask you to lie and sneak around like you did? Why didn't you just come here with your police mates and search the place properly?'

'Believe it or not, we can't just waltz into anyone's house and search it whenever we feel like it. We need a search warrant.'

'So why didn't you get one?'

'We need a good reason to get one issued to us. It could be that the intelligence we had wasn't compelling enough, or maybe we couldn't reveal that intel for other reasons.'

'What kind of other reasons?'

'All kinds. An example would be if to do so would endanger life.'

There, thinks Cody. Suck on that one. Let's see if that banged-up head of yours can join the dots I've just drawn for you.

Malcolm looks around the room. 'Endanger whose life? These kids couldn't have done anything to bring you back to the house. It's not possible.'

'No. You're right. I was just giving an example.'

This time he deliberately speaks with less conviction. If the girls couldn't have contacted the police, then who could? Eh, Malcolm? Who is the only other person who knows about this? And are you certain you really trust her?

Malcolm looks confused, frustrated. He doesn't know what the truth is, or whom to trust.

Just as Cody hoped.

'It's crap,' says Malcolm. 'You're talking crap. You're making it up.'

'I'm not, Malcolm. I'm—'

Cody halts as Malcolm dives across to him and grabs hold of his bound wrists.

'I say it's crap. The police knew nothing. You knew nothing. You got lucky, that's all.'

'You think so? You think tracking down you and the children like this could really be down to pure luck?'

'I can get the truth out of you,' says Malcolm. He digs the knuckles of his right hand into the scissor wound on Cody's thigh. Cody yells as the wound reopens.

'I saw your feet,' says Malcolm. 'I saw your missing toes. You want to lose the rest of them? I'll cut them off and feed them to you. How about that, Sergeant Cody? I can do things to you that you can't even imagine.'

Cody holds his tongue again, waiting for Malcolm to calm down.

'You need to start thinking, Malcolm. You need to realise how serious this situation is. I'm a police officer, and right behind me are a whole load of other police officers. Any—'

'Yeah, right.'

'Any harm you do to me now will only make things worse for yourself. Accept that it's over, Malcolm. Turn me loose, before this goes too far.'

Malcolm straightens up. He stares down at Cody as if seeing him properly for the first time. As if finally appreciating the ramifications of what he's done.

This is it, thinks Cody. If I don't turn him now, I don't think I ever will. Come on, Malcolm. Do the right thing.

And then Malcolm says, 'You just don't get it, do you? I already know how serious this situation is. I take it extremely seriously. That's why I'm not about to let you or anyone else split up my family.'

It's not what Cody wanted to hear. A fireball of anger rockets through him, and he reacts to it before he can stop himself.

'Family? You call this a family? This isn't a family, Malcolm. It's a prison. These girls aren't here because they want to be. They're here because you took them and locked them up. *Real* families are held together by love, not by threats and bolted doors.'

The heat in Cody's words is reflected in Malcolm's fierce expression. He gestures towards the three girls. 'I know more about family than you will ever know, than even their birth parents know. We love these girls, and they love us back. They know what's right. They know whose side they're on.' He pauses, as though something occurs to him. 'You want me to prove it to you? I'll prove it. I'll show you just how close a family we really are.'

He grabs the cotton wool then. Rips it apart and stuffs it into Cody's mouth. Cuts off some more duct tape and plasters it across Cody's face.

He draws the curtain angrily as he goes, leaving Cody with an uneasy feeling about this promised demonstration of familial love.

61

The ringtone seems to go on forever.

Answer the fucking phone, thinks Webley. I know it's late in the day, and you've probably got a wife and kids to get home to, but this is important. I've done a bloody long shift too, you know, so answer the fucking—

'DS Rockford.'

'Oh,' she says. 'Hi. It's me again. Megan Webley.'

'Hi, Megan.'

They are on first name terms now. She has called enough times to get past the formalities. She likes his surname, though. Admires its solidity, its grittiness. She has always thought of her own surname as having a certain kick-ass ring to it, but Rockford wins hands down.

'Hi, Ade.' He has asked her to call him that. She'd prefer Rockford. Or maybe Rocky. She'd prefer to hang on to her image of someone who has the dogged determination and street smarts to solve this mystery.

She says, 'You're probably sick of me by now—'

'Not at all.'

'—but Cody is a good friend, you know? And, don't get me wrong, I have complete faith in your team, but I just need to know that we're doing everything we can to find him. Is that . . . I mean, is that okay with you?'

'Megan, it's fine. And the leads you've given us have been great, but at the moment—'

'The family,' she says. She doesn't like to cut him off, but it sounded as though he was about to go all negative on her, and she can't have that. 'Did you speak to Cody's family?'

'Yes. Yes, we did. Have to say the response wasn't quite what I expected.'

She knows what this means. 'You met his dad, right?'

'Yeah. To say he didn't seem concerned would be an understatement.'

This comes as no surprise to Webley. Cody's father disowned him the day he decided to join the police. Even back when she and Cody were an item, he hardly ever spoke about his family, and she suspects he rarely sees them now. She knows only too well that his story about spending time with them at Christmas was bullshit.

She says, 'So they haven't been in touch with him, then?'

'Nope. "Haven't seen him, don't want to see him," were the father's exact words.'

She wonders how it's possible for a man to be so uncaring, so cruel about his own offspring.

'Okay. And Devon Bayliss, his ex-fiancée? I don't suppose you've had time to speak to her yet?'

'Actually, yes, we have.'

'Sorry. I'm being pushy. It's just—'

'I understand, Megan. It's okay. So, yes, we spoke to Miss Bayliss. She was very helpful.'

He halts there, and it seems so abrupt.

'Helpful in what way?'

Rockford hesitates. 'Well, I don't want to reveal too much about DS Cody's personal life. Let's just say she talked to us about his possible state of mind.'

Shit, thinks Webley. Devon has dropped him in it. Cody is going to have some difficult questions thrown at him when he returns.

'Look,' says Webley, 'I know more than most about Cody. I know about the awful attack on him, and I know how traumatic it was for him. I also know that he's fully fit now, and one of the best detectives in Merseyside. So if Devon has said something to make you think he's not all there—'

'Actually, no. She said the opposite. She said he went through one hell of an ordeal, but dealt with it remarkably well, considering.'

'Oh,' says Webley. She feels ashamed of her quickness to judge Devon. The woman has protected Cody when she could so easily have condemned him. 'But I take it she hasn't seen or heard from him?'

'Afraid not. She's worried about him, though. She's been calling me nearly as often as you.'

She wonders if Rockford is having a subtle dig at her, then realises he's probably right. To him, Cody is just another 'misper' – cop speak for a missing person. But to Webley, Cody is a colleague. A friend. An ex-lover.

'Sorry,' she says. 'I'm working on child-abduction cases at the moment, and seeing the bogeyman around every corner.'

'That's understandable,' says Rockford. 'If it's any consolation, Cody seemed perfectly fine when he left his flat.'

She struggles to make sense of his words. 'I'm sorry, what?'

Rockford pauses. 'I'm not sure you realise how seriously we're taking this case, Megan. It's all hands to the pump here.'

'Yes. Of course.'

'And one of the things we've been doing is analysing traffic data. Lo and behold, we got an ANPR ping on Cody.'

Webley feels a surge of excitement. ANPR is the Automatic Number Plate Recognition system. The 'ping' means that Cody's car number plate was spotted on a police camera.

'Where?' she asks. 'When?'

'Yesterday evening, heading away from town on Wavertree Road.'

She thinks about this. Wavertree Road? What would he be doing there? Heading towards the M62, perhaps?

'Okay,' she says. And then: 'Why do I think you've got more to tell me?'

'Because I have. We've started pulling in CCTV from the area. I'm hoping there's a lot more to come yet, but we've already got one positive.'

'You've got Cody's car on camera?'

'Better than that. We've got the man himself. Want to see?'

'What? Yes! Yes, please.'

'I'll email it to you now. Not sure where this is all going to lead yet, but it's a start.'

'Ade, you're a star. You've done so much already today. Thank you.'

'No problem. We'll find him. Check your email, and if anything else occurs to you, let us know. Take it easy, Megan.'

She thanks him again and ends the call, then grabs her computer mouse and opens up her email browser. The most recent message has the subject line: 'DS Nathan Cody'. It feels strange to her to see his name in print like that.

She opens the message, and then the attachment. She gasps at the crystal-clear image that fills her screen.

Cody.

The photograph is of the front of his car, but he can be seen behind the steering wheel. There doesn't appear to be anybody else in the car. Nobody with a gun to his head, or a knife to his throat. In fact, he seems to be wearing the expression of someone who doesn't have a care in the world.

So what happened?

Why does a man dash out of his flat, go for a drive, and then disappear into a black hole?

Webley touches a finger to the computer monitor. To Cody's face.

She prays that this is not the last ever image of him alive.

62

Cody's stomach practically howls at its emptiness.

He hasn't eaten in over twenty-four hours. Hasn't drank much, either.

The kids have eaten. Burgers, chips and beans. Cody had his nose in the air, sucking in the aromas and trying to imagine them solidifying in his stomach.

He was given nothing. Literally not a bean, baked or otherwise. He wonders if they will simply allow him to starve to death.

He doesn't want to die that way. If he has to go, let it be quick. Preferably painless, too. Slowly wasting away in the darkness is not how he pictured his end. He has always envisaged something more dramatic. A hero's parting.

But he doesn't want to think about endings. Not yet. Not while there is still hope. He's managed to unsettle Malcolm a little. Put thoughts and fears in his head that he can't cope with. Cody needs to keep picking at those scabs. Get Malcolm to start thinking about cutting his losses and surrendering.

The door again. Those damn bolts. Every time they are pulled back they seem to twist into his gut.

'Hey, girls.'

Malcolm. Shit. Cody can relax a little when it's Harriet: she appears to have no interest in what lies within the curtained-off area. Malcolm is a different kettle of fish. He is too unpredictable.

The girls don't answer. They hardly ever do unless one of them is asked a direct question, and even then it is uttered through a veil of fear.

'Who's up for a game?' says Malcolm.

No replies to that one either. Cody wonders what they'll play. Hide and seek, perhaps?

'I'll go first. See if you can beat me this time.'

It all goes quiet. Cody listens intently. And then he hears it: three soft thunks.

Darts. They're playing darts.

'Your turn, Daisy.'

Thunk . . . thunk . . . clatter.

She missed one.

'Nice darts, Daisy. Okay, Poppy. Show us what you can do.'

It continues like this for several minutes. Cody's mind begins to wander. For the millionth time, he tries to think up a way out of this.

'I'll tell you what, girls. Now that we've all had a bit of practice, why don't we make it a little bit more interesting? Why don't we bring Mr Cody into the game?'

At the sound of his name, Cody stiffens. He hears Malcolm step towards him, and then the curtain is whipped back.

Malcolm's expression is a blend of delight and malevolence that causes Cody to dread his intentions even more.

'You really want to doubt the loyalty of my family?' Malcolm whispers. 'Then watch and learn. See how we play together.'

He moves aside, drawing the curtain back all the way round the rail. Ahead of Cody, the three girls stand together and stare at him.

This is the first they've seen of him since he regained consciousness. They are transfixed. Scared and fascinated at the same time, like they're observing a vicious animal at the zoo.

Because that's what Malcolm told them, Cody remembers. That's what he has made them believe.

He locks eyes with the oldest of them. Daisy. Tries to make her understand without speaking. If any of them is capable of reading faces, it will be her.

But then she has been here for three years. How will that have affected her empathy? What kind of brutality has she suffered here, and what will that have done to her ability to connect emotionally?

He has to hope. Because he thinks he sees a spark of something in her eyes. A willingness to give him at least the benefit of some doubt.

But I could be wrong, he thinks.

'Right then, girls. Let's show Mr Cody here how good we are at this, eh?'

Nobody in the group moves. They don't know what this is, why they are being expected to put on a show.

'Come on,' says Malcolm. 'We're one big happy family. We have a good time together. Mr Cody doesn't believe it. He told me so. That's why he wants to take you away and do nasty things to you. But we're not going to let him, are we? We're going to stay here and have fun. So come on. Who's going first?'

When there is still no movement, Malcolm steps up to Daisy and drags her away from the other two girls. Cody sees how terrified she seems of his touch.

'Daisy! You're letting the team down. Show Mr Cody how you can hit that double top.'

Daisy tears her eyes away from Cody. She turns to focus on the dartboard, raises her arm to throw.

'Wait, wait!' says Malcolm. 'I almost forgot.'

He moves to the wall. Unhooks the dartboard from its nail. Turns with a look of glee on his face.

Heads towards Cody.

And now Cody understands. He finally realises what has been going through Malcolm's mind all this time.

This is his proof. His test of family loyalty. His demonstration that, given a choice between their new father and the stranger in their midst, the girls will always choose Malcolm.

No matter what that choice entails.

And so Cody watches with mounting horror as Malcolm unwraps a length of string attached to the back of the dartboard. And much as Cody tries to struggle and shout, he is powerless to prevent Malcolm hooking the string around his neck.

Powerless to avoid being turned into a human target.

63

The board is heavy. Its weight causes the string to bite into the back of Cody's neck. Perspiration breaks out on his forehead as Malcolm herds the girls together, ready to launch their missiles.

'What do you think, girls?' says Malcolm. 'Much more fun this way, isn't it? Who'd like to go first?'

Cody looks at each of the girls in turn. Wills them to see that this is not all right, that even at their tender ages they must know it's wrong to hurt another human being. His eyes bulge with the effort.

The girls stay where they are.

Malcolm remains unperturbed. Cheery, in fact. At least for now.

'Look,' he tells them. 'It's no different this way. I'll show you.'

Cody knows this man doesn't have to inflict pain. He heard each and every one of Malcolm's darts hitting the board during the earlier game. He has seen the trophies downstairs.

'But just to make it fairer,' Malcolm continues, 'I'll throw backwards.'

Cody shouts, but it is just noise. If anything, it causes the girls to recoil in fright.

Malcolm is unaffected. Slowly, he turns his back on Cody. Begins aiming a dart over his shoulder.

He's going to do this, Cody thinks. He's actually going through with it.

Cody issues another muffled cry. He strains against his bindings until they cut into his limbs.

And then Malcolm lets fly.

Cody sees the trajectory. Sees that it's wildly high, above the dartboard. He tries to dodge to his left, but he has so little room to manoeuvre, and then he feels it strike, feels it sink into his right shoulder. He cries out, then looks down at the shaft sticking out of his flesh. It is like a tropical insect, sinking its proboscis deep into his body.

Malcolm grins as he assesses his throw. 'Oops. Not a great start. I'll try again.'

Another dart comes flying Cody's way. This one hits the board. Malcolm appears disappointed.

'Only a six. I'm sure I can do better than that.'

When Malcolm lines up his third dart and makes the throw, Cody realises that its path is even higher than the first. It streaks towards him, coming straight at his head. At the last moment, Cody twists to the side and hears the dart as it sails past his ear.

Malcolm turns to face Cody, sees that his final dart lies on the floor beyond him. He looks annoyed.

He walks behind Cody and picks it up. Then he pulls the second dart from the board. Finally, he yanks the one from Cody's shoulder. Before he retreats, he gives Cody a look of sheer contempt.

'You see, girls? See how easy it is? So who's next?'

He steps up to the three girls, studies each of them in turn. Then his gaze settles on Daisy.

'Daisy, I think you should set an example, don't you? I think you should show your sisters here what to do.'

Cody sees her wide-eyed terror. Senses that she is aware of some dreadful fate that awaits her if she disobeys.

But still she doesn't budge from her position.

Malcolm drops the tone of his voice a notch. 'Daisy, I don't intend to have a discussion with you about this. We are playing a game, and it is your turn. I'm sure you don't want to ruin this for everyone. You know how angry that will make me.'

Daisy turns her head slightly then, looks directly at Cody.

And he nods. A slight tip of his head and a blink of his eyes. Giving her his blessing. Saving her.

Her own eyes begin to water. The decision is tearing her up inside.

'Daisy,' says Cody. 'It's okay.'

He knows she won't hear the words clearly, but hopes the message will reach her. She needs to know he won't blame her.

And yet she still doesn't step forward.

'Daisy,' says Malcolm, 'I'm not going to ask you again. I am your father. You do as I say. You need to show this terrible man that he can't destroy us. We stick together, through thick and thin. Last chance, Daisy. What's it going to be?'

She opens her mouth. Her lip trembles. She's going to defy him, thinks Cody. She is seriously going to tell him to take a hike.

No, Daisy. Don't do that. Not for me.

And then something curious happens. Something nobody else in the room expects.

The small, quiet one. Ellie. She moves away from the others. Takes a step towards Cody. And then she pulls back her arm and lets fly with a dart.

He is almost too surprised to react. He just manages to turn his head slightly, and the dart hits him in the side of the face. It penetrates his cheek, and he hears the grating of the metal point as it forces its way between his teeth.

He emits a stifled shriek. Then, gathering himself, he looks back at Ellie. There is no malice on her young features. Her expression is impassive, and Cody wonders what is going through her mind.

Almost robotically, she flings the next dart. Cody thanks his lucky stars as it hits the board and bounces out onto the floor.

The stars forsake him when it comes to the third dart. It's too low this time. Cody wants to shriek as the missile heads for his groin. It misses by inches, burrowing instead into his fleshy inner thigh.

And then Ellie just stands there, hands by her sides, her duty as a daughter fulfilled.

'Jesus,' says Malcolm when he gets over the shock. 'Will you look at that? Look at that!'

Malcolm strides across to Cody. He pulls the dart from his leg. Yanks the other one from out of his cheek. Cody feels the warmth of the blood as it trickles down his face and onto his neck. Tastes it as it soaks through the cotton wool in his mouth.

Malcolm jabs towards his eyes with the darts. 'See! See what they'll do? That's for me, that is. That's because they're family.'

He's actually proud, thinks Cody. He actually interprets this act of pure torture as some kind of validation of love for him.

What a warped bastard.

Malcolm takes back his dartboard. He doesn't seem interested in tending to Cody's wounds. Too preoccupied with his own smugness, he simply draws the curtain back around his prisoner.

'Well done, girls,' says Malcolm. 'I knew you wouldn't let me down. We stick together. That's what families do.'

It occurs to Cody that Malcolm appears to have forgotten that only one of the girls did his bidding. It's another sign of his instability.

And then Cody hears the door being closed, the bolts being slid home.

He tilts his head back and closes his eyes. Allows the pain to flow through his body as it must.

And he wonders what lies in store for him next.

64

Daisy keeps herself away from the other girls for the rest of the evening. She doesn't want to talk about what has happened, what she has witnessed. It's too much for her.

She can't even be bothered to explain things to Poppy, who is obviously confused by the whole episode. Every time Poppy approaches her with a question, Daisy shoos her away.

She's not sure she understands it all herself.

That Mr Cody. He's supposed to be a really bad man. Someone who has come to hurt them.

And yet . . .

It was the look on his face. Not when he was pleading with her for help. Anyone in his position would do that, good or bad.

No, it was later. When he was granting her permission to throw the darts at him.

She knows she's not mistaken. It was clear. He nodded and he blinked, and he . . .

He was forgiving me, she thinks.

He was telling me it was okay, he wouldn't hold it against me, and that I should go ahead and do it because then Malcolm wouldn't punish me.

Why would Mr Cody do that? If he really is such a terrible man, why wouldn't he hate me for doing something that might hurt him? Why wouldn't he be angry with me?

But he wasn't angry. He was trying to help me, even though horrible things were being done to him.

So what does that say about him?

Daisy carries these questions with her throughout the evening. She is thankful that Malcolm doesn't put in another appearance. Harriet shows her face once or twice, though, just to make sure they are getting ready for bed. She doesn't even mention Mr Cody. It's as if she wants nothing more to do with him.

Once in bed, and she is certain that Ellie is asleep, Daisy lets her tears flow. She does it as silently as she can, but behind her, Poppy becomes aware of the sobs wracking her body.

'Are you crying?' she whispers.

'Just a bit,' Daisy replies.

'Why? Why are you crying?'

'I don't want to talk about it.'

'Please, Daisy. Please talk about it. I want to know. Is it because of Mr Cody?'

Daisy accepts it's unfair to leave Poppy wrestling with the matter. She turns in the bed to face her.

'Yes, it's because of Mr Cody.'

'Because he got hurt? In the game?'

'Yes.'

'But . . . But he's a bad man. He came to take us away. He's worse than Malcolm and Harriet.'

'We don't know that, do we? And even if he is bad, that doesn't mean we should hurt him, does it?'

'Bad people are supposed to get punished. Everyone knows that.'

'If you're bad, you go to jail. That's the law. If Mr Cody is bad, then Malcolm should call the police.'

'But if he calls the police, they'll find us here.'

'Yes, they will.'

Poppy goes quiet. Then she says, 'What do you think about Mr Cody?'

'What do you mean?'

'Do you think he's a bad man, like Malcolm says?'

'I don't know.'

'What will they do to him? Will they kill him?'

'I don't know.'

'They don't feed him, you know. He must be starving.'

Daisy starts to cry again. She hates knowing that just feet away from her, a man is possibly dying. Good or bad, he is being slowly killed. And that doesn't seem right.

Poppy brings a hand to Daisy's cheek and wipes away the tears. 'Don't cry. It's not your fault. You didn't hurt him. I thought you were very brave.'

'Thank you, Poppy.'

'It was Ellie. *She* did it. I hate her, don't you? She's always getting us into trouble.'

Daisy sniffs. 'No, Poppy. You don't understand. Ellie saved us. She threw the darts because someone had to. If she hadn't, Malcolm would have punished all of us. Please don't be angry with her.'

Poppy goes quiet again. Daisy can picture her wrestling with these complex, thorny issues.

Eventually, Poppy's breaths become longer and slower as she falls into a deep sleep.

The night hasn't finished with Daisy, though. It taunts her with the sounds from beyond that curtain: the tiny rustles and pitiful groans of a dying man.

And she wonders if they will cease altogether before morning.

65

Sleep evades Webley, too.

She tosses and turns in her bed, but the more she fights to get away from her consciousness, the firmer it clings to her. Worse, it insists on bombarding her with imagined scenarios that only exacerbate her unrest. She keeps seeing images of Cody's corpse: hanging by a rope or dragged from a river, and then lying on a slab in the mortuary.

She gets out of bed at six, not knowing if she ever managed to drift off, but with a feeling of exhaustion that suggests she didn't.

She tries to prop her eyelids open with strong coffee, followed by a long shower.

He'll be found today, she tells herself. Alive. He'll have a story to tell – something suitably astounding to account for his dropping off the edge of the world – but at least he'll be back with us. He'll be safe.

No, he won't, she thinks. He's dead. If he's not in work this morning, then he's dead.

She cries.

Please let there be more news today. Good news, preferably, but anything will do. I can't stand not knowing.

She gets into work before anyone else. Sits there staring at Cody's empty chair, the papers on his desk still undisturbed.

Her colleagues drift in one by one. As they enter, each of them looks towards Cody's desk, then makes a mournful face at Webley. Even DCI Blunt can't stop her eyes straying towards where Cody should be as she makes her way to her office.

Webley tries to put him out of her mind and concentrate on her work. She doesn't want today to be like yesterday – not giving the missing girls the attention they deserve – but it's so difficult.

Halfway through the morning, Blunt shows her face in the incident room. She looks grave, as though she is the bearer of bad news. Webley feels sick.

'I'll keep this brief,' says Blunt. 'You are all aware by now that Detective Sergeant Cody is missing. He hasn't been seen since the day before yesterday. Nobody knows where he is. I don't want to start speculating as to what that might mean. It's too early for that. What I do want to say is that we can't allow Cody's disappearance to distract us from the vital work we do here.'

She points to the photographs of the three girls on one of the boards. 'If those girls are alive – and I would love to believe they are – then they are counting on us to save them. If we don't do it, nobody else will. And if they're dead, then we owe it to them and their families to find the man who took them. Missing Persons are dealing with Cody, and that's how it should be. If I had unlimited resources, or if things were quiet around here, then I'd put each and every one of you onto the search team. But that's not how things are. Life is never perfect. That's all I want to say.'

When Blunt returns to her office, she leaves behind a pall of silence. Detectives look at each other soulfully. From the back of the room comes a sniffle. Webley turns to see Grace Meade burying her face in a tissue.

Gradually, people return to their work. Keyboards clatter. Phone calls are made and received. Filing cabinets are opened and closed. Life goes on.

The double ping from Webley's mobile almost stops her heart. It's a text. And as she starts scrabbling in her bag for her phone, she can't stop herself thinking that this is from him – from Cody. He's finally responding to her long series of text messages. He's saying he's okay, he's saying he's—

It's from Parker.

Happy Valentine's Day. Looking forward to tonight xxx

The disappointment almost pulls her down to the ground, but she knows she shouldn't feel that way. This is from the man who, until recently, was her fiancé, and wants to be called that again. The man she thought she loved deeply is making an effort to fix things. Isn't that worth something?

And now she feels guilty. It's as though she has caught herself out comparing boyfriends, even though it has been a long, long time since she was with Cody.

Looking again at her phone, she considers calling Parker back. Telling him she can't possibly make it tonight because she has too much on her plate.

But that would be unfair. This is none of his doing. It wouldn't be right to take it out on him.

Give him a chance. Perhaps he will make everything all right for her, just as he used to.

*   *   *

It's a couple of hours later that she goes to see Blunt.

She has no good news to present to her. No significant progress on the missing girls.

What she feels now is the need to apologise. She was out of order yesterday. Blunt was quite right. There are ways of doing things: protocols to be followed. Members of an elite unit like MIT cannot allow their emotions to get in the way of the job. Webley realises that now. Much though she would love to drop everything and go looking for Cody, it would be an abrogation of her duty. It would be just plain wrong.

And so she goes to Blunt's door. Prepares herself to swallow humble pie.

Blunt will understand, she thinks. It's not as if I'm alone in having a special attachment to Cody. Blunt has her moments.

Like now, for example.

Webley pauses, her fist in the air, on the verge of knocking.

What has stopped her is the sound from within. The sound of gentle weeping.

Blunt's door is slightly ajar, and Webley cannot stop herself from putting her eye to the crack. She sees Blunt with her back to the door. One of her hands is over her mouth, stifling her cries. In the other hand is a photograph.

Webley pulls away, heads quickly back to her desk.

I shouldn't see this, she thinks. This wasn't meant for my eyes.

The image won't leave her, though. It squats in her mind, confusing her, saddening her beyond measure.

The image of DCI Blunt, crying over a photograph of her lost sergeant.

66

Malcolm, in his study, a can of bitter in his hand and two empty ones in the wastepaper bin.

He doesn't drink much these days. It clouds his already muzzy thinking.

But he's drinking now. In the middle of the day, no less. Practically unheard of for him. Harriet would have a fit if she found out.

He's doing it for the numbness it brings. The escape from the pandemonium in his brain.

He still doesn't know what to do about the cop. Still doesn't know what to believe.

Are they coming for him or not? Is there a bit of paper somewhere, a computer record, with the name and address of the Bensons on it, just waiting for someone to notice?

Cody has been here two nights. Surely his colleagues would be here by now if they were coming at all. If there is something pointing the way, surely one of them would have seen it, no matter how thick they seem.

And then there are the other questions buzzing fiercely in his head like a colony of disturbed bees. He wants the beer to drown the bastards, because they're really starting to get on his wick.

He drains the can, tosses it into the bin, burps.

He heads downstairs, and finds Harriet in the kitchen, scrubbing the grease from the hob. He sees a vase on the window sill, containing the flowers he bought her on the Internet for Valentine's Day. It devastates him that he feels the need to discuss matters of mutual trust on such a day.

He drags out a chair to sit down, and the noise startles Harriet into turning around.

'Hello,' she says. 'Fancy a cuppa?'

Malcolm feels the gas from the beer rising in his gullet. He lets it out with a belch. 'No, thanks.'

Harriet studies him for a few seconds, then she removes her rubber gloves and comes to join him at the table.

'Is everything all right?'

'Not really,' he says.

She looks worried now. 'Why? What's the matter?'

He wonders where to start. So much buzzing in his head.

'The copper. We can't keep him here forever.'

'No. That's what I said to you, wasn't it?'

'Yes, but . . . Well, it's not an easy decision, is it? I still don't know . . .'

'Don't know what?'

'What brought him here. Why did he come here, Harriet?'

'The van. He told us they had a list of people with vans.'

'I know. That's what he said. But I think there's more to it. Stuff he's not telling me.'

'Like what?'

'That's what I don't know.'

He waits for Harriet to say something, but she doesn't. It almost seems to him that she doesn't want to pursue the topic.

He says, 'And then there's the second visit.'

'The second visit?'

'Yes. Him coming back here by himself, and that ridiculous excuse about his warrant card. Don't you think that's really weird?'

'Yes. Yes I do.'

'Only you haven't said much about it. You were here and I wasn't, but you haven't told me much about what went on.'

She gives a barely perceptible shrug. 'There's nothing more to say. I told you everything I could remember.'

Malcolm thinks back to his conversation with Cody. He struggles to recall the exact words, but the gist of it is still there.

Cody was talking about police intelligence. About how it sometimes has to be kept secret because to reveal it would endanger someone's life.

As though someone might have said something they shouldn't have.

'But I'm still really puzzled,' he says. 'Don't you think it's strange that he should turn up at our door just after you sent me out for ketchup?'

Another thought occurs to him: *Had we really run out of ketchup?*

'Well, maybe he waited for you to leave. Maybe he thought he could get more out of me when you weren't here.'

'Yes,' Malcolm says. 'That's probably it.'

He stares at his wife. All sorts of unwanted thoughts are running around in his head, mutating the object of his affections into someone he no longer recognises.

Damn that Cody!

But he can't stop himself. He has to ask.

'And then the other bit I can't figure out is why he went upstairs and found the girls. That bit is really worrying me.'

Harriet blinks. Doesn't answer.

'Think back,' he tells her. 'Think back to when he was here. Are you sure you didn't say or do anything? Anything that might make him believe the girls were upstairs?'

She blinks rapidly again. Takes too long to answer. 'No, Malcolm. I told you. There was nothing. I don't know why he did that.'

Malcolm licks his lips. He needs more beer. And then he needs to have another conversation with Cody.

He gets up from the table. Harriet studies him.

'Malcolm,' she says, 'have you been drinking?'

He walks away in silence.

67

Cody wonders if they have given up on him as an item of interest.

Malcolm came to him first thing in the morning. He looked him up and down, enabled him to use the toilet, then left again. That was hours ago.

Since then, the door has opened and closed several times. Usually Harriet, tending to the girls. At one point, he heard Poppy asking Harriet what was going to happen to Mr Cody. Harriet told her she'd have to ask 'Daddy'. Cody guesses that won't happen.

He feels like shit. Every inch of him seems to radiate pain – mostly from his wounds, but also from the nylon ties cutting into his wrists and ankles, and because of the absence of food and water. His stomach feels like it's trying to strangle itself, and his muscles and joints ache from the lack of use.

And where are the police? Where are his colleagues? He knows some damn good detectives. Is it really beyond their collective wit to locate him?

You in particular, Megan. Where the hell are you? What's keeping you? You know me better than almost anyone. Use that. Think like I think. Walk where I'd walk. Come and get me.

He realises he's crying.

He pictures Megan with her platinum-blonde hair and the dimples in her cheeks, and he wishes he had never split up with her all those years ago. Wishes he had devoted more of his energies to her instead of the job.

Which then starts him thinking about Devon, the only other serious love in his life. The woman who was actually willing to have him as her husband. The woman who did everything she could to nurse him through his trauma after he was attacked. The woman who—

Shit.

Stop that, Cody. Stop being a snivelling, sentimental baby. Stop feeling sorry for yourself. Get your act together and find a way out of this.

And then Malcolm enters the room. As soon as Cody hears him talking to the girls about the headphones, he knows he's in for another little tête-à-tête with the man who holds his life in his cruel hands.

* * *

Daisy has made a decision.

It's a risk, but she needs to know.

The two men are about to discuss things behind her, things that Malcolm doesn't want her or the younger girls to hear. Why? What's so secret?

Or maybe it's not secret at all. Maybe Malcolm is just trying to protect her, because what really happens back there is that he hurts Mr Cody even more than she has seen.

She doesn't want to listen to that. If Malcolm is killing his prisoner, she doesn't want to hear it.

But what if it's not that? What if there are truths being uttered that she knows nothing about?

If he catches her, he will punish her. She is fully aware of that. He might even take his anger out on Mr Cody, so she is taking a risk for him too.

Am I right to do that? she wonders. Is it okay for me to put his life in danger?

But if I do nothing, he's probably going to die anyway. And maybe he should. Maybe he really is a nasty man, like Malcolm said he is.

But I need to know.

* * *

When Cody spits out the cotton wool this time, it alarms him to see that it is soaked in blood. He touches his tongue to his injured cheek, and balks at the touch of a large jelly-like clot there.

His first request is the same as always. 'Please, can I have some water?'

He knows he can last without food, despite the stomach cramps it's causing him. He'd read somewhere that Gandhi once went twenty-one days without eating. He doesn't want any favours from the Bensons, doesn't want to make them believe he owes them anything.

Malcolm nods slowly, then fetches a beaker of water from the sink. Cody notices how unsteady the man seems on his feet today, and when he raises the beaker to Cody's lips, he almost misses his mouth. If those clues weren't enough, the whiff of alcohol on Malcolm's breath is unmistakeable.

So, he's been drinking. In the middle of the day. What, if anything, does that mean?

Is he feeling unusually stressed, perhaps because of the mind games Cody has been playing with him? Is this whole thing getting to him?

And what effect will that have on his attitude? Will it make him more susceptible to losing control?

Cody decides he needs to tread carefully.

As he drinks, a gobbet of the congealed blood breaks loose in his mouth. Rather than appear ungrateful by spitting it out, he swallows hard, fighting to keep it from reappearing.

'Thank you,' he says.

Malcolm nods again, then leans back in his chair, studying Cody through half-closed eyes. He lowers his gaze for a second.

'What happened to your feet?'

A surprising question. The first sign of any interest in his history. An opportunity for Cody to make himself more human in Malcolm's eyes.

'I was attacked. I was on an undercover operation that went wrong. A gang of men tied me to a chair – a bit like I am now – and then started chopping off my toes with one of those branch loppers.'

'Oh,' says Malcolm. 'I thought maybe you'd had an accident with a lawnmower.'

He laughs then, a deep disturbing bray that sends shivers along Cody's spine. Cody forces himself to join in.

Look at us, he thinks. Two drinking buddies having a great time. Him on the beers and me on the blood-stained water.

When Malcolm stops laughing, it's abrupt. It's like slamming a large book closed mid-sentence, a violent rejection of all that has just been read. The humour, such as it was, is gone.

'I'll bet it was painful,' says Malcolm.

'I lived through it. That's the important thing, don't you think? We all go through pain in our lives, but sometimes it makes us better people.'

'How did it make you better?'

Cody thinks about his nightmares, his hallucinations, his violent outbursts, his insomnia, the break-up with Devon . . .

Yeah, Cody. It really improved you, didn't it?

'It made me realise that life isn't all about me. There are people around us, and everything we do affects them, sometimes more than we realise.'

Malcolm looks over at the girls, all staring at the television.

'I know what you mean,' he says. 'I used to be really selfish. Everything was about me.' He touches a finger to the scars on his head. 'I got this in an accident at work. Took that to make me start thinking more about making other people happy.'

'Just thinking about it? Or doing something about it?'

'Well, obviously doing something. You've only got to look at Harriet now to see how happy she is. Most of the time . . .'

He lets that trail off, as though something about her recent behaviour troubles him. But then he snaps out of it again.

'And then there are the girls, of course.' He gestures towards them. 'See how relaxed they are? Not a peep out of them. That's because of me. It's because of what I did for them.'

'What exactly is that, Malcolm? What have you done for them?'

Malcolm's eyebrows arch in surprise, as though the question shouldn't even need to be posed.

'Gave them a loving family. Gave them protection. Kept them safe and warm and fed. What more could any child want?'

'How about seeing the sunshine? Playing on the grass or at the beach? Running around with their friends? Going to school? They don't have those things, Malcolm.'

Cody wonders as he says this whether it's a step too far – whether it's likely to tip Malcolm over the edge again. Yet he seems remarkably calm.

Perhaps he should drink beer more often.

'They don't need all that. Sometimes in life you have to make compromises. You have to make tough decisions that are in the best interests of the children.'

'And what about their parents? I mean their birth parents. Don't they matter?'

An immediate shake of the head. 'Not a jot. I don't give a toss about them. The kids are happy, that's the main thing.'

'Are they happy, Malcolm? Are you sure about that?'

Malcolm turns his head to look at the girls again. He seems more ponderous.

'Sometimes I . . .' He shakes off the thought, turns back to Cody. 'I do what's right. The girls know that. They love me for it. That's all I need.'

68

Daisy makes her move.

She knows she can't reach up and take the headphones from her ears – that would be too obvious. She has another trick in mind.

She takes hold of the wire leading from the headphones to the three-way splitter. Starts to pull it taut.

She doesn't want it to spring all the way out. Just enough to disconnect the audio signal.

Daisy continues to pull. Beads of perspiration form on her brow.

It's not coming out. If she stretches the wire any more it could break.

She holds her breath. Tries again, praying that her actions aren't obvious from behind.

But somebody has noticed.

Ellie turns slightly towards her, then looks down at Daisy's white knuckles gripping the cable. Her eyes widen.

Daisy locks eyes with Ellie. Gives an almost imperceptible shake of her head. Ellie faces front again, but her gaze continually strays to Daisy's fingers.

Daisy tries again. Makes the wire taut. Tauter still. And then . . .

It moves! Just a couple of millimetres, but enough to cut off the audio. The shrill, joyful singing is replaced by low male voices. Malcolm and Mr Cody. Muffled through the large cushioned phones clamped over her ears, but some of it still gets through.

Scared of moving even an inch, Daisy closes her eyes and focuses all her attention on the voices.

* * *

'Why did you take them, Malcolm?'

'I just told you.'

Cody finds the conversation exhausting. He feels as though his body wants to go into shutdown to conserve precious energy. Simply getting words out takes all his effort. But he knows that his best chances of survival lie in understanding what makes Malcolm tick.

'No, I mean why these particular girls? You took some serious risks getting them. Why not other children that might have been easier?'

Malcolm smiles. 'You haven't worked that one out, then? For all your so-called "intelligence", you haven't figured out what makes these girls special to us?'

So there *is* a reason then, thinks Cody. They weren't randomly targeted.

'I have to admit we're at a loss on that score. Care to enlighten me?'

Malcolm ducks the question. 'How much else don't you know? How much else of what you've told me is just pure bullshit?'

'Don't get complacent, Malcolm. We don't know everything, but we know a lot. Others will figure out the rest, you can be sure of that.'

The donkey bray from Malcolm again. He raises his arms. 'Then where are they? All these clever men and women who know so much. Where the hell are they?'

'They'll come. It could be in ten minutes, it could be tomorrow, but they'll come. Whatever you do, don't make this any worse than it needs to be.'

'Worse? For you or for me?'

'For you. For Harriet. Think about what will happen if you . . .'

'If I what? Kill you?'

'Yes. If you kill me. That's not something you should even be contemplating, Malcolm.'

'Really? I don't see it like that. I don't see how it could possibly make things any worse for me if I'm caught. You saw Ellie's parents, didn't you? You know what I did there?'

'Yes. I saw. But from what I gathered from the evidence, they attacked you. You could argue you were acting in self-defence. This is different. This would be the cold-blooded murder of an officer of the law. Do you understand the difference, Malcolm? This would be much more serious. At your age, you would never see the outside of a prison again.'

Malcolm looks up at the ceiling, and Cody hopes he's thinking seriously about this. No need to tell him he's going down for a long time whatever the outcome. The bit about self-defence was just to make him feel better; even if he didn't break into that house with the intention to kill, he went equipped with a lethal weapon, ready and willing to use it if necessary. He knew what he was doing.

Cody says, 'And then there's Harriet.'

This jolts Malcolm. 'What about her?'

'She wasn't involved in what you did to Ellie's parents. She didn't take part in the actual abductions either. But right now she's as guilty as you are for keeping me here against my will, and if you kill me, she will also be charged with my murder. Do you want that to happen?'

'So what are you saying? That I should let you go?'

'That's exactly what I'm saying. There's no avoiding it, Malcolm. You're going to be tracked down and arrested for what you've done. That's a given. The only thing that should be concerning you now is damage limitation – for you, for Harriet, and for the girls.'

Malcolm goes silent again. He bows his head, rubs a hand across his scalp. Cody can no longer see his face.

'It's over, isn't it?' says Malcolm.

'Yes. It's over. You need to bring this to an end. I'll help you.'

And then Malcolm looks up, and his eyes are aflame. His eyes are searing.

'I mean it's over for you. Your friends aren't coming. They never were. And yes, you're right: I need to bring this to an end.'

He stands up, closes the distance to Cody.

'I need to sober up. You can have one more night of praying to be rescued. First thing tomorrow I'm taking you out of here, away from my family.'

'Malcolm, I—'

But Malcolm brings a finger to Cody's lips.

'Hush now. Don't make a sound. You won't feel a thing.'

69

She's not at all in the mood for this, but she tells herself to be optimistic. She needs a friend this evening. Someone who isn't another cop. Someone who can make her laugh, but give her the permission she needs to cry.

So come on, Parker. Fix what we had. Tell me you're sorry. Show me the man I used to know, and make me love you again.

Parker is already there when she enters the busy restaurant on Dale Street. He stands up and waves as soon as he sees her, a massive smile on his face. He doesn't look apprehensive, and that makes her feel relieved. She could do without more drama today.

She threads her way past the tables. Couples, mostly, who don't even notice her passing. But then it is Valentine's Day.

We used to be like that, she thinks.

'Hi,' says Parker. 'You look gorgeous.'

'I look a mess,' she answers. 'It's been a hell of a week.'

'You always look gorgeous to me. Have a seat.'

He pulls out a chair for her. When she is seated, he calls over the waiter and asks for a bottle of Prosecco.

Webley jumps in quickly: 'Just a diet coke for me, please.'

Parker stares at her. 'Seriously? You don't want to wind down?'

Yes, she thinks, I want to wind down. What I don't want is to get too comfortable, to say something I might regret. The shedding of inhibitions can come later, if and when we sort this mess out.

'I'm fine. Coke would be great.'

Parker shrugs at the waiter. Orders her diet coke and another large glass of Shiraz for himself. Webley wonders how many he's already had.

'I'm surprised you managed to get a table,' she says. 'Especially since we're not eating.'

'Are we not eating?'

'Parker, I told you—'

He grins mischievously. 'I know, I know. Just a drink. That's fine. I know the owner here. He said we can have the table as long as we like.'

Webley nods. As a hotel manager, Parker has become acquainted with a lot of people in the food and accommodation trades.

'So,' she says, 'how are you?'

'Okay. Busy during working hours, not so busy in my private life. I'm missing you.'

She raises her eyebrows. 'Get straight to the point, why don't you?'

'Well, I am, and I'm not going to pretend otherwise. What about you?'

She knows what he's asking. He's asking if she's missing him too. She chooses to misinterpret.

'To be honest, things are pretty shitty at the moment. I'm working on the missing girls case.'

'Wow. That's a biggie. What is it they're calling him – the Pied Piper, isn't it?'

The name conjures up unwanted images in Webley's brain. She sees a mysterious, sinister figure leading away the city's children in a long line behind him, never to be seen again.

It's that 'never' bit that worries her. It's the one outcome she fears most. The same goes for Cody. It's been another eternal day without him. Missing Persons have assured her that he is their top priority. They have interviewed her, Blunt and everyone else on the squad. They have talked again to family, friends and neighbours. And still they don't have answers.

She wonders if the Pied Piper has somehow managed to ensnare him, too. Is that possible? Could there be a connection there?

'Yeah,' she says. 'The Pied Piper. Typical tabloid response. Make everyone even more shit-scared than they already are, just so they can sell a few newspapers.'

Parker nods, but she can tell he's not really interested in her job right now. He wants a proper answer to his question.

She is glad when the drinks arrive. She uses the opportunity to divert the conversation onto several other trivial matters.

But it can't last forever. Parker eventually raises the central item on the agenda.

'Megan, can we talk about us?'

So there you go, she thinks. That's plain speaking. No avoiding the issue now.

'Of course. Isn't that why we're here?'

'Yes. And I want to begin by apologising to you.'

Well, thinks Webley. That's an unexpectedly promising start.

'Go on,' she says.

He seems surprised. 'Well . . . that's it. I'm apologising. I'm deeply sorry. Now, can—'

'What is it exactly you're apologising for, Parker? Can we be a bit more specific here?'

'The hurt I caused you. I got too controlling. I know that now.'

'Okay. That's good.' She pauses. 'I'm sorry, I'm not trying to be a pain, but I don't want this coming back to haunt us later. Just to clear the air, you're admitting that trying to break up my friendship with Cody was wrong?'

Parker takes a long slug of his wine. 'If you really want me to eat my words, then yes, I shouldn't have done that.'

'Don't do that, Parker. It's not about making you eat your words. I just need us to establish that we're agreed on this. Neither of us should try to break up the other's friendships, no matter how much we might hate the friends.'

'I don't hate Cody. I think he's a complete basket case, but I don't hate him. That's not what it was about.'

'Then what was it about?'

He stares at her, then looks away. 'Oh, forget it,' he says petulantly.

Webley struggles to maintain her calm, even though she has already registered Parker's use of the term 'basket case'.

'No,' she says. 'Tell me. We're here to talk this through, so let's talk. But we have to be honest with each other.'

He sups his wine again. 'I've already told you this. I don't know why I have to say it again. I was jealous, okay? Is that what you want to hear?'

'If it's the truth, yes. It's nice that you were jealous. It shows you cared. You just took it too far.'

She hopes that's an end to it, that they can move on now.

And then Parker says, 'You have to see it from my point of view, though.'

'Which is?'

'Well, it's not exactly a normal situation, is it? Cody isn't just a random work colleague. He's an ex-boyfriend.'

'Emphasis on the *ex*, Parker. He's not my boyfriend anymore.'

'I think it would be nice if somebody told him that.'

'What? What are you talking about?'

'He's got issues, hasn't he? Mental issues. If you ask me, he's not fit for duty. And how do I know this? Because he told you, and you told me. Of all the people in the world he could have opened up to, he chose you. And then there was that time you were a hostage on the roof. Who is it that comes running to save you like a white knight on his charger? Why, it's Detective Sergeant Cody again. Isn't that funny? And then you get injured, and why do you get injured? Because you're saving Cody's life, that's why. Do you see what I'm getting at now, Megan? This isn't exactly a normal working relationship by anybody's standards. Add to that the fact that he was seeing more of you in a day than I ever did . . .'

He lets his rant trail off then. Turns to his wine again.

Webley shakes her head in disbelief. She is stunned at the vehemence in Parker's words. His green-eyed monster seems to have been eating away at him for months. Even after all the time they have spent apart from each other, he is unwilling to let the matter go. This evening wasn't meant to be about Cody, and still he manages to find his way into the centre of her life. He is always there.

Unlike Parker, she decides. He hasn't changed, and so this isn't going to work.

She says, 'You don't need to worry about Cody anymore. He's disappeared.'

'What do you mean?' Parker says sulkily.

'What I say. He's gone. He's officially a missing person. Nobody knows where he is.'

'Really?'

'Yes.'

'Okay, well . . . Maybe it's for the best.'

Webley's mouth drops open. Did he really just say that? 'What?'

'All I'm saying is, maybe that's a stroke of luck for us. I mean, if he's run off somewhere, he won't be able to come between us again, and so—'

'He hasn't "run off". Something has happened to him. He could be lying dead in a ditch somewhere, or—'

'Come off it. It won't be like that. The guy's a nut job. He's unpredictable. He's probably holed up in a cave somewhere, thinking about the meaning of life.'

'Parker, we've got half the police force out looking for him. You don't seem to appreciate the seriousness of this.'

'Actually, I think you're making it perfectly clear to me how serious this is. To you, anyway.'

'What's that supposed to mean?'

'You're missing him, more than you've been missing me. How long has he been gone? A day or two? We split up at Christmas, and yet he's the one you can't bear to be without.'

Webley is starting to feel really angry now. While everyone else in this place is staring longingly into the eyes of their partner, Webley is on the verge of landing a punch in the eye of hers.

'Parker, you're blowing this out of all proportion. My relationship with Cody bears no comparison to what you and I had together. It's a totally different thing.'

'Well, you know what? I'm glad he's gone. I don't care if he *is* lying in a ditch somewhere. He has caused so much trouble between us. Look at us now: still arguing about him. Good riddance to the guy, that's what I say.'

Later, Webley will analyse what she says next. She will wonder what on earth possessed her. She will wonder whether it was due to tiredness, stress, desperation or just a need to strike back. Whatever the reason, the words come tumbling out.

'Parker, please tell me you don't know anything about what's happened to Cody.'

He looks as though he has been slapped.

'What?'

'I'm asking you about Cody. I'm asking you if you've seen him in the past couple of days. Because if you have, I need to know.'

Parker remains speechless for what seems like an age. Then he wipes his mouth on a napkin, tosses it onto the table and stands up, pushing his chair back noisily.

'Jesus Christ, Megan. I can't believe you just asked me that. I can't believe how much Cody has you wrapped around his little finger. I'm out of here. Happy Valentine's.'

And then he's gone. And Webley realises that everyone else has seen and heard. All the lovers who were previously lost in each other are now glaring their accusations and their pity at her.

She lowers her head to avoid the pressure of their stares. Tears well up in her eyes.

Well done you, she thinks. Good job, Megan.

She reaches for her bag, finds some tissues. As she digs them out, she realises she'll probably have to pay the bill for the drinks, too.

Damn you, Cody. Always there. Always causing me pain.

A waiter appears at her side. She begins to dab at her cheeks before daring to show him her ruined make-up. He surprises her by starting to fill her glass with white wine.

'Sorry,' she says. 'I didn't order any wine.'

The waiter gives her a humble nod. 'No, madam. It has been ordered for you. Perhaps a friend of yours?'

He nods again, this time gesturing towards the rear of the restaurant. Webley turns in her chair to discover the identity of her mysterious benefactor.

Well, this is a night of surprises, she thinks.

70

Hearing the words is one thing. Understanding them is another.

Daisy has nobody to ask what is really going on. She was brought here when she was only seven, with the limited knowledge of the world that seven-year-olds usually have. And since then her exposure to new information has been strictly controlled.

What, for example, is an 'officer of the law'?

That's what Mr Cody called himself: an officer of the law. She doesn't know what that means. She thinks the most likely explanation is that he's a policeman, but why would a policeman be sneaking into their bedroom? And why isn't he wearing a uniform? If he was a policeman and he'd come to rescue them, why did he come by himself, and why didn't he take Malcolm and Harriet off to jail?

So maybe he's not a policeman after all. Maybe he's something else. The only other people she thinks might be 'officers of the law' are judges and all those who wear wigs in court, but that doesn't seem to make any sense at all.

Or maybe he was just lying. Making stuff up so he can escape.

And then there was what they said about other people who might arrive. Malcolm asked where all the 'clever men and women' are, and Mr Cody said they were coming.

Who are those people? Are they really coming here?

Daisy cannot deny that the thought frightens her a little. She doesn't know if they are good people or bad people. She has this vision of hundreds of evil men descending on the house in the middle of the night.

Because that's the big question, isn't it? Who is good and who is bad? She knows that Malcolm does bad things sometimes, but what if Mr Cody is even worse?

And there's one other worrying bit of information she managed to pick up from the conversation.

They talked about what Malcolm had done to Ellie's parents.

They weren't specific, but the way they talked about killing Mr Cody suggested that what was done to Ellie's parents was just as bad.

Ever since she caught Daisy unplugging the audio cable, Ellie has been giving her searching looks. Although she still refuses to speak, her eyes seem to be filled with a million questions.

Daisy wishes she had a few more answers.

* * *

Webley feels it would be rude not to drink the wine that has been so kindly bought for her. Ruder still to quaff it and not convey her gratitude.

So she stands up. Walks with trepidation to the table in the far corner.

'Thank you. You didn't have to . . .'

'You looked like you needed it,' says DCI Stella Blunt. 'Care to join me?' She gestures towards the empty chair opposite her. It is clear that she has just eaten, and is now on a coffee and what is left of her wine. It is also clear that she has dined alone.

'Er, sure. Okay. Let me just get my things.'

Webley heads back to her own table and grabs her bag and wineglass. Thinks to herself, What am I doing? Why did I say yes?

She returns to Blunt's table and settles herself into the empty chair. Tries to put some words together that aren't just gap-fill.

Blunt beats her to it. 'I often eat here. Forgot it was Valentine's night, though, or I mightn't have bothered sitting here looking like I've been left on the shelf. Still, now you're with me, anyone coming in will probably think we're lesbians.'

Webley laughs nervously. She's not sure how long she'll be able to keep up the pretence of wanting to be here.

'That was your fella, wasn't it?' Blunt asks. 'The one with the funny name.'

'Parker.'

'Yes, Parker. That's it. I always think you're calling him by his surname. Bit like Cody.'

Blunt sips her coffee, acting as though her remark was totally innocent. But Webley knows better. Connecting the two names like that wasn't just a throwaway comment.

'I guess . . . I suppose you saw what happened between me and Parker just now?'

'I got the gist. Do you want to talk about it?'

Webley blinks. Suddenly the woman in front of her has transformed from her boss into her agony aunt. Blunt has never offered to discuss personal matters with her before.

'I don't think there's much to say. It was probably as much my fault as his.'

'I doubt it,' says Blunt.

What is this? thinks Webley. Leaping to my defence like that. What's going on?

She takes a long draught of her wine. 'Actually, you're right. It's not my fault. Parker was a complete arsehole tonight. He had no right to humiliate me like that.'

A hint of a smile forms on Blunt's lips. She puts down her coffee and picks up her wineglass. 'Chin chin,' she says.

Webley clinks her glass against Blunt's. 'Cheers, ma'am.'

'We're off-duty, Megan. You can call me Stella.'

'Er, right,' says Webley. She has no intention of using Blunt's first name. She would rather avoid calling her anything than get so awkwardly familiar.

'What a week, eh?' says Blunt.

Webley nods. 'One of the worst I can remember. I could down a whole bottle of this right now.'

'Drink up, then. I'll order some more.'

'No, I didn't mean—'

'Megan, it's fine. Drink the sodding wine and put aside your worries for a short while.'

Blunt signals a waiter and places her order. Webley admires the woman's confidence, her absolute self-assuredness.

'That's the problem, though,' says Webley. 'The relief is only temporary. The stress will be back in spades tomorrow.'

'As it should be.'

'Ma'am? I mean . . . How do you mean?'

'We get stressed because we care, Megan. I'd be worried if you weren't stressed. Especially with what's going on with young Cody.'

There she goes again, thinks Webley. Sneaking Cody into the conversation. But then again, I'm pretty shit at hiding his importance in my life. I might as well have a big red 'Cody' sign on my forehead.

'Yeah,' she says. 'To explain that . . . I don't know whether you're aware of it, but Cody and I used to . . . well, we used to be an item.' Hastily she adds, 'A long time ago. Not recently.'

Blunt's smile is more pronounced this time. 'Get away,' she says.

'You know about that, then?'

Blunt leans forward conspiratorially. 'Megan, I knew about that before I brought you onto the team.'

Webley feels like she has just been jabbed on the chin. 'You . . . You knew? And you still wanted me?'

Blunt shakes her head in bemusement. 'You lot make me laugh. You seem to think I just stomp around all day, breathing flames and quoting regs and breaking balls. Believe it or not, I also put a lot of effort into getting the best out of my team. And when I take on a new member, I do my research. People think I don't know what's going on, but I do. I know things about you, and I know things about Cody, even though he believes nobody can see through his disguise. But I don't give a rat's fanny what you and Cody got up to in a past life. All that matters to me is that you do a good job. So far, I think you've proved I made the right decision.'

'Even after yesterday?'

'Yesterday?'

'I gave you some grief in your office. About Cody.'

'You were upset. You were anxious. I get that, Megan. I'm a human being too, you know. I do have feelings sometimes.'

Webley is starting to realise how true that is. She drinks some more of her wine, and starts to welcome its effects. Starts to feel the tingling sensation as her inhibitions dissolve.

'I came to see you again today,' she says.

Blunt shows her puzzlement. 'When?'

'I didn't come in. I went to knock on your door, but you . . . you were preoccupied.'

'Go on.'

'You were looking at a photograph. A picture of Cody.'

Blunt looks across at the single red rose in its slim vase on the table. 'I see.'

'You were . . . well, you seemed pretty upset. So I guess I'm not the only one who's missing Cody.'

Blunt goes quiet for a long time. She continues to stare at the rose.

'Shit, I'm sorry,' says Webley. 'I shouldn't have said that. It's none of my business. I was just trying to let you know . . . trying to share . . .'

Fuck, thinks Webley. I should never have touched the frigging wine. Shouldn't have come out this evening at all. What a crap day.

Blunt reaches for the bag hanging over the back of her chair. Webley thinks she's getting ready to leave, and starts thinking up new insults for herself.

'Ma'am, I—'

'Just a second,' says Blunt. She slips her hand into a partition in the bag. Pulls out a photograph. 'I think this is the photo you caught me looking at today.'

She hands it over. Webley takes it, stares at it.

It's not Cody.

It looks like him, certainly. From a distance, it could easily be taken for him. Similar hair and cheeky grin. But it's definitely not him.

'Who is it? If you don't mind my asking.'

'His name's Evan. He's my son.'

Another surprise, and this one's a doozy. Webley almost falls off her chair.

'I didn't know you have a son.'

'Most people don't. He's not around anymore.'

'He . . . he died?'

'He went missing. About ten years ago. Not long after that picture was taken. He'd just turned eighteen.'

'What happened?'

'I don't really know. His dad and I divorced, he became a sulky teenager. We argued a lot. And then one day he just left. I got a text from him saying he was okay, and not to look for him, and that was it.'

'Did you try to find him? Did you report it?'

'Yes to both. I got nowhere. The official line was that he was an adult who was free to go wherever he wanted if that was his choice. Without support, I had no chance of finding him.'

It all suddenly makes sense to Webley. If he is still alive, Evan is now about Cody's age. That's why Blunt mothers Cody so much: she sees her missing son in him. It also explains why she has been so affected by the abductions of the girls. Kids going missing must be her worst nightmare.

Webley continues to stare at the photograph, but she's not really seeing it now. She is thinking about the woman sitting opposite. Thinking about how, for the most part, she is just the Boss; the one they call Ma'am; the one who winds up the mainspring of her team each day and sets them running.

But now she is so much more. What she said earlier about being a human being seems such an understatement. Even through the alcohol-induced fog, Webley can see Blunt's fears and emotions with painful sharpness and clarity.

Webley could cry at the intensity of this moment. And later she knows she will.

'You're not to tell anyone else about this, Megan,' says Blunt.

Webley shakes her head. 'No. No, I won't . . . Stella.'

71

The clowns visit Cody that night.

He's been expecting them – is surprised they've left it so late – but it doesn't make their appearance any less terrifying.

Even though he hasn't slept a wink, he has no idea what time it is. It feels as though the girls went to bed several hours ago, but his concept of time has been distorted. There are too many forces pulling at his brain and body, dragging him away from the here and now.

The fire of pain is everywhere. His head, torso and limbs are all aflame. Hunger gnaws at his insides. Thirst seems to shrivel and desiccate his every cell.

And then there are the mental pressures – of what has been and what is to come. If Malcolm is to be believed, Cody has no life remaining. This is his last night on earth. It is a staggeringly profound realisation. He might have hours left, possibly even minutes. The next time that door is unbolted and the light comes on will herald his oblivion.

Hope is the thing with feathers.

Tad optimistic, Emily Dickinson, he thinks. My bird is just a crushed ball of feathers now.

The clowns hear this. They listen to his despair, his sorrow, his pain, and it calls them forth. They delight in opportunities such as this, when his strength and morale are at their lowest.

It begins with the rustlings.

Tiny noises in the blackness. Like the quick, scuttling movements of rats. His wayward mind leaps to make connections, and he sees a long, snaking line of the whiskered fiends as they scamper in the wake of the brightly clad Pied Piper. Except, in Cody's version, the Piper has the grinning, rotting, blood-streaked face of an evil clown.

And then footsteps. Soft on the carpet, but betrayed by the occasional creak of floorboard.

Cody knows they are trying to sneak up on him. His divorce from reality leaves him in no doubt about this. The clowns are here, in this room, and they are searching for him. They can taste his odour in the air, but they cannot see him. For now, the curtain shields him from their gaze.

They have knives. He is certain of that, too. Long, sharp blades, ready to part the flesh from his bones, slice by agonising slice.

I mustn't move, he thinks. Mustn't make a sound.

But it's so difficult. The pain. The fear. I can't halt my breathing. I can't stop my heart pounding like a drum.

And then there is light.

It must be the light that signals his execution. But it is not the full-on glare of the ceiling light. It is so dim it barely casts a shadow.

And there has been no sound of the door being unlocked and opened.

They are here, though. He knows they are here. Doors are no barriers to the clowns. And they create their own deathly light.

They surround him now. They are touching the other side of the curtain. He can smell their fetid breath as it seeps through the insubstantial cotton.

Movement.

He is certain he sees movement in the curtain. They have found him. They are closing in.

He lets out a moan. It makes no difference now. He cannot save himself.

A hand appears. He sees it as having the yellow skin of the dead, with inch-long dirt-encrusted nails. Its fingers curl around the cloth, begin to pull it aside with excruciating slowness. The scraping of the metal curtain rail is like the sound of long fingernails being dragged down a chalkboard. Cody lets out another moan. His breathing turns to panting. He strains against his bindings, rocks in his unyielding chair.

And then a figure appears in the gap.

It is just a silhouette – a hole punched into the darkness. But Cody's mind fills that space with the slavering, knife-wielding form of his worst nightmare. His moans turn to muffled cries for help. He throws his whole weight from side to side in a desperate attempt to demolish the chair that grips him so tightly in its embrace.

But the clown gets closer, closer. It opens its mouth to reveal sharp serrated teeth, dripping with blood-tinged saliva.

And it demands to know. It insists on knowing.

'Why did you come here?' it whispers to him.

And he has no answer. He doesn't know what answer could possibly satisfy this demon. He doesn't fully comprehend the question. He just wants this to end.

If I am going to die, let it be now.

And the clown reaches for him. It touches him with its ice-cold fingers and speaks to him again.

'It's okay. I won't hurt you.'

A void intrudes. An interval while the imaginary switches places with the real. An unbearable moment of relief as the burning dies down and the fear subsides.

Because this is not the voice of a monster.

It is the voice of a child.

A child by the name of Daisy.

72

She has turned on the television. It is not attached to an aerial, and there is no DVD playing; the only thing it displays is a piece of text that leaps around the screen, saying 'No Signal'.

But the important thing is that the screen gives off light. Not much, but enough for her to see where she is going. It does not have the strength to wake the others, or to seep under the door and alert Malcolm or Harriet should they wander past.

Daisy hasn't slept yet. She lay there for hours until she was certain the young ones were lost in the deepest of slumbers.

But now she can find out.

Mr Cody seems scared – more scared than she is of him. Perhaps it is simply because he knows he will die soon. Perhaps everyone gets that frightened when faced with the certainty of death.

And yet she suspects there is more to it. Mr Cody does not seem like someone who would fear death. He is not cowardly. Look at how he gave her permission to hurt him so that she herself would not get hurt.

No, something else is bothering this man. Something dreadful. His muffled cries and moans are like those of an injured animal. He needs help.

She never thought she would dare to get close to him, but here she is. Reaching out to him. Touching him. Telling him she won't hurt him.

He becomes less agitated. His breathing begins to slow. He blinks, as if struggling to see her properly in the murky gloom.

And then he breaks her heart.

He breaks it with his tears. They flow freely down his cheeks and across the tape covering his mouth. His head drops, and his shoulders heave with his sobs. A single hot tear splashes onto her hand.

'Please,' she whispers. 'Don't cry. I just want to ask you something.'

He lifts his chin again. Looks her directly in the eye. Nods.

She has thought about removing the gag, but she reckons that Malcolm would be able to tell it had been disturbed. She is also not quite sure that she is willing to take the risk with Mr Cody. He seems so convincing, but what if he's the big bad wolf that Malcolm claims he is? Or what if he simply talks too loudly and wakes everyone? She is not supposed to be doing this. Malcolm would punish her badly if he knew.

'You said you were an officer of the law,' she begins. 'Is that true?'

He nods. Yes.

'Is that the same as a policeman?'

Yes.

'You're a policeman?'

Yes.

'Why did you come here? I mean, did you come here to take us away?'

Yes.

The answer alarms her. Malcolm told them that Mr Cody wanted to take them away. But then she realises she needs to be more specific.

'To hurt us? You want to take us away to hurt us?'

An emphatic shake of the head. No.

'Then why? Did you come to help us?'

Yes.

'To rescue us?'

Yes.

'Then why didn't you? Why did you let them do this to you? Where are your friends, the other police?'

He looks confused, and she realises she has bombarded him with too many questions, none of which can be answered with a head gesture.

She tries again. 'You said other people are coming. Did you mean other police?'

Yes.

'Then where are they? Are they coming to get us?'

Mr Cody considers this one carefully. His answer is a long time in the making. When it arrives, it's a sorrowful shake.

No. They aren't coming. Nobody else is coming to help.

His response surprises her. This is the opposite of what he told Malcolm. He could easily have stuck to his story, and yet he hasn't.

Does that mean he is being honest with her? Does it mean that only she is entitled to the truth? Or is it just a ruse to get her on side, to make her believe he can be trusted?

She is also saddened by his answer. If what he says is true, then there is no escape for anyone. This man in the chair is already doomed. Even if he were to get free somehow, he is too weak to do anything now. Malcolm would squash him like an insect.

'Is Malcolm going to kill you?' she asks.

Another pause. Then a yes.

'Are you afraid of him?'

Yes.

She hesitates. 'There's one more thing I want to ask you.'

He nods.

'Ellie's mum and dad. Did Malcolm kill them?'

Yes.

'Was she there? Did she see it?'

Yes.

Daisy stands there for a while, taking in what she's heard, trying to figure out what is true and what is not. Trying also to decide what difference such knowledge would make.

She takes a final lingering look at Mr Cody. Searches his eyes for honesty, for decency, for goodness.

'I have to go now,' she says. 'Malcolm . . .'

She waits for Mr Cody to protest. Waits for him to scream at her to help him.

But he doesn't. He just nods, as though he understands. As though he is grateful to her just for daring to grant him a few brief moments of her company.

She turns, slips through the curtain.

When she sees the figure standing there like a phantom, she almost screams.

Ellie stares back at her, pale and mute. Daisy wonders how long she has been there, how much she heard, how much she saw.

'Back to bed, Ellie,' she whispers. 'Come on, before we get into trouble.'

She escorts Ellie to the bed and tucks her in. Then she turns off the television and gets into bed herself.

She cuddles into Ellie, strokes her hair to comfort her.

And she tries to make her mind up about Mr Cody.

73

Mornings here are instantaneous. There is no gradual lightening of the room as the rising sun forces its way through curtained windows. No gentle encouragement to ease from sleep into wakefulness. Instead, there is blackness one moment and blinding brightness the next. The day is proclaimed with the flick of a switch.

Cody hopes his death will be as quick as that. He hopes that Malcolm will not think like the clowns, who would want his final moments to be as prolonged and painful as possible.

Malcolm's cheery voice seems so at odds with what is to occur here this morning.

'Good news, girls!' he says. 'You're going to get your bedroom back today. I've found somewhere else for Mr Cody to stay.'

There is a moment's silence, and then Daisy asks, 'Where? Where will he go?'

'I'm going to clear a space in the garage for him.'

Cody doesn't doubt that he will end up in the garage, but only for a few hours. His corpse will likely be dumped behind one of the vehicles there, ready to be transported when darkness falls again. Malcolm has obviously figured out a way to dispose of his body.

'The garage?' says Daisy. 'He's going to live in the garage?'

Careful, Daisy, thinks Cody. Don't give yourself away. Don't land yourself in trouble on my behalf.

Malcolm's voice betrays his irritation. 'Yes, Daisy. The garage. Now will you stop asking me stupid questions and listen to what I have to say?'

There is no reply.

'Right,' says Malcolm. 'As I was saying, Mr Cody is leaving here this morning. I'll be giving him something to make him sleep, and then I'll move him. You won't have to worry about him any longer. How does that sound?'

Again, no answer.

'Good. I knew you'd be pleased. Okay, then, get dressed. After breakfast, Mummy wants to read a story to you.'

And that's it, thinks Cody. That's all the kids are getting. Soon I'll be gone, and they will forget I was ever here. They'll return to their own kind of normality. An unvarying, mind-numbing existence in a windowless, soulless room.

Before Malcolm leaves, he pops his head through the curtain.

'Not long now,' is all he says.

* * *

Everyone is missing.

Webley has hardly slept. The wine knocked her out for a couple of hours, but then she woke up in a cold sweat. She has tossed and turned in her bed ever since then, but all she has been able to think about is the people who have disappeared.

The girls. Cody. Blunt's son.

She has decided she would like to do something about Blunt's tragedy. The eye-opening encounter with her boss last night has established in her mind a mission to locate Blunt's son, dead or alive.

But that's for another time.

There are other priorities now. The girls, of course, but also Cody. She has decided she can't leave this to Missing Persons any longer. She needs to play a part. Even if it means spending every minute she has outside work, she needs to do something to help. She will hate herself for ever if she doesn't even try.

And, by the way, Parker can go fuck himself.

She throws her covers aside and climbs out of bed. Takes a shower while thinking about Cody. Gets dressed while thinking about Cody. Eats a bowl of cereal while thinking about Cody.

She looks at the clock. Still early. Too early to head into the station.

I should do something with this time, she thinks. Something productive. So . . . what should I do?

Okay, put yourself in Cody's head.

You've just spent a ridiculous amount of time checking out stupid white vans. You go home. You enter the building on Rodney Street. The people in the dentist's downstairs are long gone by now. You go upstairs to the flat. You go into the kitchen. You're desperate for a cup of tea, so you make one. You unload all the junk from your pockets. You take off your jacket and your tie and sling them over the back of a chair. And then . . .

What?

Something happens.

Yes, but what?

It's not a phone call. Someone at the door, perhaps?

Maybe.

You let them in. They're not the nice people you think they are. It all goes wrong . . .

No, that doesn't fit.

No sign of a struggle. You're not the type of guy who would go without a fight. And on the CCTV image there was no sign of anyone else in your car.

So what, then? What could have possibly occurred to make you drop everything, get in your car and drive away? It's that important, you don't finish drinking your tea. You don't intend to be gone for long, because you don't even take your wallet, change or mobile phone with you. All you've got are your keys . . .

Wait, wait, wait.

Something is wrong here.

What is it? What's missing?

Look again. See it with your mind's eye. Wallet, phone, change, tissues, notebook, pens . . .

But no warrant card.

Are you sure? Yes. Absolutely.

Cody's warrant card wasn't on the kitchen counter.

So he took it with him. Which suggests he was going out on police business.

But hang on. What was this suddenly urgent business that nobody else on the force knows about? Cody is an experienced cop. He would have called it in, logged it. He would also have taken his mobile phone with him.

It still doesn't make sense.

Unless . . .

His card was never there in the first place.

Okay, slowly now. Think about this.

You empty your pockets. You realise your warrant card isn't among your possessions. You panic. Where the hell did you leave it? And then you remember. You know you're going to need it tomorrow, and it'll only take a few minutes to fetch it.

Yessss!

Or no.

This could just be the most tenuous, ridiculously manufactured explanation ever.

So continue the thought process, Megan. You were with Cody for most of the day. Where might he have lost his warrant card? When did you last see him with it?

We were looking at vans. He had it with him then, because he flashed it without fail every time we knocked on a door.

Except the last call. The – what was that weird couple called? – the Bensons, that's it. Mr Benson took Cody's ID from him so that he could have a proper gander at it inside.

Yessss!

Or maybe no. They might have given it back to him. Webley can't be certain.

But it's a possibility. His car was spotted on Wavertree Road, which would fit with a drive from Rodney Street to the Bensons' house in Childwall. Maybe he called there, and maybe he gave them a clue as to where he planned to go next.

Maybe. A big *maybe*.

But it's something. Even if all she does is rule it out, it's a contribution.

She looks at the clock again. Still too early to go knocking on someone's door, especially on a mere hunch.

She decides to leave it a little bit longer.

It probably won't make any difference.

74

Daisy, Daisy, give me your answer, do.

She has no answers. She doesn't know what to believe, whom to trust.

What she *doesn't* believe is that Malcolm is giving Mr Cody a nice new home in the garage. She thinks he plans to kill him.

She doesn't know how she feels about that.

If she could be certain that Mr Cody came here to hurt her and Poppy and Ellie, then Malcolm should do what he needs to do.

But if Mr Cody came here to rescue them, then that's different.

Or is it? Because what can she do about it anyway? Mr Cody has already said that nobody else is coming for him, so how can his death be prevented? She can't be expected to stop a big, powerful man like Malcolm. He would kill Mr Cody and then he would kill her too. Even if she were willing to take the risk of setting Mr Cody free, she has no way of removing those cable ties.

He said he's a policeman. But he doesn't look like one. He seems too young, and he doesn't dress like one either. He didn't act like a policeman when he came here, sneaking into their bedroom like that.

So is it all lies? Is he just trying to save himself?

But he was nice to me, she thinks. He tried to save me in the darts game. He didn't even ask me to help him when I came to see him last night.

And he cried.

She hasn't seen a man cry before. Not even her father. It was one of the saddest things she has ever seen.

Best not to get too emotional about this. Whatever she would prefer to happen, Mr Cody is going to die, and that's that. No use crying over spilt milk. Or spilt blood, for that matter. Forget about him.

Except that she doesn't think she can forget. Doesn't think she will ever forget Mr Cody.

*   *   *

Hard to believe, but this is it. This is the end of his short, tumultuous life.

He finds himself filling his final moments with goodbyes. To Devon, to Webley, to his family, his colleagues; to all the people he has known and loved; to the three girls in this room. He also apologises to the girls. He regrets not doing more for them. His only hope is that someone else will rectify that one day.

And when he's done, he wishes to be kept waiting no longer. He wants no time for fear to creep up on him, for self-pity to start gnawing at him.

Bring it on, Malcolm, he thinks.

And Malcolm responds.

He draws the curtain back with a wide, almost ceremonial sweep. In his free hand he carries a full hypodermic and a pair of scissors – larger and stronger this time, to cut through the cable ties. He brings no cotton wool or duct tape – he has no further need for them.

He looks over his shoulder at the children huddled together on the bed.

'I'm just going to give him something to make him sleep now,' he tells them. 'So he won't struggle when I move him.'

Cody knows differently. He knows that the contents of the syringe are likely to be much more potent this time. Lethal, in fact. He won't wake from this particular sleep. He will die, here in this chair, and the girls will be none the wiser.

Malcolm approaches. He puts the scissors down on the shelf. Pushes Cody's sleeve further up his arm.

Malcolm utters no last words. He simply wants to get on with the job.

He raises the syringe, looks carefully at its deadly contents.

And then he touches the tip of the needle to Cody's flesh, and Cody holds his breath in preparation for nothingness.

75

Damn!

Of all possible times, why does it have to be now?

Malcolm freezes. Starts to count. If he gets to ten, he'll assume they've gone away.

But no. There it is again. A more insistent ringing at the door this time, followed by a rap of the knocker.

It will have to be answered. It will have to be dealt with. Only, he can't trust Harriet to handle it. Not the way she's been acting lately.

He looks Cody in the eye. 'Back in a minute,' he promises.

He lays the hypodermic down on the shelf, next to the scissors.

And then he leaves the room, locking the door behind him.

* * *

Daisy gets off the bed.

'Daisy,' says Poppy. 'What are you doing? You mustn't.'

Daisy ignores her. She moves steadily across to Cody.

'Daisy! No! You'll get into trouble.'

She stands inches away from Cody. She stares him in the eye. He stares back.

And now she's the one who starts crying.

'I don't know what to do,' she says. 'I don't know what's right.'

Cody shifts his gaze. She follows it, sees that it alights on the syringe. Then he turns his eyes on his exposed arm.

'No,' she says. 'You don't mean it. You want that to happen?'

He breathes out heavily through flared nostrils. Turns his head towards the shelf again. Nods. Says something.

She looks once more.

Scissors.

He wants me to use the scissors. And now he's looking at his arm. The ties around his arm.

She takes a step back.

'I can't. I'm so sorry. I can't. Malcolm will kill me. He'll kill us all.'

Cody stares at her. And then he nods, closes his eyes, and bows his head.

* * *

Malcolm recognises her as soon as he opens the door.

It's the woman detective. The one who came here with Cody.

He feels his heart hammering in his chest. Is she alone? Are they about to raid the place?

'Hello,' she says, showing her ID. 'Detective Constable Webley. I don't know if you remember me, but I was here the other day, with DS Cody?'

'Yes, I remember,' he says. 'Something about vans.'

'That's right. Don't worry, there's nothing to be alarmed about, but I just want to ask whether my colleague has been back to see you since then?'

Malcolm forces out a laugh. 'Wouldn't it be easier to just ask him?'

Webley smiles. 'You'd think so, wouldn't you? The problem is, we're not quite sure where he's got to.'

'What, you mean he's disappeared?'

'Er, yes. It's looking that way.'

'A copper has disappeared?'

'Yes.'

'Well, now I've heard it all. And you think he might have come here? Why on earth would he do that?'

'We're just trying to work through all the possibilities at the moment. I thought that DS Cody might have accidentally left his warrant card when we were last here. Bit like this one?' She points to her own ID.

Malcolm shakes his head.

'You haven't seen it, then?'

'No. I'd have phoned you if I'd found something like that.'

'And DS Cody didn't call round asking the same question?'

'No. Sorry.'

He sees her shoulders slump, and he almost smiles.

'Okay,' she says. 'Thanks anyway.'

And then she walks away, and Malcolm closes the door, and he lets that smile find its way out.

Stupid coppers.

He heads back upstairs. Unbolts the door. Enters the bedroom.

The girls are still on the bed, still uncertain. Daisy in particular looks terrified.

Cody is still in his chair, still bound and gagged. The scissors and hypodermic are where Malcolm left them.

All is well.

He moves across the room to stand in front of Cody, then he bends at the waist.

'Thought you should know,' he says. 'That was your woman friend. Webley. She's gone now. She won't be back.'

He watches Cody's eyes for a reaction. Some sadistic streak within him wants to see the pain of abandonment there.

But he doesn't find it.

Something is wrong here. Very wrong.

And then he sees that the cable ties around Cody's wrists are much looser than they should be.

They have been cut through.

76

He knows, Cody realises. Malcolm knows.

He seizes his opportunity, because it's the only one he'll have.

It's not like in the movies. In a film, he would demonstrate the power of good over evil by finding a sudden enthusiasm to win, and then boxing the bad guy to the ground with his superior fighting skills. Every strike would be a resounding cymbal-crash in the name of right versus wrong.

This isn't like that.

In this version, Cody's arms and legs are weak and ineffective after several days of inactivity. What is supposed to be a spring into action turns into more of a flop forward, and the intended rapid-fire battery of blows becomes a sequence of pathetic slaps that are easily batted away.

It becomes messy then. The two men grapple with each other, scrabbling for an advantage as they whirl around the room, bouncing off walls and knocking furniture over. The television topples and smashes. Books and toys tumble to the floor around them.

Cody feels Malcolm's power. Realises he could lose this.

It's driven home to him when Malcolm finds an opening, hammering Cody with a roundhouse punch that splits his cheek and sends him reeling backwards.

Cody hits a wall, and then Malcolm is on him again, and he tries to retaliate with a blow of his own, tries to do something, anything, to stop this bulldozer of a man. But his arm is slapped away and Malcolm lands another punch, this time into his empty gut. It is so powerful it seems to drive through his abdomen and connect with his spine, and Cody collapses to his knees and tries to find oxygen even though his mouth is still taped, tries to find energy and willpower and luck and anything else that will help him survive this onslaught.

But Malcolm isn't done. Malcolm has already decided Cody will die, and die he will, by injection or by being physically torn apart – it's all the same to him.

And then he is standing over Cody. Applying a headlock. Crushing his windpipe and twisting his head until it feels as though his neck will snap like a twig.

And what Cody focuses on now is the girls' screaming. Because he knows he has failed them. Worse, he has endangered them. Malcolm will finish him off, and then he will turn on his own brood. That is the kind of animal he is.

And then the screaming begins to fade, and the dark mist rolls in.

* * *

'Stop! Stop it!'

Daisy's yells go unheard. Alongside her, Poppy is also screaming, but to no avail.

She watches Malcolm pummelling Mr Cody. He's going to kill him, she thinks. And then he's going to kill us. And it's all my fault. I'm the one to blame. I shouldn't have interfered. I should have stayed out of it.

She glances at the other girls. They are scared out of their wits. Even the usually impassive Ellie looks terrified.

They don't deserve to die, she thinks. Please, God, let him punish me, but not the others. They did nothing wrong. It was me, only me!

And then Malcolm is squeezing Mr Cody's neck, just as he did with Poppy that time. She managed to stop him back then, managed to make him listen to reason. But that won't work now. He won't listen to her ever again.

And suddenly she is moving.

She hears Poppy shouting at her, but she doesn't stop. She has to do something.

She grabs the scissors. Opens them up. Launches herself at Malcolm's back.

The blade sinks in deep. Malcolm howls and releases Cody, who collapses to the floor like a bag of bones.

Malcolm reaches behind him, first around his waist and then over his shoulder, but he can't quite reach the scissors embedded between his shoulder blades.

He turns, his face a spittle-covered mask of fury and hatred, his eyes burning with a passion for death and destruction. He lumbers towards her. She runs, heads for the door, yanks it open.

And on the other side she sees Harriet, brandishing a rolling pin and screaming at her like a banshee.

Daisy dives back into the room, but the change of tack has cost her. Malcolm grabs hold of her long hair with one hand, and slams the door closed with the other. He pulls hard, spinning Daisy and slamming her into the wall. He takes hold of her dress below the neck, bunches it in his hand, begins to slide her up the wall until her feet are inches above the ground. He brings back his other hand and forms the biggest fist Daisy has ever seen – a sledgehammer of a fist that will smash her skull and spread her brains across the wall.

Daisy closes her eyes and waits for the inevitable.

Which doesn't come.

She opens her eyes again. Sees that Malcolm's face has taken on a curiously puzzled look.

He lowers her almost tenderly. Then he turns around and looks down.

Daisy stares past him, sees what he sees.

The tiny, pale, waif-like figure of Ellie.

Malcolm takes a step towards her, but Ellie stands her ground. He takes another step.

Daisy cannot believe what she is seeing. Cannot understand it either.

But then her eyes shift again to Malcolm. The scissors are still buried between his shoulders, but further down, protruding from the back of his leg, is the hypodermic syringe.

And it's empty.

Ellie has injected the whole contents of the syringe into Malcolm's bloodstream.

One more step from Malcolm, and then his knees buckle. His kneecaps slam into the carpet. He reaches a hand out towards Ellie, who stares dispassionately back at him. He remains in that kneeling position for a full five seconds, and then he tips forward, his nose making a cracking sound as his face connects with the floor only millimetres from Ellie's feet.

77

Cody drags himself to his feet. The scene around him is like a battlefield –
the dead, the wounded and the lost strewn among the rubble.

He grasps the tape covering his face. Rips it away from his mouth, leaving
it still hanging from one cheek. He breathes again, he coughs, he splutters.

The girls stare at him, waiting for his guidance. The king is dead; long
live the king.

'Wait here, girls.'

He heads for the door, but before he can reach it, it is flung open and
Harriet rushes in – too terrified to enter earlier, but now wielding her
rolling pin and emitting a cry shrill enough to shatter glass.

Cody grabs her arm, wrests the weapon from her grasp, then pushes
her up against the wall.

'Shut the fuck up,' he tells her. Then, as an afterthought, he pulls the
duct tape from his cheek and plasters it across Harriet's mouth.

She sees then. Sees her husband lying prostrate on the floor, the
scissors and the hypodermic firmly stuck in him as though he has been
turned into one of his own dartboards. Harriet loses what little fight
she had in her, and she slumps and sobs in Cody's grasp.

'Go,' he tells the girls. 'Knock on the neighbours' doors. Get them to
call the police. Tell them a police officer needs urgent help. Go!'

* * *

It's hard enough for Daisy to leave the bedroom. She has never done this
before. Never stepped beyond this threshold. Poppy has to grab her hand
and lead the way.

They head downstairs. It seems so strange to Daisy that she has lived in this house for three whole years and never seen the landing, the stairs, the hallway, the pictures on the walls, the carpets.

And then they're at the front door. The way out of this prison.

'Come on!' Poppy cries. 'We need to get help.'

Daisy finds herself rooted to the spot. She cannot move.

'For God's sake,' says Poppy. She opens the door herself, goes running outside, hand in hand with Ellie.

Daisy lets them go. She knows they won't travel far. They'll try next door, and if that's empty, each one after that until they find someone.

Daisy has other things on her mind.

She stands in the doorway, on the line between here and there, between incarceration and freedom, between the small and the large.

And just look at how big that world is! It's enormous. It's gigantic. It's heaven.

She sees real grass, flowing like waves. She sees the spiky skeletal fingers of trees, denuded of their leaves. She sees sculpted shrubbery, in a thousand shades of green. Beyond a line of perfectly geometric hedge she can see parked cars and streetlamps and a road and litter. In a window across the street sits a grey cat, staring curiously back at this stranger in its territory. How she longs to stroke a cat or a dog.

And, above it all, the sky. The colour of pewter now, but still making her blink to stare at it. And look! An aeroplane! Showing her just how limitless her boundaries are now.

All this movement. All this life.

She takes a deep breath. Steps forward.

A breeze flicks at her hair, rustles her dress and caresses her cheek and legs. And it makes her want to laugh and cry at the same time.

She is free, and the world is welcoming her back.

78

This makes it all worthwhile, thinks Oxo. It doesn't happen often, but when it does it's magical.

The best he can usually hope for is that a perpetrator is brought to justice. The murderer of a loved one is found and arrested. It can bring a little relief, a little closure, but it can never bring back the dead. It can never mend broken hearts.

But this – this is almost a resurrection. It has to be the best news ever.

And he gets to deliver it.

He rings the doorbell. Maria Devlin answers. She wears the expression of someone who has come to expect at best promise but no substance from these updates. A possible lead, a shiny new nugget of information, but not her child standing on her doorstep. That would be too much to hope for.

She lets him in without even being asked. It has become a ritual for her. Bring the policeman in, offer him tea and a biscuit, listen to his news, send him away again. And repeat.

Oxo doesn't tease. This isn't the announcement of the winner of a talent show. It would be unfair of him to keep them waiting. He reveals his news as soon as Maria and Craig are sitting in front of him.

'You're probably sick of me telling you there's been a development, but there has. We've found Poppy, and she's alive and well.'

There. All out. He didn't even pause after 'We've found Poppy', because he knew they would picture her dead.

Maria's hand jumps to her mouth. Craig brings shaking fingers to his temples.

'What?' says Craig. 'She's alive? Our Poppy? She's alive?'

Oxo nods and smiles, and then he can no longer keep the tears from his own eyes. They all jump out of their chairs, they hug and kiss and dance and cry and yell, and the room spins, the world speeds up, the brightness floods back in.

And then the questions come. Who, why, where, when? Oxo does his best to deal with them without saying what he can't, but it's less of a problem now. This couple are more accepting of anything as long as it means they get their daughter back.

'So when can we see her?' asks Maria breathlessly. 'When do we get our Poppy back?'

'Soon,' says Oxo. 'We have to check the girls out, make sure they're okay, both physically and mentally. And then we have to debrief them. We'll interview them separately, using officers trained to deal specifically with young children.'

Maria nods. 'I understand.' She smiles at Craig. 'What's another couple of hours, after all this time?'

* * *

He waits with them. Chats to them, drinks tea with them, enjoys the moment. He listens to the sheer unadulterated joy in their cracking voices as they phone friends and family. This is a time to savour and to remember.

When the call comes in on his mobile, he sees how the couple shuffle forward to the edges of their seats.

'Oxburgh,' he says.

'Oxo, it's Megan. I'm outside the house. Do you mind coming out here for a few minutes?'

He's puzzled, but tries not to show it to the parents. 'On my way.'

He ends the call. Maria and Craig are almost falling off their chairs in anticipation.

'Two ticks,' he says. 'Just need to confirm a couple of things with one of the other detectives.'

They nod, but he can see how frustrated they are. They just want to cut through all the red tape that lies between them and the daughter they miss so much.

He gets up from his chair, sees himself out of the house. Gives them a reassuring smile as he leaves. Because, to be honest, he's worried. Something is wrong.

He walks along the driveway, to where Webley is waiting for him on the street. She looks serious, and that causes his stomach to tighten.

Please don't ruin this, he thinks. Please don't shatter the happiness I have just given them.

Webley is not alone. Footlong Ferguson is sitting at the wheel of the unmarked police car. When he looks at Oxo, he simply raises his eyebrows in greeting. No smiles.

'Problem?' he asks Webley.

'Yes. A big one.'

'What's up?'

She tells him. And as she speaks, he cannot prevent himself glancing once or twice at the house. And he is certain he can see Maria looking back at him through the bay window. He is certain she is trying to read their lips, their expressions, their body language.

He wishes he could send her a signal of some kind – something to comfort her. Because now he knows his own face is betraying a sense of what he is hearing. He can feel his mood darkening, souring. He is turning as grey as the clouds.

And suddenly his moment – his glorious moment – has turned to shit.

He sees the gaudy squad cars coming up the street and pulling in behind Footlong. Uniformed officers pile out, and then Ferguson gets out to join them. He looks at Webley, and she nods back, and then Ferguson leads his pack up the driveway.

Oxo watches the shifting dark figures through the window, and he wants to cry. He feels Webley's hand rubbing his arm, and that just makes it worse.

Too sensitive, he thinks. I'm too sensitive for this fucking job.

They exit the house then. All very quick and efficient. The real work will be done back at the station. That's where the recriminations, the accusations will all come to the fore. That's where fresh tears will be shed as lives are ripped apart again, so soon after they were last devastated.

And one of the things that will haunt Oxo for ever is the look of confusion on Maria's face as she is brought out behind her husband. Her utter lack of comprehension. Her total astonishment at how the universe could possibly treat her so harshly, so unjustly.

It gets to Oxo. There and then it overwhelms him. He remembers the conversation at the kitchen table. Recalls with burning shame how he allowed himself to be sucked in. He finds himself stepping forward, unable to control his actions.

'Bastard!' he says to Craig Devlin. 'You fucking bastard!'

They manage to drag Oxo off before he can do much damage, and he wishes they wouldn't. He wishes they would just let him get this out of his system.

Because now it will just sit there, bottled up inside.

She thinks he looks pale and thin and broken, even though he has been gone only a few days. Her heart hurts as she looks at him staring out of the hospital window, and she struggles to find the energy to lift his spirits.

'You swinging the lead again, mate?' she says.

Cody turns at the sound of the familiar voice. 'Megan!'

He smiles and seems suddenly to fill out a little. He spreads his arms widely to embrace her. She fills the space he creates for her, encircling him with her own arms – gently, for fear of causing him pain.

She remains there perhaps a little too long, and when they finally break apart, she feels the glow in her cheeks.

'Bloody hell, it's hot in here,' she says in excuse.

'Hospital wards are always too hot. I'm tempted to strip off completely.'

'Ew. Don't do that. Remember there are cardiac patients knocking about.'

He chin-points at the paper bag she's carrying. 'That for me?'

'What? No. I just bought myself a snack for later.' She pauses. 'Course it's for you, soft lad. Here.'

She tosses the bag to him, and he starts to open it.

'If these are grapes, I will eternally question your ability to use your imagination.'

But then he peers inside and sees the sweets it contains.

'Chocolate peanuts! I love chocolate peanuts.'

'I know you do, you big kid. Enjoy them. If you're allowed to, that is.'

'I won't tell if you don't.'

He pulls open a drawer beside his bed and slips the bag inside.

'So,' Webley says. 'What you in for?'

'Everything. Various injuries, including the whoppers on my bonce.' He points to the bandage on his head. 'Dehydration. Hence this get-up.' He points again, this time to the drip in his arm. 'Starvation, exhaustion and severe stress.'

'Jesus, that's quite a collection. You're . . . you're okay though, aren't you?'

She cannot hide her deep concern, and she doesn't care. He should know that people have been worrying about him.

'I'm okay. They want to keep me in for observation, but they think I'll live. You can tell Blunt she won't need to go looking for a new sergeant just yet.'

'She was upset, you know. Blunt, I mean. We all were. I thought . . . we thought . . .'

Shit, she thinks. Look at me. I promised myself I wouldn't lose it, and I'm losing it.

Cody reaches out a hand. Grasps hers briefly and then releases it again.

'I'm fine. I'll be out of here in no time.'

She looks away as she wipes her eye, then nods. 'Are you able to talk about it? About what they did to you?'

'Sure. How long have you got?'

'As long as it takes. Since when did I ever refuse to listen to your problems?'

So he tells her everything, from start to finish.

Well, not everything, she feels. The facts, yes. The sequence of events. But not what went on in his head during his time in that house. Not the really intimate stuff – the stuff that might expose his vulnerability and the true extent of the damage done.

But it is dramatic nonetheless, and by the end of the story, Webley is gobsmacked.

'Frigging hell, they really did a number on you, didn't they?'

'I've been through worse,' he says.

Which is true, but it doesn't make it any better. She wonders how much punishment a man can take. Cody wasn't in the best of health before he was incarcerated. What kind of state will he be in now?

'How are the girls?' he asks.

'They're okay, but they've been through a lot. They're going to need counselling. Especially Ellie.'

Cody nods. 'What about the other two? Have they been reunited with their parents yet?'

Webley hesitates. 'About that . . .'

'What? What do you mean?'

And now it's Webley's turn to tell a story. The story she heard from Harriet Benson in the interview room. The one that she in turn related to Jason Oxburgh outside the Devlin house.

It's a story that began more than three years ago, when two disturbed individuals were in desperate need of something to make their dysfunctional lives complete. In the pursuit of his fabled pot of gold, Malcolm turned to the Internet. He spent hour after hour every day there, looking in places most of us wouldn't dream of looking.

What he found there was a young girl named Daisy Agnew.

He did more research, much of it on the Internet, but a lot in the real world too. He found out all about her family, her school, her hobbies, her friends, her holiday arrangements. He followed her, took photographs of her. Made plans for taking her.

And then he explained his thinking to Harriet.

At first she was horrified. It was too dangerous. They would get caught and go to prison.

But he allayed her fears. Told her he'd thought through every detail. It couldn't go wrong. They could have the family they'd always wanted.

Above all, he told her, it was the right thing to do. It was the right thing for Daisy.

'I don't get it,' says Cody. 'Why were they so convinced they were justified?'

Webley takes a deep breath. 'The place where Malcolm found Daisy wasn't something like Facebook or Twitter or Snapchat. It was an area of the dark web.'

'Aw, shit,' says Cody. 'Please don't tell me . . .'

'Afraid so. It's a child pornography site. But Malcolm didn't go there looking to get his kicks. He went there because it made him furious that people could do such things to little kids. He wanted to do something to help those children.'

Cody groans in despair. 'How did Daisy get on there?'

'Her mother's new boyfriend. The way the website works is that to be able to download stuff you have to upload some images of your own. The site organisers tell you how to do it in a way that's supposed to be undetectable if anyone searches your computer later. I don't know how true that is – maybe the people at GCHQ or someone like Grace could crack it – but the tech guys certainly didn't come up with anything on the Devlins' computer. To be fair, none of us had any reason to think it might contain anything like that, especially once they were dropped as suspects.'

'So it happened to Poppy, too? And Ellie?'

'Yes.'

'How bad? I mean, do we have any idea what these girls went through?'

'We're hoping it's nothing too traumatic. They've had enough to deal with since then. According to Harriet, the video of Daisy was of her playing in her paddling pool in the back garden. Perfectly innocent to most of us, I know, but there are some sick bastards out there. Anyway, that's how Malcolm tracked her down. In some of the images there was a "for sale" sign outside the neighbours' house, which gave the name and phone number of the local estate agent. Harriet said they could also hear Daisy mentioning the name of her primary school. A quick search of the estate agent's website was all it took to find out where they lived. I'm guessing there were similar clues in the videos of Poppy and Ellie.'

Cody puts his head in his hands, groans again.

'What?'

He looks at her. 'It's never straightforward, is it? Never black and white. I got out of that house today hating the Bensons. I was glad Malcolm was dead. I could quite easily have punched Harriet's lights out. But now? In a way, I can understand what they did. They were trying to help little kids. Malcolm told me as much. He said they were doing what had to be done, to protect the girls.'

Webley nods. 'I guess the Pied Piper was the perfect name for Malcolm. In his head, he wasn't taking children to hurt them, but to punish the bad parents.'

'Exactly. Obviously their whole approach was completely warped, but are they the monsters I thought they were? I'm not sure anymore.'

Webley shrugs. 'Let me know when you figure out what makes people tick. I don't even know how *you* work.'

He smiles. 'I like to be enigmatic.'

'Yeah, right.' She glances at her watch. 'Listen, I should get out of here, let you rest.'

'Okay. But just before you go . . .'

'What?'

'I want to thank you.'

'What for?'

'For saving my life. Again.'

'What are you talking about?'

Cody looks uncomfortable, and not merely because of his injuries. 'Yeah, I might have left out that tiny detail. Malcolm was about to inject me with the syringe. The tip of the needle was actually touching my arm. And then you rang the doorbell. I was literally saved by the bell. *You* saved me. For the second time since you joined the team.'

The revelation hits Webley hard. She thought she had accomplished little, believed she could have tried much harder.

But what if . . . ?

What if she hadn't spent so much time thinking and worrying about Cody? What if she hadn't realised what was missing from his flat? What if she hadn't turned up at the Bensons' house when she did?

It says something profound to her, but she's not sure what it is. There are few people whose lives we get to save once, let alone twice. It suggests some kind of connection over and above the mundane, physical kind.

It suggests . . .

Well, never mind what it suggests, she thinks.

'You're welcome,' she says, playing it down.

She stands, ready to leave.

Cody says, 'By the way, how did your date go? With Parker?'

She thinks about telling him. About his central role in that particular rendezvous. And about the outcome.

'Yeah,' she says. 'It went okay.'

Because right now that seems the safest reply.

ACKNOWLEDGEMENTS

I would like to thank my editors, both past and present, for everything they have done for me: Joel Richardson, who got me this gig in the first place, and who will be sorely missed; and Sophie Orme and Bec Farrell, for their amazingly scrupulous work on knocking this book into shape. A massive shout-out, too, to the rest of the team at Bonnier Zaffre; you are the best.

Big thanks also to agent Oli Munson and the gang at A. M. Heath. Being a member of Oliver's army is an honour and a privilege.

To family, friends, colleagues and anyone else who has given me support: I owe you my gratitude for keeping me sane enough to do this.

And to the booksellers and the book buyers: you are the ones who make this all worthwhile. Your passion for books is the fuel that drives my fingers at the keyboard. Thank you.

A message from David . . .

If you enjoyed *Don't Make a Sound*, why not join the David Jackson Readers' Club by visiting **www.bit.ly/DavidJacksonClub**?

Dear Reader,

The inspiration for *Don't Make a Sound* came from the story of the Pied Piper. As you might recall, the Pied Piper is called into the town of Hamelin when it is overrun by rats. The Piper successfully rids the place of the rodents, but when the time comes for payment, the town's officials refuse to honour their debt. In retaliation, the Piper leads all the children out of Hamelin, and they are never seen again.

Like many of you, I first heard that story when I was very young, but it has always lingered in my mind. The idea of someone undertaking a mass abduction of children is both terrifying and haunting, and a great premise for a novel.

Turning a concept like that into a modern crime thriller isn't straightforward, however. It gives rise to all kinds of questions. Who is carrying out the abductions? What is their motivation? How are they committing the crimes, and doing so without getting caught? How does the case unfold for Cody, Webley and the others on the Major Incident Team?

It is in attempting to answer all these questions that I eventually produced *Don't Make a Sound*, and if you've just reached the end of the novel, I hope it's whetted your appetite for more books in the series.

If you'd like to receive advance notice of new books before they appear, you might be interested in joining my Readers' Club. Don't worry – it doesn't commit you to anything, there's no catch, and I won't pass your details on to any third parties. It simply means you'll receive occasional updates from me about my books, including offers, publication news, and even the occasional treat! For example, sign up now and you'll be able to download an exclusive short story, completely free of charge. I won't bombard you with emails, but if you ever get fed up of me, you can unsubscribe at any time. To register, all you have to do is visit **www.bit.ly/DavidJacksonClub**.

Other ways of reaching out to me are via the contact page on my website, www.davidjacksonbooks.com, or on Twitter, where I exist as @Author_Dave. One way or another, I hope to hear from you soon, and that you continue to read and enjoy my books.

Thank you for your support.
Very best wishes,

David